Fair Weather by Noon

a novel by Karen Chalfen

Order this book online at www.trafford.com
or email orders@trafford.com

Most Trafford titles are also available at major online book retailers.

© Copyright 2009 Karen Chalfen.
All rights reserved. No part of this publication may be reproduced, stored in a retrieval system, or transmitted, in any form or by any means, electronic, mechanical, photocopying, recording, or otherwise, without the written prior permission of the author.

"Us Two" from NOW WE ARE SIX by A. A. Milne, copyright 1927 by E.P. Dutton, renewed © 1955 by A. A. Milne. Used by permission of Dutton Children's Books, A Division of Penguin Young Readers Group, A Member of Penguin Group (SUSA) Inc., 345 Hudson Street, New York, NY 10014. All rights reserved.

This is a work of fiction. While settings may be familiar, specific places, names, characters and incidents are the products of the author's imagination. Any resemblance to actual persons, living or dead, is entirely coincidental.

Note for Librarians: A cataloguing record for this book is available from Library and Archives Canada at www.collectionscanada.ca/amicus/index-e.html

Printed in Victoria, BC, Canada.

ISBN: 9781-4251-651-4-7 (soft cover)
ISBN: 9781-4251-651-5-4 (eBook)

Our mission is to efficiently provide the world's finest, most comprehensive book publishing service, enabling every author to experience success. To find out how to publish your book, your way, and have it available worldwide, visit us online at www.trafford.com

www.trafford.com

North America & international
toll-free: 1 888 232 4444 (USA & Canada)
phone: 250 383 6864 • fax: 812 355 4082

In memory of my father, who delighted in the small details that make life beautiful, and for my children,

Jonathan and Jennifer

A number of people have read the manuscript for this book—in parts or as a whole. I am grateful to Kai Maristed and Allyson Ross Davies for their recent readings and comments for the cover, and to Anne Moses Bennett, Paula Marshall, and Leslie Wheeler for perceptive edits of earlier drafts. Special thanks to my husband, Richard—for his support and for the cover photo—and to my talented step-daughter, Claire Chalfen, for the cover design. Finally, for his early and sustaining encouragement, I will always remember my mentor, the late Martin Robbins.

PART I

Chapter 1

December 1963

AS THE TRAIN slowed into Stamford, Cassie scanned the platform looking for Peter. The conductor took her bag and extended a steady hand as she stepped down from the train. Shoving her suitcase ahead of her, she cut a path through the crowded smoke-filled waiting room to the washroom. He was late, so she'd have a chance to make herself presentable. Before a blurred mirror, she brushed her hair away from her face, then let it fall to her shoulders again. Back in August, she'd worn it up, but then she was summer blonde. Her winter-dark hair looked better loose. Last summer, tan and rested, she hadn't even worn lipstick, but today she needed foundation, shadow, the works. She dribbled water onto a folded paper towel and gently dabbed her face. She had concealed the dark circles, but her eyes still looked more grey than blue.

She and Peter Lawson had met the first night of her seventh camp season. She had spotted him at once—a newcomer, at six four the tallest person on staff, and the most handsome. From a distance she had admired his coppery square face and chestnut hair, already streaked from salt and sun. Later, when he approached her, all she seemed to see were his eyes—deep, green, flecked with gold. He'd spoken softly, with a slight Southern accent. She'd fallen in love with his voice.

The waiting room crowd had thinned, and Cassie found Peter sitting alone on one of the long oak benches, feet apart, elbows on his knees, studying the timetable. Cassie hurried toward him. On the phone he had sounded eager to see her, but she hadn't given a thought to what she'd say. She tapped him lightly on the shoulder and heard her own voice—faraway, breezy.

"Hi, Peter. Were you…"

"Cassie! I thought I'd fouled up the schedule somehow." Peter stood up and beamed down at her. "You look great, Cass, just great." He moved closer, but didn't give her a hug. "My car's right outside. Why don't we get going." Stuffing the schedule into his pocket, he picked up her suitcase and strode to the door, leaving Cassie to catch up.

With each block of stoplights and shopper traffic, Peter grew more tense. The suburban congestion did make driving difficult, and he was resisting her attempts at conversation, so she stopped trying. Banks, service stations and bakeries were swagged with red and green or sparkling tinsel. Cars passed with trees sticking out of trunks or lashed to roof racks. All of the holiday activity just made Cassie more excited.

Once the shopping centers were behind them, the snow along the road was smooth and clean. Stone walls and stands of trees, bare black against the sky, separated one meadow from another, one farm from its neighbor. Winter offered clear vistas from the ridge road across rolling hills. Dusk—the last cold daylight glowing blue in the snow, warm glimpses of life through amber windows. Cassie's favorite time of day in her favorite time of year.

"Lovely, isn't it." Cassie broke the silence.

"What?"

"The countryside, the snow, the season..."

"Damn cold is what it is. My folks have the right idea."

"What's that?"

"Florida for the winter. They're down there already. I'm heading out in a couple of days."

"I'm glad we could get together first."

"Well, I was sort of curious." Peter pushed up the heat lever and slid his hands into his gloves. "Wondering if you'd be the same."

"Well am I?"

Peter glanced at her and chuckled. "Better," he replied. "Definitely better."

Cassie disagreed, but smiled at the compliment.

"Nice of your folks to ask me to dinner."

"They were glad to. After all, you saved them a trip to the station. Besides, Mom's curious, too. She's asked a couple of times what happened to 'that nice young man you met last summer.'"

"Wondered that myself."

"We're almost there. I'll explain when we have more time." Cassie hadn't decided what she'd say to him, since she wasn't sure herself. "Take the next left. The driveway's the first one on the right."

Candles shone in every window of the house and the porch railings, twined with laurel garlands, welcomed them. In her earliest happy memory Cassie was lying alone under the Christmas tree, looking up through the branches at the lights and ornaments, listening to "Christmas Candlelight" on the radio, believing that the man with the kind voice played the songs and told the stories just for her. She was going to keep that feeling in this Christmas. Nothing would spoil it. Not sooty slush, or the sight of mothers snapping at their children, not people who didn't share the spirit.

Her mother would be happy. No one to spoil the holidays. When Cassie had brought Julia home last year, she hadn't fit in. Her mother seemed to resent her presence. Cassie had thought her mother just felt uncomfortable having a stranger in the house at a family time. But then, Julia had aggravated her by staying home from church on Christmas Eve. If she were orthodox, and stayed home on principle, Cassie's parents might have respected her religious conviction. But Julia wasn't the least bit religious. She'd just said she'd skip it. Well, Julia had her own life now.

Before Cassie could reach for the latch, the walnut door swung open. Her mother's coiffed hair shone in the light from the brass chandelier. Her forest green velvet skirt and satin blouse were too much, but she looked lovely.

"Cassie, dear." Her mother hugged her tight. "It's good to have you home!"

Cassie looked around the foyer—at the holly arrangement in its place on the table between red candles in brass candlesticks, the brass chandelier with its sprig of mistletoe, the wood floors, buffed for the holidays with lemony wax. It was good to *be* home. Her mother held out her hand to Peter as Cassie introduced him.

"I'm so pleased to meet you, and so glad you could come." She put her left hand on his wrist as they shook hands. "We always like to get to know Cassie's friends. She'll show you to your room. Why don't you freshen up and then join us in the study."

Cassie's favorite room. With a fire going, they'd start with cocktails, then spend the whole evening here, rather than in the living room with its chintz cushions and pale plush carpet. Even with a Christmas tree, the living room was fussy and formal. The study shelves filled with books and pictures, cherry paneling, indigo carpet and seascapes made her feel at peace. A fire snapped in the fireplace. When she and Peter walked in, her father folded his paper neatly, rose to welcome them, then offered Peter his leather chair.

"Only because you insist, Mr. Lindemann. Thank you."

"Well, Peter," her father said, sitting down next to her. "Thank you for meeting Cassie's train."

"Glad to do it..."

"Are you headed home for the holidays?"

"Yes, sir. Well, sort of."

"Where is home?" her mother interrupted.

"Maryland. But I'm headed further south. May do some sailing."

"So you're a sailor!" Her father leaned forward.

"Peter taught at Cassie's camp, Eric. Remember? That's where they met."

"Oh, yes. I'd forgotten."

Cassie's mother smiled, pleased with herself for being the one who remembered.

"Maryland. On the Chesapeake?" she asked.

"Yes Ma'am. We used to summer there, but since my folks sold the Virginia house, they're there longer, from April to December."

"A sailing family, then." Cassie's father nodded.

"To be honest, my folks would rather ride." Peter looked around the room at the seascapes. "But I love being out on the water."

"Do you own a boat in Florida?" Her mother, sitting in her wing chair by the fire, sounded curious, but not deeply interested.

"Yes. Well, the title's in my dad's name. It's sort of a winter business for him, booking charters."

"What is she?" Her father wanted details.

"Morgan 30. And yours?"

"Oh, I don't own. Just crew with friends. Racing more than cruising. Morgan, eh? Fine boat."

"Fine boat."

Cassie listened to the hissing fire, the clink of ice in their glasses. The twenty of or twenty after silence, she thought, wishing she had a watch.

"What's his summer business?" her father asked.

Cassie hated it when her father was so blunt, but Peter didn't seem to mind. He answered the questions gladly, but didn't ask any himself.

"He sold real estate when we lived in Virginia. Did pretty well. Retired early and moved to Florida."

"Lucky man."

Her mother excused herself to tend the dinner. Cassie knew she should help, but for now she'd rather sit and listen to the men. Her father had always been good at pulling information from her dates. When he didn't approve of a person, or his answers, he could chill the conversation, but tonight wasn't one of those times. Peter sat with his right ankle on his left knee, tracing the stitching of his cordovan loafers with one finger, answering questions. By the time her mother came back, Peter had explained how he happened to find a job at the Cape, why he'd chosen Brown.

"I like it, except for the cold."

"How are you doing there? Her father eyed Peter's glass as he got up to mix a drink for his wife. "Refill?"

Peter shook his head. Between answers he'd hardly had time to drink his first.

Her mother took up where her father left off, as if she'd been there all along.

"What are you studying, Peter?"

"Economics."

"We were just getting to that." Mr. Lindemann handed his wife a glass and sat down again. "Preparing for law? Politics?"

"Maybe investment banking," Peter continued in his drawl, "But I haven't narrowed my options."

"Good field. You want to avoid production. Too many headaches."

"Must we talk business, Eric?" Her mother sipped her drink, staring at Peter, and Cassie wondered what she wanted to talk about.

"Do you have brothers or sisters, Peter?"

"None."

"Pity. Cassie and Christopher—she's told you, I'm sure, about our son—have always been close, and my husband and I both come from large families. You must have been lonely growing up. I can't imagine it, myself."

"I guess I can't, either. Having anyone else, I mean. The other way around."

Her mother looked at her watch.

"Dinner's ready. We'll take our drinks along to the dining room."

Silver and crystal gleamed in the candlelight as they took their places at the long cherry table. Her mother had prepared an elaborate dinner. During the meal they chatted about the food, the weather and vacation plans.

"And what is Julia doing for the holidays this year?" They were almost finished when her mother asked.

"I don't know what her plans are, Mom." Cassie got up and began to clear the plates, avoiding her mother, who took two and followed Cassie into the kitchen.

"That's odd. I thought you and she were inseparable, though I never could understand it."

"We were. I mean, we are...close, that is. Let's not talk about Julia tonight, Mom." Cassie rinsed the dishes and stacked them in the sink while her mother took down a stack of dessert plates.

"Fine," she said, handing them to Cassie. "Just tell me—will she be coming here? During the vacation?"

"No. She won't, so you can relax, OK?"

Whenever her mother spoke of Julia, rancor seemed to harden her voice, erase her smile. When they returned to the dining room and found the men still discussing business, she turned over another shovelful of the past.

"I'm glad she's not coming," she murmured to Cassie as she served the cake. "Because from what I can see, you've started to think for yourself. Take Peter...such a gentleman. He's the sort of young man who's right for you, not one of Julia's crowd."

Cassie picked up her fork calmly. That remark just proved that her mother didn't know Julia at all. Julia, who never had a crowd. If her mother found out that Julia had left school, she'd consider it further proof that Julia was not a "good association," as she had asserted all along. Were Cassie to defend Julia now, the erupting arguments could ruin the evening. She didn't want the turmoil. Peter *was* a gentleman. That had been part of the summer attraction. She felt safe with him. She hoped he hadn't heard her mother making too much of him.

"Peter is a friend," she whispered, then turned deliberately to her father.

"So, Daddy, have you and Peter decided where the market is headed?"

"We hadn't come to that. What do you hear, Peter?"

The diversion tactic worked. Peter reported, they listened, and enjoyed her mother's chocolate cake in peace.

Chapter 2

PALE YELLOW FLAMES curled along a fat charred log as Cassie and Peter finished their coffee in the study.

"Daddy probably thought we'd go up, too, or he'd have stirred the fire." Cassie nested Peter's empty cup in her own. "If you'll put another log on, I'll pour us some cognac."

When she returned with the snifters, Cassie switched off all but one low lamp. She settled into a corner of the sofa, tucking her feet under her, and watched Peter work on the fire, as she had many times last summer on the beach. He seemed at home here in her favorite place, among the marine antiques and her father's memorabilia.

"Your Dad's all right, Cass. Easy to talk to."

"If he likes you. And I can tell he does."

"Your mother? She sure gave me a warm welcome, but she seemed kind of serious at dinner."

"She likes you, too. She told me so. But we started to talk about Julia."

"Your roommate."

"Ex-roommate. She left school. She's living in New York. With someone." Peter looked up, surprised. Shocked? Cassie wished she hadn't told him. "Mom doesn't know at this point, and I'd like to keep it that way."

Peter shrugged.

"Julia must be something. You talked about her enough last summer. I thought I'd get to meet her this fall." Peter set the poker in the stand next to the fireplace. "But..." He came towards her to take his snifter of brandy, then sat in one of the wing chairs by the fire.

"Peter, at the end of the summer, I *did* think we'd get together this fall. That you'd come up some weekend..."

"And?"

"A lot of things happened..."

"You were too busy." Peter watched the brandy swirl in his glass.

"When I got back to school, I had a heavy course load, with tons of reading. Summer just seemed *over*." Cassie didn't know what else to say. She turned around, took a photo album from the table behind her, and turned up the light. "I'm sorry I didn't invite you up. Here, I'll show you some pictures."

Peter came and sat next to her.

"Here's one on Mountain Day. October of freshman year. No one's supposed to know what day it will be, but we usually guess. When they ring the bells in the morning, it means no classes. But we have to spend the day outdoors."

In the snapshot, three girls were sitting on a blanket, bicycles lying behind them almost buried in golden maple leaves.

"There's Julia, next to me. By then we were friends, though it's a wonder."

"Why?"

"Because we'd spent the first couple of weeks 'thinning out'. Her term for getting rid of my clutter. That's what she called my things—making room for her treasures." The fire sparked and settled. "In the woods that day, we were drinking tea laced with brandy."

Peter sipped his.

"Fun," he said, stifling a yawn.

"And one more," she said, flipping past sophomore year. "Of Junior Show. I was a dancer. Julia had one of the leads. Here she is, playing her seduction scene."

Peter leaned closer, squinting at the pages. "All women in this show? It's hard to tell."

Cassie nodded.

"Our class did everything. Music, lyrics, choreography. It was so good. The best in years..."

"Does she always look that fine?"

Another admirer for Julia. Cassie closed the album.

"Almost always."

"No pictures of this year?"

None. Only an academic record to show.

"Everything changed this fall. Julia left, and..."

"You idolize her."

"No! But I miss her. At first I thought she was bossy and self-centered. But rooming with her made me see the world differently."

"Through her eyes?"

"You sound like my mother! No. Just started to *see* it. Period. Enjoy it."

Peter started to say something, then took a deep breath. He thought some more before speaking.

"I can't comment. I don't know Julia." He closed his eyes and breathed the brandy. "But did you decide to write me, out of the blue, a couple of weeks ago, only because you're lonely without her?"

Cassie swallowed the last liquid in her glass.

"No...it was a hard fall. First Julia leaving, then the assassination...it was all so terribly sad. After about a week, I couldn't stand to stay in the dorm with all the sobbing. I hid in the library for a month. When I wrote you I guess I was ready to have some fun, like we did last summer. I'm so glad you answered my note."

"I am, too." Peter put his arm around her and kissed her gently. "Some of my curiosity has been satisfied, but I'd still like to meet Julia."

"You'll have to." The embers glowed hot but the room was getting cool. Cassie shivered, rubbed her arms to get warm. She stood up and took Peter's empty snifter.

Peter got up to revive the fire.

"When do you have to be in Florida?"

"I'm on a night flight tomorrow."

"I have an idea. Could you make it the day after, and the four of us could get together tomorrow night in the city?"

"No chance of switching tickets this time of year."

"I guess not. But maybe we could spend the day with them."

"I'd like that," he said softly, and kissed her ear. "Enough about Julia."

Yes, enough. Cassie moved her left hand from the soft hair on the back of his neck along his strong jaw. Peter kissed her, then pulled away and smoothed her hair. They sat quietly for a few minutes the way they had on the beach in the summer, watching the fire as they had watched the waves in the moonlight.

"It's good to be with you again, Cassie."

It is nice, Cassie thought, feeling warm again.

"But I'm ready to turn in." Peter stood up. "How about you?"

"Not yet," she said, studying his eyes. They were dark in this light—forest green. "You go ahead."

He touched her cheek.

"Goodnight, then."

She must have offended him with too much talk about Julia, she thought when he had gone. But she'd really told him so little. She turned back to the beginning of the album.

On the first page, a picture of Cassie and her mother, in wrap-around skirts, standing in sunlight by the steps of the dorm. And one of Cassie, waving goodbye to her parents from her window.

Cassie had been leaning out, staring down at the granite steps, hollowed by generations of 'girls with aspirations,' her mother had said, when someone in a scarlet cape dashed up the steps and disappeared into the dormitory. Seconds later she was standing there in the room.

She was different. Wearing that heavy cape on such a hot day, and blue jeans instead of a skirt. Her eyes were dark and flinty, like her hair. Shining smooth and black, it swung back into place when she tossed her head. It was cut just to her square jaw, which she thrust forward before speaking.

"You must be Cassandra."

"Cassie."

"Alright—Cassie. But I hate nicknames. I'm Julia. Julia Kramer. She flung the cape across a desk and flopped onto the bed. "Couldn't you die with this heat? No one told me fall in New England would be like this."

So she was from somewhere else. That might explain the clothes, but something in her tone made Cassie want to defend New England from this invading stranger.

"Today's warm for September. Where do you live?"

"You mean where am I from? San Francisco. But I guess this is where I live." Julia looked around the room. "At least for now."

Cassie pretended not to notice Julia's disdain.

"Did you drive all the way? Have your parents left?"

"God! Mother come cross-country to deliver me to college? She has better things to do."

"And your Dad?"

"Never met him. They divorced before I was born. I came myself, by bus. 'Go Greyhound,' *et cetera*. Hey, did you bring everything you own?"

"No..." Cassie was now embarrassed by the boxes and luggage piled on her side of the room. Julia had arrived with only two suitcases and her cape. "It's too bad my parents had to get back to Connecticut by four. They'd have liked to meet you."

"We'll meet soon enough, I'm sure. Right now we have to make this place livable. First, let's get rid of your boxes."

The day her trunk arrived, Julia had followed the delivery men up the stairs, ordering them to be careful. She relaxed as soon as they left and closed the door behind them. Cassie watched from her bed as Julia knelt on the floor and unbuckled the black leather straps. She took a key from a chain around her neck, unlocked the trunk, and lifted its lid.

Lying on top was a slubbed wool throw, hand-woven in rich shades of royal blue, teal and fuchsia. Julia held it to her cheek, then shook it out and laid it over the foot of her bed. Next she unwrapped a lead crystal perfume bottle—a teardrop shape, about five inches tall, with a heart-shaped stopper—and set it gently on the desk.

She reached again into the trunk and brought out a long piece of linen with a cross-stitch border of muted blues and browns. Smoothing the folds, she covered the stained, splintered surface of the cheap oak dormitory dresser. "Now, isn't that an improvement?" She didn't wait for an answer from Cassie, but placed the perfume bottle on the dresser, and stepped back to admire her composition.

"Lovely," Cassie said. "Is the bureau scarf old?"

"Not very. It's the first thing I worked up when I learned to embroider. Eight or nine years ago."

"You did that when you were ten?"

"I used to spend hours with my grandmother. She loved doing that kind of thing. And she loved teaching me." Julia was nearing the bottom of the trunk, where she'd packed pens and inks, paints, pastels and sketch pads. "I don't do it anymore, though. Too monotonous," she said, taking out a covered round wicker basket. "My treasures are in here."

Cassie couldn't have imagined the things that Julia would create from that collection of yarns, gold and silver threads, silk flosses and snippets of fabric. Ornaments, pillows, gifts for her friends.

Next Julia took out stoneware mugs and teapot, a trio of antique tins, a walnut tray with a rich, hand-rubbed sheen, and one last package. She slammed the trunk shut and shoved it into place in front of her bed, where it would serve as a table, then set the tray on top for the tea set. She hummed as she unwrapped the package, a squat pottery lamp, and set it at the rear corner of her desk, where it illuminated her work surface and warmed the entire corner of the room. Like Julia.

"Now it's time," she said, lining up the tin. "The grand one is for goodies, this next for sugar, and this one for tea....Here, Cassandra—sorry, Cassie. Smell."

From that day on their room had felt like home and smelled like oranges and cloves at teatime.

That September and October had whirled by, bright with foliage and first times. Cassie knew a few girls in the class from summer camp and prep school weekends. The elite emerged after the first round of fall mixers, when they found they knew many of the same people, up and down the East Coast. They moved around campus in clusters of shetland and tartan, laughing, greeting each other as they passed. Elected officers at the first class meeting, they were on their way up.

In the first weeks Cassie had coffee after English class with one group and walked back and forth from the quad to the gym with another. But as comfortable as she was with those girls, Cassie discovered she preferred to walk by herself. She liked moving among many kinds of people, feeling part of something new. And she liked the academic pressure. The course work wasn't difficult, but the professors, hoping to find the most determined students for their departments, loaded it on and watched to see who survived, or better, excelled. Cassie pushed herself hard.

By November the leaves had fallen, and the leaden sky settled down around the Massachusetts hills. Her need to be alone and a growing sense of the limits of her past had separated Cassie from the comfortable crowd. She began to wonder if she'd pulled away on her own or if Julia had lured her from familiar people and patterns.

They were so different. Even in high school, when Cassie had spent weekend evenings at parties, dances or movies, she had cherished days or late nights of reading, writing. She welcomed the energy that came with her ideas, even the exhaustion that followed her struggle to get them down on paper—rapidly, as they came to mind. That part of her had thrived in the college atmosphere, despite Julia's example.

Julia had been content to keep up—never a problem for her—and had worked in brilliant bursts, leaving time to spare for her art. Cassie, struggling with chemical equations or German vocabulary, used to like to hear Julia humming as she sketched designs. But after midnight, sitting in bed with a circle of light on an economics text, she had hated the sound of Julia's even breathing across the room in the dark.

Cassie looked up at her reflection, framed in one of the study's French doors. She didn't look very different now from the way she had looked in the pictures, but three years rooming with Julia had changed her. She had arrived at college needing to feel she belonged, needing to feel accepted. But Julia, who had seen more of the world, was way ahead of her, ahead of most of them. She seemed to know that she only needed to like herself, and didn't care about approval. She had welcomed anyone to their room, even those considered eccentric by the crowd.

Cassie hadn't shed all of the patterns of behavior and dress that had made her popular in prep school, but she'd left many of the people behind. Of all the friends who had visited the Lindemann house over the years, Julia was the only one who hadn't fit in.

The one thing Julia didn't tolerate, in herself or anyone else, was hypocrisy. She had said that when she left in September. In the three months since, Cassie had wished many times that that day had been different.

Watching Julia pack her trunk with the treasures she'd brought, and the ones she'd acquired over three years, Cassie had voiced her thought, hoping to persuade Julia to stay.

"Three years have gone by so quickly...senior year might seem shorter still."

"Cassandra Lindemann, an inane remark like that makes me wonder if we know each other any better than the day we met."

"I don't know what you mean."

"You do so. You and I know you're about to give me the 'Julia, you're ruining your life' speech. I don't want to hear it again. Sometimes, Cassie, you are so like your mother it's infuriating."

"That's not fair. I just don't want you to do something you'll regret."

"So? What's your advice? Stay here, in this place I hate, read these goddamn books, pretend that it's going to make some difference in my future? You know I hate hypocrisy. They say success comes down to the man you snag, anyway."

"Nonsense."

"Are you so sure, Cassie? Your mother certainly believes it. Maybe you do, too. I've found my man, and I'm leaving. So relax and stop meddling."

"I'm sorry you see it that way. I won't say any more. It's your life." She had wanted to add, 'I'm just trying to be the best friend I can be', but if she had, Julia would have known she was crying. Instead she had turned to the wall and pretended to memorize art history notes.

Julia must have had doubts about leaving school, even though she seemed so sure. She'd brought up Cassie's mother, the way she did whenever Cassie touched the truth. They might look alike, but Cassie wasn't like her mother, and it hurt whenever Julia said she was. Cassie had always defended Julia. She liked her and wished she would stay.

Julia had just shrugged when Cassie told her the next morning that she hoped she'd be happy, as if she didn't care. Cassie had watched from the window as Alan's car disappeared down the drive. The tin in Cassie's hands was all Julia had left behind.

The 'grand' tin. Julia had always restocked it on Saturdays, preferably with imported biscuits. If she went off campus on a weekend, she brought back treats from fancy bakeries. Occasionally Cassie's mother had sent a batch of her best butter cookies. Even those had been rationed, like the rest of the sweets. They had to last the week. Julia had left the tin. "To see you safely through senior year." Cassie shook it gently. Empty.

Like the world after November 22. She couldn't sit in the dorm, staring at those images—the horse with no rider, the veiled widow, John-John in his little woolen coat touching the casket. She'd spent the next few weeks in the library. When the thick door clicked shut behind her, it shut out the hollow sounds of drums and caisson wheels.

There the sunlight seemed distant, slanting through lead-paned windows in thick stone walls. She felt isolated, immune. She climbed the curved stairs to the main floor, then the narrow flights up through the stacks, to her retreat, the top level of carrels. She stayed there for hours at a time, preparing for senior seminars, forgetting even to eat meals. There were no aromas to make her hungry, only those of aged leather and paper. There she could suspend time until the lights blinked at quarter of ten to signal closing.

Walking back to the dorm one night, with the air cold on her face, she heard the tower clock chime ten and realized that it was almost Christmas. Time was again passing quickly. The isolation had been good for her work, but bad for her social life.

The dorm committee had decorated a tree that evening, and the nightly hot chocolate and cookies were being served in the living room. Cassie dropped her book bag by the front desk and joined the gathering in front of the fire. She stretched her hands toward the flames. Too bad no one was looking for a fourth for bridge. She'd have liked to play, to unwind a little.

Later that night, gazing at the moon through the bare branches outside her window, she smiled in the dark. If Julia were here she'd accuse her of brooding. She'd say it was time to get on with it. It was time to start making plans for Christmas.

She had written Peter the next morning. Because she missed Julia, he thought. Cassie got up and poked at the fire. She lifted a log from the brass tub by the hearth, then put it back. Enough staring at the fire, enough thinking for one night. It didn't matter now *why* she'd written, because she was glad to have him here, and tomorrow he'd take her to New York. Tomorrow he'd meet Julia.

Chapter 3

FRIDAY MORNING'S BLUE sky made it hard to believe a snowstorm would reach New York by early evening, so despite predictions, Cassie and Peter left for the city around ten.

"Tell me something about this guy Julia lives with," Peter said, after Cassie had directed him to the Parkway.

"His name's Alan. Alan Goodman. Julia met him the spring of our sophomore year. She was painting sets for a theater production, and he was the student director. She really fell for him. Pursued him, which was not her style."

"I wouldn't think," Peter said, as if he already knew Julia.

"He could direct without offending anyone, and that fascinated her."

"Thought she could learn something?"

"No," Cassie said, annoyed by Peter's smirk. Why didn't he remember the good things she'd told him about Julia? "Alan's warm and kind. And funny. Anyway, except when she had to be in the dorm, they were together for the rest of the year. Then they found jobs for the summer in Provincetown."

"That sounds like the right place for Julia."

"For both of them. Alan was an apprentice in a summer theater, and she worked as a waitress. They had one room with a water view in a cramped old house near Town Hall. In the middle of the hubbub, but they probably weren't trying to sleep, anyway." Cassie wished she hadn't spoken that thought.

"Does it bother you that Julia's living with Alan?" Peter kept his eyes on the road.

No grass or trees grew in the narrow median separating them from the northbound traffic. The 'Mamaroneck' sign flashed by. Peter drove fast, close to the dented metal divider that made the concrete curves more threatening.

"Why would it bother me?" Peter's question surprised her. Cassie watched him, waiting for his answer.

He shrugged.

"It doesn't at all. They love each other."

"You don't feel left out?"

"Never." Cassie clicked on the radio and dialed WHN. Gershwin filled the quiet space. *Rhapsody in Blue* for the Manhattan skyline rising ahead.

The Greenwich Village street was quiet, and it felt more like a Sunday than a Friday morning. Cassie rang at number twelve, a black door in a sooty ochre brick wall.

"You're sure this is it?" Peter studied the storage buildings that lined the block.

"Goodman/Kramer." Cassie had her finger on the names when Alan opened the door. She thought of dancing bears whenever she saw Alan. He was over six feet tall, and broad, with a big voice, black curls, a boyish face, and a smile that lingered in his eyes. He hugged her around the waist, lifting her off the ground.

"Cassie. Ravishing, as always!"

When she got her breath, she introduced Peter. Alan shook his hand warmly, grasping it with both of his, and pulled Peter through the doorway.

"Come on!" Alan said, "Let's get out of the cold."

He led the way through another door and across a courtyard, bright even in winter, with holly bushes and the red, yellow, green and blue doors of the four apartments that faced it. Cassie could imagine being there in spring, the mulched beds filled with flowers, the small fish pool with water.

"This is the most fantastic place! How did you ever find it?"

"We got lucky. A professor of mine is on sabbatical in England. He sublet it to us for a year for almost nothing because he fell in love with Julia and wanted her to take care of it for him."

"Sure," Cassie looked over her shoulder and smiled at Peter. "Same old story."

"Sounds like a good woman to have around."

Alan didn't comment.

"This is the only split-level apartment in the building," he explained, as they followed him up the narrow stairs. An ornate ceramic umbrella stand filled one corner of the cramped entry hall. Cassie would have liked to look closely at the clusters of framed photographs lining the walls, but eager to see Julia, she kept Alan's pace. In the living room, Julia was waiting.

She was wearing a red suit, the same color as her old cape. The straight skirt, or maybe the high thin heels, made her look taller than Cassie remembered, and with her hair pulled back from her face she looked older. Julia hugged her. Her perfume was strong, spicy.

"You look fabulous!" Cassie said, standing back to look at her.

"Don't sound so surprised. So do you!"

Cassie looked down, past her blue tweed skirt, at her flat rubber boots.

"I wish I'd dressed for the city, but with the forecast..." She gave Julia another hug, while Peter and Alan stood like strangers at a family dinner.

"And you must be Peter." Julia mocked out a frame with her hands, as if she were taking his picture. "No wonder Cassie enjoyed last summer. I'm glad she brought you by." Peter flushed as she took his hand. "Listen, you two. If we go out to lunch we'll pay a fortune just to battle the crowds, so we're eating in. If you want to window shop—I'm sure you want to see the Christmas lights, Cassie—we'll do that later. No arguments. Besides, it's too cold to tramp around when we can settle in here."

Cassie agreed, looking around. It was a man's room. Two deep leather armchairs, almost large enough to sleep in, stood on either side of the fireplace. Opposite them, in front of the sunny windows, was a shabby grey tweed couch, with a thick trestle table behind it. The professor must have had at least one cat, Cassie thought, noting the couch's pulled threads. Framed woodcuts covered the white walls, and the walnut bookshelves were crammed with well-worn leather-bound classics and art books.

Julia had conquered the comfortable, if stodgy, male environment. Over the deep grey carpet, in front of the hearth, lay a *rya* rug, splashy with reds, purples, and touches of orange. At the far end of the room, a round oak table was set for four, with red and white checked mats, white plates, and a cluster of narcissus blooming in the center.

Alan hung their coats on an antique brass rack on the landing, then disappeared into the kitchen.

"Peter. Don't be so formal. Sit down." Julia gestured toward one of the leather armchairs. "Cassie." She patted the cushion next to her on the couch. "Here. I want to hear all the news."

"I've spent most of the semester in a carrel."

"How depressing. *No* news?"

"They might eliminate curfews next year..."

"Now that I've left, of course. That place is such a prison. Have you been up for a visit, Peter? Been part of the great one AM lineup?"

"No, Cassie only..."

"And the work! I had to get out of there. If you didn't resist, the place swallowed you whole, like Jonah and the proverbial whale. I didn't realize how close to gone I was until I came to the city."

Still exaggerating for effect, Cassie thought.

"Julia, you were hardly gone! You were hardly *there*...always with Alan."

"True. Snatched me from those whale jaws, Alan did."

"What did I do?" Alan appeared with a tray of drinks.

"Rescued me from the belly of the whale called school."

"Let's just say you escaped. Here, Cape Codders—vodka, cranberry juice. Healthy stuff. Remember them, Cassie?"

"The night we all had dinner in your room! Alan had the most wonderful room at school, Peter, complete with fireplace. One night he and his roommate staged an elaborate meal—probably the best in fraternity history."

"To impress you two!"

"Which you obviously did, since I still remember it—and Julia's here."

They reviewed the menu of the memorable dinner, and other events of years past. Julia rose abruptly and went into the kitchen.

"I almost forgot these," she said, returning with a bowl of cured olives.

"Peter," she said, holding them in front of him. "Enough about old times and places you don't know. Let's talk about you."

Cassie sipped the cool drink, enjoying the warm sunlight on the back of her neck. The leather squeaked under Peter as he squirmed.

"I don't know what Cassie's told you..."

"Hardly a thing. What are your passions?"

"Boats and money." Peter answered her with a direct gaze and his most charming smile. That sounded so shallow, but Cassie hoped Julia could tell he was kidding.

"Ah. Women, too, I'd bet."

You'd lose, Cassie thought. But she was surprised to see shy Peter raise his eyebrows suggestively.

"It would be rude of me to answer."

"A real diplomat, Cassie." Alan winked at her. "And he's already figured out that he doesn't have to answer all Julia's questions."

Julia gave his beard a tug as she left the room again.

"Anything I can do?" Cassie called. She hoped Julia would invite her to help, so they could talk in the kitchen, but "not a thing" was her reply. Because she and Peter had spent most of their time alone last summer, before last night Cassie hadn't seen him with many people. Alan's questions—less specific than her father's, less biting than Julia's—seemed to relax Peter, and Cassie was comfortable in the space between her daydreams and fragments of their conversation. "...farmers. Yankee schools..." Leave it to Alan and Julia to find an apartment that looked like a theater set—different levels, good light, rich details. "...better for business." "...complete change." Easier now to feel that Julia's choice was not a mistake—not for her.

Julia returned with a platter of steaming spaghetti covered with a light sauce. "I remembered how you love clams. These are canned—but you won't hold that against us?"

The aromas of butter, garlic and herbs drew them to the table.

"Did holing up in the library pay off, Cassie?" Julia asked when she'd served them all.

"I guess. My grades are good."

"Why do you need all those As? You're not going on to graduate school?"

"I don't know yet."

"No?" Peter sounded shocked.

"It's only December! I still have five months to decide."

"Take them," Alan said. "Choices make *you*."

"Regretting yours?" Julia stared at him.

"Not at all," he said, without a pause.

"Exactly what *do* you do?" Peter asked. "Cassie said something about theater."

"I'm studying drama at Columbia..."

"But that's not his passion," Julia interrupted.

"And I teach children's theater on Saturdays. That's the greatest."

"The point is it's the real world he enjoys, not school. You should come work in the city next year, Cassie. It could be like old times."

Just what Cassie had been thinking while Julie prepared lunch. Cassie wondered if it could be, whether it even should be, now that Julia lived with Alan. Something about the two of them was different. About the three of them. Maybe because they were four today and Peter was new to the group.

"Where will you be, Peter?" Julia continued.

"Business school somewhere," Peter said, finishing his first helping of spaghetti.

Julia sighed at his answer.

"Even if it isn't fascinating, I suppose learning to make money will have its rewards."

"Plenty," Alan said, heaping more spaghetti on Peter's plate and his own. "Anyone else?" Julia and Cassie, who smiled at the pun, declined.

Alan cleared. He set a bowl of pears and grapes on the table, as Julia took a small pipe from a red suede pouch and filled it with tobacco. The smell of applejack mingled with pungent paper-whites, then French roast coffee as Alan filled their cups.

"So, Cassandra," Julia said, puffing to get her pipe going. "How many diamonds in the dorm?"

"What?" Cassie tried to appear unfazed, by the pipe and by the remark.

"How many people engaged?"

She wondered if Julia was honestly curious or up to something.

"None...that I know of...lots of pins..."

"Ah, some of those will turn to stones over this vacation."

"Hinting?" Alan's smile said he was joking. Cassie looked through the smoke at Julia's eyes. She wasn't.

"Julia wants to prove a point she made before she left," Cassie said, hoping Peter wouldn't think Julia was hinting on her behalf.

"I guess I can't. Maybe all those girls will turn out to be 'uncommon women' after all."

"Like you?" Peter asked.

Julia didn't answer.

Peter folded his napkin and pushed his chair back. The sky had begun to cloud over when they sat down to lunch, but no one had seemed to care.

"It's almost three, and my plane leaves at five," he said, looking out at a deep gunmetal sky.

"I hope you'll beat the weather," Alan said, handing Peter his overcoat.

Peter put on his left glove. "Thanks for the hospitality," he said, shaking Alan's hand before putting on the other.

"I'll walk you down." Cassie said.

The scent of snow hung in the air as they crossed the courtyard to the passageway.

"I'd drive you home if I had time." Peter turned up his coat collar.

"That's OK." Cassie didn't even want to think about going home.

"You probably want to stay longer, anyway."

"You did like them," Cassie asked. "Didn't you?"

"Sure. But I have to go. Merry Christmas."

"To you, too, Peter. And a Happy New Year."

Peter took both her hands and looked into her eyes. His leather gloves felt cold already, but even without a coat, Cassie was warm.

"Think I can be part of yours?"

Cassie nodded.

"Good." Peter kissed her, harder than he had the night before, squeezing her hands, then dropped them and walked through the passageway. "Take care, Cass."

She didn't answer, but watched the door close behind him, wishing he could stay, relax, celebrate. As she walked back across the courtyard the first fine flakes began to fall. It would be a white Christmas.

Chapter 4

ON THE WAY back up, Cassie paused to look at the photographs, mostly snapshots taken abroad, many in England. There were few faces among the scenes of cottages and castles, though there were a couple of cricket teams and city children in the collection. Alan had said that the professor was on sabbatical in England. He was clearly an Anglophile whose pictures suggested he cared more for the place than its people.

"It's started to snow!" She was excited to bring the news.

"We'll have to keep you here for the night, then. Getting out of town now will be chaos. Besides, Alan and I have a great idea."

"Julia's right. You have to stay. We'll head up Fifth Avenue. Look at all the windows and the tree at Rockefeller Center."

"Sounds like fun, but I should let my parents know that I'll be staying in town."

"So call them," Alan said.

"Not so simple. I haven't told them that Julia's left school, so I didn't say that Peter and I were going to see you two today."

"Oh, I don't believe you, Cassie. *So* your mother doesn't like me! You have the right to choose your friends. I can't believe you let her get away with that narrow-minded crap."

"Don't, Julia." Alan rubbed Julia's back lightly. "Why don't you call and say that you're staying in town because of the storm, that you knew Julia was here, staying with a friend, and you're going to stay there, too. True, right?"

"Right." Alan could make everything seem so easy.

"You can call from the bedroom," Julia suggested, "Across the landing."

Cassie went down to the landing, then three more steps to the bedroom. It was furnished with massive mahogany Victorian furniture, ornate and ugly, Cassie thought, but again, Julia had made the most of what was there. Her wool throw was arranged diagonally on the huge bed. The trunk at the foot, even without the tea tray on top, looked so familiar. On the far wall was a large armoire and next to it some sort of chair, buried under a pile of clothing, mostly Alan's. Julia had shoved the furniture together at the dark end of the room to make a place for herself at the sunny end. There she had set up a long worktable, leaving barely enough room to work. Her little pottery lamp, assorted stoneware crocks filled with paintbrushes, pens and charcoal pencils, and piles of sketchbooks took most of the space. In the center of the room Cassie saw something new—a loom. On the floor next to it was a cardboard carton filled with brilliant yarns. Standing in the doorway, Cassie could feel Julia's pleasure in that room, and her own jealousy.

She found the phone on the floor next to the bed and sat for a moment before making her call. Running her hand over the throw, tears in her eyes, she realized how much she'd missed Julia these past few months. All day her friends had made her feel there was room for her here, and there had been moments when she had felt at home. But this is their place, she thought, looking around the room—one large bed and a jumble of their possessions.

Her mother sounded annoyed that she wouldn't be back for a family dinner—her brother had arrived that afternoon—but relieved that she was safe.

Snow was falling steadily when the three of them left the apartment. The subway was crowded with people trying to beat the rush hour. With Christmas only a couple of days away, some offices had closed early, traffic was heavy and snarled, though the sound of blaring taxi horns was muffled by the snow. People who remained in the city that evening, whether by resignation or choice, were there to stay, and shared a festive spirit.

Cassie, Julia and Alan began their window shopping at Macy's and worked their way uptown, along sidewalks jammed with last-minute shoppers. Fresh white snow veiled the city soot, fell silently around the chorale singers at Rockefeller Center. So many things she loved—new snow, the magnificent tree shimmering with lights, sacred music and feelings of friendship—Cassie felt secure and happy as she had as a child at Christmastime.

They skipped in step along Fifth Avenue—Alan in the middle with an arm around each girl—catching snowflakes on their tongues, laughing and singing. They had to rest when they reached 58th Street and FAO Schwartz. In the window was a miniature Alpine village, complete with an aerial tramway, chalets and tiny mechanized skiers. Alan was eager to go into the store. Julia motioned for Cassie to accompany him and lingered outside at the display.

Inside, Cassie left Alan watching the electric train and went to look at the dollhouses. Such patience in all that perfection, she thought. Most of the houses had little families, and some even had food on the table and antique furniture. She must have been dreaming there for ten minutes before Alan came up behind her with a hand puppet policeman who demanded in a gruff voice that she clear the aisle.

"O.K, officer, I'll move along," she said, laughing. "Where's Julia?"

"With you, I thought."

"I left her outside, looking at the village in the window."

"Ah. Probably feeling a little sad. Her mother's in Switzerland on a ski holiday."

"So? Her mother travels around all the time. It's never bothered her before."

"She hasn't shown it, but she really envies your family, Cassie."

"Oh, sure..."

"No, I mean it. Even the problems you say you have with your mother—Julia would take a tenth of them to have any relationship with her mother. I swear, she hardly blinked when Julia left school, just sent a note that Julia had to do what she thought best. We invited her to come for the holidays, but she declined. Wouldn't you think the woman would at least like to meet the man her daughter is living with?"

"Yes..."

"She doesn't care. Let's go."

They found Julia where they'd left her. She wiped her eyes when she saw them come out and forced a smile. Alan bowed, pulled a small package from his pocket, and presented it to her.

"Pour toi, chérie." He turned to Cassie, pulling a box from his other pocket. *"Et pour toi, Mademoiselle.* But neither of you may open them until we get home. Come on. O.K. if we head back, Julia?"

Julia kissed him on the cheek and nodded quietly.

Cassie followed them across Fifth Avenue, through the slush toward the subway.

By the time they reached the Village, Julia was cheery again. "We'll have a light supper by the fire, and then, ta-da, present time!"

"I like the fire part. I'm freezing." Cassie shivered as they entered the courtyard. None of the other tenants had come in or gone out, so the snow sparkled smooth in soft light from the windows.

"Why don't you go ahead up. Start the fire, Alan, so Cassie can get warm," Julia said, as she lay down carefully in the middle of the path. She began to move her arms and legs. "Angels!"

Making angels had been a ritual whenever it snowed at school. Cassie couldn't resist. The two of them decorated all of the courtyard paths with angels. Then, breathless, they stomped and shook in the lower hall before trudging up to the living room, where they fell giggling into the leather chairs.

"The kettle's on for tea, Julia." Alan called from the kitchen. "Omelets for supper?"

"Perfect. Isn't he a gem, Cassie?"

"He is. You really seem happy here, Julia. Do you miss school at all?" Cassie blew on her fingers.

"Not a bit. I miss you, of course, but other than that...no. I have my projects." Julia dangled her legs over the arm of the chair, swinging her toes closer to the fire.

"I saw the loom in the bedroom!"

"That's one. But with no studying I have time to read, think, draw, cook...anything I want. I'm never bored."

"How about your job? Do you really like it?"

Julia hesitated.

"The people are fascinating. I'm working with the art director mostly, and I get to meet lots of the illustrators," she said, staring into the fire. Then her eyes met Cassie's. "I like it, but to be honest, all I really do is type, file, and run errands."

"Here we are, ladies." Alan waltzed into the room with a towel over his arm, carrying a large tray. "Would you care to dine at table or here at the fireside?"

"Oh, right here, thank you." Julia gestured for him to put the tray down in the middle of the *rya* rug. "A winter picnic." Cassie and Julia slid out of their chairs, and the three of them sat cross-legged in the purple and orange grass.

"I enjoyed meeting Peter," Alan said. "Nice guy."

"He seems nice *enough*, Cassie," Julia said, twirling a string of Swiss cheese around her fork. "I just wish I could have gotten more out of him. He seemed defensive."

"Not surprising, the way you went at him," Alan said. Cassie had to marvel at the way Alan could needle Julia with the truth.

"He could take it," Cassie said, proud of the way Peter had handled Julia's grilling. "I had told him about both of you, but I think he felt a little like odd man out."

"Even man, actually." Alan winked to be sure they'd caught his quip. "Have you been dating him all fall?"

"No. We're just picking up where we left off last summer."

"He's more pleased about that than you are."

"You think so? I hope *he* didn't."

"Maybe not," Alan assured her. "You were polite—kind."

"Well, *he* is. We'll be seeing more of each other."

"All this small talk," Julia said. "Can we open our little boxes now?"

"Not yet, Julia. Cassie's big box first."

"My what?"

Julia jumped up and ran into the bedroom. Alan gathered the dishes and took them to the kitchen, returning as Julia entered the room with a large package, wrapped in red and white paper.

"Oh! What have you two done?"

"You'll see." Julia grinned, kneeling next to Cassie.

"It's really Julia's doing," Alan said.

Julia reached for Alan's hand, and he knelt beside her as Cassie opened the box. Inside was a wool blanket, almost like Julia's, but with an added bit of purple. Cassie wiped away tears, speechless.

"That's hardly the reaction I expected. Did I do that bad a job?"

"It's beautiful! I'm...overwhelmed."

"I know that you always coveted mine, and I couldn't leave you up there in the frozen north without anything cozy to wrap around you during those late nights."

"It must have taken so much time...I'll treasure it, Julia."

"I've been out a lot." Alan winked. "Julia's needed an outlet for all her energy. You know how she gets, Cassie."

"In that case, thank you, too, for being out so much. That does sound strange," she said as they laughed. Cassie rubbed the throw against her cheek. "Such a lovely day.... Now, I have a little something for each of you, though nothing I made myself, I'm afraid." Cassie got up and took the packages out of the shopping bag she had tucked under the table behind the couch.

At Cassie's request, Alan opened his first, and found a heavy red canvas apron.

"I know Julia probably has you doing a lot of time in the kitchen—you might as well be dressed properly."

"Right. Thanks, Cassie. Now I have my own apron strings, so I don't have to be tied to hers!" He leaned over and kissed Cassie on the cheek. Julia opened her gift, a rectangular crystal bud vase.

"Cassie, I adore it. I *love* Swedish glass—you knew that. This one's such an unusual shape. It's going right on that sill, where it can catch the sun."

"Alright, ladies," Alan said. "Now you may open your toys."

Alan watched Cassie and Julia open the little boxes he had given them outside the toy store. They each found a glass orb with a wooden base. Inside Cassie's was a Christmas tree, inside Julia's a snowman. Both were surrounded by swirling "snow."

"From Santa. To remember today."

"The tree is just like the one we saw! I won't forget today. What a thoughtful gift."

"Well, it's been good to have you here. I think Julia's missed your talks. Now, I have a theater class with fifteen kids tomorrow morning, so I have to turn in. Want me to build up the fire a little?"

"No, thanks," Cassie said. "I like to sleep in a cool room. Goodnight."

Alan hugged her, then headed down to the bedroom. Julia had already pulled out the couch.

"I'll help make this up, then say goodnight myself," Julia said, unfolding the bottom sheet. They each took a side and tucked in the corners. "We can talk more in the morning, when Alan's at class. I'm so glad you came."

"Me, too."

In the darkened living room, Cassie reviewed the day as the glowing coals faded to ash. Peter had met her friends and promised to see her in the new year. She stroked her new blanket. Such a beautiful gift from Alan and Julia—from Julia, really, who was hiding some sadness behind her cheery holiday façade. Maybe they'd talk in the morning. Only two days 'til Christmas and so much to celebrate.

Chapter 5

CASSIE HEARD ALAN creep down the stairs and close the door behind him. She was sorry not to see him today, to thank him for being so kind to Peter, bringing him into the group. The sun glinted off the top row of windows across the courtyard, throwing white squares on the wall over the fireplace. She was dressed and ready to leave when Julia came in.

"Did Alan wake you?" she asked.

"No, I just woke up thinking I'd better get home."

"No breakfast?" Julia went to the window and rotated her new vase in the reflected light. "I guess I'll have to wait until afternoon to see the full sun in it." She rubbed away her fingerprints with the hem of her nightgown. "Want to talk?" she asked, setting it back on the sill, keeping her back to Cassie.

"I'd like to, but I really can't stay. It's Christmas Eve, and you know what that means at home."

"No way to fight that. Besides, the storm's over, and you wouldn't want them to think you were here by choice."

"Julia..."

"Never mind. Just come again soon, will you? When you can stay longer?"

"I will. This is such a warm and welcoming home. It is hard to leave."

"But you must. You can get a cab to Grand Central right down at the corner."

Easy to spot with his coppery curls, her brother was waiting for her train. He was also the only one without a coat. Even on the coldest days he wore just a sweater, and maybe a scarf tossed around his neck. Stepping down to the platform, Cassie realized that her little brother was now taller than she.

"Good to see you, kid. But I guess I can't call you that anymore!"

"Guess not!" He put his shoulders back, trying to look even taller.

"Sorry I didn't make it back for your first night home from school. Am I in the doghouse?" Cassie asked.

"Not really. Mom carried on some about you staying with Julia, but she likes that Peter guy you were with, so it balanced out. Mom and Dad both like *him*."

"You will, too, I think. He's a fellow sailor..."

"Oh, yeah?" He took her bag and tossed it into the trunk.

"Watch it! How do you know I don't have fragile presents in there? Want to stop for coffee somewhere?"

"We'd better get home. Mom will think we're trying to get out of helping."

Aromas of orange, fennel, cardamom and allspice welcomed them at the back door. Mrs. Lindemann was bustling around the kitchen, surrounded by trays, platters and crystal dishes.

"Hi, Mom. It smells heavenly in here." Cassie kissed her mother on the cheek. "Looks like you could use a little help."

"Not just now, dear. Everything is organized, but I'll need you later to set the table and put the food out." She pushed Cassie's hair away from her right eye. "How was your day yesterday? Did Peter get off to Florida?"

Cassie lifted the cover of a large pot on the stove and tasted a meatball. "Mmm. Now I know I'm home. Peter? I assume so."

"And you saw Julia. She's staying in New York for the holidays?" Her mother drained the water from a pan of hardboiled eggs and began peeling them, tapping the wide end on the counter and sliding the shell away in two pieces.

"For good, actually." Cassie took an egg from the bowl and tapped it, but the shell clung in small pieces to the papery skin. "She's left school."

"Left? Just like that?" Her mother took the egg from Cassie, slid her thumb across the top, removing all the irritating bits, and placed it, undented, in the bowl with hers. "Oh, she'll probably change her mind after the vacation."

"She left in September, right after we got back."

"You never said a word!"

"No."

"That girl. Imagine! To go through three years in a school like that and then just walk away, so close to the end. What a waste." Her mother sliced each egg and dropped the hard yolks into a small bowl.

"That's what I tried to tell her, but I couldn't persuade her to stay. Her own mother didn't seem to care."

Cassie's mother either hadn't heard or wasn't interested, focused as she was on whisking the yolks with mayonnaise and spices.

"So Julia's in New York," she tuned back in. "Doing what?"

"She has a job in a publishing house."

"However can she afford to live? Does she have a roommate?"

Cassie went to the refrigerator and poured herself a glass of juice, keeping her back to her mother.

"Uh, yes...she lives with Alan. You remember him?"

"The theater person. That figures."

"She couldn't stand school anymore. She spent almost all of her time with him last year, you know."

"And you spent too much of yours with them, as I recall."

"Not that much, Mom. The point is, she's happy. I'm glad it's worked out for her."

"I don't suppose they're married," her mother said, squirting detergent into the sink.

"No, but they're so devoted to each other. It was wonderful to see them again. I've missed them."

Her mother dipped a cloth into the suds and began to scrub the counters.

"I just don't know what you see in people like that, Cassie. I do not understand their values." She nudged Cassie out of her way, continuing around the kitchen, scrubbing stubborn spots with a small brush. "There are right ways and wrong ways to do things, and Julia always seems to choose the wrong way."

"Mom, no more. Alright?"

"I suppose we should be thankful that she's left school. Ya," she inhaled, the Scandinavian sigh. "Now you can concentrate on what you're there for, instead of flitting about with her and her friends."

Cassie glanced at Chris, wishing he'd say something, change the subject, but he was sampling cookies. Her mother looked his way and saw him with his hand in the jar.

"Christopher! Leave some for the party!"

"Sure, Mom. What time are they coming, anyway?"

"Five as always, so I'd suggest that you two go up and get ready. Come down to help me around four-thirty."

He clicked his heels together, giving her a mock salute.

Cassie, who had already escaped to the dining room, called back to them. "I'll be doing some last minute wrapping in my room, so everyone keep out."

Chris always took steps two at a time and he caught up with her in the upstairs hallway.

"Is that the whole scoop on Julia?"

"Yes. I wish you'd changed the subject..."

"I wanted to hear! Besides, Mom wouldn't have let me," Chris said.

"Well, it's out now, and if Daddy doesn't bring it up again, maybe this family will enjoy the holidays."

"He won't. He doesn't like you and Mom to argue. And I think he liked Julia."

True, Cassie thought, closing the door behind her. She did have wrapping to do, but mostly she just wanted an hour or so alone in her room. The womb, Julia had named it last Christmas. The deep raspberry wallpaper, antique spool beds and cherry dresser made it warm, cozy, while white cotton bedspreads and dust ruffles and starched organdy curtains at the small-paned windows gave it a crisp edge. In one corner, behind a soft armchair, her books were arranged by category in built-in shelves—American literature, novels in French, political science paperbacks, favorite childhood storybooks. Her desk, painted white to match the woodwork, was tidy, except for the blotter, with years of notes, numbers, sayings and boys' names—the life and loves of Cassie Lindemann in a two by three desktop space. *That* had to change.

Her mother hadn't changed anything. All was just as Cassie had left it—not last September, but three years earlier, when she'd gone off to college. She looked around. At prep school banners hanging on the wall over the bookcase; at the old school books that filled two shelves; at a stuffed dog, autographed by her ninth grade friends, that still sat on her pillow; and at the dried senior prom gardenia, hanging by a puckered elastic wristband from the mirror frame.

Suddenly it all looked silly. This week she'd clear it away. Pack things she couldn't part with. Stash them in the attic. She opened the top drawer of her dresser. More remnants—old handkerchiefs, tubes of lipstick, odd gloves. She took out a small box with 'Baby Jewelry' penciled on the lid in her best adolescent handwriting. Inside she found a tangle of gold chains with a dark coat of soil. A bracelet of miniature pearl-covered books—each meant to hold a precious photo. Several books had been lost, and all but one of those left had lost their opalescent bindings. They were supposed to be little Bibles—a confirmation gift. She pulled out a loose charm—engraved '18th'—with a faded replica of her birth flower, a marigold, under glass. Perhaps she'd treasured these things too much, too long. She closed the box, then the drawer, and began to unpack her suitcase. She took out the blanket that Julia had made for her and folded it neatly across the foot of her bed. It clashed with the wallpaper, but its newness in this familiar setting pleased her.

Her favorite aunt and uncle came exactly at five. Cassie couldn't imagine Christmas without them. When she was a child, six pairs of aunts and uncles and assorted cousins had gathered on Christmas Eve for the traditional feast, rituals and dancing. With job changes and marriages, most had moved away, but Uncle August and Aunt Tina remained.

August had changed jobs many times, always finding work that included travel and had hundreds of stories to tell about places he'd been, people he knew. He loved people, good food, and good books. Cassie remembered sitting in his huge lap when she was a little girl, telling him what she was reading as she twirled the ends of his blond handlebar moustache. He looked especially distinguished tonight in a green velvet jacket.

From the top of the stairs, Cassie watched him come in with Aunt Tina on his arm. He had met her backstage after a local production of *Kiss Me, Kate* and married her a month later. She was a talented actress, but there was nothing feigned about her affection for August. She looked at him the same way she had ten years ago, the first Christmas she'd joined the family. She was as slender and elegant as she had been back then. Cassie ran down to hug her, wanting to whisk her off to a corner for a good talk, but the food was on the table and her mother herded them all into the dining room before they could settle elsewhere.

Silver and lace had been put away for Christmas Eve. The table was decorated with colorful woven cotton runners, straw animals and *Dala* horses, and the red hand-painted wooden candleholders from Sweden, unpacked every year on December 24th. Even with extra leaves, there was barely room for all the traditional dishes. Cold ones—tangy herring, pickled beets, and cucumbers, stuffed eggs and glistening veal in aspic. Next to them a basket of fennel-fragrant rye bread and crisp hardtack and a platter of smoked meat and liver paste. Then a wheel of golden *bundöst* cheese, and small bowls of pickles, lingon berries, and mustard.

At the other end of the table the air was steamy with aromas—savory meatballs, sugary sliced ham, chunks of sausage, and bubbling potato, onion, and macaroni casseroles. More than enough for six people—stuffed eggs and aspic were always left over—but nothing traditional could be left out.

Assorted sweets covered the sideboard—soft round butter cookies and crisp *pepparkakor*, raisin-heavy spice cake with thick cream frosting, and egg-glazed coffee cake. At the far end, the bowl of hot rice pudding, *gröt,* with a cinnamon shaker and a pitcher of warm cream, next to the coffee urn, which Mrs. Lindemann would keep full and hot until the evening ended.

They served themselves, and moved to a smaller table in the living room, where Mr. Lindemann filled their glasses with aquavit and beer.

"*Skol*! *God Jul*!" The evening began officially with the toast. While they ate the cold foods, they reviewed the holiday plans of family members who weren't there, as if to include them at the table in spirit.

"Your roommate didn't come home with you this year, Cassie?" Aunt Tina asked.

Cassie shook her head.

"Charming girl," said Uncle August. "Her name again?"

"Julia." Cassie glanced across the table. Her mother's expression was cool, neutral. "She's in New York."

"New York..." Aunt Tina sighed the words. "My favorite city."

"Cassie brought a young man home the other night." Her mother leaned across the table toward Tina, and lowered her voice as if she were sharing a confidence. "She was in New York with him yesterday."

"Aunt Tina," Cassie said, before she could ask any questions. "Why don't you and I lead the way."

The others followed to the dining room for clean plates and hot foods, while her mother collected the soiled ones.

"So it's college for you next year, young man," Uncle August said to Chris when they returned to the table. "Where are you headed?"

"Annapolis, I hope."

"Annapolis!" Cassie didn't mean to sound so shocked, but her little brother, her sweet little brother, at military school...."There's more to the Navy than sailing, you know."

"Of course he knows." Her father ruffled Chris' hair as he moved past him, refilling the aquavit glasses. "I'm sure he's considered all the angles."

Cassie wasn't sure he had. Chris was so carefree he wouldn't consider the hard ones for long. Or he'd decide it was best because it wouldn't cost Mom and Dad a cent. And it would make them proud. Somehow he always made them proud.

"And you, Cassie? What have you been reading lately?"

Uncle August always asked and Cassie was ready.

"Dos Passos. *Manhattan Transfer*."

"Don't know it. *USA*, but not that one."

"I just finished a long paper about the symbols of destruction, the unity of humanity and the city's power to destroy it. He uses transfers, from one character to another, from one chapter to another..." Cassie heard her voice rising against the others' silence. "I'm going on. If you haven't read it, there's no point. Sorry, Aunt Tina, Dos Passos doesn't agree with you about New York."

"Do you?"

"Yes! Well, it's not my favorite place, but even after writing the paper, I'm thinking about going there next year, after graduation."

"Well, dear," her mother said, "You never know what may transpire between now and June." She leaned to her left, toward August. "Such opportunities these young people have today."

"Not like our day," he responded.

Cassie knew those lines by heart, as she knew all the rhymes they would recite, for good luck in the coming year, before eating the rice pudding. Over the years, dozens of people had hoped they wouldn't spill any *gröt* on their brand new shirt, or said it wouldn't hurt to have more *gröt.* Every year at this moment Cassie promised herself she'd come up with something original next time, use internal instead of end rhymes. But it was her turn, and she had nothing in mind.

"We've come to dessert, and my favorite is *gröt.*" Chris smirked at her. It was one of her worst ever, but it was bad luck to criticize, so he couldn't make a snide comment. Everyone rushed their recitations, because they felt shy or silly or because they were eager to enjoy the warm rice—with just a little sugar and cinnamon and lots of cream—or because they couldn't wait to see who got the almond. As young teens, she and five other girl cousins had tittered when the older boys found it, flushed if it turned up in one of their own dishes. This year there weren't many possibilities.

"Ha!" Chris pointed at her when he spotted it in hers. "*Cassie's* going to get *mar*-ried."

"Aren't you a little old for that?" Cassie laughed, but she still flushed. Too old to tease, but not old enough to get the almond. She was the logical choice, if there was one. Was it fate? Wasn't it possible, that no one would find it, that it would remain in the serving dish?

"Is this true, Cassie?" Aunt Tina asked. "Maybe the young man your mother told us about?"

"It's only a superstition, and he's only a friend."

As her mother brought their coffee, her father and Uncle August began their litany—the hardships and limitations they had faced. The stories had been told so many times that the younger generation often drifted away from the table when they began. Chris did, clearing quietly, but Cassie sat still, listening and nibbling on cookies.

Her parents and uncle had come so far from the farm days they recalled, from their small village in the central flatlands of Sweden. Uncle August told his story about her father chasing a chicken around the first time he was told to catch one and kill it for dinner.

"You didn't do so well with the pig. August had to take the pig to town to be turned to ham, but the pig got away."

"I chased her longer than you chased the chicken. You're right."

"August told Papa she slipped out of the lead, but I know he let him go. I never told though. The pig was his friend." Her father winked at August. "Too bad she wasn't faster..."

As a child, Cassie had believed every word, but sometimes now she wondered how much her father exaggerated. Her mother remembered baking bread for the week, round loaves with holes in the center, and carrying them to the attic to hang on a pole under the eaves. Tina hadn't lived in Sweden, but Cassie saw her eyes fill up sometimes as she relived the experiences with the others.

In those days, or even the early ones in Waterbury, they would have skimped for a year to produce a feast like tonight's. Hard work and good spirits had brought them success, and abundance that erased need, but not memory. And what they remembered, Cassie realized, was not what they lacked in the old days, but the special things they had then. This was the time a grownup usually asked each child what he or she wanted from Santa. In the old days, one of the uncles would come in later, dressed as Santa, with one special gift for each of them. Chris and Cassie were too old, but Uncle August asked anyway.

"What are you hoping Santa will bring?"

Chris said skis, Cassie a stereo.

"Do you know what was the best, the very best, thing I ever found in my stocking?" her father said. They all did, but no one said. "An orange. The most beautiful thing. In Sweden! In the middle of winter! How it smelled...stronger than this," he said, picking an orange out of the fruit bowl on the table and raising it to his nose. "And sweeter. It was brighter, too." He cupped the orange in his hands as if it were the original, or a crystal paperweight. The rest of the world might respect her father for what he had achieved, acquired, Cassie thought. But she loved and respected him most for what he hadn't lost—his humility. He knew what mattered. He had been kind to Julia last Christmas. Her mother had reacted reflexively to her brusque manner, but he had overlooked it.

Cassie was convinced he had put the almond in Julia's rice pudding. Its prophecy was almost right. Julia hadn't married within the year, but she had started a new life in New York. Perhaps she was struggling, but Julia had always done a lot with very little. Cassie was quite sure Julia was happy with Alan. Maybe with him Julia would have the kind of family closeness she had longed for.

The others had left the table. On her way to help Chris with the dishes, she paused to watch them. When the needle dropped on the first of the old scratchy records, Uncle August bowed to her mother, her father to Aunt Tina, and the four of them began to move around the foyer, in patterns as traditional as the food, a swirl of red and green. They would dance until close to midnight and time to go to church.

Chapter 6

JANUARY WAS FRIGID. Storms buried New England the first Friday and again the next, stranding Cassie and Peter on their own campuses, foiling their plans to be together. The third week, wrapped in her new blanket and sipping tea, Cassie studied in her room between exams. Five days and five bluebooks later, Peter arrived for semester break.

"Friday's fish night in the dorm, so we're going to Glessie's," Cassie informed Peter when he arrived. "They have the best burgers in town, so it's worth standing in line." She didn't mind waiting, watching girls eye Peter. When a booth emptied, it was at the back. Cassie and Peter paraded past the others, hung their coats and scarves on the end post, and slid in next to a print of sailboats at Argenteuil.

"Remind you of Florida?" Cassie nodded toward the bright boats, rubbing her palms together, and blew on her fingers. "It must have been nice to be warm!"

"But after being there it feels even colder here!"

"Let's have chowder," Cassie said, checking the box on the order pad. They could start February as they'd ended August. "We can pretend it's summer while you tell me what you did down there."

"Explored the Keys by boat."

Cassie could picture turquoise water, almost feel long days of sunshine.

"Had a nice time with my parents. How are yours?" Peter asked. "Did you ever tell them about Julia?"

Cassie nodded. "It wasn't as hard as I'd expected."

"Did you see her again?"

"No, vacation was a quiet family time. I spent most of it cleaning my room," she said, glancing over Peter's shoulder to see if their order was ready.

"I did that the year my parents moved. You wouldn't believe the junk I found in the bottom of my drawers."

"Like what?"

"Oh, I don't know..."

"Think...while I get our soup." She might get to know him by what he hoarded. He still had no answer when she returned with the chowder. She sprinkled a generous helping of pepper into hers, while he dropped oyster crackers into his bowl one by one, in time with the opening chords of Handel's "Water Music."

"Foreign coins," he said finally, after a couple of spoonfuls. "A slingshot, and a squirrel tail..."

"Oh, please!" Cassie shivered over the hot soup. She didn't want to hear more about that over supper. "Coins from places you've been?"

"No, my parents always brought me the leftover change at the end of their trips. I stayed home."

Stayed home or been left home, Cassie wondered. Maybe he'd been a difficult child, though that was hard to believe. Maybe he didn't like the places they went, or going places with them. Maybe he had other things to do.

"By choice?"

"Not always."

Cassie waited for him to say more. When he didn't, she tried a new tack.

"How did your exams go?"

"OK, I hope. I need to keep my averages up for Wharton. Have you thought any more about what you'll do?"

"No." She was so tired of the question. "I love school, but I don't want to teach, so there's no point in going on." Besides, seeing Julia out in the world made her want to be independent. "I might like to work in publishing. I've written some letters...and I'm going to New York during spring vacation for interviews."

Peter nodded. "To stay with Julia again?"

"Of course."

A waiter brought their hamburgers, covered with onions, and a single plate of french fries.

"Julia. On the outside, friendly and warm, but so cold inside," Peter said, as he squeezed ketchup over the whole pile of fries. "I can understand your fascination with her."

Fascination seemed a strange word, Cassie thought, salvaging clean fries from the bottom of the pile. She hated ketchup.

"Funny you had that impression, Peter. People who know her say the opposite."

"She's certainly beautiful." Peter stared past her, as if he were trying to conjure Julia. "But I didn't get a word in," he said, smiling.

Cassie remembered Julia's questions, his quick answers. He had done better than most. And he talked more that day than he had so far tonight.

"Alan's a nice guy...I wonder how he stands up to her."

"He adores her!"

"But she calls all the shots. He can't like that much."

Cassie didn't want to start the weekend with an argument.

"They both liked you—they said so." Peter popped a cluster of fries into his mouth and didn't respond. "We had a terrific time after you left, tromping around in the snow." She watched him eat the last of his hamburger and offered him half of hers.

"It's getting late," she said, eager to get to the movie. "It's *The Seventh Seal* tonight. You haven't seen it, I hope."

"No, I avoid Bergman films. Too weird."

"There's no other choice in this town on a Friday night."

"I'll live," Peter said, as he finished. He paid the check, and they headed down Main Street to the auditorium, walking fast, as much to keep warm as to be on time.

Peter had studying to do, so they spent Saturday morning in the library reading room. Even on break Cassie wanted to read—just for pleasure—so she curled up in one of the soft chairs behind the card files. At one of the long oak tables, not far from her, Peter had spread out his books and papers. He seemed unaware of the clock, chiming away the quarter hours, and of Cassie. She occasionally looked up from her book to reassure herself that he was still there.

This was the first time she had seen him in eyeglasses. The light on his bowed head highlighted his chestnut hair and the tortoise shell frames. He looked good. Intelligent, earnest. Afraid he might catch her staring, she went back to her book and reread a paragraph for the third time. Of all the days she had spent in this library, this was the one she might remember most.

When they finished lunch around one, the air had turned spring-like, despite the snow. With the February sun on their faces, they started out on a walk around the lake. Along the far shore, snow and rain and foot traffic had created ruts and bumps in the path and the going was slow. Squeals and reassurances came from the lake, where another couple had ventured onto the sun-weakened ice.

"We might have to use our lifesaving skills!" Cassie said.

"When they're that stupid, I wouldn't feel obliged."

"You're kidding, of course." Cassie watched his face.

"No!" Peter smiled. He had to be kidding, but she couldn't tell.

By the time they reached the head of the lake, the voices were distant, and the afternoon sun had gone pale. Cassie stopped to take in the glacial beauty of pine trees in snow, to listen to the birds warning of intruders.

"Cardinal," Peter said.

"What?"

"I hear a cardinal. Surprising. We should be able to spot him."

Peter led her quietly toward the call until, almost under the tree, the bird flashed away, scarlet against the green and white. "Male."

"Do another," Cassie said.

Next they chose blue jays, then chickadees, and finally a woodpecker. Following the sounds, they moved in random directions through the hushed woods.

"You really know your birds," she said. They had come to a wooden bridge over a frozen brook.

Peter shrugged. "I'm a country boy."

She'd never thought of him that way.

"Let's take a look." Peter said, leading the way down the steep bank to where the brook wound off under ice into the woods. The ice was wind-rippled in places, with rough patches of drifted and crusted snow here and there. On a smooth, thick stretch Peter ran and slid along the stream. Cassie followed him, but stopped several times, convinced she heard cracking under them.

"You said they were stupid. The couple at the lake," Cassie reminded him.

"That was a lake, this is just a shallow brook."

He laughed as he showed her the source of the ominous cracking sound—birches, hanging over the banks of the brook, moving in gusts of wind, tapping the ice.

Further along they came to a small drop, where the ice hadn't taken hold on the moving water. The trickle and sloosh echoed in the hollow chamber under the ice, and Cassie felt as if she were within the sound. They were in unknown territory by then, far from any sign of habitation. Even Cassie, used to winter weather, was freezing. Her fingertips had gone white and numb, and her jeans seemed to absorb the cold and harden on her tired thighs.

The chill penetrated her heavy boots, and she slid more and walked less. Just up from the south, Peter must be even colder.

"Are you sure we're heading in the right direction?" he asked.

"Positive," she said, though she wasn't sure. Almost, but not completely. "It was your idea to explore."

"But this is your territory." He sounded angry.

Over the hollow cracking of the trees, she heard a dog barking, and children's voices, growing louder, and then a whirr—snow tires. At last—the road back to the dorm.

Under the bridge, Cassie picked a branch of empty milkweed pods for her room, to remind her of their afternoon. Peter, who had climbed the bank to the road, reached down to help her up. She could feel the warmth of his hand through her glove. They walked arm in arm the rest of the way back.

Chapter 7

FROM GRAND CENTRAL Cassie took a taxi. Better than lugging a suitcase on the subway, and she felt safe in the sunken leather seat—even as the cab swerved through Park Avenue traffic. Safer than she would have felt jostled by strangers on a train lurching through dank tunnels.

Julia met her in the courtyard, wearing jeans, her hair loose on her shoulders, looking like a student again. She grabbed Cassie's suitcase.

"I could have managed." Cassie said, following her to the apartment door. "It's just one bag!"

"Of course you could, but I've been waiting for you all afternoon." Julia nodded toward the stairs for Cassie to go first, and trudged up the stairs behind her. "I called in sick so I could be here when you came. I'm so glad you're interviewing in New York. It is the *only* place to be."

While Julia put water on for tea, Cassie glanced around the living room. Only the flowers had changed. Arcs of yellow blossoms now filled the crystal vase on the windowsill.

"I didn't see any forsythia bushes in the courtyard."

"I snipped it after dark from a garden a couple of blocks over," Julia answered. "Just a few branches to brighten my spirits."

"You seemed fine at Christmas."

"I was. I am. But you know...those February doldrums." Julia returned with the tea tray. "Alan's staging a play, so he's at school all the time. Tonight, too, so it's just us for dinner."

Cassie was glad. They'd be able to talk, as they probably should have at Christmas, if she had stayed. Even at school, through the long snowy winter, Julia had never complained. But the flowers were a good sign—Julia wasn't giving in.

"Like old times," Cassie said, after a while, tucking one leg under her. But she couldn't remember ever having waited in silence for the tea to steep. "Have you made many friends at work?" she asked.

"No close ones. Alan and I have friends, but they're theater people, too. All involved with the same thing." Julia poured the tea and put a couple of biscuits next to each cup. "Enough. I'll survive. What about you? Seen much of Peter since Christmas?"

"We got snowed out for most of January, but he came for semester break. And I spent last weekend with him in Providence."

"Really!" Julia raised her eyebrows, teasing. She was hardly in a position to disapprove, even if she did.

"Peter lives in the fraternity," Cassie said, wanting to be very clear just the same. "I shared a room near campus with his friend's date." Cassie sniffed the steam from her cup. Smoke, not spice. "New tea?"

"Lapsang souchong. Like it?"

"I may get used to it," Cassie said, wrinkling her nose at the surprising smoky scent. She missed the sweet old kind. "Anyway, there was a dinner dance at a private club. An old English Tudor place on a steep hill. All the rooms had really low, beamed ceilings and Peter had to duck through the doorways. The floor actually sloped in places! It's a gallery most of the time, I think—there were gorgeous watercolors on the walls. You'd have loved it, Julia. Saturday night the place was filled with round tables, candlelight, flowers...."

"Sounds romantic."

"Peter and I had never danced..."

"He looked dashing, I'm sure. He *is* handsome, that Peter."

"He looked magnificent, if I do say so." Cassie flushed, recalling the dance, the evening spent in his arms.

"This sounds serious. Do your parents like him?"

"They think he's terrific. Perfect, in fact."

"Really? Better grab him then. We know how hard they are to please. How does he feel about you?"

Cassie might have guessed that Julia would ask the question she'd asked herself. Though kind and affectionate, Peter never talked about his feelings. She had understood this during the summer, when she thought they were just friends, and even at Christmas, when he perhaps questioned her motives for contacting him. But lately things had seemed more serious, and she was surprised by his reserve. Tired, too, of keeping her own deepening feelings to herself.

"He hasn't said. He's very quiet."

"Couldn't help noticing that. I think he's afraid of you."

What could give Julia such an idea. Especially when she'd talked to him for all of three hours. "Afraid?"

"Maybe not of you specifically. Of getting involved. He seemed interested, but afraid to move too quickly. Deliberate, like he'd have to consider every inch of ground ahead before he'd take a step."

"He's sort of..."

"Dispassionate?"

"No..." Cassie remembered looking up at Peter from time to time as they danced, pictured his smile. "He can be very affectionate."

"Have you met his parents?"

"No, and he hasn't mentioned introducing me."

"Then it can't possibly be serious!" Julia laughed, stacking the teacups on the tray. "I'm famished! Let's make dinner."

"You make everything look so easy," Cassie said a few minutes later, as Julia set a casserole, topped with golden, bubbling cheese, next to the salad on the table.

"Everything I cook is easy. And cheap."

"Is it hard to get by? Will I be able to manage here, living alone?"

"If you get a break on a place. Alan's hardly earning anything, so two of us are really living on one rather measly salary. Then again, we don't see any Broadway shows." Julia served them both and filled their wine glasses. "Or have wine very often. Thanks for bringing it."

"Tell me more about Alan's play," Cassie said.

"I can't. It's about fathers and sons, but he hasn't asked me to read it. The script was accepted, and now he has to show proficiency in production. What a colossal waste of time when he'd rather write. He'll never be a producer."

Cassie thought it sounded exciting and said so. "But then I don't know what's involved," she added, when Julia looked impatient. "What do you think he'll do, then, when he finishes school?"

"We haven't talked much lately, thanks to the play." Julia toyed with her food, moving the chicken pieces and mushrooms around in the rice. "I suspect he'll end up teaching and write on his own time. He works at a children's theater near here on Saturdays. Loves it."

"I'll bet he's good with children."

"He is. Says they give him something back. Not like the grownups, all puffed up and temperamental. His heart's with children."

Julia emptied her wine glass and filled it again. Cassie ate quietly.

"What are *you* working on these days? Still weaving?"

"Now and then. It keeps me from being bored...but not always from being lonely," she said softly. "Maybe I'm ready to try something new," she said, more to herself it seemed than to Cassie. "Seconds?"

Cassie shook her head. She was full. She didn't want more to eat. She wanted to hear more about Julia's life.

"I've made a sinful chocolate cake," Julia said. "We can have it with coffee in front of the TV. Tonight there's a great old movie, *Affair to Remember*. Know it?"

"God, yes. Saw it several times in high school. A six Kleenex film, as I recall."

"That's why it's so good!"

Julia fixed a tray while Cassie filled the sink to wash the few dishes.

"Like *Black Orpheus*? You nearly flooded us out of Chapin."

Counting scoops of coffee to herself, Julia didn't answer.

"Or *Gone with the Wind*?" Cassie asked.

"That was during freshman exams, and you shed a few tears yourself. I'll take these things in. When the coffee's ready, just bring the pot along."

Cassie wondered if Julia cried only at movies. Julia had always hidden her tears from Cassie. Sitting on the counter in the tiny kitchen, listening to the coffee perk, Cassie wondered why and if Julia hid them from Alan, too. Maybe next year, when Cassie had a place of her own in the city, when she and Julia could get together more often. Then neither of them would have to be lonely.

Julia had set the tray in the center of the bed and settled in, with double pillows behind her, on one side. Cassie made herself comfortable on the other, and the two of them spent the next hour and a half drinking coffee, nibbling at the chocolate cake between them, and sniffling through the movie.

Alan tromped up the stairs just before ten, looked down into the bedroom from the landing, and laughed loudly.

"What a scene."

"Hush up, Alan," Julia scolded. "This is the best part! Heat up the coffeepot, and get a cup for yourself. There might be a piece of cake left, too, if you behave."

Alan saluted, then tiptoed dramatically out of the room with the coffeepot.

"That should keep him busy 'til the end," Julia muttered. But he appeared on the landing again before it was over.

"Who's been sleeping in my bed?" he boomed.

"Oh, no. Papa Bear's back. You can tell he spends too much time in children's theater, can't you?"

Cassie smiled. Alan's antics always tickled her. She'd seen the movie before, anyway, and the ending was so sad that Alan's comic relief seemed just what they needed. He sat down sheepishly on the chair next to Julia and drank his coffee quietly for a moment. Then, with a wink at Cassie, he reached for a Kleenex and began to dab his eyes, pretending to sob. Julia glared at him, trying to look stern, then burst into laughter herself.

"You goof. Cassie and I were having a good cry. Now you've changed the whole mood."

"For the better, I'd say. All that despair and melancholia isn't healthy."

"Surely you've heard of catharsis."

"If you want me to, I'll leave."

"Don't bother. It's over now."

"Actually, *I'll* leave," Cassie said, getting up. She was feeling like an intruder in their bedroom. "I should get to bed early so I look my best tomorrow."

"Julia tells me you have a couple of interviews."

"Yes. I haven't given them much thought tonight, but suddenly I'm feeling nervous."

"Just be yourself, and by tomorrow night you'll be weighing job offers."

"He gave me the same advice," Julia said. "Worked for me."

"Here's hoping. Goodnight, you two."

Leaving the kitchen tidy was no chore. Cassie would do that when she had a place of her own. Her stomach churned a little. Coffee and nerves. But Alan was right. She should just try to be herself.

A silent elevator took Cassie from the marble and steel lobby to the seventeenth floor in as many seconds. When she stepped off, the receptionist greeted her warmly and asked her to make herself comfortable. Cassie was content to wait.

The reception area, paneled in richly grained rosewood, was furnished with soft suede chairs and filled with an array of glossy magazines and best sellers. She didn't know what to read first and found it hard to concentrate. Two tall dark-suited men strode by. She strained to hear their conversation, but their voices were muffled, lost like the sound of their footsteps in the plush forest green carpet. A woman joined her on the couch. Probably an author, Cassie thought, with a manuscript in the box under her arm. A soothing hum enveloped her, calming the excitement that made her heart pound. She remembered Alan's admonition.

The first publishing house had been cold, austere, and she hadn't cared if they hired her or not. She'd been relaxed, even disinterested, and a place in their training program was hers if she wanted it. She smiled. Perhaps haughtiness was a prerequisite there and hers had won her a place. Here she hoped that eagerness and enthusiasm would count for something. Both would be hard to hide. She was sweating, and knew dark wet crescents were growing under the arms of her best silk shell. She'd have to keep her jacket on.

"Miss Lindemann? I'm Miss Rowan." She looked up at a tall, thin woman, dressed in a smart brown suit the color of her skin. "Please come with me. We'll see how you type." Even the lilt in her voice and the subtle swing in her walk didn't put Cassie at ease. She followed down the hallway to the left, to a cubicle bright with travel posters of Jamaica.

She sat down in front of the typewriter, bright blue and huge. Miss Rowan clipped a piece of paper to the typing stand at the right of the typewriter. Cassie was used to keeping her copy at left. She wondered if she should ask to move the stand, but there wasn't room. She'd have to move the typewriter.

"All set? Just type until you hear the bell. Ready...begin."

The machine was new and sensitive. Cassie was used to punching the keys on hers. This one could put letters on the paper as soon as she read them unless her clumsy fingers got in the way. She tried to slow down, lighten her touch, concentrate, ignore her heartbeat. She heard the door click shut behind her, then the bell at the end of the first line. Her right hand went up, slapped for the lever to return the carriage. None. Just touch the big key. Little finger. It was hard to keep her eyes on the copy. The little ball flipped across the page. Crisp letters clicked onto the paper, faster this line than the last. Her hand didn't go up. The ball jumped left and started right again. And again.

Five minutes flew by, and Miss Rowan returned, pulled the paper from the machine, sat down at the desk, and began circling mistakes with a red pen. Cassie couldn't watch. She stared at the blue water over the coral reefs, imagined escape.

"I've never typed on an electric before."

"So they all say." Miss Rowan put numbers in the margin at the end of each line. "Can you find your way back to the reception area?"

"Yes." She'd failed for sure.

"Good. Please wait for me there."

The "author" was gone, so Cassie sat alone, barely believing her chance was over. She had typed a lot of material in five minutes, but she'd made a lot of mistakes. She picked up *Publishers Weekly* and flipped through the pages. If only she'd had practice time to get used to that machine.

"We may have a place for you," Miss Rowan said when she returned. She led Cassie down another hallway, past a small sign pointing to the editorial offices. Cassie crossed the fingers on her left hand for a second chance. They entered a room with two desks, both piled with manila envelopes and boxes. Only one was occupied, by a slight blond man, probably about twenty-five, who barely looked up as Miss Rowan passed.

"He's expecting us, Stephen. We'll just go right in."

Mr. Timothy Simonds, as the sign on the door read, sat behind a huge cluttered desk. He rocked back in his chair, so far that it seemed only his feet on the desk prevented his toppling backwards. When they walked in he was reading, biting on a pencil, running his fingers through his disheveled brown hair and humming to himself. After a few seconds, realizing they were there, he started and jumped to his feet.

Only slightly taller than Cassie, he was wearing a shapeless green tweed jacket—with worn leather patches at the elbows and a hemline that hung lower on the right than the left—that he might have worn every day for years. His bow tie was crooked. Mr. Simonds was the antithesis of the silvering gentlemen who had passed her in the halls.

"Ah, Miss Lindemann. Do sit down." Miss Rowan left them and Cassie looked for a place to sit, but both chairs were piled with folders. "Oh, pardon me," he said, moving one pile to the floor. "I'll just move some of this chaos. There, now. Miss Rowan tells me you're a crackerjack."

"She does?"

"Just the person who can straighten all of this out."

"Well, I..."

"And she's a good judge of these things. You'd be ready to work when? May? June?"

"June."

"Dandy. Stephen and I can muddle along until then, I suppose. He tries to keep up, but as you can see, we've fallen a bit behind."

"Will I be doing clerical work, Mr. Simonds?"

"At the start, to be sure. But you'll be training to be my editorial assistant and doing some first readings. Interested?"

"Definitely." Her pulse was racing.

"Wonderful. Then we'll look for you in June. Miss Rowan will go over the salary details with you in her office."

Cassie guessed the interview, if she could call it that, was over. She hesitated, then stood up and moved toward the door.

"And Miss Lindemann," he smiled and winked at her. "Good luck on your final examinations."

"Thank you. See you in June, then. Goodbye." He had already returned to his reading as she closed the door gently behind her.

"Excuse me. Stephen, is it? I think I'm supposed to go back to Miss Rowan's office. Would you point me in the right direction?"

"Glad to." He stood and shook hands with her. The trousers of his glen plaid suit had a fresh crease, and the paisley handkerchief in his pocket matched his tie. "Stephen Gillette. You're going to be joining us?"

"Not until June. I'm Cassie Lindemann."

"Nice to meet you. Too bad you can't start today. We need help."

"You do look swamped. Have you been short-handed for long?"

"We always are. You young ladies don't last."

"Why not?"

He shrugged and looked at her sideways. "Don't ask me. Tim's a peach. We read more than most...but then we discover more new talent than most."

"He seemed very kind. Didn't grill me at all."

"Of course not." Stephen sounded as if he knew more than he'd tell. "He's a bit of a maverick, but I like working for him."

"I'll let you get back to it, then. Which way to Miss Rowan's office?"

"I could use the stretch." He stood up. "I'll walk you down." He led her briskly through the hallways, back to Personnel, where he shook her hand again.

"Don't let me scare you off. I'm sure you'll do fine. See you in June?"

"If *you're* still here."

Cassie wasn't going to be scared off. She and Miss Rowan went over the details—health insurance, vacation time, and salary. Salary was low, only about $80 a week, but intangibles were more important. Convinced that this was where she wanted to start, Cassie signed the papers.

Chapter 8

ON ANY OTHER Thursday at ten AM she'd be listening to Mr. Ciarciello read Dante as it was meant to sound—in Italian. But in the middle of April, mud season in Massachusetts, Peter had offered her a ticket to spring. Only eight weeks from her diploma, with a job waiting, she could do what she wanted.

Cassie boarded the plane and strapped herself in. Heart pounding and holding tight to the arm of her seat, she watched the ground fall away as the plane headed south over the eastern end of Long Island. She saw few signs of life among the small inlets and ponds. The marsh grass was a dull tan, the trees still bare, but sunny stretches of gale-smoothed dunes looked warm and inviting. Near the center of the island, summer houses clustered around the water in a patchwork of squares and triangles. Here and there peninsulas stretched into small bays, forming canals, lined with docks. As the plane moved out over open water, only an occasional tanker or freighter made dotted lines of the waves.

She pushed her seat back and trying to imagine the coming summer, her first away from the ocean, she fell asleep, dreaming the wash of waves on the shore, laughing gulls, the jingle of shells in a painted tin bucket. She woke up sad to be twenty-one, longing to be ten again, with summer ahead, inviting as a sandbar in a retreating tide.

When the pilot announced the descent, Cassie again pressed her forehead to the window. They were flying over a barrier beach and a bay with a green shoreline. Here the houses were farther apart, some stately, some ordinary, brick and white among blooming trees.

Time had passed quickly. As they touched down, she closed the book that had been open in her lap since takeoff. Now for Peter's parents. If meeting them went half as well as the flight, she'd be glad she came. When the plane finally came to a complete stop at the terminal gate, Peter was the only person waiting.

In the middle of the tarmac, Cassie stopped and tipped her head back to feel the noon sun on her face. Peter laughed when she reached him.

"Same old sun-worshipper," he said, patting her back as he hugged her.

"It's spring here!"

"Our best season! Welcome to the south. How was the flight?"

"Fantastic! What a way to travel!"

"Sure is quicker than the train."

"It's fascinating to look down and see everything so clearly. I was nervous at the beginning, with the strange noises..."

"Wait." Peter stopped in the middle of the terminal. "You mean to say you'd never flown before?"

Something about his question, or maybe the way he asked, made her feel silly. Once, years ago, at a family picnic, her favorite cousin had smiled at her the same way. She'd taught herself to do a perfect cartwheel and tracked him down to show him. He'd stood with his arms crossed while she did her trick. Then, without a word, he'd executed four front flips, one after another, across the lawn before flashing her that same deflating smile.

"No," she said keeping her excitement to herself. She wouldn't bore Peter with the details of what she'd seen. "I couldn't work very well on the plane. Between my trip to New York and this one, I'm falling behind."

"Well, forget it and relax for today. We're going sailing."

"I can try." The top was down on Peter's red sports car. Cassie dropped her book bag into the back and sank into the hot leather seat.

As they crossed the bridge at Annapolis, Cassie looked down at the bay, which extended as far as she could see north and south. Peter turned off the main highway, and drove narrow roads at the same speed, past fields neatly plowed and patterned with shoots of summer crops. The smell of rich soil laced the salt air.

Cassie wondered what would make her feel this good after she moved to New York City. Sometime she'd ask Julia, though she might not be able to answer. Turning leaves, quiet snow, tender spring flowers—nature never seemed to affect Julia. Then again, she did, after all, pick flowers from other people's gardens. Perhaps her response to the seasons was to draw, or weave, and her art was a way of sharing those feelings. Cassie noticed details and sometimes talked about them, but never turned her thoughts into anything tangible. Images stayed in her mind, coloring her inner landscapes, but affecting no one else.

"Cassie." Peter snapped his fingers in front of her eyes. "We're here."

A river widened to a natural basin. Most of the marina docks were empty, but four large boats rode quietly on their moorings. Cassie held up her hand, testing, showing off her expertise.

"There's not much breeze," she said.

"Not yet, but it'll be up in a while. It's always quieter in here than around the point. Come on. We'll head out."

Cassie grabbed the picnic basket from behind the seat and followed Peter to the dinghy. He rowed a straight and smooth course to the farthest mooring, to a thirty-foot sloop. The deep blue hull mirrored their faces and their shimmering reflections. Teak rails, freshly oiled and smooth, gleamed in the sunlight. Cassie climbed aboard and stood in the cockpit, stroking the surfaces while Peter secured the dinghy to the stern. How her father would love this boat.

"Peter, this is gorgeous! She's yours?"

"Dad makes her pay in the winter—books charters—but when she's here she's mine. My folks only sail when I invite them. Usually I head out alone, for a few days at a time." He unlocked the door to the cabin. "Come see the quarters."

Cassie followed him down the shiny wooden ladder.

"It's hot down here—it's been all closed up. But later you'll see it's very comfortable."

It was cozy, inviting. The galley was small, but adequate, and everything was orderly and secure. She sat down on one of the bunks.

"I could certainly sleep well here."

"Sure. With a gentle sea to rock you."

Cassie had always dreamed of sleeping on a large boat. She and her brother had spent a night on their small sailboat once, but their sleeping bags were soaked with dew in the morning and they hadn't had any of the comforts that would make staying aboard this boat a pleasure.

"Want to try?" Peter sat down next to her and pulled her close. She did, but put her hands on his chest, keeping him at a distance for now.

"Tonight? What about your parents?"

"Just kidding. Not tonight." He smiled at her. "But soon."

Cassie felt his hand on her waist under her sweater and knew that it would be soon. She liked being held, feeling his thigh against hers, knowing that he wanted her. She responded to his kisses, thinking, but not daring to say, "not soon enough." He let her go and stood up.

"We'd better cast off if we're going to have much of a sail. I promised we'd be on time for dinner." He climbed up to the cockpit, the skipper, the man in charge. "I'll hoist the main, then you can cast off and hoist the jib once we're under way."

Cassie sat on the bunk, wondering why he'd left the cabin so fast. Well, there'd be other times.

On the deck, she did what he told her without question or delay, even coiled the jib halyard when she was finished. When she joined Peter in the cockpit, she studied the set of the sails, the direction of the wind, the heading he was taking and trimmed the jib perfectly without being asked. In the light breeze, the boat sliced through the water leaving little trace behind.

"Well done, crew. We make a good pair. Want to sail her for a while, to get the feel of it?"

"I was hoping you'd offer." Cassie changed places. "Where are we headed?"

"Sail for the mark just off the point there. Leave it to port, and then it's open water. I'll go down and serve up some lunch. You're hungry?"

"Ravenous."

Cassie was comfortable at the helm. Weekday traffic on the bay was light, so she could even scan the shoreline as she sailed, look at the mansions and cottages, their grass and gardens like new paint boxes with shining circles of color.

"So, how are we doing?" Peter popped his head up. "More breeze out here?"

"Not much."

"Just as well. We won't have to anchor for lunch. Here you go." Peter passed her a plate and a plastic tumbler of iced tea, then ducked below to get his own. "I was hoping for fried chicken, but we'll have to settle for sandwiches." He sat to leeward, opposite her. "These are the best, though. Chicken salad. Always took these on picnics. In Virginia, at our old place, there was a pond on the property, a mile or so from the house. I'd take a lunch and go there to play. I made little boats out of sticks and leaves and push them around for hours while my pony waited under a tree."

"You had a pony?" Where Cassie was from, people either rode or sailed—rarely both.

"Had to in our family."

Cassie sipped the iced tea. Cool and minty.

"I'd expect that as an only child you'd end up doing what your parents did."

"Hold on!" A power boat roared past, throwing up a wake. Without wind to drive her, the boat was tossed by the swells, the air shaken from her sails. "Stinkpot," Peter muttered, trimming them again. "Where was I?"

"Your parents."

"They expected me to do certain things..."

"You didn't like riding?"

"I did. But when they bought this summer place, I found the water. Some fluke I guess. Even this close to it, everyone else rode. At least everyone else we knew."

"So how did you take up sailing?"

"I'd go exploring, you know, and see the boats out on the bay, and I'd stand on shore and say to myself, 'I want to be out there.' I started hanging around the marina, doing chores for people, and when they got to know me they let me crew a few times. I loved being on the water."

Cassie leaned back and listened, enjoying his accent, the sun's warmth and the sea smell.

"And what did your parents think?"

Peter shrugged. "They lectured me about neglecting my horse, skipping shows on weekends. They were kind of baffled. Disappointed, too, I guess."

"But they bought you a boat!"

"A graduation gift. By then they'd given up. And I already had a horse!"

"So you just did what you wanted to do, and they finally accepted it."

"Sure. Whose life is this?"

"You sound like Julia."

Peter rolled his eyes when she mentioned the name.

"How is Julia, anyway?"

"OK...A little lonely, I think. Looking forward to having me in New York!"

Peter looked away, back toward the point.

"Sun's getting low," he said, collecting the plates and cups. "We should head in so you don't get cold. Bring her about, Cassie."

Peter took over to navigate the channel and Cassie went up to the deck to be ready to catch the mooring. She lay on her stomach and reached down with one arm, trying to touch the water that curled up from the bow.

As they drove to the house, the late sun striped the road with tree shadows and glinted on the water. When Cassie was a child, she'd loved to sit on her window seat at this time of day, feeling safe at home, watching the dusk go dark. But this twilight, soothing as it was after the day in bright sun, made her restless.

The Lawsons were standing in evening shade on the front steps of the house. Mr. Lawson, who was even taller than Peter, leaned down and grasped Cassie's hand when they were introduced. Peter's mother, who was close to six feet tall herself, extended her hand, as if to have it kissed.

"It's a shame you arrived so close to dark. One can't see any of the view now," she said.

"There'll be plenty of time for her to see the view, Mother. Besides, she's probably had enough sightseeing for one day."

"I'm a little tired," Cassie said, "But it's been a lovely day. I especially enjoyed your picnic lunch, Mrs. Lawson."

"I had Letty pack Peter's favorites. Let's go inside. It's chilly this evening."

They followed her into the house, where in the light Cassie could see the physical resemblance between Peter and his father, who was trim and tan. Even with flecks of grey in his light brown hair and deep smile lines around his deeper brown eyes, the father looked only ten years older than his son.

Like Peter, Mrs. Lawson had chestnut hair. Hers was pulled back and twisted into a tight chignon at the nape of her neck. Because she wore no makeup and had a matronly figure, she looked older than her husband. Her eyes were blue—a light, icy blue—almost grey, like the silk shirtwaist dress she wore. The lady of the manor, Cassie thought, with a shiver that she could not blame on the evening chill.

Manor was a good word to describe the house. Cassie might have expected blues and frosty greens, but not mahogany, damask, marble and pale Oriental carpets. This may have been a summer house, but it was elegant, not informal.

"You haven't long to dress for dinner. I told Letty that we'd dine at seven. It's nearly that now."

Cassie followed Peter up the curved staircase and down a broad hallway. She would sleep in an antique bed with an arched canopy of ruffled white eyelet. She didn't have much time, but stepped into the shower briefly to rinse off the dust and salt. The day's fresh air and sun had colored her cheeks, so she needed only lipstick to look presentable. She slipped into her dress, a raspberry linen sheath, put on her pearls, and looked into the mirror. The back of her hair was wet from the shower, and her dress still had creases from the suitcase, but she felt refreshed when she met Peter, waiting for her in the sitting area at the top of the stairs. With a smile and a slight bow, he offered his arm and they descended to the dining room.

Mr. and Mrs. Lawson were already seated at the ends of the long oval table. Even on Peter's arm, Cassie felt out of place. He had said she looked dazzling, but she felt garish in the dining room's colorless neutrality.

Her discomfort only deepened as Mr. Lawson's early attempts at conversation reached dead ends. She could admire horses from afar but she'd never understood them, nor cared to. They terrified her, so she had never learned to ride. Steeplechase and dressage, favorite topics at the Lawson table, were only vocabulary words to Cassie.

When she mentioned her plans to live and work in New York, Mrs. Lawson went on about the merits of the Met and questioned her about operas she had seen. Having seen none, Cassie couldn't keep that subject alive, either.

She could tell when the topic of school was raised that Peter's mother was convinced of the superior value of a history major. That had been *her* choice. Medieval, specifically. When she remarked that an English major "must be fun," Cassie couldn't comment. Surely, she thought, the insights of literature are as valuable as the lessons of history. But her mind spun when she tried to speak. Churning inside, she ate and smiled graciously, nodding apparent agreement with every opinion. Letty's interruptions, to serve successive courses in silence, were welcome.

At the end of the meal, they moved from the grey dining room into the blue living room to have coffee. Cassie was relieved to have Peter beside her on the sofa, rather than out of reach across the table. She felt his arm against hers as he talked quietly with his parents. That afternoon he had told her a little about his past. She wanted to know more. She wanted to understand how he had grown up with these two people and become the Peter she knew.

She crossed the room to look at the collection of silver-framed photographs on the grand piano. There were standard family portraits—the Lawsons on their wedding day, Peter and his parents at Peter's christening, and Peter, when he was a year old, she guessed. The rest were snapshots, less formal, but hardly candid, showing the Lawsons and their son with horses and ponies in many meadows, through successive seasons—from Peter at two, in a pony cart, his father by his side, to mother and son, astride hunters when Peter was older. The last picture of him was another formal portrait, probably his prep school senior picture. It was as if when he went away to school, out of range of their cameras, Peter had ceased to be the focus of their lives.

"You can't find those very fascinating." He had come up behind her.

"You were a cute baby..."

His face flushed. Maybe he wasn't used to compliments.

"Are you too tired to take a walk?" he asked, changing the subject.

"A short one?" She looked past Peter at Mrs. Lawson. "Are your parents coming?" she whispered.

"No. They'll probably go up soon themselves." He took her hand. "Mother, Cassie and I are going to take a walk, so we'll say goodnight now."

Mrs. Lawson rose and turned her cheek to receive her son's kiss. Cassie shook her hand again, thanked her for dinner, and asked her to say goodnight to Mr. Lawson, who had dozed off in his chair.

"And Peter," she called after them, "Do be on time for breakfast."

As they stepped out onto the porch, the night air felt warm.

"Let's walk down to the river. The grass will be wet, so leave your shoes."

Cassie did, and walked beside Peter down the sloping lawn. Glistening with dew in the light of a half moon, it felt slippery under her stocking feet. They sat down on the dock at the river's edge. Where the lawn ended on their side, woods took over, tall trees and dense undergrowth limiting the view. But along the opposite bank Cassie could see the lawns and lights of other estates. With no breeze to stir its surface, the dark water slipped by.

"The house in the pictures on the piano...that was the one in Virginia?"

"Right."

"I think I know why you like this place better. The river."

"Yes." Peter put his arm around her. "Warm enough?"

"Fine. I was just thinking about the ocean. Sitting here like this reminds me of the Cape."

"We've had a good day, Cassie. I feel so comfortable with you." The peepers and the owls filled the spring night with sound. "I'd like to have you with me all the time."

Cassie stared at the lights across the river, barely believing that Peter was talking this way. He was always so reserved. He'd never spoken about his feelings with her. "I guess what I'm saying is that I'd like to marry you." He held both her hands. "I know. This is sudden, but I feel close to you. I think we can have a fine life together."

It was too dark to read his eyes.

"OK. You need to think about it. Don't answer tonight."

"I can't." Cassie pulled her hands free and hugged her knees to her chest. "You'd have surprised me anytime, talking like this, but tonight? After that disastrous dinner..."

"What was disastrous about it?"

"It was so awkward. You *must* have felt that. I'd bet if you asked them your parents would say I'm not a proper match for you."

"I wouldn't ask them. This is my decision. But even if I did, I think they'd approve. And when they get to know you . . . "

"Your mother wants you to marry a history major who loves opera!"

"I hate opera! Always have."

"And I can't ride..."

"...but you can sail!"

Cassie laughed. "You aren't going to let me off the hook, are you?" She reached for his hand. "Of course I'll think about it." As if she'd be able to think about anything else.

Peter stood up and pulled her to her feet.

"I think I've loved you for some time, Cass. Maybe since summer." He held her close and kissed her as he hadn't before, deep and long. She wanted to tell him how she felt, but when she tried to speak, he put his finger on her lips.

"Tomorrow. We'd better get back."

They held hands as they walked to the house, now dark except for the light on the stairs. Peter kissed her again at the door of her room, gently this time.

She fell asleep thinking of him in the next room...the next bed.

Chapter 9

THE ROOM FACED north toward the river, so no sunlight announced the day. Smells of freshly brewed coffee and smoky bacon drifted into Cassie's dreams before she was aware of the morning. She turned over and nestled deeper under the covers, thinking it was pleasant to be home, to be coaxed awake, not startled by a strident alarm. She forced her eyes open, turned over, and stared at the white canopy over her head in the pale grey morning light. This was not her rosy room. Then she remembered.

She sat up, shook her head and squinted at the clock. Nine AM. She'd missed breakfast, after Mrs. Lawson had specifically reminded Peter to be on time. He should have wakened her. Too excited to read the night before, she had turned off the light right away to think about Peter's proposal, then fallen asleep without an answer.

In the time she'd known him—almost a year—Peter had always been courteous, respectful. He had never tried to take advantage, even when she thought her desire must show. His eyes stirred her most, green on gold, like burnished brass. They could have beautiful children, and she hoped the children would get his eyes. The thought surprised her, as if she had come upon an answer delivered in her dreams. Cassie liked the way people watched when she and Peter walked by, liked being a couple. They'd do things together. Sail, especially. Peter's boat was big enough to take the children along. She wouldn't stay home with them, as her mother had when her father was racing. Her mother would approve. Peter was a "gentleman." Both parents would approve. They wanted the best for her, they always said.

She stepped out of the shower and dried herself with a towel the size of a sheet. EML. His mother's monogram. Cassie's would be a C between two Ls. Lindemann to Lawson. Her initials wouldn't even change. She wondered what Mrs. Lawson's maiden name had been. She knew so little about the Lawsons. Cassie suspected they disapproved of her, but Peter said she was wrong. Being this late for breakfast wouldn't help. She put on a pink shirt and grey slacks. She'd brought jeans, thinking they'd be perfect for the country, but this house didn't feel like the country. She slipped into loafers and headed downstairs.

Peter met her at the bottom of the stairs.

"Good morning," he said, giving her a hug. "Sleep well?"

"Too well. Are your parents annoyed?"

"I made it down in time for breakfast with them. They've gone off for their morning ride. I told them you had a lot of reading to do last night and would probably sleep late. Let's find you something to eat."

Despite the aromas that had drifted into her dreams, Cassie's appetite for breakfast had faded when she thought of facing Mrs. Lawson. She felt hungry again, knowing she'd been excused. Letty had left a plate of hot biscuits and bacon in the oven. Cassie put it on a tray set with honey, butter, cream and sugar, while Peter poured them coffee.

"It's cloudy. Too damp to eat on the verandah."

Cassie didn't mind the kitchen. Anywhere but that dining room.

"Did you get some reading done?"

"None." She smiled at him across the table. "I had other things on my mind."

"Such as?" He smiled back.

"Such as when to marry you."

"When! You mean you're willing?"

Cassie nodded.

He came to her side before she could speak, leaned down, and kissed her ear. Then he sat down again, pulled his chair in and shook the fold from his napkin. "We'll have a fine life, Cassie. I promise you."

Cassie didn't doubt him.

"Did you tell your parents you'd asked me?"

"No. I didn't know if you'd accept. I didn't want to get their hopes up. We'll tell them today, though."

"No. I think we should wait," Cassie said, breaking bacon into pieces to fit her biscuit. "You haven't spoken to my father. He may refuse you my hand!" She thought he'd guess she was teasing, but his eyes told her he didn't.

"Do you think so?"

"No. But he takes being a father pretty seriously. He'd be offended if we just assumed his approval."

"Then I'll ask him tonight. We'll leave after breakfast, drive up there." Peter beamed at her, proud of his impromptu plan. "I'll take you back to school tomorrow."

"We can't just leave! What about your parents? Their plans?" A quick exit might be her *coup de grace* with the Lawsons, but she'd end this visit without having to get on a horse.

"I'll tell them you have to get back," Peter said, patting her hand, assuring himself. "Work to do."

"Lots. *Sometime* today I have to tackle my reading."

"You can do it in the car. Call your folks after breakfast. Tell them we're on our way."

"You're determined!" Cassie drizzled honey over another half biscuit and popped it into her mouth. "These are divine, but I can't eat three. Want mine?" He nodded, so she fixed the last half for him and reached across the table to feed it to him. He took it from her hand and ate it himself.

When they drove down to the barn—to see the horses and to say goodbye—Mrs. Lawson shook her hand and praised Cassie's dedication to her studies. After working hard all year, she wanted grades to show it. For the first few minutes Cassie enjoyed the scenery, but she opened her book as soon as they were on the interstate.

"Cassie?" She'd only read a couple of pages when Peter interrupted. "We didn't decide when."

"We can't. My parents should have some say, since they'll be throwing the party. And there's my job..."

"You can tell them your plans have changed."

She'd promised Mr. Gilbert she'd start work in June. She knew they could find someone else, but she wanted the job. "I could work for a year..." She noticed Peter's jaw tighten. "Even six months. We could be married around Christmas time." Perfect, she thought. Dark velvet dresses and candlelight.

"Take a job for six months? Move in, move out? That's not practical, Cassie. I thought we'd get married this summer. Early, then spend some time sailing up and down the New England coast before I start school."

"Then what? I'll have to find another job."

"You shouldn't have trouble. You landed the one in New York, after all. I just can't see waiting around—you in New York, me in Philadelphia. I love you, damn it. I want you with me."

"I love you, too." The words didn't sound right, slipping out as a retort in a discussion. She needed time to think. Time to read *The Great Gatsby* without thinking. She hated this struggle. She wanted life to be simple, her choices to be clear. "Your plan sounds irresistible," she said, putting her hand on his knee. "A whole summer living on the boat...but I can't decide now. Can't we talk about it later?"

"I can wait."

At the first Philadelphia exit, he interrupted again.

"This is a pretty big city. There must be good jobs here. And it's not that far from New York. You could get up to see Julia in no time."

"It's not about Julia! It's the job I don't want to give up!" She couldn't see anything out of the side windows in the heavy rain. Peter fidgeted with the wipers and vents, trying to stop water from dripping on her foot. The cities *were* close. They could all get together on weekends, one place or the other. She doubted she'd find another job like the one she had, but she could at least look before she dismissed the possibility.

"Just wanted to make that point," Peter said. "Give it some thought."

Along the Jersey Turnpike they stopped for a late lunch. The cafeteria offerings looked old and dry, so Cassie had soup and watched Peter eat a sandwich.

"Is something bothering you?"

"No."

Cassie knew better.

"I haven't refused your proposal!"

"But you haven't accepted, either. I get the feeling you'd rather go to New York and hang around with Julia."

"Not rather, but she and I had talked about next year. Things are set...I've been looking forward to it. Your proposal is sudden, that's all. Nothing's planned."

"It can be." He crinkled up the cellophane and his napkin, stuffing them into his empty cup. "Had enough to eat?"

Cassie nodded. "I was spoiled by Letty's cooking."

"We'd better keep moving."

Back on the turnpike Peter was still tense, but the rain let up, and he didn't have to strain to see where they were going. They skimmed along in the fast lane, bursting through the clouds of spray thrown up by tractor trailers. Peter took the Tappan Zee, avoiding Manhattan, the streets and the subject. Cassie watched the miles click by on the odometer. They had traveled a long way in two days.

No one answered when Cassie rang the bell. She was taking out her key when her mother appeared, drying her hands on a striped kitchen towel. She hugged Cassie, and Peter as hard, happy to see them both.

"I'd love to sit right down and visit, but I have to get a cake into the oven. Make yourselves comfortable. Dad should be home shortly," she called from the kitchen.

"The man I came to see," Peter quipped as they climbed the stairs. "I'm not sure I need to. Your mother acted like I'm already part of the family. Do you think he'll offer a dowry?"

"He's not *that* old-fashioned. I hope you weren't counting on one."

"I'll settle for the daughter." He set her suitcase inside her bedroom door and kissed her hard. Cassie pulled away.

"Mom might come up! I'll see you in the study."

"Maybe I'll let him have a drink first."

"And read the paper? And..."

"Right. No point in stalling. Just get it done." He closed the door.

He'd always seemed so sure of himself that his anxiety surprised her. Pleased her, too, in a way. But he didn't have to worry. Her parents were of one mind about almost everything. Her mother's warm greeting meant Peter would do fine with her father.

He was settled in his chair, but jumped up to embrace Cassie when she entered the room.

"What a nice surprise! Beautiful as always, sweetie."

Cassie hugged him tight. "Same dear old Daddy. You remember Peter..."

"Sure." He extended his hand. "Good to see you again. Sit down. Can I fix you a Scotch?"

"I'd like that, sir."

"Not for me. I'm going to see if Mom needs help in the kitchen." Cassie ducked out the door, leaving them alone.

In the dining room, before pushing open the swinging door to the kitchen, she identified the aromas.

"Mom, you said you'd keep it simple. Leg of lamb? Chocolate cake? Too much fuss."

"You haven't come home for many weekends over the years, so this is a special occasion."

Cassie hugged her mother around the waist. "You're working too hard. What can I do?" She asked knowing she'd be sent to the dining room to set the table. Her mother liked to cook alone. Cassie had observed a trick or two the times she'd sat on the counter chatting, but her mother had guarded her recipes and never taught her to cook. This was an occasion, so Cassie spread the best linen as a backdrop for her mother's treasures. Cassie had been twelve before she was allowed to handle the crystal, but for years before that she had loved the sparkle and the ring of glasses and laughter whenever family and friends gathered around the table.

Placing the candles around the centerpiece of narcissus, Cassie remembered the way Julia had set the table for their first luncheon in New York. It had been her signature as this was her mother's. Soon Cassie might be signing a new name, setting her own places, making her own choices. Facing all that lay ahead, she took comfort in being here, where everything was familiar. She refolded the napkin at Peter's place and went back to the kitchen.

Her mother had finished frosting the cake. She handed Cassie the knife to lick and pointed to the tray of cheese and crackers, ready to go to the study. Cassie stalled, not wanting to interrupt.

"Cassandra," she said, pushing her toward the door, "The men should not be left alone for so long without food."

"Coming. Coming," she said when she met her father in the foyer.

"About time! Peter's hungry in there. Go ahead. I want to have a word with your mother."

He spoke softly, soberly, without the slightest smile. Peter was staring into space when she entered the study.

"How did it go?"

He shrugged. "He asked a lot of questions, about what I wanted to do, where I thought we'd live. He listened to everything I had to say, but he never said anything, just pondered. Then he got up and left. To find you and the crackers, he told me."

"He told me he wanted to 'have a word' with my mother. That's serious. Fix me a drink while we wait? Whatever happens, you'll enjoy the dinner. Mom's outdone herself—and Letty!"

Peter was dropping ice into her glass when her father came back, followed by her mother.

"Stop! Don't pour that!"

Peter couldn't tell from the sound of the voice that Mr. Lindemann was smiling, and he whirled around with a shocked expression. Her father was standing in the doorway with a bottle of champagne and glasses.

"Scotch will not do, young man." He poured champagne for himself and his wife. "Anna and I want to welcome you to this family." He passed each of them a glass. "And toast to your happiness."

Mrs. Lindemann took one sip, then put down her glass and hugged Peter again, then Cassie.

"Darling, I'm so thrilled. Didn't I say he was right for you? Oh, there's so much to plan and do. We'll have such fun working on it together. Of course, we'll have the reception in the garden."

"I was thinking of getting married around Christmas time."

"Nonsense. Christmas is Christmas, and so it shall stay. Summer is for weddings. It must be the summer."

Peter glanced at Cassie.

"I feel the same way, Mrs. Lindemann. I hope we can be married early in the summer. You see, I want to take Cass on a long cruise."

"A cruise? On a ship!" Her smile radiated approval.

"No, on my boat. But it's very comfortable. I thought we'd sail up the coast to Maine or Nova Scotia. If that seems too soon, we don't need an elaborate wedding."

"Need? Nobody needs an elaborate wedding, but Cassie is our only daughter. I've looked forward to her wedding for years. We'll manage. We'll get everything done on time, won't we, Cassie. By late June. The garden is lovely at that time of year."

Cassie had danced as a sea nymph in a ballet recital once, behind a gauze curtain that made everything look soft and dreamlike. She felt now as if she were looking at life through that curtain. Everything looked dreamy and inviting. She might have known her mother would love to plan a family wedding. Her father was quizzing Peter about the boat and the planned trip. Neither of them asked why she'd wanted to wait until Christmas. Maybe it *was* silly to wait, to move into New York and out again in six months. Everyone else seemed delighted with the idea of a June wedding. She sipped her champagne. She'd draft a letter tomorrow.

Dear Mr. Gilbert....

Chapter 10

March 1965

AFTERNOONS WERE ALWAYS long at Wallingford Press, but this one was passing more slowly than most. Cassie stared at the clock over the vault, watching the second hand sweep away the minutes. Three more hours and she'd be on the train to New York.

The silence and the stagnant air were suffocating. Once—probably on an afternoon like this—her predecessor had thrown the window open, and a March gust had cleared the desks, scrambling the illustrations for six texts. Maintenance had arrived the next day to nail the window shut, and it hadn't been opened since. She often went to the window when she felt sleepy—tired of pictures of hearts and lungs—to look at the people and the flowers in the park across the street. Today a young woman was sitting on a green bench among the daffodils, her face to the spring sun, one hand rocking a baby carriage, reading.

Only a year ago, Cassie had given up a chance to read manuscripts for a living and come to Philadelphia to do layouts in the medical division at Wallingford—until something opened up in the trade division. They'd praised her neat work and given her a raise after two months, so she'd stayed. But whenever she asked about the promised transfer, they said they couldn't do without her where she was. This spring she was trapped inside, working with pictures instead of words. She went back to her paste-up. Sometimes the smell is the best part of this job, she thought, brushing rubber cement on the back of an illustration. Julia would find that amusing. Pathetic, but amusing.

The cab stopped in front of a row of houses. Cassie checked the address again and before leaving the shelter of the backseat, paid the driver an extra couple of dollars to wait, in case there was some mistake. The gutter was filled with discarded paper and broken glass, and several people were clustered on the steps, laughing, smoking. They stopped talking and stared as she ran up to 137, rang the bell, and waited. Seven months had passed since she had seen Alan and Julia. They would bring her to life again.

Through the cracked window she saw Alan jump down the last two steps. He opened the door, kissed her hello, and waved the cab off.

"The buzzer's broken," he said, taking her bag. "And it's a long climb. Not like the other place....my professor came home, so we had to move."

Thin rubber treads on the stairs were torn and curled at the edges, and the walls, streaked and gouged from furniture, were grimy with handprints and graffiti. Not like Julia's old place, with its collections of photographs. Cassie's apartment was in a row house, too, and nothing special, but at least it was clean. She wondered how her old friend tolerated this approach to her home.

Julia had painted the top story walls white, put up three posters of anemone blossoms—red, blue, and purple—and given the door a coat of red enamel. She was standing on the landing, waiting for them, wearing a short sweater dress and black fishnet stockings, and high-heeled red pumps. Her hair was long, pulled to one side in a shiny braid that fell over her left shoulder. She looked different, but she gave Cassie a hug as always.

"I'm glad you came," she said stepping back. "Looks like you're surviving. Come meet everyone." She broke through a circle of six people to turn down the music.

"Hey! You're killing the mood." The protestor was handsome, with a tan that said he traveled. He had a slivery blonde at his side.

"Too bad. I want you to meet my old friend. She defected to Philadelphia, or you'd have met months ago." Julia introduced them, people who worked with her in the art department at Hawkins House. Ignoring the woman who clung to his arm, stroking his sleeve, one man winked at Cassie. The woman squinted at her.

"Why Philadelphia?"

"My husband's in school there," Cassie said, fingering her rings.

"But tonight she's alone, so make her feel welcome."

Cassie wished Julia hadn't singled her out.

"This our art director," Julia said, putting her hand on a tall man's shoulder. "My boss, some might say."

He nodded without speaking, and smiled. Even though his dark moustache turned up at the corners, he seemed cold. Both men, one in midnight blue worsted and the other in tweed, looked surprisingly conventional. Cassie had expected Julia's city friends to be bohemian, more like her. Paul, who worked with Alan, looked more like an artist. Despite his full red beard, he seemed too young to be a university teaching assistant. He said hello, then pulled Alan aside.

"We were arguing a point when you came," he apologized to Cassie over his shoulder.

"As always." His wife put her arm around his waist. "He must be winning this one, since he won't let Alan off the hook." She was no more than five feet tall, with dark hair, and a genuine smile.

"Go ahead, you two." Julia put on more records and turned up the music again. "I'll look out for Cassie."

"I'd like to change," Cassie said.

"No need. You look fine. Besides, pretty soon the room will be full of people, and it won't matter what you're wearing."

Maybe not, but Cassie felt dowdy in her navy suit. "I came straight from work!" she said.

"Follow me, then." Julia led the way to the bedroom. "I'll wait, if you don't mind." Julia flopped onto the bed, kicked her shoes off, and stretched her legs out straight. "I'm not much for this crowd tonight."

"They're your friends!"

"Colleagues, mostly. Alan's and mine. I'd rather talk to you. What is it since your wedding? Nine months? Seems like a year. And I had to twist your arm to come tonight." She played with the end of her braid, coiling it in the palm of her hand. "Why wouldn't Peter come?"

"Not wouldn't—couldn't." Cassie didn't say that he had turned down the invitation without discussion the day it arrived in the mail. That he had never even offered to try to get his work done so he could come. That she had begged him the night before, but that he had refused. "He has to study—can't take even half a day away from his books."

"Too bad. Now Paul and Ingrid are the only 'old marrieds' here."

"They seem nice."

"They're good friends. Alan and I see a lot of them. Movies, dinners. You know..."

Cassie didn't know. She and Peter rarely went out.

Julia got up and went into the bathroom across the hall, leaving her red shoes behind on the goatskin rug. Cassie could hear water running. Julia sat down on the bed again when she came back.

"Are you OK?"

"Fine. Just not in a party mood." Someone turned the music up and there were more voices. "New arrivals. We'd better get out there. Then later you can tell me about married life."

The living room had filled with people, maybe a dozen more. Cassie was glad she didn't have to make a solo entrance. Julia threaded through the crowd toward Alan without stopping to introduce her, so Cassie followed, nodding and smiling as though some of the faces were familiar.

"There you are! I had to serve this without your taste test," Alan said, ladling out some punch for Julia. "Pass?"

Julia nodded scanning the room. "I see my friend has arrived."

"He's been looking for you."

Cassie watched Julia move into the crowd.

"My old professor," Alan said, handing Cassie a cup of punch. "The one who rented us the first apartment. He's nuts about Julia. She goes there for tea once a week, takes him cookies."

"He must love that." Cassie remembered college teatimes, the tin. So long ago. "It seems years since we've seen you two. We got your postcards. How was your trip?"

"Fantastic! We rented one of those little French tin can cars and drove all over the place. No itinerary, except to see some of the out-of- the-way spots Julia remembered from her childhood."

"I didn't know she'd spent that much time in Europe."

"She hadn't, but she had pictures in her mind—places she'd been with her grandmother. She could lead us right to them!"

Cassie wasn't surprised. Julia sustained her memories of her grandmother by doing things she had taught her. Their connection showed in gestures like taking sweets to the professor, making gifts for her friends.

Neighbors from the old building came over for more punch, and Alan introduced them. She joined in the talk about buildings, rents, and where there were deals, shocked them with the low Philadelphia prices. Julia, across the room, seemed to be back in a party mood, miming some story. Cassie would have liked to slip into that circle next to her, but couldn't think what she'd talk about with that group. Ingrid joined her at the table and only half filled their cups by tipping the bowl.

"I'll get Alan to top it up," she said. "Looks like he could use an interruption." The blonde had detached herself from her escort's grey sleeve and was leaning on Alan.

"Time to play host, thank God," he said when he had broken away.

"Do you think her feet hurt?" Cassie asked.

"Why? They don't bear any weight!" Alan laughed. "Nasty. You're waiting," he said, noticing her empty cup. "Coming right up. I didn't tell you the revelation of the trip," he said, opening a can of pineapple juice. "I met Julia's mother." Alan lowered his voice. "The mysterious Mrs. Kramer."

"I lived with Julia three years and never met her! She avoids her mother!"

He handed her a bottle. "I guess Julia planned the meeting in London because she thought things could be different."

"Can they?" Cassie poured the ginger ale while he poured the juice, then the rum.

"You tell me. When we showed up for dinner at her hotel she told us we were a disgrace. Without a hello or how are you! No wonder those two go years between meetings. And we were wearing our neatest traveling clothes!"

Cassie knew Julia's traveling clothes, remembered her own first impression. Jeans had probably not been welcome in the hotel dining room.

"For Mrs. Kramer's generation..."

"You're too kind Cassie. Mrs. K. won't fit your image." Shaking his head, Alan took a bag of ice from the freezer. "That woman is rare. Gorgeous, in a tinselly way, like that blonde in the living room. Maybe natural, probably not. Looks only a couple of years older than Julia," he said, tapping the block to break off some small pieces. "If you don't look too closely. Very well dressed and jeweled. Cold as ice and poker hot." He dropped a couple of cubes into her glass and into his, and eased the block into the bowl.

"But did she like you?"

"She flapped her green eyelids, caressed my hand... Seemed to like me fine, but she wasn't thinking about her daughter."

"How horrible. Poor Julia!"

"Poor me?" Julia came in with an empty platter.

"London," Alan said.

"Oh, that! You told her? Shocking, isn't it? I have a new motto where she's concerned," Julia said, arranging frozen pastries on cookie sheets. "Expect anything, expect nothing." She slid them into the oven and closed the door firmly. "Ten minutes." She put her arms around Alan's waist, her cheek against his chest. "You can stay here while these cook—Cassie, make sure he takes them out on time—but then you'd both better circulate." She tucked a loose strand of hair behind her ear and went back to the party.

"She's gotten over it, it seems."

"She had steeled herself for the meeting. Or so I thought. But face to face, Julia withdrew. She was no match for her mother."

"Julia outdone?"

"Not really, but she must have thought she could be, because she didn't fight back. Seeing them together was very revealing."

Clearly Alan was thinking more than he was saying, making Cassie wonder if Peter ever compared her with her mother, thought as deeply about their relationship.

"All those two have in common is height and pride." Alan put the empty bottles in the trash. "It was the pride that brought Julia back."

Cassie smelled browning cheese and peeked into the oven. "We'd better rescue them." Alan held the platter while she lifted the pastries one by one from the hot sheet. "These are darker than the last batch. Maybe they won't notice. The trip wasn't spoiled, though?"

"No, we had a perfect summer. How about you and Peter? A whole summer of cruising...not hard to take."

"We weren't free the way you were. We had harbors to make by the end of each day, and most of them were familiar. It was relaxing more than exciting."

Alan offered her first pick from the platter. "I'd better take these around now, while they're warm."

Alone in the kitchen, Cassie realized that she missed Peter. On their honeymoon they had been together almost all the time, except when she wanted to be alone, for a little while each day. Since he'd started school they'd seen each other only at dinner and in bed. They hardly ever talked.

She spotted Ingrid and Paul, who were with strangers, but drew her in when she approached their circle. She didn't have to work at the conversation, and it felt almost like the old days, like one of the Provincetown parties. This wasn't the first time she'd been by herself among Alan and Julia's friends, but tonight was different.

"Missing your husband?" Ingrid asked.

"A little." But what she missed most was the fun. She had always loved Alan and Julia's parties. Talking, dancing, laughing with their other friends. This was a roomful of people—acid and basic, but no chemistry.

Ingrid and Paul stayed. The others were gone, and so was the tension, replaced by the feeling Cassie had missed all evening. The five of them lounged on floor pillows, sipping espresso and comparing impressions of the party. Cassie looked at her watch—one AM and only the friends are here. Ingrid was fighting sleep. Her eyes slowly closed, flashed open too wide for a second, then closed again.

"I'd better take this little lady home," Paul said holding out both hands to help her get up. "It's way past her bedtime."

"I'm a night nurse, remember?"

"That's reassuring," Alan said. "When the night nurse falls asleep at midnight...must be the company."

"Sort of." Paul grinned. "The baby!"

Ingrid put her hand over his mouth. "We weren't going to tell!"

When she and Cassie had talked earlier about babies, Ingrid had confessed that she too dreamed hours of each day away thinking about them, that she too noticed the pregnant women first wherever she went. But she hadn't even hinted at the news. Alan shook Paul's hand and gave Ingrid a hug. Next to him, she looked like a child, and Cassie couldn't imagine her having one.

"When?" Julia had to ask, but sounded like she didn't want to know.

"Between Thanksgiving and Christmas..."

Perfect! Cassie was going to say, but decided not to when Julia said nothing.

"We didn't plan it," Paul said, filling the silence.

"That's two embarrassing remarks. Let's go, before you make any more." Ingrid nudged him into the hall. "Goodnight all."

Julia started collecting glasses before the door had closed behind them.

"I'll do that, Julia," Alan said. "You talk to Cassie."

"You talk to Cassie," she said, disappearing into the kitchen. They heard her slam the refrigerator door, then begin to stack glasses. When Alan took the punch bowl in, she came out.

"Ingrid's news upset you?"

"Just surprised me." Julia shook her head and lit a cigarette. "So, Alan's talked to you all night. My turn to catch up. What's new?"

"Not much. And we didn't talk all night. Just about your trip, your mother."

Julia puffed without inhaling, creating a veil of smoke.

"Speaking of mothers, how's yours?"

"Fine. We were home for Christmas."

"We spent the holidays in Montreal. What a madhouse!" I love the Goodmans. Alan's father's a professor. History. At McGill." Julia tossed Cassie a couple of pillows, tucked one under her, and rolled onto her stomach. "His mother's too good to be true," she said, resting her chin in one palm. "She cooks and bakes and sews and soothes....She's beautiful still. And Alan's sisters were there with their kids and husbands, so she had all of them to fuss over. I had a good dose of family."

"You make it sound like foul medicine!" Cassie could imagine a Christmas like that in a year or so.

"Not foul! Alan's mother is happy being a slave to their every wish. His father hides in his study, keeps out of the way, but when he appears he tries to tell stories over the din. He bounces the babies on his knee, sings them little songs..." Her voice faltered, and Cassie let the silence be. "Want a brandy?"

Cassie didn't, really, but the rum had worn off some by now, and she didn't want Julia to drink alone. Cassie wanted to keep her talking, though odds were she couldn't pull anything out of Julia that she wasn't ready to share.

"Finished." Alan bent down and sipped from Julia's glass.

"Join us?"

"No. My head will be bad enough in the morning, when those kids descend on me with those voices..." Alan winced.

"You're still doing children's theater?"

"Are you kidding? He'd give up almost everything before that!"

"Almost everything," he concurred. "I love those kids."

Cassie moved to get up, but he put his hand on her head. "Stay where you are, Cass. Goodnight."

Julia crossed her ankles, pulled up her dress, and lowered herself smoothly to the floor. "Need another pillow? The rug is about the only thing that was mine in the old place. We bought this table and the pillows. I suppose we'll have to get chairs, too, at some point, but I like sitting around like this, don't you?"

"Yes, because it's truly comfortable. You were talking about Alan's family. So you felt part of it?"

"Part of it! It was like a whirlpool swirling around me, sucking me into the center. I'd get flashes I'd dreamed it or something... weird."

"Did Alan understand?"

"He couldn't, any more than you would." Julia lit another cigarette and shoved the pack toward Cassie, who decided to have one. Peter hated the taste on her lips and the smell in her clothes, so it had been months since she'd smoked. The first puff made her dizzy.

"Your families envelop you, color your world view." Julia drew lines in her old ashes with the glowing tip.

"You feel free because you haven't had a family?"

"Sometimes. But most of the time I feel like I'm outdoors at night, looking into warm rooms of laughing people."

Cassie loved driving at night, being able to do that. She never felt like an outsider. Maybe because her childhood was happy, she put herself into those scenes.

"The problem is Alan. He wants so much to be married. But I'm afraid I'll feel confined." She sat up and looked straight at Cassie. "What if I get to depend on all that love and care, and then can't survive without it?"

"Why would you have to?"

"I have to know I could. I had my grandmother, but when she died....Damn! If I give in to this..." She got up and went to the kitchen.

Retreating again, Cassie thought.

"Look at *you*," Julia said, returning with the brandy bottle. "The change in *you*."

"You're changing the subject."

"Not at all."

Cassie put her hand over her glass, so Julia refilled her own, sank back into her pillows, and raised it in a silent toast. "You add to my doubts," she said.

"Why?" Julia had seen so little of her. What could she know?

"Let's start with Alan's mother. She lives for everyone else. She's happy, but what would happen if they all let her down?"

"Do you have to think about the flip side of everything?"

"And his sisters," Julia continued, ignoring her. They're completely dependent on their husbands and don't have a waking minute to themselves with the babies. They don't have time to think, much less do anything creative."

Things were never that way in Cassie's daydreams.

"And you're sure a different person than you were a year ago."

"Who isn't?"

"Don't be glib. You were full of energy, ready to come here to live, work. Now you're only half here. Halfhearted."

"I just felt a little awkward tonight, without Peter." Cassie's back was beginning to ache. She massaged the muscles along her spine, longing for something to lean on.

"No, when you decided to sail off with him you tossed your own goals overboard."

"I wanted to marry him, so I modified my plans. You can hardly criticize! Who dropped out of school to follow Alan to New York? What about your goals?"

"I did what felt was right at the time."

"Well so did I." Cassie said.

Julia unbraided her hair, pulled it all forward, over her face, then flung it back like a mane. "But I'm at least working in the art department, doing some things I like. Can you say the same? You shouldn't be pasting pictures. You hate it!" Julia always found clues. Cassie hadn't had to tell her. "Being married has changed you."

"You don't know everything about me."

"I know you're a giving person. Like Alan's mother. But you give yourself away trying to make other people happy. Give away too much and you won't get it back."

When threatened with a truth, Julia still turned it around and struck with one of her own. Cassie would think later about what she'd said. Now she wanted to keep after Julia.

"We were talking about you. I doubt Alan expects you to be like his mother."

Julia blew smoke rings, thinking.

"My mother didn't find me very fulfilling. She couldn't take the demands..."

"Come on, Julia. You're very different. Alan sure thinks so."

"But I can learn from her! I don't have to make the same mistakes. I don't have to get married. I don't have to have a child, I don't have to give up my work...." Julia rapped the table with her knuckle after each 'have to.'

"No, you don't have to do any of those things if you don't want to. But I think you do. Why don't you stop trying so hard to imagine how everything will be." Julia had changed, too. When she was determined to take off from school to follow Alan to New York, she had said logic had no place in some situations. "You used to say you had to listen to your heart. Haven't you been happy? Have you regretted leaving school?"

"You used to say I'd ruin my future if I did." Julia laughed quietly. "Why are we arguing about this. I am happy. No regrets."

"So trust your heart again. Your instincts will get you by."

Julia shook her head slowly, unconvinced.

"And Alan wants to be a father. The whole burden wouldn't be on you." Cassie paused. "Even if it were, children grow into fine people in spite of their mothers. Look at you," she added, wishing she hadn't.

"Or you..."

"Sorry. You know how I meant that. You've made your life what you want it to be, and it's good so far. Why would that change?" Craving another cigarette, Cassie reached for the pack. Julia leaned over to light another for herself from the same match, and inhaled deeply.

"I don't know. What happens? What's made you so sad and quiet? Is your life what you want it to be? Can you do anything without Peter?"

"I'm here..."

"Because I insisted."

"My ideas of what I *wanted* to do have changed. All I think about now is having a baby. I *do* hate my job. I was jealous of Ingrid tonight." Of her friendship with Julia, of the dinners and movies, not just of the baby. "Some days I feel like I'm the only one in the world who isn't pregnant."

"Nope." Julia smoothed the front of her dress, showing off her flat abdomen. "Have you talked to Peter about this?"

"Too many times. He won't talk about it anymore. He says we're not ready to have children. He wants to be established first."

"Established! God, you're the most established couple I know! Old stodgy logical Peter."

"He's right! We should wait."

"Your instincts? Or is that the Cassie who wants to please?"

"Neither. He has another year in school. I have to keep working." Cassie swallowed the last of her brandy.

"So here we are. Me—married, dying to start a family, with a husband who says the time isn't right. You—with a man who wants to marry you, have a child, and you're not ready." The wee hour quiet gave Cassie's words more weight. "I guess it's true what they say about the grass..."

"Even in New York City." Julia smiled. "At least we can still talk, though we never find any answers. I wish you had come here to live. For both our sakes."

Chapter 11

August 1965

CASSIE ROLLED OVER, stretched, and inched her fingers into the warm sand. The midday sun on her back and the buzz of the cicada lulled her in and out of dozes. She barely heard the bob-white whistle. She dreamed Julia arrived wearing a heavy satin wedding dress, appliquéd with teardrop pearls. Down the road to the beach, holding her veil up out of the sand, Alan followed.

Cassie opened one eye, squinting to see the time. In ten minutes her campers would descend on her, clamoring for their boat assignments. The limp flag on the signal pole by the boathouse meant no wind and a long and lazy afternoon. A break in the routine would make it seem shorter—she'd let them make their moorings early and swim off the raft for the last half hour.

Peter came over the hill and flopped down beside her.

"Everything's all set. I switched my office duty, so I'm free."

"Wonderful!" she said, and kissed his cheek as he glanced around to see if anyone was watching. "Maybe we should take them to a fancy restaurant...no, a cookout's better. But there's still so much to do." She sat up, checking her watch again.

"I know. Back to work." Peter did three quick push-ups, then ran toward the water. "I'll get the raft," he called and dove in. As she folded the blanket, Cassie watched him swim out to the mooring, admiring his stroke, his powerful shoulders, wishing the afternoon were over so they could make love. Last summer, on the boat, she could indulge her midday desires. Here at camp every minute was scheduled. Still, she was glad they'd come back to where they'd met—to work the waterfront together one last summer.

Cassie walked to the office along shiny needle-fragrant paths under the pines, then across the parade field, the grass brushing the rhythm of her stride against her loafers. Far behind her, down the hill, one of the youngest campers shouted "ready or not" and raucous laughter came from one of the teen cabins ahead. She was happy here. If she could take this energy back with her to the city, this might be a better year, even if she didn't have a baby.

A VW beetle pulled into the parking lot, and Cassie ran to meet it when she saw the New York plates. The man at the wheel didn't look familiar, but as soon as the car stopped Julia got out and rushed toward her.

"Mrs. Goodman!" Cassie said, trying the name on Julia.

"Same old me."

"Alan—no beard! What happened?" She frowned at her old friend. "You didn't make him shave it off..."

"No! Why would you think that? Tell her, love."

"The rash move of a desperate man, Cassie. I threatened to shave if Julia didn't marry me, and when she didn't take me seriously, I had to go through with it. Then she felt guilty and had to give in."

"So that's how you snagged her...congratulations." She kissed him, then stepped back and looked him over. "The new you isn't bad. We'll get used to it."

"This marriage isn't supposed to change us. He's going to grow it back." Julia patted his cheek and looked around the parking lot. "Where's Peter?"

"Down at The Grove..."

"The Grove?" Julia drew out the word, rolling her eyes at Alan. "How quaint."

"Now don't be cynical," Cassie said. "Here all the special places have names. Our cabin is near there. We can drive down in your car."

Cassie climbed into the back seat, and the three of them drove down the sandy hill toward the bay. A column of smoke rose from the clearing next to their cabin. Peter had started the fire. She left Alan and Julia to change and joined him. He had spread blankets, dragged up two huge driftwood logs for backrests, and strung colored paper lanterns in the trees. Cassie put her arms around his waist and gave him a squeeze.

"Wherever did you find lanterns?"

"The prop room at the theater. Think anyone will mind that I borrowed them for the evening?"

Cassie shook her head. "Julia and Alan wanted to change. Can we start cooking when they get here?"

"With a few more coals." Sparks flew up around his hand as he poked with the end of a stick and the pine logs crumbled into orange chunks. He tossed two more on top, and set the cooking rack in place. "While the lobsters steam, we'll have a round of champagne."

"Here you are!" Julia and Alan had shed their city clothes for jeans. "Good timing!"

"Looks as though marriage has done something for *you*," Peter said, shaking Alan's hand, staring at his beardless chin. "You look very civilized."

"Peter..." Julia put her finger to her lips. "You don't know the details. You're looking great yourself. Too refined for this uncivilized setting."

"Rustic, lady. Rustic." He kissed her cheek. "Congratulations." His greeting was spontaneous, sincere. That pleased Cassie. "Now," he said, pulling a bottle from a bailing bucket—also borrowed, from the boathouse. Moët. Peter hadn't scrimped. "When we heard you all had gotten married, we thought we'd better plan a celebration. Help me out here, will you Cass?" As he popped the cork and filled each of their paper cups, she took over the speechmaking.

"When we were married, you two were there, wishing us well. So...we're glad to have a chance to toast both of you. And wish you happiness."

Peter raised his cup. "To the newlyweds."

Alan took a sip. "And to friends who know how to celebrate."

"Peter planned it all." Cassie patted his back, then stroked a circle with her palm.

"To Peter, then," Julia added. "I see you really went all out. I'm famished. Did I hear 'lobster'?"

Peter lifted the cooler lid to show her. In a bed of seaweed, four lobsters glistened green, stirred at the sudden light. "You all sit down and I'll put them in."

Cassie filled a bowl with potato chips and set them in front of Julia. "Mostly simple pleasures here," she said, joining them on the blanket.

Alan leaned back against the log, closed his eyes, and sighed. "This camp stuff could be habit-forming. Good to get away from the books, Peter?"

"I'll say."

"So will I." Cassie liked being with him more of the day, even if they weren't alone.

"This is a great place," Alan said. "But you have the boat. Why not take off?"

"Finances. Last summer, the honeymoon, was a luxury. I've chartered her this year. She makes more money than we do."

"But we have fun," Cassie added.

"You quit that deadly job, then. Good." Cassie could have closed her eyes and believed she was back in their dorm room on the first day of college, with Julia surveying her boxes. "What are you going to do in the fall?"

"I don't know," she said, kicking off her loafers, wishing Julia hadn't asked. "This is summer." She wiggled her tan toes. Signs of a sailor—tan toes and faded shorts. She looked out over the bay, past the stranded Mercurys on their moorings, at the sandbars that stretched for miles at low tide. She couldn't have wished for a better evening. The air was warm and dry and still. "Just look at that light."

"Looks like the gods sneezed gold dust," said Alan.

"If I walked toward the sunset," Cassie wondered out loud, "How far could I go?"

"A quarter of the way to Barnstable before the tide came in," Peter said.

"Sure, but if it didn't..."

"Pointless question, because it does."

"Is this a regular topic around here?" Julia scowled at her. "It's a good thing you're going back to civilization soon. Really, Cassie. You must have some idea what you'll do."

She did, but didn't want to discuss it. If you spoke a wish it didn't come true. "None."

"You'd have had more choices in New York."

"But then I wouldn't have been able come back here." Cassie crossed her legs Indian style. She could feel the prickly grass through the wool blanket. She refused to argue with Julia tonight. "When did you two get married, anyway? I was so excited when you called, I forgot to ask."

"The first of August. We'd been talking about it—Alan had been talking about it—for months. Then one hot day, when he knew I didn't have any fight in me, he dragged me down to city hall."

"Just like that?" Cassie couldn't imagine such an important occasion with no ceremony.

"Just!"

"Lucky you," Peter said to Alan. "I had to go through months of planning with Cassie and her mother. Nothing was spontaneous with us."

"I'm sure not," Julia said, not quite to herself, and popped a chip into her mouth. "Alan's mother didn't let us off scot-free, though. We're on our way back from Montreal."

"I thought you called from New York."

"No. Montreal. Does it matter?" It mattered that this wasn't the first celebration since their wedding. Cassie had wanted it to be, but that was selfish. "*La Mère*—that's what I call her—started planning as soon as she heard the news. Gathered all of their friends, family." The light had turned rose, coloring Julia's pale cheeks. "It was a huge party."

"They're happy then?"

"Thrilled," Alan said. "They've been telling me for years to marry Julia. When I told them she wouldn't have me, they thought I was joking, stalling."

"Because your mother couldn't believe I didn't jump at the chance to marry her son."

"I can see her point," Cassie said.

"Hear that, Peter?" Julia tapped his foot with hers. "What's that supposed to mean?"

"That he's nice," Cassie said, not daring to look at Alan.

"Then I'll let it pass." Julia elbowed her. "The point is she thinks I'll make him happy. And she hopes I'll make him babies, so she's delighted."

Peter cleared his throat, got up, checked the pot, and refilled their cups. Encircled by the scents of pine, wet sand, and wood smoke, they listened to the singing that drifted from the cabins on the hill and watched the rainbow sky go dark.

"We even have background music," Julia said, filling the silent space after the song. Cassie, her own eyes misting, could tell she wasn't being sarcastic.

"'The Ash Grove Round'," Peter said. "We got lucky. They could have blessed us with another favorite—the one about laughing when a hearse goes by—every verse, always *every* verse."

"But they're fun," Cassie said. "I know why you like working with kids, Alan. Other summers I felt like one of them, or like I had to work to be "in charge." This year I've just relaxed and enjoyed them. They've made me think about things."

"Made you? How? They haven't done a thing." Julia waved her hand and turned away. "You thought about things," she said, her eyes reflecting the fire. "Can't you take that responsibility?"

The evening wasn't supposed to be like this. Cassie's eyes stung.

"O.K. Being around them has changed me."

"I know what Cassie means," Alan said. "I look forward to fall, getting back to my bunch. They keep me honest."

"Not you, too!" Julia shook her head.

"They do! They demand reasons, and I'm forced to find them—at least to try. Sometimes I find answers to questions I've wrestled with for months."

Cassie listened to his words, to their echoes in her mind.

"When I'm in charge, I don't give reasons." Peter stood up and lifted the pot from the fire. "Enough rambling. It's time to eat and enjoy adult privileges. After a summer of hot dogs, burgers, peanut butter and jelly, this meal will change my life." He placed a steaming lobster on each plate and poured butter into paper cups. "Use your fingers—no fancy crackers or forks here."

"Cassie's always said it's the only way to eat lobster anyway." Julia put her arm around Cassie's shoulder. "And she's right. When we were in Provincetown, we'd buy pound bags of lobster knuckles, all cooked, for forty cents—or something like that—and eat them as we walked along the beach. Remember, Alan?"

"Do I! I can smell the wharves—the oil, rope and fish—popcorn, fudge...."

Cassie pulled a small leg off her lobster and sucked the juice from the end. She knew just what Alan meant. In the salty taste were the memories of all her years on the Cape, by the sea. This would be her last at camp.

They had finished when taps sounded at nine. The bugle notes hung in the summer air. Still warm, but Cassie could feel fall coming.

"Do we have marshmallows?" She asked out of habit.

"On top of lobsters and champagne? I hope not!" Julia just had no sense of camp.

"I knew I forgot something," Peter said, snapping his fingers.

"It's O.K." Cassie snuggled against his shoulder. "You remembered everything else." But she had wanted to sit around toasting marshmallows one at a time to a butterscotch brown, blowing them out and eating the warm crusty shells, sucking the soft centers from a stick. She buried her feet in the cool sand, until she could feel the day's warmth underneath.

"How about another log? It's getting chilly."

"One more, then we should let it die. Before you know it they'll be blowing reveille."

Cassie didn't want to let it die. She looked at him, at her friends, in the firelight, and put her hand on his knee. He covered it with his. Alan was lying on the blanket, hands behind his head, staring at the brightening stars while Julia played with his curls.

"Isn't it great to see the heavens like this? Hey! Look!" Alan pointed straight up, then lowered his arm toward the horizon. "What's that?"

"A shooting star," Cassie said, just as it seemed to fall into the sea.

"I missed it," Julia said. "I've never seen one."

"Lie down next to me." Alan patted the blanket. "Maybe we'll see another."

"Probably lots tonight. Meteor showers." Peter got up and started collecting trash, packing the cooking utensils into crates. "We should do this before the fire dies, Cass."

She got up and helped him, glancing now and then at Julia and Alan pointing at the sky, counting, laughing. She took a deep breath of salt air. She didn't care about morning. She wanted to stay here all night.

PART II

Chapter 12

August 1966

STILL NO SOUNDS from the street below. Julia put her daughter, satisfied and sleepy, on her stomach in the basket next to the bed. Now, curl up next to Alan and try to sleep a little longer herself? Or wake him so they could get out of the city before the sun was high and hot.

He'd slept right through three feedings. His tranquil breathing, amplified in the clammy night air, had made it harder each time for her to sink back to sleep. Tired as she was, Julia couldn't wait another couple of hours to get out of New York, to be on the road. Alan had slept enough for both of them.

She grabbed his beard and tugged. "Time to get up."

He tried to turn over, away from her, but she tugged again.

"Too dark. Go away."

"Don't growl at me. It's getting light fast, and I want to get moving."

"Moving?"

"To Cassie's. Our long weekend in the country? Remember?"

"Sure," he said, rising to his elbows. "Early start." He squinted at her and tried to rub the sleep from his eyes. "Have you been up long?"

"Shh. Whisper! Not long, but lots. Your daughter got your appetite, but not your sleep genes. Three times during the night," she said, shaking three fingers in front of his face.

"You must be dead. Still want to go?"

"*Yes* I want to go. And soon. I can't get back to sleep anyway. I'll shower, and you'd better be up when I'm done."

"Yes, Ma'am." He saluted her. Julia turned her back quickly to leave, hoping he hadn't seen her smile.

"Damn," she muttered, measuring out extra scoops of coffee so they'd have some for the thermos, resenting the way he could always dissolve her anger with a joke before she was ready to let it go.

But she hummed as the warm water washed down her back and rinsed the bitterness away. Her shower was now a sacred ritual. Mrs. Sanders, the head maternity nurse, had given Julia the best baby gift of all the day after delivery—permission to take a shower. Each one since had been one more step back to normal life, if there was such a thing. Julia stepped right under the shower head. The streams of hissing water formed a wall, separated her from the daily demands, created a silence where her own thoughts weren't drowned out by the mysterious whimpers of her new daughter.

She could see her toes again. No small event. Losing sight, and in that sense, touch, with part of herself had disturbed her. Lathering her stomach, she celebrated the slow restoration of her body. Maybe the old desires would return, too.

Most of her fatigue vanished with the water down the drain, and she pushed the shower curtain aside to face one more day. Now that she was almost her old self, she looked forward to seeing Cassie. A distance had grown between them, along with her belly. Now, with that gone....

Alan sat on the edge of the bed, smiling down at Gillian.

"She's still asleep, I hope."

He nodded and whispered, "I've been very quiet."

"Why are you just sitting there? You should be getting ready to go."

"I was waiting for you to give up the bathroom. I need to shave."

"You cannot fool me. You were mooning over her again. God, you should be her mother. You'd be better than I am in the middle of the night." Alan came up behind her and put his arms around her.

"No one is better than you are in the middle of the night." He nuzzled her neck. She raised her shoulder, wriggling away.

"Please don't, Alan."

Releasing her, he threw up his hands, let them slap to his sides and disappeared into the bathroom, slamming the door behind him.

Gillian stirred. Julia crossed her fingers, as she'd done for the last month, hoping she wouldn't wake up. Not yet. At first she'd been scared that the baby wouldn't wake up, then that she wouldn't know what to do with her when she did, that she'd hurt her somehow. They were getting used to each other, but the tension didn't go away. Her own mother must have felt like this.

In the dark bedroom's mirror, Julia could barely look at herself most mornings without tears. You can resume normal sexual activity, her own doctor had said, more than a week ago. She couldn't—kind and gentle as Alan had been. Why didn't he understand that it made her feel worse to reject him? Couldn't he wait for her?

They said motherhood would make her feel more of a woman. She buttoned her blouse over the thick cotton bra, a strait jacket of straps and flaps, feeling less like a woman than she had in her life. So that she'd be cool in the car, she brushed her hair back from her face and braided it high, off her neck. She pulled a clump of hair from her brush before sticking it into her purse. Two handfuls a day. At this rate, she'd be bald in another month.

She tiptoed to the kitchen, poured two mugs of coffee, and the rest into the thermos, over ice, for the road. The bathroom door was still closed. With no free hand she had to kick the bottom gently to get Alan's attention.

"Coffee." He opened the door a crack and reached out for the cup. "May I come in?"

He hesitated, then opened the door, and turned on the hot water tap. Julia placed his cup on the shelf above the sink and sat behind him on the edge of the tub, watching his face in the mirror as he shaved. Like a sculptor he could change the contours of his face, his whole image, with that razor.

"I'm glad you have your beard back," Julia said, trying to catch his eye in the mirror.

"Not half as glad as I am. Shaving was a drag."

"What do you call this, if not shaving?"

"Edging. It's easier." He agitated the razor in the soapy water, adding black whisker flecks to the ring in the basin.

"I guess I'm trying to say I'm glad to have the old you back... that I'm sorry you don't have the old me yet. I'm getting there, though. I am, and I do love you." She stood up, put an arm around his waist, pulling him close to her hip, and faced him in the mirror. "Don't we look like the same people we've always been?"

Alan smiled under his suds. In his eyes Julia saw the smile she'd missed most in the last couple of months.

"Hurry up now, Papa Bear. We have a kid to show off!"

Sultry August. Stagnation month in the city. Julia looked back through the smog at the midtown skyline and felt glad to be getting out. Despite the heat, she rolled up the window to close out the caustic stench of the New Jersey lowlands. She'd never really noticed the neighborhoods here. People actually lived in the spaces between factories and highways, hung clean wash to dry in soot-laden air. In one yard a sunflower stretched toward the sky, rising above the asphalt. Like that flower, she supposed, they and their children survive.

Gillian would know other worlds. A glance over her shoulder assured Julia that the baby was still sleeping soundly, soothed by the engine and a symphony on QXR.

"Last night is catching up with me. Mind if both your traveling companions snooze?"

"I'll wake you when we get there."

"If she doesn't wake me first...."

There was no more motion. Or music. The pleasant absence of sensation turned to stiffness in her neck and swelling in her breasts. When she opened her eyes, everything looked green. Startled and wide awake, she realized that she was alone in the car, parked in the deep shade of an oak tree. Outside, sitting on a blanket against its trunk, Alan rocked their daughter on his knees. Gillian gazed up at the moving light and shadow in the branches above her. Julia watched for a few moments, then joined them.

"She started to complain a little so we stopped. I got her out of the car so you could sleep."

Letting herself down slowly, she leaned against his arm. "And I did. You two seem to be enjoying yourselves."

"Absolutely. Aren't we, Gilly?" The voices made Gilly whimper. "Just a temporary diversion, though. She thought she might be hungry, but now that you're here she's sure. You take over. I'll get our snack."

As he rose to go, Julia grabbed his hand, pulled him closer, and kissed him. "You are wonderful. You know that."

"It's nice to hear that now and then."

After fussing and several false starts, Gillian settled down. Sitting in the shade, listening to the smacking sounds of her nursing child, Julia felt she could breathe again. Some of the fear was gone. Alan came back. They lingered for a while by the highway, hardly aware of passing traffic, drinking iced coffee with

Danish pastry and peaches, smiling down at the baby between them.

By the time they reached Crossbrook, the sun was almost directly overhead. Even with the windows wide open, the air in the car was humid and close. It seemed hotter here than in the city. Looking up from the directions, Julia saw a store with a rusting refrigerator case on the porch, metal Moxie signs tacked to the walls. She'd expected Cassie to live in the suburbs, not the boondocks. The road was narrow and winding. Stone walls snaked away, marking pastures that spread up the hill on one side and down the slope on the other.

"A few sheep and I'd think I was back in England!"

"That place up on the ridge even looks like a castle," Alan said slowing the car. "They live in a cottage?"

"A gatekeeper's cottage."

Within the arc of iron gates that must have stood open for years, wildflowers grew undisturbed. Hollyhocks and delphiniums lined the fence, a pink and blue backdrop for the rest of the garden. When Julia stepped out of the car, she heard only the sound of bumblebees working blossoms in the noon sun. Then Cassie was there, tan and strong, hugging her.

Julia sucked in her stomach. "So this is the cottage."

"Peter found it and surprised me. Isn't it great?"

"A little more ivy and it could be a dorm!"

"Hardly. Wait 'til you see how small it is." Cassie peered around Julia's shoulder toward the car. "Speaking of small, where's the baby?"

"Alan's bringing her. She slept most of the way."

"She's good, then?"

"Of course she is, aren't you, Gilly." Alan came toward them, the baby in his arms. "She already likes to travel, just like her mother. Gilly, this is Cassie. She's family, almost. Want to hold her?"

"I'd love to."

Alan kissed Cassie's cheek as he placed the baby in her arms.

"I can't believe this." Cassie smiled at Julia. "Your baby. She's beautiful."

"Like her mother?" Julia nudged Cassie with her elbow, but didn't get the compliment she was fishing for. Cassie was stroking Gillian's tiny hand. Gillian grabbed Cassie's finger and held tight. "She likes you already, see?"

"She'd better. I love her already. She looks like you, I think. Maybe a little like her dad."

More like him, Julia thought, with those curls.

Alan came back with a suitcase in each hand, a package under his arm, and a drop of sweat running down his nose. Julia held the screen door and let Alan pass sideways ahead of her into the cottage. Cassie turned into the first door on the right.

"The couch opens to a bed."

Julia peeked around the corner into Peter's den—barely big enough for the desk and leather couch, much less a bed.

"Where?"

"It works. Honest. Though you won't be able to dance in here, and the person on the inside has to crawl over the other one to get up."

Alan stuffed the luggage under the desk, out of the way. "OK to put Gilly's car bed on top?" he asked.

"Sure. Let me move all this stuff."

"Peter won't mind?" Alan asked, helping Cassie lift piles of glossy corporate reports to the floor next to the desk.

"No, he's not going to work this weekend, anyway. I'd have moved them myself, but I thought you'd put the baby in the nursery."

A little distance. Julia liked that idea.

"You're not saving the nursery for someone special?"

"For Gillian. I put up the curtains just yesterday. Come see."

The room across the hall was a bit larger than the den, and cooler. Organdy curtains, still stiff with fresh starch, brushed the sill in a bit of breeze. Filtered light brought green indoors, washing the white walls with summer. Folded at the foot of a day bed was the throw Julia had woven for Cassie—its blues, greens and purples the only color in the room.

"The bed's made up, if you need to be near her."

"I need a night's real sleep. I'm going to take the far side in the other room. Papa can get up and bring me the hungry child in the night," she said, patting Alan's arm.

But she wanted Gillian to sleep here, in the cradle by the window. She knelt and placed her among tiny white pillows embroidered and trimmed with eyelet. "You can look at the leaves again," she whispered, rocking her gently. "This cradle's lovely, Cassie. With room to grow. Was it yours?"

"Peter's. His mother's before that."

"Getting some pressure from the Lawsons?"

"They want a grandchild." Cassie answered without a blink.

"Julia, do you need anything else from the car?"

Julia shook her head. Alan didn't have to interrupt, try to cut her off. She knew it must be hard for Cassie, living with other people's hopes, with visits from other people's babies. She was just trying to let her know that.

"Gillian and I thank you," she said. "And we brought you something. The package, Alan?"

"I'll get it."

"Lunch is ready, whenever you're hungry."

"I am," Alan called from the den.

"Figures," Julia said. He was always hungry lately, so she let him cook. She didn't have the energy or the desire. And she wanted to be thin again. Looking at Cassie, trim in her print slacks, made her want it more. She collapsed into one of the chairs at the table. "Why didn't you leave her in the cradle?" she said to Alan, who was settling the baby in the car bed next to her.

"All alone?" Cassie asked.

"She has to learn to be alone." Julia resisted the urge to put her head down, close her eyes, sleep. The table was set—pink linen mats, china plates with tiny roses and scalloped edges, napkins that looked like freshly-cut bouquets from the garden.

Julia liked being a guest. She watched Cassie set a pottery tureen in the center of the table, take a silver ladle from the sideboard. "Sit a minute," she said. "Open your present."

"This looks intriguing," Cassie said when Alan put it on her lap. "Something of yours, Julia?"

"Not the way you mean."

"It is Julia's," Alan said. "This artist came in one day with his portfolio. Julia's stuffy boss—remember him?—didn't like the work. But Julia did and told him so. The next day a messenger delivered two sketches."

Julia watched Cassie as she tore away the wrapping. Puzzled, disappointed for an instant, then a pleasant smile. She didn't like it. Julia could tell.

"You do know what it is."

"Of course! The bridge! Washington, not Brooklyn."

"It's not valuable," Alan said. "Yet. But I agree with Julia. The guy's good."

"Thank you, Julia. Both of you," Cassie said, setting the print on the floor against the wall. "That was so thoughtful."

Damn right. Julia had spent half the week's food money for just the right frame—for the sketch and for Cassie. She couldn't afford an expensive housewarming gift, but had thought this would mean more. Especially the bridge. A reminder of the old days. She wished Cassie wouldn't pretend to like it. Would tell the truth and give it back. She never could appreciate good graphics. Hard lines. Black and white. Julia should have remembered that watercolors were Cassie's thing. She would never hang the sketch here. Even if she did—because she thought she should—Peter would probably make her take it down. It didn't "fit."

Cassie set a platter in front of Alan. Sandwiches, the kind Julia remembered having in Copenhagen—rare beef on thin dark bread, each with a sprig of watercress and a dab of golden remoulade sauce.

"I thought you'd want something more substantial than cold soup. Ladies lunch, Peter calls it."

"He comes home for lunch?" Alan looked surprised.

"Never! We'll be lucky if he's home in time for dinner. He loves his job." Cassie filled their bowls. "Long hours and all. And now, with school behind him, he doesn't have to study when he's home. Tomorrow we'll take off on the boat."

"Hear that, Gilly. Cradle one night, a yacht the next. Not bad at one month! Travel's good for a child," Alan said. "This is our first trip. Julia hasn't wanted to go anywhere. My family's been begging us to visit." He looked at Julia for a sign. "But that will have to wait."

"Maybe in the fall." Julia sighed.

"You have to admit that baby was an angel on the way down. And there hasn't been a peep out of her since we arrived."

He could go on so. "Shh. You'll jinx us." Gillian was always good during the day. She raised her hell at night. "I'll admit it's good to get away."

"A change of scene always does wonders." Cassie sounded so knowing.

"The miracle country cure," Julia mumbled, spearing a tomato in her salad. She ignored Alan's foot nudging hers. "What's in this soup?"

"Summer vegetables, mostly—some chicken broth."

"Tastes like pure cream!"

"A bit of that, too. Don't you like it?"

"Love it. It's good and rich. Alan's been cooking for us, but his repertoire is limited."

"You're never hungry!"

"Today I am." Julia helped herself to seconds. "I need to eat well. I'm nursing."

"That's why I thought you might need to sleep near the baby."

"Not that near." Though at the moment the thought of sleeping alone, away from both the baby and Alan, was appealing. Julia tried to guess the vegetables in the soup, but no one flavor was stronger than another. Maybe she'd ask for the recipe, serve it herself sometime, if she ever entertained again.

"You're a good cook, Cassie," Alan said. "Peter's a lucky man."

"Is this a pink plate special," Julia asked, "Or do you always eat this well?"

"I do a lot of cooking lately."

Probably not much else, way out here. Julia tried to imagine the days, the kind of people Cassie might know.

"I'm surprised you left your job."

"In the summer it's a long, hot commute. It didn't seem worth the trouble when I planned to stop in the fall anyway..."

Planned or hoped. Julia didn't ask.

"...and I needed to work on the cottage."

"It looks fine," Alan said.

"Here are the 'before' pictures." Cassie took a small album from the shelf of the hutch, and handed it to Alan. "What you see now is two months of hard work."

So Cassie stayed thin by hard labor. Labor hadn't helped Julia. She wondered if Cassie's friends helped out, talked to her while she worked. Life looked pretty horsy out here. Not Cassie's scene.

"How's your social life?"

"Next you'll want to know if she's joined the local women's club," Alan said, slowly turning the pages of the album, without looking at Julia.

"I don't have time," Cassie said. "I don't even know if there is one. We're away on the boat every weekend, sometimes with Peter's clients."

Julia only half listened to Cassie describe the cottage as she'd found it, all the projects she'd tackled. She looked out the window, past sills crowded with pink begonias. Old glass, clouded in places with bubbles, rippled in others, distorted the view of the fields.

"This country cottage scene is just too perfect," she thought out loud.

"Let up, Julia," Cassie snapped. "I happen to like it here. I love my new home..."

Gillian started crying.

"...and that's the only thing that's missing!"

Julia threw her napkin on the table, scooped Gillian out of the car bed and ran to the nursery before anyone could see her tears. Cassie called after her, something Julia didn't hear after she closed the door.

"Poor baby," she said, holding Gillian close. She could hear bowls being stacked, Alan's voice, but not his words, a chair scrape on the brick floor, then his footsteps.

"We're fine here," she said when he opened the door. "Don't worry about us."

"Why did you leave? What's wrong with you? Poor Cassie's having a hard time. She wants a child, you have one. She makes an effort, invites us here, and you keep rubbing it in."

"*Poor* Cassie? Look around, Alan. China, silver, flowers—she didn't even appreciate the sketch. I'm supposed to feel sorry for her? I'm sick of her self-pity." She looked up at him, looming over her. "And why all this sympathy for Cassie? Why can't you try to understand *me*?"

Alan sat down next to her and put his arm around her shoulder.

"I'm trying, Julia. If you'd talk to me, tell me what's wrong..."

"I wish I knew." She didn't want to talk about it now. "This is nursing time. I'm supposed to be tranquil."

Alan rubbed her back in circles, his fingers seeking the knots. Gillian sucked on, staring through her.

"I thought Cassie was over her jealousy," Julia said. "Guess I was wrong."

"Maybe you're the one who's jealous."

Julia was going to cry again. She had to fight it. "Jealous! Why would I want to trade places with her?"

"I didn't say you would."

"Whatever you said, it was ridiculous."

"Maybe you just need some rest. I'll take her and you have a nap. Come on, Gilly. We'll go for a walk." He held his daughter to his shoulder, whispering in her ear, hiding her head with his hand. The door closed. "And Julia!" he said, opening it again. "Just sleep."

As if sleep could make it all go away. She could hear their voices in the garden. She tried to listen, but her pulse raced, pounded in her ear against the pillow, drowned out their words. Jealous. This was probably Cassie's first real conversation in months. Peter had clients, but did she have friends? Jealous? She'd go mad here, herself. Oh, the cottage was lovely. Cassie had made it hers. But with the work done, she wants a child to fill her days. She doesn't know how a child does....

Like limes, the light in this room. Lime rickeys in frosted glasses, with lots of sugar, shared with Gran on scorchers. The breeze on her forehead. Gran's touch.

Chapter 13

CASSIE CLEARED THE table. They hadn't even stayed around it long enough for dessert—fruit and homemade lemon cookies, served from Julia's tin. Yesterday at this time—while she'd chopped vegetables for the soup, cut and arranged flowers, pressed the napkins—she had pictured the three of them sitting there after lunch, talking while the baby napped, making up for the months she hadn't wanted to see them. She'd gone cold at Christmas when she'd heard the news, and hadn't been able to face a radiant Julia, mother-to-be.

She collected the napkins and used them to push the crumbs into her left palm, then buffed the wood. She loved the warm color, the rich grain. Her parents would be pleased that their gift was the centerpiece of her home. Sitting at the table with Peter, or even alone, she felt settled. But today Julia's edginess had rubbed off. Too perfect, she had said. Which meant she didn't think Cassie's life was perfect at all. She never would.

Leaving the dishes for later, she went out to the garden. At the sunny end, the cosmos and coreopsis drooped in the afternoon heat. Getting ready for company, she'd forgotten to water yesterday. The soil was cracked, and smelled like dust. If she watered now she'd burn the leaves and the petals. She knelt and yanked out every weed within reach, so the roots wouldn't have to compete to survive.

"This is quite a garden, Cassie. It must be a lot of work." Alan's voice startled her. She hadn't heard the screen door.

"It looks like work." She stood up, pushing her hair off her forehead with the back of her hand. "But I love tending flowers, watching them grow."

"Julia needs to sleep for a while. Gilly and I are going for a walk."

"The road's too narrow to walk the carriage safely."

"I'll carry her. Can you come, too? Show us around your estate?"

"That would be a short tour! Only this corner is ours. But we could walk up the lane. It's not too hot for her?"

Alan pulled a bonnet from his back pocket. "Your hands are free. Mind tying it on?"

"Free, but filthy. Just a second."

Cassie turned the nozzle of the hose coiled by the step, and rinsed her hands in water hot from the sun. She dried them on a linen towel, hung on a hook by the door. "That's better," she said, showing him her palms. She tied the bonnet while Gilly squirmed. "I can see why you needed help."

"She hates hats."

"She'll probably love them when she grows up. Big bright straw ones with wide brims." She didn't know how she knew that. Because Gillian looked like Julia didn't mean she'd be like her. "Is Julia OK?"

"Tired."

"I'm sorry I lost my temper."

"She was needling you," Alan said, as if he didn't believe she had to apologize.

"Sometimes I just can't take her superior attitude."

"She doesn't feel superior," Alan said. "We both know that."

"I don't." They walked in the shade along the drive leading to the main house. "Ever since I married Peter instead of moving to New York she's held it against me, made me feel bad." The words came out before Cassie thought about them. "I shouldn't have said that. Especially to you."

"I won't repeat it."

"She compares our lives..." Cassie tried to think of specifics, of times the comparisons had hurt. "Take the drawing she gave me today. It was a message. 'You should have come to New York.'"

"So that's it! Julia's upset because she really wanted to give you a special gift and she thinks you don't like it."

Even with their voices and the stones crunching underfoot, Gilly had fallen asleep on Alan's arm.

"I like it...I'm just not sure where to put it." It wasn't large enough to fill the big, obvious spaces, and except for those, walls were scarce. The cottage was all doors and windows. And she wasn't sure how good it would look. The living room needed more color, not black and white. If Peter liked it, maybe she'd hang it in the bedroom.

"Julia does compare." Alan said. "Who doesn't? And she envies your life. Always has, I think."

"Because of my family. I know. But she's traveled all over, done what she wanted, lived where she wanted. And now you two have Gillian."

Alan took a deep breath and let it out slowly. "The cows look contented, at least," he said. "Sweet grass."

"It's the lawns you smell." Cassie pointed toward the main house, where the gardener had been working all morning. Tractor rows striped the grass. "And they're not cows. They're cattle. From Brahman bulls. You have to be careful about those distinctions around here. Everyone raises some strain or other, and everyone thinks theirs is the best."

"See? Everyone compares!" Alan smiled at her. "One of the good things about living in the country must be the smells."

"And sounds." She put her hand on his arm, and they stopped and listened to the crows calling across the fields, the orioles singing in the sycamores above their heads. "Peter can tell the songs apart,"

"Can he!"

"Oh, yes! Don't be fooled by the business suit. He's a country boy at heart. She left the path and sat down on the stone wall. "He's taught me...I can name almost all of them now. And there are owls at night." She stroked a patch of moss, thinking that the best things in the country were the little things you didn't notice unless you lived there. "Look at these tiny flowers," she said. "But being from the city, you probably think all this is boring ..."

"Not at all," Gilly's eyes fluttered open then closed. He waited quietly until she had settled again. "But I notice the silence," he continued softly. "Not really silence—a hush that roars. Montreal's not New York, but there I used to hike up the mountain, listen to the birds over the far sound of the city below. And at Amherst, walking on campus at night, you could feel the silence, something you almost had to push through to get where you were going."

"I used to try to guess by the sound how far away things were. A dog barking, a train." Cassie remembered ten o'clock walks home from the library—the quiet in which she felt alone but never lonely. "Same at the Cape, with the gulls, the foghorn. But there, when I heard the waves, I'd think of the silence they came from, how far that went." Cassie looked out over the pastures. "I miss those sounds. That's why I like to get out on the boat on weekends."

"Your life sounds good, Cassie."

"Too perfect, Julia says. But she can't appreciate this. She needs excitement. People."

"She's been really down since Gilly was born."

"Why?"

"Baby blues? At least that's what I thought, but I'm beginning to think it's more than that."

"If she and I talk later, maybe she'll give me some idea. How are *you* doing?"

"I don't know. Today, on the way here, we stopped for a picnic. No place special. I sat with this little one under a tree, watching her look up at the leaves. I'd like her to be able to do that all the time."

Gilly was sleeping soundly. If only she'd wake up. Cassie wanted to carry her for a while.

"She's missing *these* leaves," she said." Julia would say Gilly can see leaves in Central Park. One can do anything in New York, you know. Have you two talked about this?"

"We don't talk much these days."

They got up and started walking again.

"Where would you go if you left the city? What would you do?"

"I haven't thought that far. These are new feelings."

The stone walls along the lane were hidden now by formal shrubs and flowers. They could see the rows of large windows reflecting the afternoon sun.

Cassie put her hands in the pockets of her pants. She usually wore a skirt when she walked near the main house, in case she was invited in. "They're friendly people, but I think we've come close enough."

Alan stared at the place for a moment before turning around. "It's like a manor house."

"The owners are wealthy, but not titled."

"Do you and Peter know them? Have you had them to dinner?"

"Oh, no! Peter wants to wait until the cottage is finished." She doubted he'd ever think it was finished enough for the Yardleys. "You and Julia are our first guests, other than family. Though you're sort of that."

"I think it looks terrific. You've done great work. I'm glad you invited us. Julia was so happy."

"And I'm glad you came. I behaved so badly at Christmas. I was afraid it might have spoiled our friendship." As they started back down the road, Cassie kicked a stone ahead.

Alan kicked the stone when they caught up to it.

"That's history. No need to talk about it."

There was no need now. Alan had made her feel better. She wished she could do the same for him. She could tell he was worried about Julia. Now she was, too. They were quiet the rest of the way, taking turns kicking the stone.

They found Julia reading in the garden.

"Feeling better?" Alan kissed her forehead.

"Much. Where have you been?"

"Sightseeing." Alan laid the baby in her lap.

"Working up a thirst," Cassie said. "I'll get us some iced tea."

"Cassie," Julia asked. "Do you have any limes?"

"Plenty—for Peter's G and T's."

"I'd love a lime rickey."

The boat barely moved. Port and starboard lamps reflected on the water, red and green bugle beads on black satin. Lights from a few windows still wavered among the trees onshore, but the cove was dark, except for the glow of their lantern. In the circle of light the four of them sat close around the Monopoly board, crowded with clusters of red and green buildings and piles of small cards. Tucked under the edge in front of Peter were thick sheaves of paper money, while just a few bills remained in front of the others. The only sound was the tock of the dice in the hollow cup of Alan's hands. He spilled them out onto the board and moved his silver car swiftly around the corner to a dark blue space in front of a red hotel.

"That's it," Alan shouted. "Can't even build a play fortune." He stood up and handed his few bills to Peter. "Take it all."

Julia grabbed his wrist.

"Sshh! People are sleeping!"

"Sorry. Listen, its been a great day on the water, but a long one. Anyone else ready to quit?"

"I concede to Peter," Cassie said. "As always."

"You should have told us you always win," Julia said, pushing her money toward Peter. "You'd have saved us a lot of yawning. I'm ready to end this torture, but I can't go to sleep yet. I have to feed Gillian so she doesn't demand a meal at three."

"I'll keep Julia company," Cassie said. "Go ahead down, Peter. I'll secure everything."

Alone above deck, Cassie collected the empty beer cans and packed up the game, then stretched out on one of the seats. Their masthead light seemed one of thousands of stars. The day had been fun. After grumbling about the late start, Peter had resigned himself—things just took longer with twice as many people and a baby. He'd had a wonderful afternoon teaching Alan to navigate, while she and Julia lay on their stomachs, talking, dangling their arms over the bow toward the water. Cassie had told Julia about her jealousy and now it had eased.

"Are you asleep?" Julia whispered.

"No, just looking at the sky. The stars seem so close." Cassie sat up and pulled her knees to her chest under her sweatshirt. "I didn't hear you come up. Is she awake?"

"Not yet." Julia gently shook the bundle in her arms.

"Maybe this was the night she was going to sleep through."

"Very funny, Cassandra," Julia said, pulling back the corners of the flannel blanket. "I'm not taking the chance."

"Should you unwrap her? It's cool out here."

"Just this much." She snapped the sole of Gillian's tiny foot with her thumb nail.

"Julia!"

"Don't worry. The nurses in the hospital did this. It doesn't really hurt—just stabs at the sleep."

"How do you know?" It hurt Cassie to watch. "How does anyone know? I think it's cruel."

"Nonsense. It works. See?"

Once awake, Gillian was eager to nurse. Her little fist opened and closed in rhythm with her breathing, the soft nails tracing lines on Julia's breast.

"Your instincts certainly came through."

"What?"

"Maternal instincts. Remember when you didn't think you had any? You're both doing fine."

"We're surviving."

"It must be so satisfying."

"Sometimes. Remember, I came to this reluctantly." Julia reached out and squeezed her arm. "Sorry. That was unfair, especially after what you told me this afternoon."

"It's OK. It would have hurt last winter, but I'm trying not to think that way anymore. I haven't been jealous since yesterday," she joked, trying to convince herself.

"Cassie, don't while away your life dreaming of a baby. Soon enough you'll have one, and then..." Julia turned away, out into the darkness. "There's no way to prepare. Sometimes I feel she's sucking me away. Then other times, when she looks at me, something comes back. The feelings change...like breathing in, breathing out." Julia put Gillian over one shoulder and stroked her back. "I'm exhausted."

"Alan can't help?"

Julia threw her head back and sighed at the stars. "He tries. He's dear, very patient. But he can't sleep for me."

"Does he get up, talk to you?"

"He's offered, but I prefer to be alone."

"I guess I should have gone to bed with Peter, then. I'm sorry. I just presumed..."

"I don't mean tonight! Poor Alan. Most nights I tell him I'd rather he slept through, but when he does I hate him for it. Everything's so confused."

"He's good with Gillian."

"He adores her! And it's mutual. He's going to spoil her terribly, I know."

"Is that so bad?"

Julia didn't answer. "I love seeing them together. I never had a father." She closed her shirt and stood up. "Listen, I'm starting to ramble, I'm so tired. Can we call it a night?"

"Sure."

"Thanks for the perfect day, the air, the sunshine..."

"I had nothing to do with all that."

"For asking us to come, then. It means a lot to me. So, let's hope we've seen the last of this little character until after sunrise."

"I'll take her while you go down the ladder." Cassie held the baby close for a few seconds. Kissing her sweet ear, she whispered, "Goodnight, Gilly," before handing her back to Julia. She blew out the lantern, and waiting for a shooting star so she could make a wish, sat in darkness long after mother and child were asleep below.

Chapter 14

October 1966

THE LINE AT Beau Geste trailed out the door onto the avenue and around the corner. Julia peered through the picture window's blinds at the crowd, veiled in sun-striped smoke, crammed into vinyl booths at Formica tables covered with plates of heavy food. Yesterday Alan had insisted on a cafeteria for lunch, today a glorified diner. Famous places maybe. But today she'd prefer *café blanc* and *petit pain*, outdoors—in Old Montreal, where cobblestones and narrow casements let her imagine she was back in Europe.

Ahead of her women chattered in French. Some were turned out for the day in pants, others in mini dresses, wide belts on negligible hips, bright stockings, bold jewelry. Julia had on her favorite black sweater—over jeans, because they made her look thin. No one could see that they were zipped only halfway and unbuttoned, but she felt inelegant. Drab and fat. She did not need a heavy brunch. Alan's mother had been offering her home-baked specialties all weekend. Julia always declined, intending just to taste Alan's, then ended up eating more than her share. She wished she could resist sweets.

Alan scanned the line behind them.

"Looking for some old flame?"

"Just for familiar faces," he said. "Beau Geste has always been the place to be on Sunday."

"To see beauties," she muttered.

He smoothed her hair on her shoulder. "That's why I brought you!"

She didn't feel beautiful, not in this crowd.

"Haven't you been looking at the men?"

The women, too. And she'd caught several of them glancing at Alan. Their men were shorter, neater, dressed in tweed jackets, belted trench coats. Most had moustaches, wore cologne, kept their hair trimmed. Alan's curls, still damp from his morning shower, hid the collar of his fisherman's sweater. In the sun Julia could see deep red, strands of gold, even white, in his dark beard, which held the scent of his sandalwood soap. He never tried to look good and had no idea that he did.

"New York men are sexier," she said, squeezing his arm against her waist.

"Every Sunday when I was growing up, our whole family used to come here. My sisters would look at the boys, I'd look at the girls, our parents at the other parents and other children. All of us were on our best behavior, trying not to get caught staring."

Families. Once inside, Julia counted a few singles at the counter and some couples in the small booths, but all the large ones were crowded with families—some of three generations. Most of the parents looked the way she imagined the Goodmans would have. Not envious. Not critical. Proud.

"Wishing we'd asked your parents and brought Gilly along?"

"Nope. This weekend is your break," he said, squeezing her hand. "Though I'm sure they wanted to come so they could show off their fifth grandchild."

"I keep waiting for the novelty to wear off."

"She's the first Goodman!" Alan laughed. "Imagine if she'd been a boy!"

As much as Alan's parents doted on Gillian, Julia knew a grandson would have been more welcome.

"This way, please." A man with grey hair and a white apron over his tie and starched shirt, showed them to a booth near the back. "I know you," he said to Alan, as he handed them menus.

"You did, Mr. Skolnick."

"I don't forget, even behind that beard. The Goodman boy!"

"Alan." They shook hands. "And Julia, my wife."

"What a pleasure. Such a long time! I knew him since he was this high," he said to Julia. "You see my boy is helping out now." He gestured to a young man about Alan's age who was pouring orange juice behind the counter.

"But here by yourselves! Everyone is healthy?"

"Fine! They're home with our baby."

"Ah! Good," Mr. Scolnick said, listening, but keeping an eye on the door. "Here's another stranger who wants to cut the line. They don't know. Excuse me."

"He seems successful enough," said Julia. "Why doesn't he stay home, sleep late on Sunday morning? Let his son deal with the headaches."

"It's his life, his place."

"I like it here," she said, sipping the fresh juice, savoring the sweet beads of orange.

"Good. Have the special. Lox and cream cheese on a bagel. Better than New York."

Julia had meant she liked Montreal. Last night she'd stood by the window in the dark, looking down at the lights below, the way she had at Gran's, when she was eleven or so. She'd lean on the sill and watch the fog turn out the lights of San Francisco, thinking hard until she could see her father's face, smiling. He would want to see her someday and come back.

The Goodman house was built on rock, dwarfed by old trees, surrounded by old gardens, but the new buildings of *centre ville* looked close enough to touch, and that made her feel again that anything was possible. When she opened the steel casement, the cold air that rushed in didn't smell of the sea, but slipping into the already warm bed next to Alan and pulling the comforter to her chin, she felt like part of a family.

Julia liked Beau Geste, too, now that she was part of the scene. Lox did look good—and was something they never had at home. Alan's father had handed him money for brunch, a final occasion in a weekend filled with them. A Sabbath meal on Friday, dinner at The Queen Elizabeth on Saturday, and three days free to roam Montreal—just the two of them—while grandmother hovered over Gillian. And late yesterday, after buying her perfume, Alan had hailed a horse and carriage to take them to the old city for coffee and Napoleons at a sidewalk cafe on Jacques Cartier. She sniffed her wrist.

Alan smiled at her. "Still like it?"

"Love it. It's different today." Mixed with smoke, salmon, and onions instead of horse, leather, autumn afternoon air.

"You must have had such a good life here. Why did you leave?"

Alan shrugged. "Maybe the same reason you left San Francisco. For something different."

One of Julia's high school teachers had encouraged her to head East, so with Gran gone and little to keep her in California, Julia had. But Alan had left family and his country.

"When your education would have been free? You gave up so much!"

"Nothing's free." Avoiding Julia's gaze, Alan kept his eye on the waitress, waiting to catch her attention. "We need more coffee."

There had been moments all weekend when he'd seemed only half there. Maybe because he had to divide himself among parents, a daughter, a wife. He'd take Julia to one of his favorite places, tell her stories about it, then go quiet.

"Why won't you tell me?" His fingers slipped from hers as he pulled his hand away and turned over the check.

"Another time."

"Are you wishing you hadn't left?"

"Not at all."

"You could move back," she continued. "Why don't we move back?"

"It won't work." As if it ached, he put his head in his palms.

"It seems like a perfect solution to me." Julia passed Alan the last bite of her bagel and leaned back, stuffed. "Manhattan isn't right for us anymore. This city makes me feel so good..."

"I know you think it's great here." He looked around to see if anyone was listening. "You think it's romantic hearing French, feeling like you're back in Paris, but you don't know. The government tells people they have to speak it, write it. Think it!" he whispered.

"They don't tell you how to think..."

"No, but teach kids in French, they'll end up thinking in French. I'll be damned if I'll write in it!" He bunched up his napkin and dropped it onto his plate.

"Why would you have to?"

"To get anything staged." Alan downed his cool coffee, tucked two crisp bills under his empty glass and stood up. "Let's go home."

Julia woke early. Where was she? Maybe they had moved. She squinted at the ceiling, let the room come into focus around her. New York. Back to the real world. The weekend away had been good for them. Last night they had moved Gillian's basket into the living room and made love for the first time in months. She moved closer to Alan and rested her head on his shoulder, draping her arm across him. She'd almost forgotten the pleasure of being close.

"Say I'm not dreaming," Alan said, pulling her on top of him. He squeezed her tight then opened one eye. "Good morning, gorgeous."

"Good morning. I didn't mean to wake you."

"I'm glad you did." He kissed her. "I hear Gilly out there," he said, still holding her close.

Gillian was cooing to herself. Probably staring at strange shapes and shadows of the living room.

"New surroundings."

"Plus she can't see you."

"It's time to move her out of the bedroom." Julia nuzzled in his beard. "So we can have some privacy."

"Maybe I'll build a screen..."

"And I'll paint it. I need a project."

"Or a move?" She could feel his heart beating harder against her chest. "Should we move in the spring, Julia? Out of Manhattan?"

She rolled off onto the bed and stared at the ceiling.

"I'd consider it. But not suburbs. Conformity would bring out the worst in me."

"The burbs wouldn't be good for either of us. But everything depends on what I can find. With a drama degree I can hardly step into some firm and move along the track to junior partner."

"Like our friend Peter?" She took his warm hand, twining her fingers with his. "Thank God."

"Anyway, be thinking about it." He sat up, but she held on to his hand. "I have a class at ten."

"Then you may go, for now." She let his hand slip away.

He stood, then knelt on the bed and kissed her again.

"Welcome back, Julia. It was lonely without you. I'll grab something to eat on campus. You stay in bed."

Nothing better to do. Julia leaned over and rummaged through the stack of books on the floor. Nothing caught her interest. She craved coffee, but to get it she'd have to pass Gillian's basket, and if Gillian woke up the long day would begin. Alan had made it past, but she wouldn't push her luck. She bunched her pillow under her right ear, drew the blanket over her head, and spent an hour drifting in and out of dreams. Dreams of color. Vermillion, sienna, green, gold. She covered herself with color, became color.

She opened her eyes and stretched, then got up and tiptoed to the basket. Gillian still slept soundly. Julia loved the crescents of long, thick lashes along the curve of her eyes. Her hair, the color of bittersweet chocolate, curled in wisps on her forehead.

The closet door was stuck, but Julia managed to force it quietly open. Her tubes of paint had hardened, but she found a box of charcoal stubs and a pad. She sat down cross-legged on the floor next to the basket and began to sketch, her hand moving freely, setting down the curves, then the shadings.

The phone rang, startling both of them. Julia jumped up and grabbed the receiver too late. Gillian grimaced and started to whimper.

Ingrid. Wanting to hear about the weekend. Wanting to talk about the weather, wanting to meet in the Square. Now Gillian was wailing. Julia wouldn't be able to draw anymore. She might as well go to lunch.

"OK. I'll be there. Eleven thirty." Damn. Julia stood with the dead receiver in hand. She just wanted to draw. She wiped her blackened fingers on her nightgown and picked Gillian up. "Soaked, smelly and starved."

The crying stopped.

Julia hurried toward Washington Square. The air snapped with autumn, made her think of Mountain Day. Yesterday, when she and Alan had stopped on their way home to buy apples, Julia had told him how she and Cassie would always stop at an orchard on the Notch Road for a half bushel—Macs for Cassie, Jonathans for her—and cider. Back in the room, they'd drink it warm—instead of tea—stirring it with cinnamon sticks sent by Cassie's mother. Here in New York fall was different. Leaves went yellow then died and dropped, mingling with litter in the gutters. The advancing chill was the only thing she noticed.

Students were different, too. There were lots of them in the Square today, passing joints, circulating petitions, while the old men played chess, hunched over the boards, weighted down by age and ancient black overcoats. Already cold in October.

Ingrid had found a sunny bench in the northwest corner. Ten month old Andy stood on her knees, bouncing up and down, gripping her thumbs for balance. They were giggling and didn't notice Julia. She parked the carriage and lifted Gillian and a bag of apples out into the sunshine.

"Here. Something from the country." She set the bag on the bench. Andrew grabbed for an apple at once, dropped it, grabbed for another. "Oops. Bad idea." She moved the bag to Andrew's stroller. "Looks like Andrew's full of it today."

"I didn't want to lose the bench, but now that you're here, we'll walk a little." Ingrid set Andy down and stood up. "That's what he needs."

"I wonder how long it will be until Gillian's on her feet." Gillian sat quietly in her lap, sucking on her pacifier. Julia tried to imagine painting with her underfoot. Little hands grabbing for brushes as Andy had for the apples.

"Don't wish! I have to watch him every second, and it can only get worse as he gets faster. But I want to hear about your terrific weekend."

Julia reviewed everything they'd done, told her about the galleries, the great stores, the fashions.

"Furs...boots..." Julia sighed. "I wanted to be rich."

"I'd have been depressed, seeing all those things I couldn't buy."

"I wasn't!" She told her how Alan's father had been so generous with his money, his mother with time. "Alan and I were alone for the first time in months." She faced the sun. Yesterday noon they'd been standing in line for brunch. "We're thinking of moving."

Ingrid stopped walking and sat down.

"When?"

"In the spring, when he's finished school."

"Where?"

"Who knows?" Certainly not the country. Driving home yesterday she'd tried to imagine life in one of those upstate villages where smoke curled from every chimney. She couldn't. "Right now we have to figure out how to exist where we are. Our apartment's too small. I'm going crazy. I need to do something."

"Go back to work."

"I'd like to, but who'd take care of Gillian?"

"If you found a job part time, I'd look after her a couple of days. We could switch off. Home with one, what's one more?"

"One's enough for me!" Julia realized that she must have sounded reluctant to take Andy. "Full time, that is."

"It wasn't easy for you, was it, deciding to have a child."

Was it that obvious? Or had Alan told Paul?

"Anyway, I understand. You need something besides mothering." Ingrid looked at her watch. "I've got to think about lunch and get this boy home for his nap by two. If he's awake much beyond that he won't sleep at all, and then he'll crank up into a rage by the time Paul gets home. Let's walk toward my place. There's that deli with the great shrimp salad."

"I stuffed myself all weekend. I shouldn't eat at all, but I'm starved. There wasn't time for breakfast."

"Did I wake you?"

"No." For once. Ingrid called a couple of times a day, not to talk about anything important—just to gab. "I was up. Sketching Gillian. She looked so angelic, asleep in her basket..."

"Then I woke her. I'm sorry."

So was Julia. But she'd get back to the drawing.

When they parted at two, Julia strolled back toward the Square, considering Ingrid's offer. She could do some freelance work a couple of days a week. But what would she do the rest of today? She didn't want to go home. Gillian was wide awake and might not nap after sleeping so late.

They crossed through the Square this time and walked west a few blocks into the old neighborhood, toward the factory facade, right past the door of their old building. How she'd loved that place. Maybe because of the courtyard. Or the different levels that surprised visitors. Maybe because with all the professor's books and pictures it really felt like a home. Or because it was their first, and everything seemed like a sweet dream. She wanted to sit on the old tweed couch, have tea, and talk with the professor. She stopped and turned back, drawn toward the black door.

"Since you're not sleepy, how'd you like to visit an old friend?" She barely touched the buzzer, hoping he'd be home, but hesitant to interrupt his work. She hadn't called him since the baby was born. Maybe he'd be hurt. When no buzz came back, she leaned harder. Still no response. "Too bad, Gillian. Not in. We'll have to go back to our place for tea."

She wandered around the block to Alan's favorite bakery and picked up an apple tart—dessert to dress up last week's leftovers—wishing she had enough money for wine so they could celebrate. What? The return of desire. To love, to work. Possibilities.

She stopped in at her old art supply store. New faces, old temptations. Tubes of paint, shiny and smooth, with uncreased ovals of color on the labels. Brushes—squared, angled, thick, thin. Wishing she hadn't spent her money on the tart, she bought charcoals. She'd have to work before she could afford new paints.

By the time they reached the top of the stairs, Julia's eyes had adjusted, but the apartment's shadows were close, confining after a day in the open. She set the baby on her blanket in the middle of the living room and switched on two lamps. Refusing to be pulled down by the purple gloom, she put the kettle on for tea, and while she waited for its whistle, started right in on a sketch for the screen. That morning the project had seemed like a good idea—a cure for their space problem and her boredom. This afternoon it was a reminder of both. She'd given up weaving because she wanted to paint. But she needed room, light, materials. Before she could have any of them, she needed some assignments. Maybe her old boss needed some help. She might just catch him. It wasn't quite five. His secretary said he was out of the office and would return her call. Not this afternoon, he wouldn't. Julia knew that 'out of the office' meant cocktails with a lady friend. Damn.

She sat down on the floor next to Gillian to drink her tea, picked up the bright wooden rattle, shook it. When Gillian reached up, Julia pulled it away slowly so she'd have to move and stretch a bit. Tonight their usual game was frustrating, and Gillian let her know with tears. Julia picked her up and held her close, hugging her hard.

"OK. OK. I'll fix your bath, and you'll be all ready for bed when Alan gets home."

She poured the rest of the hot water from the kettle into the kitchen sink and added warm from the tap until it seemed right. Easing Gillian down slowly, first one foot, then the other, she cradled her and dribbled handfuls of water on her arms and tummy until she was used to it. Some nights Julia loved soaping her daughter's skin, the feel of the round little body, her soft giggles. But tonight Gillian whimpered and squirmed, so Julia skipped the shampoo, wrapped her in a towel and took her to the bedroom.

"Too long a day for you. For both of us." She slipped a pink cotton gown over Gillian's head, brushed her damp curls with a fur baby brush, and settled down on the bed.

At least the afternoon hadn't been routine. The trip to the park was nice, but she couldn't be content with daily rendezvous, maternal strategy sessions, and one-way conversations with a child. Ingrid was right. She did need more. She stared down at Gillian in her arms. Her sucking had tapered off to a reflexive quiver, and her eyelids fluttered, then remained closed. There were moments, at this time of day, at the end of the last feeding, when Julia felt satisfied, at peace with herself. She drew the string at the bottom of Gillian's gown and tied it in a bow, then tiptoed out to wait for Alan.

Mondays he could as easily be home at eight as six, so there was little point in heating the meatloaf now, drying it out. She drained the bath water from the sink, scrubbed and peeled a couple of potatoes—putting them in a pot of water so they wouldn't turn brown—and made a salad. There were no lights on in the apartment across the alley. A wall of darkness. Trapped.

Moving. She thought about it again, as she had on and off all day. To Montreal. She set the table—candles tonight—and put on some Brubeck to sketch by. The phone again.

Cassie.

Julia smiled. Would Cassie believe she had just been remembering their Mountain Days? She reviewed the weekend again.

"I wish I felt that comfortable with Peter's parents," Cassie said. "That's sort of why I'm calling. I mean I don't, and the Lawsons will be here for Thanksgiving. It would be much more fun if you and Alan could come, too, maybe for the whole weekend?"

"OK, but you have to let me pitch in." They agreed that Julia would bring a mince pie. "Regards to Peter," she said, but Cassie had hung up.

Julia lifted the needle and carefully lowered it to start the record over. She hummed with the music as she studied the screen design. Thanksgiving. Knowing Cassie's reverence for family occasions, she felt honored to be included, even with the Lawsons. She remembered meeting Peter's mother at Cassie's wedding and knew why Cassie wanted other company. She couldn't imagine Mrs. Lawson taking over a grandchild for an hour, never mind a day. Couldn't imagine wanting her to.

But Alan's mother...if they lived in Montreal, she'd have more peaceful times like this, time to herself. Time with Alan. And Gillian would have a grandmother to love her.

Julia looked around the room, trying to picture the screen. One corner or another. It would be tight. And what if the baby were sleeping here in the living room now? Julia couldn't enjoy her music. She and Alan couldn't have their candlelit dinner. The only answer was to give over the bedroom to Gillian, move their mattress out here. She'd bury it in pillows.

Alan walked in around seven.

"You look comfortable," he said. "Where's Gilly?"

"She couldn't keep her eyes open. She didn't nap, so she was cranky."

"You had a hard day, then."

While he riffled through the mail, Julia put the meatloaf in to warm.

"Not really." She filled the water glasses and put them on the table. "We were out all afternoon. I walked Gillian over to Christopher Street. I rang the bell at the old place, hoping to see the professor. Is he away?"

"No, I've seen him around."

"I loved that place. Too bad we can't go back there. But I've been thinking more about moving—why *not* Montreal? Your family would love to have us all around."

"No! I told you—I can't go back!"

"Not all that stuff yesterday about writing in French...there has to be a better reason."

"I don't want to talk about it now. We just said we'd think about moving. Not that we'd decide today." Standing in the middle of the room, he looked like a man with his back to the wall. Alan usually wanted to talk things through, but something in his eyes told her not to push.

"Maybe not today." She put her arms around his middle. "But we *have* to talk about it."

"We don't." He pulled away. "I'll start the screen this weekend. We'll get along here a little longer."

"Forget the screen," she said, tearing the sketches from her pad. "I did some designs today, but the basic idea is flawed. Just before you came home Cassie called..."

"Cassie? How is she?"

"I'll tell you in a minute. My point is, Gillian will never sleep through all that goes on here, screen or no screen. She has to stay in the bedroom."

"But this morning..."

"She stays in there and *we* move out. The mattress can go there, in the corner." She ignored Alan's skeptical look. "Gillian's going to outgrow that basket any day. And there's play space in the other room, even with a crib."

"Play space?"

"For Andy. Ingrid and I are talking about swapping off a couple of days a week. To give each other free time."

Alan flopped down on the cushions. "You've had trouble coping with one quiet little girl. Now you want to take on little Mr. Hell-on-wheels?"

"I have had trouble. With no time to call my own. No stimulation. I called Hawkins House today to get free-lance work." She ripped the screen sketches in half. "This sort of thing isn't enough for me. Besides, a little extra income would help."

"If you can bring it all together, great."

Good. Sold. She tore the sketch halves into small pieces.

"So that takes care of the winter, but where do we go in the spring?" She sat down next to him. "What's *wrong* with Montreal?"

"Plenty. Believe me, I've thought about it a lot. Let it go, Julia."

Maybe he'd been thinking half the weekend.

"When I make it, it will be in the States," he said. "I told my parents that when I came to school here. Sure, I could have gone free there, lived at home like everyone else." He shook his head. "Couldn't do it. I said I wouldn't cost them anything, and I haven't. And every hour I've had to work to do it my way has been worth it."

"But doesn't that mean you can go back now? They must respect you for all you've done."

"What does it matter? Even if they do, back there it would start all over. You shouldn't do this. You should do that. You heard Mr. Scolnick. 'The Goodman boy.' Even after I had white hair like his, and grandchildren, I'd still be the Goodman boy. Someone would always be measuring. My brothers-in-law are successful lawyers. Both of them. Life would be one long lunch at Beau Geste."

"I thought it would be nice for Gillian, having her grandparents nearby. And for me."

"Maybe sometimes, but it's not worth it. Gilly would be smothered. I want her to grow up to be what she is, not what they want her to be."

Families. Julia just didn't know enough about how they worked. Maybe not having a close one wasn't so bad. Anyway, she liked Alan's wish for their daughter. Gillian was lucky to have him. She put her hands on his cheeks, kissed his forehead.

"You never told me this before," she said. "Why not?"

"What was the point? You liked my family, they liked you. You never guessed?"

"How would I? We were away from them, in our own world."

"That's how it has to be, Julia."

"Time for dinner," she said. She got up and lit the candles. "Dessert's from Marie's."

"Can't wait for that." He came up behind her, put his hands on her shoulders. "It must have been some day! You're wearing your new perfume," he said, kissing her neck. "It's good to see you with some energy. I just hope you're not taking on too much with Andy, and the idea of starting work. You're just getting back to being yourself."

"That's the point!"

"What brought this on?"

"The weekend, I think. Or maybe what Cassie used to call fall fervor."

"You said Cassie called."

"To invite us for Thanksgiving—for the whole weekend, if you can spare the time."

"You'd like to go, wouldn't you?"

"Of course. I told her so. She's counting on us."

Alan lifted his goblet.

"I wish we had wine," he said.

"I only had enough cash for dessert and pencils."

"Here's to fall fervor." They sipped their water. "May it last through the winter."

Chapter 15

JULIA'S SKIN PRICKLED, making her want to peel everything off, but even in Alan's turtleneck jersey, pajamas, and socks, she shivered under the covers. Every time she forced a swallow, her throat felt as if it would stick shut, and her joints throbbed. There was no way she'd be ready to go to Cassie's tomorrow. Even if she felt better, Gillian wasn't well enough yet to travel. Not in cold weather.

Poor Gillian. Now Julia knew why she had slept so little, cried so much. She was crying again, or maybe Julia was dreaming. She opened her eyes and turned over. Alan was across the room, reading.

"Is that Gillian?"

"I thought she might go back to sleep. I didn't want to disturb you."

"I feel so lousy."

Julia propped her pillow against the wall and tried to sit up, but her head pounded and the light made her eyes sting and water. She couldn't even remember when she'd last had something like this. Her flu had started with a sniffle. Andrew's. He'd brought it the first time he'd come to spend the day and by the end of the next week Gillian was sick.

"Here she is." Alan nudged her shoulder and set Gillian down on the mattress.

Julia put an arm around her daughter, who last week would gasp for breath after only a couple of swallows and now sucked again in peace. She closed her eyes and listened to the dial click, wishing she had the strength to go to the phone.

Beside her, Alan slept. It must be late. She opened her eyes. The room was dark. The baby was gone. Julia swallowed, testing her throat. Still raw. She should get up, get water. She rolled off the mattress and knelt on the floor, gathering strength to stand.

"Julia? Are you OK?"

"I need some water."

"I'll get it. Close your eyes." The light went on. He was running the water, waiting until it was cold. Alan lifted her hand and helped her hold the glass.

"Want something else? Toast maybe?"

"No, thanks." She held the glass to her mouth to moisten her parched lips. "What time is it?"

"About eleven thirty."

"Gillian settled down?"

"She fell asleep here with you and never woke up when I moved her. I called Cassie. You won't believe this—she was about to call us. She's sick—some stomach thing—and can't have anyone for Thanksgiving. So you don't have to feel miserable about missing out."

Just miserable.

Almost three weeks, and she still had this damn cough and no energy. Hawkins had called twice, asking for drawings she'd promised, and she couldn't even tell them when they'd be ready. She couldn't work. Hardly up to taking Andy, she couldn't ask Ingrid to care for Gillian, who rolled around on the mattress during her waking hours. Julia had to force herself to feed her and play.

Even the short days of December were too long. When Gillian napped, Julia tried to sleep them away. On the best days, she didn't wake up until she heard the key in the door, until Alan came home to take over. He gave Gilly baths, cooked dinners, shopped for food, soothed her, smiled at her.

Sometimes Julia wished he'd blow up, tell her off for lying around, but he was cheerful, considerate, and certain that he knew what was best for her. Now, when she could barely get out of bed to go to the bathroom, he wanted to pack her off on some romantic drive to God-knows-where. She'd have to go. He said it was her Christmas present, so how could she refuse? Going would be her gift to him. She had no energy for shopping and couldn't think of anything else—anything that would please him more.

She suspected—and was sure when they crossed the bridge over the canal—that Alan was taking her back to Provincetown. Most of the traffic was heading the other way.

"Everybody else is going home." Growing up, she had never celebrated Christmas. But rooming with Cassie, Julia had come to love the holiday. Every year since she'd gone "home" to the Lindemanns', Julia had planned some little celebration, believing in the spirit, if not the story, of Christmas.

This trip might revive her. Every time Alan convinced her that they needed to get away, she ended up feeling better. She wanted to. Wanted to be excited about New Year's—to be excited about something. Provincetown wasn't a bad idea. They'd been happy there.

It was late afternoon when they arrived. Closed since September, the house was frigid and damp. Julia hugged herself, rubbing her upper arms hard to warm up.

"You expect us to sleep here tonight? It's colder than outdoors! I'm just getting well, and Gillian..."

"We'll turn on the heat. Jeff said it warms up fast, and he said there's plenty of wood for a fire. I'll bring some in. Here, take Gilly."

Julia took Gillian under the arms. Bundled in her snowsuit, she didn't bend, but she giggled when Julia hugged her.

"OK, kid. If you can grin and bear it, I guess I can, too. Let's check our quarters."

There were four bedrooms. Julia walked into the largest. Hooked rugs had slipped out of place on the slanty painted floors. An ornate iron bed creaked under the weight of a thick cotton mattress and swayed like a swing when she sat down. The room ran the length of the house on the water side, and windows filled three full walls. She could look straight out to the bay and along the waterfront, east and west. She imagined summer mornings, the glint of the sun on the water.

With Gillian snug on Alan's back, they started down Commercial Street toward the heart of town, toward the sunset, cooler than the brassy summer ones Julia remembered. Thin wisps of clouds turned pale pink, lavender, grey. Empty windows, boarded or hazy with dust and watermarks, lined the deserted sidewalks. Here they marked the change of seasons as much by the rise and fall of the tourist tide as by the temperature. A man shuffled past them, pale as his bushy white beard.

"Do you suppose the natives welcome winter?"

"I would—at least at first." Alan put his arm around her shoulder.

Julia missed the summer, when nights seemed to dance into town. Missed the bright windows shining down on narrow streets. Contented cats settled on plant-lined sills staring at the passing crowds. Morning glories and nasturtiums cascading from window boxes, the scent of roses in the salt air.

Tonight darkness crept in, and by the time they reached the center of town, black windows reflected the last steely purple of twilight. The first open restaurant they found was a small pine-paneled place with unmatched chairs and paper placemats. But it was warm, and only one table was taken. The waitress led them to the rear corner.

"Very Capey," Julia said. "Probably good home cooking. I'm going to have chowder to warm me up and celebrate our return to town."

"So you're glad you came!" Alan said. "You weren't easy to convince."

Steaming chowder arrived, in deep bowls heavy with potatoes and clams. A thick layer of melted butter floated on the surface and coated Julia's spoon when she dipped it in for her first taste. *This* was chowder. Alan blew on a spoonful to cool it off, and fed a taste to Gillian, who reached toward him, opening and closing her fingers, begging for more.

"See, she's a Cape Cod kid. She loves it."

"No more, Alan. It's too rich. We'll be up all night if it upsets her."

"Sorry, kid. Your Mom says that's it. Here." He put the spoon in her hand to distract her. "Four years ago could you have imagined us back here?" Alan asked. "As a family?"

"No." Julia wasn't sure she could believe it even now. She nodded at Gillian. "She's being a sweetheart tonight."

"She likes adventure." Alan ripped open a second package of oyster crackers and dumped them into his bowl. "Do *you* still?"

The challenge in his smile made Julia hedge. "Depends."

"How about moving here?"

"To this sand spit? It's a hell of a way from New York City!"

"When we talked about moving..."

In October. It seemed so long ago. Gillian dropped her spoon, so Julia pulled a wooden toy out of her bag. 'Not too far away,' he'd said back then. This was like the end of the earth.

The waitress took the bowls away and brought oval platters, mounded with golden fried cod and french fries.

"What would you do?" Julia asked him.

"Try and find a teaching job. I could write in the summers."

Summers. Plural. Winters in between. He was thinking they'd be here for years.

"And you could paint! We could find you studio space." He lifted Gillian out of her chair into his lap and bounced her on his knee. "We'll come in the spring, get summer jobs until something steady comes up. Our first winter might be tough, but we could live on less here."

Three years of graduate school and they'd be starting over—working a summer resort, pinching pennies. He looked so eager, so sure. And studio space...

"We could look around tomorrow," she said. "At places to live."

"You'd go along with this!"

When the coffee arrived Alan slipped Gillian back into the highchair. She pouted and breathed fast, but Julia stuck the pacifier in her mouth before the cries came.

"I'm not going along, Alan. Just because you had the idea doesn't mean it's yours forever. I'm buying in—now it's *our* plan."

Gillian threw her head back and began to wriggle. In another minute she'd start to fuss.

"Time's up." Over loud protests from Gillian, Julia zipped up the snowsuit. "I'll wait outside while you pay the check."

The cold air on her face was welcome, and it quieted Gillian. Julia took Alan's hand when he came out. They picked up some brandy and walked back without words. While she waited for Alan to unlock the door, she could hear the rustle of dead leaves, swept by the north wind against the picket fence in the garden. Maybe she'd get used to the stillness. She vowed to try.

Alan carried the baby right up to bed. From the dark living room, Julia watched the lighthouse beam sweep the silence. Except for a near full moon, rising over the harbor, it was the only light. She struck a match and started the fire. The flames and their reflection in the windows banished the darkness.

"She's sound asleep already." Alan sat down next to her and poured brandy into small juice glasses. "To this place. All it will mean for her—sun, fresh air, the ocean."

"And for us," Julia added.

She lay awake long after they went to bed, missing the sirens and horns that usually punctuated her nights. Waves slapped the shore and sleep came in spells. With no clock in the room, she measured the passing night by the moonlight. It had spread across Alan's side of the bed when they came up and now shone on her face through the west windows.

She had dreamt about her studio, woke and could see it again—small, cluttered, bright, full of color. Why did color make her so happy? She wished for morning, so they could get up and begin the search. She slept again, only to make time move faster, to bring the day.

Warm sunshine woke her. She was alone. How could he have left without a creak or sway of the bed? She must have slept soundly, after all. She didn't hear Gillian, but smelled coffee. Dear Alan had already made it, so she wouldn't have to get up. But she heard no sounds downstairs. He must have gone out for food. She hoped he'd return before the baby woke up. She wanted to make love in the sunlight. This would be the last time she'd let him wait on her for a while. She'd been lying around for a month. It was time to get up again.

When Alan appeared, he set a tray of coffee and doughnuts in the middle of the bed.

"Sorry, no Portuguese bread this morning." He handed her *The Advocate*. "I didn't look yet. It might be too early for summer rentals,"

"We'll look later." Julia dropped the paper on the floor.

Alan sat down and reached for his cup.

"Oh, no. Breakfast in bed means both in bed. Take off those clothes and get back in here with me."

"An invitation I can't refuse." Alan tossed his sweater across the room, dropped his jeans on the floor, and settled in. "It's warm today. Like October."

October. Before she got bitchy. "I was awake on and off all night," she said.

"Sorry."

"No I am. For the way I've treated you this last month."

"You've been sick!"

"Still..."

"It's OK, Julia. You're excited about our move, happy to be here—that's enough. You even attacked me last night!" He whispered in her ear. "When I was too sleepy to enjoy it." He grabbed her cup, put it on the tray with his, then set the tray down on the floor.

Julia took the next to last bite of her doughnut and crammed the rest into his mouth.

"I never got to feed you wedding cake."

"A tradition I was glad we escaped. Better done in private."

The day changed. By ten the blue had faded from the sky and the water. They watched a silver haze slip in from the sea and wrap around everything in town. Alan fed Gillian while Julia made a shopping list. They left the house around eleven.

There were more people out than there had been the night before, and excitement drifted with the fog through the streets. People who stopped to exchange holiday greetings and discuss travel plans ended up talking about the coming storm. The aisles of the small market were impassable in places, crowded with full carts, with people stocking up for the long holiday weekend.

The clerk at the register studied their purchases, then their faces. "You folks visiting for the holidays?"

Alan nodded.

"Where'bouts you staying?"

"The Leitner house in the East End."

"Heavy seas tonight. You'll feel the storm. Better leave your car up on Bradford. East End could be pretty wet in the morning."

"Thanks for telling us. How about the power? Are we likely to lose it?"

"Never hurts to be prepared."

"Julia, is there anything here we can eat if we can't use the stove?"

"I'm afraid not."

"Then we'd better reconsider." They backed out of line past the glares of the shoppers behind them.

"What are we going to do?" Julia asked. "Buy hot dogs and toast them on sticks in the fireplace?"

"We can cook a steak. Let's put the eggs back and get cereal and milk for breakfast. And stuff for sandwiches instead of soup."

"Let's keep the soup and get some good bread, lots of cheese, and fruit. And sweets for tea."

"And we'd better have candles."

"That's it. Now, can we check out? That nosey clerk will probably want to know what we're planning for dinner."

"It was considerate of him to warn us about the car. After all, we're outsiders. He could have said nothing. In the morning, when the car had washed out to sea, there'd be someone right there to tell us we should have parked it elsewhere."

She wanted to look at houses, and at this rate, by the time Gillian had her nap, there wouldn't be any day left.

"Enough! Let's get out of here."

The wind had freshened while they shopped, and by the time they returned to the house, Julia was glad they had kept the soup. They'd need something warm before going out again. Alan scanned the real estate ads while Julia served lunch.

"Some prospects here. Listen. Artist's dream. Two bedroom duplex with studio. Quiet street. Eight hundred for the season."

"Eight hundred!" That's a lot of waitressing hours, and no time to paint. Even if they could live on less, food prices were high. "Too much."

"If we're both working?"

"And Gillian?"

"We'll stagger our schedules...."

"And never see each other."

"Julia, does the place sound good or not?"

"Too good."

"Then let's at least look. If we like it, we'll find a way."

Julia got up to clear, but before taking his bowl away, leaned down and kissed him. "That's one thing I love about you. You're impulsive."

"That's a positive trait?"

"Living with someone totally practical would be a bore. Take Peter—he'd have to analyze every angle before making a move. He'd be sure they could afford it before he even went to look."

"No, he'd figure out if he could make something on the deal before he went to look," Alan said.

"And he'd never have the fun of just taking a chance."

"He's a broker. He takes chances for a living!"

"But not in life."

The second-floor walkup was in a narrow West End alley, away from the lively center of town that Julia loved. Oh, well. Waiting tables she'd have plenty of contact with crowds. The quiet would be good for painting. So would the place.

Even today, when it was dark and grey outside, the studio was bright, with lots of storage space—open shelves and cabinets—and a deep double sink. Rain began, a staccato ting on the skylight. She hadn't heard rain on the roof since she was a child, tucked tight in her bed, lying still in the darkness, listening. Nor had she had this feeling of being where she belonged. There was no need to look at other apartments. Even if Alan was right, and the second floor turned out to be hot in the summertime, they could go for a swim, open the windows, sleep naked. Julia had made up her mind.

It was pouring hard when they finished the paperwork with the landlord and drove home. The wind had picked up. They parked on high ground and raced through the cutting rain to the house. Julia dashed upstairs with the baby and turned on the hot water.

"We're going to give you a hot bath, little one." She took out corduroy overalls, a long sleeved shirt, a little sweater and laid them out on the bed in the big room.

When they returned to the bedroom, the surf was pounding and sucking at the seawall beneath the windows, sending plumes of spray past the second story. The sight, as much as the cold, made Julia shiver. She dressed the baby quickly, pulled on dry jeans and a pair of heavy socks herself, and hurried back downstairs.

Alan was standing at the windows. Upstairs there'd been spray on the panes. Down here sheets of water, hurled against the glass, rattled the casements.

"How can you stand there and watch? It's terrifying!"

"Exciting! In the city we only hear about things like this."

She sat down with Gillian in front of the fire and tried not to look.

"We're lucky it's rain. It could as easily have been a blizzard this time of year. Don't worry, Julia," Alan said, sitting down beside them. "These houses have been here for years, weathered hundreds of storms. Enjoy the adventure!"

Alan had made tea. She poured a cup and added a slice of orange.

"Maybe your father's right, Gillian. Think of the stories we can tell about of surviving a winter storm at the seashore. We might as well get used to it. This wild place is going to be our home."

Chapter 16

December 1966

JULIA FOUND HER old self in the mirror. At Thanksgiving, down with the flu and still fat, she'd thought she would never look this good again. Tonight, wearing her favorite black dress, she looked forward to her New Year's Eve celebration, a real party—a small dinner with their closest friends. She was hiding one last pin in her hair when the buzzer sounded.

"It's co-o-ld out there!" Paul said, pulling off a wool cap. His red hair, full of static and standing straight up, looked almost as full as his beard. He put Andy down and embraced Julia.

Standing eye to eye and trying not to laugh, she smoothed the top of his hair.

"There. Your dignity restored."

"You look recovered—to say the least!" he said. Alan takes you out of town and you come back looking like this!"

"I had the whole day to work at it, thanks to Ingrid." Julia took her daughter from her friend's arms. "We'd have never managed with you underfoot," she said, pulling Gillian's hood down. "Were you good?" She lifted Gillian out of her snowsuit and set her among the cushions on the floor.

What could be keeping Cassie? Julia had expected her to arrive early, and it was now after eight. She went to the window and pressed her forehead to the cold glass. No snow. The roads should be clear.

"Tell me about your holidays," she said, sitting down next to Ingrid, "You went to Buffalo..."

"That says it all." Paul handed Ingrid a drink.

"To Paul, Buffalo means total confusion," Ingrid explained. "My sisters blow in with their kids, everybody talks at once, there are too many toys—all noisy—and endless meals with piles of dishes to dry."

"And too many names and faces to match up," Paul added.

"Every time we go there he takes his briefcase and looks for a quiet corner."

"There's no such thing."

"So leave your work at home and enjoy the family."

Julia wished they'd left their tensions at home.

"I used to dread visiting Alan's parents."

How that had changed. She'd even thought of moving to Montreal to be near the Goodmans. But she didn't say so. Ingrid would want to know where they were going. The buzzer sounded and Alan ran downstairs again. Julia held up her hand and Paul pulled her to her feet.

"Finally!" Julia said as Cassie climbed the last few steps. Her soft tweed coat looked warm, but her cheek was icy. "I was beginning to worry. Traffic?"

"Peter doesn't like driving at New Year's or parking on the street, so..."

"We rode the Pennsy, then the BMT," Peter said, giving Alan's hand one strong shake. He sounded so stiff when he tried to be casual.

"You should have taken a cab," Julia said. He could certainly afford one.

"You all remember each other," Alan said.

"Andy, too? He's changed a lot since you saw him last year," Ingrid said. Andy had climbed into her lap with a book.

"They grow up that fast?" Cassie knelt by Gillian. "And Gilly! Just since August! May I pick her up?"

Cassie studied Gillian. "Such enormous dark eyes. You, little girl, are a cherub," she said, twisting a curl around her finger. "Julia, you both look so good, it's hard to believe either of you was sick."

"Miserable! Alan had to take us away for a rest cure."

Alan was at Cassie's side. "Shall I take my daughter off your hands?"

"Please do," Julia said, putting her arm around Cassie's shoulder. "Notice whenever there are compliments she's his daughter. Peter, you'll have to get your own drinks. The bartender is busy."

"Fine. Everything's right here. Cass, want anything? Ginger ale?"

Julia hated to hear Peter call her friend "Cass." It sounded hard, didn't suit her. "Give me a hand," she said, nudging Cassie toward the kitchen. "I hoped you'd come early."

"I wanted to...I've really missed seeing you," Cassie said, instead of what she'd started to say.

"You've recovered from that bug? You look a little thin." She was wearing a mini dress—great line, but dark brown wasn't good on Cassie. It washed the color from her face. Julia handed her a box of crackers. "You can arrange these on the plate after I do this..." Julia inverted the mold onto a platter and lifted it slowly. "*Voila*! Out clean on the first try. A good sign for the rest of the evening. Here, you get the first taste." She spread a thin layer of paté on a cracker and offered it to Cassie.

"Thanks anyway," she said, looking away.

"Are you sure you're well?"

Cassie laughed. "Very. Julia, you're slipping. I expected you to take one look at me when I walked in and guess."

Julia threw her arms around Cassie. "God, am I dense! You're pregnant!"

"Shh!"

"First you refused a drink," Julia said softly. "Then my paté. Oh, I'm thrilled for you. Now we have two things to celebrate tonight."

"Two?"

"Your baby, and the New Year." She had almost slipped. "When are you going to make the announcement?"

"Peter wants to. He'll be annoyed I told you first."

"Then I won't let on." She glanced at her watch. "It's way past Gillian's bedtime. I'd better get her down. Do me a favor and take this in."

Julia was startled to find Peter holding her daughter. Last August he'd shown no interest in her. Gillian wasn't used to neckties—Alan hardly ever wore one. Peter's rep stripes were bunched in her little fist, and he wasn't objecting. Maybe he'd be a more patient father than husband.

"Sorry to interrupt, Peter, but it's time to pack this little girl off." Andy was pulling record albums one at a time from the bookcase, and dropping them at his feet. "Time for Andy, too, isn't it?"

"Oops. Guess so." Ingrid traded her son a book for an album sleeve and lifted him to her hip. "Excuse us."

When Julia and Ingrid returned, Peter was describing Mrs. Lindemann's Christmas feast, and just getting to the hot dishes.

"Peter!" she said when he started to itemize the desserts. "This is torture! Dinner isn't ready, and it can't match a Lindemann spread. I was there one year, so I know. Unforgettable."

The food, the feelings. Cassie had talked for weeks about her family celebration, and had tried to make Julia part of it. But at the Lindemann's you were one of them or you were not. Julia was "not," but Peter seemed to fit in fine.

"Mrs. L. will remember this as the year that Cass didn't eat a thing," he said. Silence. "I hope she'll do better tonight, but if not, you better know it's the baby objecting, not Cass." He paused. Everyone looked puzzled. "We're going to have a baby," he added, grinning. "Along about July."

"That is *great* news," Julia said, giving him a hug. Alan added congratulations. He kissed Cassie, then raised his glass.

"I'd like to toast the three of you, which is *not* the same thing as the two of you, as you will learn."

Paul raised his glass. "Hear, hear. Welcome to the club."

"We told our parents at Christmas," Cassie said. "The first grandchild on both sides. Everyone's thrilled."

"Is there anything I can get you, Cassie?" Julia tried to remember her own cravings.

"Milk would taste good, but I know you hate it, so you probably don't have any."

"Alan prefers it to tea."

He appeared with milk, in a wine glass, and handed it to Cassie. "For a fellow connoisseur. Now you have a glass to raise for the Goodman news."

Julia placed her fingers on his lips. "Wait until dinner, when everyone's seated."

Paul laughed out loud. "You two aren't going to have another one? Not already!"

"God, no." Alan laughed. "We'll tell you at dinner."

They all shouted for him to continue, now that he'd started.

"All right." Alan relented. "Will you all drink to our new home? We're moving in the spring. To Provincetown."

Julia waited for exclamations, congratulations—instead, silence.

"Come on, people," she said, "That's exciting news!"

"I'm stunned," Cassie said. "You're such a city person! It's hard to imagine you so far from the action. Are any of your old friends there?"

"I've no idea. But it doesn't matter. Alan didn't mention the best part. We found an apartment with a real studio! I'll have a place to work."

"So, Alan," Peter said. "I assume you've nailed down some sort of position?" Julia had predicted he would be the first to ask.

"I'll take something seasonal at first, then look in the fall for something permanent."

Peter shrugged.

"It's no more chancy than the academic track these days," Paul said. "Did you see the predictions for fall? Bleak."

"The brokerage business can't be too solid either," Alan said. "Where'd the market close yesterday? 460? For the year?"

"But back from October!" Peter sounded confident.

"I'm jealous," Ingrid said. "I'd love Andy to grow up in the country."

"Well, you can all come visit once we're settled. But not all at once. The apartment has two bedrooms. Any chance you could make it this summer?" Julia asked on her way to the kitchen. Maybe that would excite them. She put six cups on a tray and set it on top of the refrigerator while she heated the soup. This kitchen was not the place to create elaborate dinners.

"Cassie? What are you and Peter doing this summer?" Alan asked.

"We'll be homebound. I'll be trying to survive the heat, while you're swimming in the bay."

Julia could hear the strain in Cassie's voice, though she couldn't see her face. Last August they were supposed to feel sorry for her because she wasn't pregnant, and now because she was. Sure, Cassie would miss the Cape, but there were worse places to spend summer afternoons than the garden in Crossbrook. Besides, Cassie knew what to expect. When Gillian was born, Julia had had no idea. Cassie was getting what she wanted.

"Who knows?" You might be ready to travel by the end of August," Alan said. "We visited you last summer!"

"We'll see," Cassie said. I'm superstitious about planning."

"Me, too. I didn't buy any baby clothes until after Andy was born," Ingrid said. "It's dangerous to take things for granted."

"She didn't buy anything!" Paul said. "While she was in the hospital, I had to shop—for all kinds of little things with strings and snaps and strange names."

"Peter will have it good. A summer baby, like Gilly. Just diapers. All you'll need to worry about," Alan said. All he had to worry about. Not so easy. Life had been hell, and all this talk about babies was bringing it back. That was over. This summer was going to be different.

Carrot and scallion slivers floated on the surface of the consommé, bright and still crisp—just the way she'd wanted them. The right light touch between the rich paté and the beef.

"This tastes wonderful," Cassie said.

Peter laughed. "She hasn't said that in some time."

"Maybe if you stopped talking about it, she'd feel better." Julia smiled at him. Enough was enough.

"The table's beautiful," Cassie said. "I love the white roses against the evergreens."

"Pine and juniper for the season—from the Cape. Alan brought me the roses this afternoon, so I stuck them in among the branches. They don't really go together."

"The roses stand out like snow against the needles. They look even more elegant than they would in a vase by themselves." Cassie stared at the centerpiece, as if she had more to say.

"Perhaps. I didn't think about it at the time," Julia said, getting up to clear.

"You didn't have to," Ingrid said. "You create beautiful things without thinking."

They all agreed.

At the sink, Julia ran the water hard to rinse the cups and drown out their voices. It was embarrassing hearing them go on, like overhearing some juicy bit of gossip, something she wasn't supposed to know. They were all so sure she was good. None of them knew how badly she wanted to be.

She wished now that she'd made something more dramatic for dinner, something to command their attention. But she hadn't been trying to impress them. She'd planned simple food, perfectly cooked, to be a background for conversation, not a topic. She'd expected excitement, curiosity about their move, and all they'd talked about was pregnancy and babies.

She poured the peas and pearl onions, shining with butter, into a glass bowl, and tasted a slice of potato, crisp and golden with garlic, cheese and cream. Cassie's favorite, but if she didn't eat, so be it.

Paul poured the wine while she and Alan served the food.

"Mind if I make the first toast?" he asked Alan.

"Not at all."

"Peace in Vietnam. A truce—not just for New Year's but for the whole year."

"To peace."

Everyone was silent.

"Noble thought," Julia said. "But I doubt our wishes make much difference. We should drink to something closer to home. To Cassie and Peter's baby."

They all raised their glasses again. Julia waited for someone to toast them, wish them luck.

"Every voice counts," Paul said instead. "That's why the letter to Johnson was so great."

"What letter?" Julia hadn't read a newspaper in days.

"The one from students, from all over the country. Hundreds of them signed it! Now he'll have to listen."

"Come on, Alan. The man's got a job to do. Now I'm not saying he's doing a good one," Peter said. "Hell, this war would be over if we'd elected the right man. But why should he listen to people who don't know anything about it telling him what to do?"

Julia stared at Peter's sleeve. Narrow pinstripes on banker grey—not hard to guess that he wouldn't find any allies in this group.

"You voted for Goldwater?" Paul smirked. Fuel for his cause. "Then you probably think we're justified in bombing the north."

"I think we have to stop the threat from there. If that's what it takes..."

Paul sawed at his meat, though it was really very tender.

"Next you're going to tell me the war is good for the economy," he said.

"Don't politics usually come after dinner? With the cigars? In the drawing room?"

Politely put, Cassandra.

"No! That's the trouble!" Ingrid said. "I agree with Paul. We need more voices in this country. I don't give a *damn* about politics, but I want the killing to stop. I'm lucky—Andrew's only one. But what if he were eighteen!"

Julia had never heard Ingrid speak out. Being a nurse, she saw plenty of suffering. Did she feel it less? More?

"I don't much care for politics, either," Julia said. "Especially at dinner."

"I think the point of the letter was just to ask Johnson to be clear." Alan—the voice of reason at the head of the table—changing the subject without changing it. He had to get his bit in. "The States sort of backed into this thing, he continued. "If they really want a settlement, then how can they justify escalation?"

"Alan..."

"You academics. We're fighting an enemy! You think Charlie will negotiate when the hippies in this country say 'We won't fight. We'll go to jail first'?" Peter whined an imitation. "And Canada doesn't help—taking them in."

"Why aren't *you* fighting, then?" Paul glared at him.

"Bad knees. 4F."

"Rich boy with bad knees. Your local draft board probably sent a few peons over to fight for you."

"Easy, Paul," Alan said.

"And you?" Peter's gaze was direct, but showed no feeling. "You're not there either."

"I'm a student. And teacher. And father, as you will be."

Ingrid looked proud of Paul. Cassie looked pained.

"Listen," Julia said, grabbing Paul's and Peter's wrists. "I'm going to make you boys change places if you don't change the subject. This is a party!" She hoped Alan would back her up.

He smiled at her, and raised his glass.

"Great food! Besides, Julia didn't tell you yet about the storm."

"What storm?" Cassie asked.

"In Provincetown, at Christmas."

She told them about stocking up on food and candles, about the waves smashing against the seawall, threatening to drag them out to sea, about feeling scared but strangely safe.

"It was even worse here," Ingrid said. "We had thunder and lightning and a blizzard on Christmas Eve! Crazy."

Julia was weary. She could talk about movies, but they rarely went anymore and Cassie and Peter never did. And who had time to read these days—anything except the damned *Times?* All people read about was killing and hatred and ugliness. She couldn't wait to get to Provincetown. There she wouldn't have to be informed. She could go to her studio and paint.

Alan urged the others to get up and stretch while he helped Julia. She pushed the scraps of her celebration dinner into the trash and began rinsing and stacking the plates.

"I'll do all this later. You've done enough work." Alan put his arms around her waist. All night he'd been at the other end of the table, a war zone in between. His beard against her cheek felt good.

"Dinner was a disaster."

"It was superb!"

"Not the conversation. It was *good* that Paul toasted the truce. But then Peter's diatribe..."

"He was pretty hard on the academic community."

"On you and Paul."

"He didn't mean it personally, Julia. I didn't take it that way."

"You wouldn't." She watched him wrap what was left of the roast, put the leftover vegetables in small containers. He hated to throw things away. "You're too damn forgiving. Paul was proud of the students for signing that letter—some of his did, you know—and Peter cut him right down."

"Keep your voice down, Julia. Paul was the one who got personal. Peter was just having a gentlemanly debate."

"Why are you defending him? You like him?"

"I don't dislike him. He's Cassie's husband—I accept him."

"I've tried, but after tonight..."

"They'll still be our friends. You can't make them all think alike. And we both know you'd be bored with them if they did. You should be glad they all feel they can be honest. Now, what's dessert?"

"Chocolate mousse," she muttered. Bored. That's what she was, and annoyed with him for trying to humor her. But maybe he was right. She glanced into the living room. They were all talking to each other as if they'd never argued. She took the bowl out of the refrigerator and put it in his hands. "I guess we'll serve it in front of the TV."

"Good. Then we'll watch the ball come down," Alan said over his shoulder.

"And dance to Guy Lombardo," she heard Cassie say. A tradition at the Lindemann house, no doubt.

"Julia?" Alan bowed to her after dessert. "Care to dance?"

He held her close, and they swayed in their small space. She glanced past his shoulder at the screen, at the crowds jammed in Times Square.

"Our last New Year's in New York. And we've never gone to Times Square."

"Are you sorry?"

The cameras had cut to the ballroom at the Waldorf Astoria—black and white images of women in ball gowns and men in tuxedos. She closed her eyes, saw Cassie's parents and aunts and uncle whirling around the foyer. When she opened them her friends were dancing, too.

"No. This is better."

"Gonna take a sentimental journey," he sang in her ear.

"Sentimental jour-ur-ney home." He kissed her. "Happy New Year, Julia."

Chapter 17

July 1968

THE SKY OVER the road shimmered silver with heat. As a child, Cassie had believed the waves in the air meant water over the next hill, and her father had never told her it wasn't true. Twenty years later, Cassie still watched the horizon ahead, hoping to be first to glimpse the sea. She'd wanted to visit last summer, but eighteen steaming hours of July labor had ended with a Caesarean. Now she felt fine, and Sara was such a good little girl. Peter, she knew, would rather have spent a week on the boat closer to home than waste three days of his vacation driving to the Cape and back.

"There's the sign," said Cassie. "Truro. Finally!"

"I saw it."

"What a long drive! Aren't you glad we spent last night with my parents?"

"I guess."

She got so tired of working Peter out of his moods. He'd agreed to visit Alan and Julia this summer, so now why did he have to act as if he were being forced into it?

"You'll be able to swim this afternoon," she said. "The beach is walking distance."

"A swim will feel good."

"I wonder what the house will be like. I can't wait to see Julia."

They took the third exit and, beyond the wall of heat that lined Route 6, found themselves on a narrow road that wound west under deep and dappled shade. They passed tidy shingled houses with old, imperfect lawns, converted barns with north roofs of glass, driveways with discreet name signs. Cool, green and eternal, this place. They burst into sunlight again when the road crossed a shining golden salt meadow dotted with cedars and wild roses. Cassie breathed deeply. The water was near. When they reached the top of the meadow, she saw the bay and the clear summer green of the marsh for just a moment before they turned right and drove northeast.

"This can't be right, Peter. Now we're heading away from the bay."

But there it was—precisely the kind of house Cassie had imagined, a Cape with lots of angles and irregular windows and doors in unexpected places. Its shiny side faced the road, the cedar shingles polished to silver by strong south sun and salt air. The windows were so close together the black shutters overlapped, and the weathered panelled door, with its own row of tiny windows above, seemed narrowed and squeezed between them. A copper ship's lantern, greened by the sea, was mounted on the trim, for lack of a free wall. No fancy shrubs flanked the foot-thick granite slab that was the front step, but lilac and forsythia marked the corners of the dooryard, daylilies tangled with wild roses for space along the picket fence, and four tall cedars clustered by the driveway.

"This place is much bigger than it looks from the road!" Peter brightened as they pulled in. "Hey, there's a barn! Even a tennis court!"

Cassie looked at the level area to the right of the driveway. It had been a tennis court, but the chicken wire fencing was torn and hanging, and weed clumps dotted its gravelly clay surface. "It doesn't look like anyone's played for a long time."

They heard a screen door slam when Peter switched off the engine, and there they were. Gilly led the way, running toward the car.

"Stop at the driveway," Alan called.

"Car stopped, Daddy." She paused and looked back at him for permission to keep going.

"Even so, Gillian," Julia warned. "Do as Daddy says."

Cassie got out. She knelt and gave Gilly a squeeze. The child kept her arms at her side and didn't hug back.

The tide was out, and the sun through the shallow water cast shadows on the sand bottom. Perfect for Sara's first day at the beach. Lots of little things for her to look at, and no big waves to frighten her. Gilly ran right to the edge and sat down, laughing and slapping the water with her hands.

"How'd you get her to do that?" Peter asked.

"Go in? I don't know," Alan said. "She just took to it."

"She's right at home," Cassie said. "Like it's her bathtub. See, Peter? Babies need to feel the water's a friendly place. We've been arguing about this for months," she explained to her friends.

"All well and good," Peter said. "But Sara's going to be on the boat, where she could fall into deep water. She needs to learn to swim."

"She needs to like the water to do that!" Cassie stooped down, and dipped Sara's fingers into the water.

"Peter wants me to take her to one of those swimming classes for infants. All those shrieking babies—she'd be terrified. I'm glad I waited. Now she'll see how Gilly loves it."

"I'll give her this week...."

"Oh, Peter, listen to yourself!" Julia said, giving him a disgusted look. "This is the seashore, not the stock exchange! We'll give you a week. To relax. How's that?"

Cassie wished Julia wouldn't pick on Peter, at least not until he'd cooled off. If they started carping at each other this soon, it would be a long, difficult weekend.

Alan started back to the blanket, and Gilly ran after him. He wrapped her in a towel, then lifted her in the air.

"Daddy's hungry. Gilly's yummy." He opened his mouth, as if to take a big bite, and Gilly squealed and wriggled.

"Not Gilly, Daddy. Not Gilly."

"No?" He paused, holding her in mid-air, looking into her eyes. "What then?"

"Sandwich." He put her right down.

"Of course. A sandwich." He scooped up some sand and pretended to eat it. Gilly couldn't stop giggling at him.

"No, Daddy. Julia's food."

Julia handed him a sandwich. "Here, clown. Sit down and eat. It's ham, appropriately enough. And cheese for you, little girl."

Gillian took the slice, walked around the edge of the blanket to Sara. She sat down, tore her cheese in two and held out a piece to Sara, who stared for a second or two, then took it and put it in her mouth.

"Give kids a chance. They'll take care of themselves, and each other." Alan smiled.

"Sara gets to have cheese instead of that jarred stuff you brought," Julia said. "And you don't have to feed her. You can just take it easy."

"But I like to know she's getting enough of what's good for her," Cassie said.

"I read somewhere that babies balance their own diets," Alan said. "Of course, you can't ask them what they want, but you can let them show you."

If you spend time with them, Cassie thought.

"Enough of this baby talk," Peter said. "I want to know how you two found that house!"

"We got lucky." Julia poured out juice for the girls. "Shortly after we moved here—what, Alan, a week or two? Alan found out that the Playhouse was looking for new playwrights, actors, technicians...."

"So not only were we in Provincetown, but I landed a job in theater! Odd hours and very little money, but..."

"What does this have to do with the house?" Peter popped open a beer.

"Everything! There was a terrific guy on the board. Tobias Hilton—nothing to do with the hotels. He's a playwright. An attorney, actually, with a summer place in Truro. But he only practices law to make a living."

"Never heard that one before," Peter said. "But if you're going to do something just to make a living, law's the thing!"

"Some people take seats on boards, do their civic duty and don't care that about what goes on," Alan said. "For Toby it was a way to be part of what he really cared about."

"I think he admired Alan for not selling out to make money," Julia said. "For taking a chance...."

"Maybe that was it at first. He asked me one day if I'd read one of his plays. I did, and asked for another, and another...All great! He had no confidence. Writing was just something he did for himself, because he loved it. His family thought he was plain strange. His wife liked to travel in the summertime, used to say he wasn't good company." Alan shook his head. "He deserved better."

"Then Alan produced one of the plays," Julia said. "Under another name, because Hilton wanted to remain anonymous. When it turned out to be one of the best of the season, rumors started going around that Alan was the playwright. I'd deny it, looking guilty, which only reinforced their suspicions."

"Those rumors got me my teaching job, I swear. Our meal ticket for the winter."

"But you make enough to rent that house?" Peter asked.

"No. Toby offered us the house for the winter." Alan's words came slower, softer.

"Where is he?" Cassie asked. "Now that it's summer."

"Dying, and there's not a damn thing I can do." Alan got up and walked back down to the water.

"He really loves that old man," Julia said. "He's been so withdrawn this summer, except with Gillian. I'm glad you all came. Maybe he'll dwell on it less with you here."

"You know, Cass has told me how things always seem to work out for you two," Peter said. "Luck just must follow you two around."

Julia began to collect the picnic trash. "Alan *was* lucky to meet Toby."

Getting up to help Julia, Cassie wondered if Peter really thought it was lucky that Toby couldn't be there this summer.

Gilly, who'd eaten all she wanted, ran to Alan's side and wrapped her arms around his legs. Cassie watched him place his hand on her head. He knew she was there, but still stared out to sea. Alan said you couldn't ask babies what they wanted, but you could let them show you. Maybe it worked both ways.

Peter put Sara on his shoulders and joined them. Maybe he was learning something from Alan about being a daddy, not just a father. Cassie and Julia packed away the food, then stretched out on the blanket, eyes closed, faces to the sun, and listened—to the steady slap of the sea on the sand, the red-wing blackbirds trilling over the marsh, doves and bob-whites whoo-ing and whistling in the woods beyond. Peace.

"In your element?"

"Mmmm," Cassie answered, close to sleep. "You?"

"Every now and then."

"And in between?"

"You know, Cassie. My old restlessness."

"Was it there in Provincetown?"

"Not as much. I had the studio, and people around."

"It's not far from here, Julia." Cassie said, rising to her elbows.

Julia sighed, staring across the water toward Provincetown. "No...the monument looks close enough to touch, doesn't it?" She scooped up a handful of sand and let it sift through her fingers. "They call that Land's End, but this place *feels* more like the end of the earth."

"I like that feeling. It must be wonderful in winter."

"It's wild. When the town was first settled they called it Dangerfield, and I know why. Some nights the wind hurls itself at the houses, even the ones in the lee of the hills. On stormy nights there's this constant roar—wind and surf. I'll never get used to it."

"The house must be cozy, though, with the fireplaces and low ceilings."

"Drafty, mostly. I'm always cold. I keep warm by drinking gallons of tea."

"*That's* nothing new! Right now it's hard to imagine being cold. Walk down to the water with me?"

Cassie created patterns with her feet in the damp sand at the water's edge, the way she used to do when she was a child. She spoke first.

"When you had your studio, did you do a lot of work?"

"Some, but I was so scattered."

"I'd love to see some of your paintings."

"When I'm ready." Julia looked away down the beach, where the men walked with the girls.

Cassie liked seeing Peter with Sara. Maybe he'd grow to enjoy her as Alan did Gilly. But Alan had been thrilled with his daughter from the start. That was clear. Sometimes Cassie still heard Peter's voice in the delivery room as she was coming out of anesthesia. 'I wish she'd had a boy'. Cassie dove into the water, washing the words away.

"Alan's really happy with Gilly, isn't he?" she said when she surfaced."

"Of course!" Julia was lying on her back, sculling quietly. She flipped over and began to swim toward the others.

Cassie let her get a head start, then broke into her best camp crawl and caught up. They didn't race, but swam side by side without talking, back to their families.

The next morning, after an early breakfast, Cassie, Julia, and the girls set out for Provincetown, where Cassie parked the station wagon at the East End of town. She unbuckled Sara from her car seat, and settled her into a stroller. Julia, who despite Cassie's cautions had held Gillian in her lap for the drive, slipped a harness over her daughter's shoulders and attached a long leash.

"Don't look horrified, Cassandra. Surely you've seen these?"

"Not on children...."

"It's the only answer for this kid. She wouldn't ride in that contraption. She has to do everything herself."

Cassie had noticed, and smiled at Julia's exasperation. "Think you might have been that way?"

Julia eyed her, then turned and gestured for Cassie to follow her across the street.

"This is where we survived the Christmas storm."

The white house and its white picket fence were peeling. Its grass and gardens were protected by the houses next door, but its east, south and west sides were open to the wind and waves.

"This house is practically in the water on a *calm* morning!" Cassie could believe Julia's tales of the storm. "No wonder you were scared!"

"I wasn't, really. After all, these houses have been through hundreds of storms."

Gillian was trying to undo the catch on the gate.

"She couldn't possibly remember..."

Julia grabbed her hand and took up the slack in the leash.

"A friend of ours lives here. He's a photographer. Loves to take pictures of her. Too early, Gillian. He's sleeping. Let's go see the boats."

It was 8:30, and quiet enough to hear the click of an approaching bicycle, the whirr as it coasted past. Gulls clamored over a school of fish across the harbor.

"Here's the Beachcombers'. Men only. On Saturdays they take turns cooking and then sit around drinking and telling stories. Alan's been invited a couple of times."

"Is there one for the women?"

"Sewing circles, quilters, maybe, but nothing like this, I'll bet. To be honest, I never looked. I needed solitude when we lived here."

"To paint."

"Right. Between waitressing, street sketching..."

"Street sketching?"

"For Starving Artists. They do portraits and caricatures down near the wharf. I filled in there when I could." Julia stopped, picked a white rose, stripped the soft thorns from its stem, and tucked it into her hair.

"Still picking other people's flowers, I see."

"These are wild! Here, one for you, too. I hope Maia's at the wharf today so you can meet her. Maybe she'll do a sketch of Sara for you. She's great with kids."

"Maia? See Maia?" Gillian repeated any word.

"Gillian knows everyone! Another friend?"

"Yes. A good one. She's a painter, too. But she's only here summers. She spends the rest of the time in the Village. Funny—I know more people in the Village now than I did when we lived there!"

Funny, but Julia didn't sound amused. Gillian ran ahead, tugging on her harness, pointing to the wharf.

"Boats. See boats now."

"Alan used to take her every day to watch them bring the catch in. I'm afraid we have to walk the wharf."

Sara liked sightseeing. She sucked quietly on her thumb all the way out the wharf and back. Gillian ran again and again to the edge and squinted at the green-brown water, looking for fish among the beer cans. By the time they left the wharf, Cassie was tired, more from worry that Gillian would fall in than from pushing the stroller over the rough planks. At the corner of Commercial Street, the mingled smells of dead fish, salt-water taffy, fudge and foot-long hot dogs made her feel sick.

"Can we sit somewhere, Julia? I'm pooped."

"Yes, yes. I just want to see if Maia's in yet."

The sidewalks were crowded with day-trippers in Cape Cod t-shirts and clip-on sunglasses, scanning windows filled with miniature lobster pots and clam shell ashtrays. At the Starving Artists' lean-to, tacked up between two buildings, behind a wooden stairway to a second floor apartment, lines were forming for twenty-minute masterpieces.

But Maia was not one of the day's artists. Julia left a message telling her to join them at the sidewalk cafe next to Town Hall before work.

Julia ordered cappuccino and pastries for two and water ices for the children. Sara had never had one, but Cassie decided not to say so. Her legs felt like jelly, and her back ached from pushing the stroller. Even the hard wire chair felt good. The beach would feel better. She hoped Julia wasn't planning a full-day tour.

"Is your old house much farther?"

"Quite a way. Don't give out on me now, Cassie. Have some coffee. Quick energy."

Cassie poured two sugars into the center of the milky froth and stirred carefully so she wouldn't spoil the foam. She liked to sip through it. Sara stayed in the stroller and took small spoonfuls of watermelon ice from Cassie. Gillian sat in Julia's lap, feeding herself, her shirt and the concrete floor, still littered with last night's butts. Julia lit a cigarette and inhaled.

"Sorry," she said through the first puff of smoke. She held out the pack to Cassie. "Want one?"

Cassie shook her head. She had never liked to smoke in the morning. And now, even outdoors, the smell made her sick.

"I thought you had quit."

"I didn't smoke for over a year..."

"Well, the young mothers." The voice behind her was deep, but female. A tall woman took a chair from an adjacent table and sat down between them. "What a scene."

Maia had an Afro. Frizzed gold, her hair looked more like a hat she'd have to take off to sleep. She also wore a tie-dyed t-shirt and short cut-off jeans that drew attention to her long brown legs. They too were covered with thick golden hair, shining in the sun. Maia wore no jewelry, no makeup.

"Hi. The Gerber baby?"

Julia answered before Cassie had decided whether she was being funny or critical.

"That's Sara. And this is my friend, Cassie. They're here for a few days."

"Great...great...." Maia took a fingerful of Gillian's ice and popped it into her mouth. "You missed a good trip at Tony's last night. He had some really good stuff."

Trip. Stuff. Drug words. Cassie looked at Julia, but she turned away.

"We stayed late at the beach," she said quickly, "And with Cassie and Peter here, we didn't finish dinner until late. Listen, Maia. Do you have time to do Sara for Cassie?"

Julia had skirted the subject. Maia did mean drugs.

"Not now, Julia...not today," Cassie said. "I'm feeling off. I'd really like to go home."

"You haven't seen my old studio!" Julia looked annoyed.

"I know, and I'm sorry. I think I need to get out of the sun."

"So? I can sketch in the shade," Maia said.

"Never mind." Julia stood up and put her hand on Maia's shoulder. "We'll go." She stuffed Gillian into the stroller behind Sara.

"I thought she wouldn't ride," Cassie said. Sara was going to get all sticky.

"If you want to get back fast she'll have to. I'll push. So long, Maia."

"Another day...." Maia put her grimy bare feet up on the empty chair and pulled the plates closer. Cassie tried to think of something to say. She watched Maia help herself to the half-eaten pastry and cool coffee, then turned to catch up with Julia, who had already crossed Ryder Street. Julia pushed on so Cassie couldn't catch up. Hurrying made her feel sicker, so she walked at her own pace. If Julia was going to sulk about not going to some old house, she could do it while she waited at the car.

"Not nice, Cassandra. You save your manners for your suburban friends?" She didn't offer to help with Sara or the stroller, just took Gillian, flopped into her seat and slammed the door.

As she secured Sara in the back seat, Cassie protested.

"Since when is it rude to be ill?"

"Ill! Maia was too much for you." Julia lit another cigarette.

"I wish you wouldn't smoke in the car, Julia. There's not enough air."

"Since when have you been so prissy about smoking? You used to be a shameless mooch." Julia carefully knocked the burning head off the cigarette and slipped it back into the pack for later.

"I don't mind your smoking, Julia..."

"Just the other stuff, right?"

"What other stuff?" Cassie didn't know what she'd do with the answer, but stalled for time, asking the question anyway.

"Hash. Maybe even acid."

"You're the one, Julia, who changed the subject when Maia brought it up. You're the one who acts like it's something to hide."

"From *you* it is."

Julia didn't speak again until they'd left town behind.

"See these places, Cassie?" They were driving past rows of rundown cottages, squeezed between the bay and the road. "Depressing, right? And not just because they need paint. They're deadly because they're all the same. Is that how people have to be, Cassie?"

"No, but drugs..."

"Why is it easier to blame drugs," Julia said, "Than to admit our differences?"

"I just don't understand." Cassie glanced at Julia, at Gillian in her lap. She should be more responsible. "What about your daughter? Future children..."

"There won't be any."

"What?"

"I'm not having any more children. And I don't want to talk about it. We're almost home. It's not discussed there. This is my decision, not Alan's. Drop it, Cassie."

When they pulled into the drive, the men were on their hands and knees on the tennis court, pulling out hunks of grass. The posts had been straightened and the rusted wire pulled down. Julia jumped out of the car before Cassie turned off the engine and strode down the hill.

"Looks like you two have had a constructive morning!"

"Sure have. We thought we'd resurrect this thing." Alan stood up and wiped his hands on his shorts before picking Gillian up. "And you had...let me guess...watermelon ice?"

Gillian nodded.

"So, will you two be ready for mixed doubles by tomorrow afternoon? Alan and I have booked the court."

"Not unless Cassie feels better," Julia said.

"Julia says you're not feeling well," Peter said, following Cassie to the house. "What's wrong? Anything I can get for you?"

"No...I'm just beat. Could you give Sara lunch? I'm going to lie down." Without waiting for him to agree, she hurried inside and let the screen door slam behind her.

She woke up in a quiet house, with no sense of time or place. Windowpane shadows lay across the wide white floor boards. From the west window. Damn. She'd missed most of her afternoon at the beach—sleeping. She could have done it there. She got up and pulled on her suit. Gillian's room was empty. The children weren't napping. They'd all gone without her.

Chapter 18

ON A MUGGY mid-Atlantic August day—the kind that made her miss New England most—Cassie waited, slip stuck to her skin, in the familiar air-conditioned office. The woman across from her, possibly into a tenth month, had to be feeling worse. Cassie knew—she'd been there last year. She didn't need the test or the exam to know this would be the first of monthly visits. She had denied the signs, so welcome before, as long as she dared.

"Back so soon!" the nurse had said when she came in. "With a doll like yours I'm not surprised you want another."

Cassie couldn't say she did. At least not now. And Peter? This pregnancy would foul up their five-year plan to build equity in the cottage, then move up. But he couldn't blame her—she'd taken every precaution. She had stuffed the damn thing in her purse this morning—properly powdered in its little pink case—so the doctor could tell her if it was defective. She wanted to throw it now onto the nurse's desk, and...what? Demand a refund? It was too late. Being angry was pointless. They'd have to move. She was resigned to that, had even brought along the real estate section of *The Bulletin* to scan while she waited. She loved the cottage and was sad to have to leave, but it wouldn't be fair to blame the baby. Even now the three of them were tripping over toys and each other. They needed something bigger. Better? Hard to find on their budget. She pulled out the listings. She'd decided one thing—if Peter was going to keep working such long hours they'd move closer to town. She wanted him there for the children's bedtime. And she wanted to live closer to Kate.

Kate had been Cassie's roommate in the maternity ward and they had clicked at once. Their daughters had stared at each other for weeks, put fingers in each others' eyes at six months, and last time they met ignored each other. Soon they might decide to play, and then it would be nice to be within walking distance, in Gladwyne.

Having daughters was only the first of many things Cassie and Kate had in common. Since the week they bought the same patterned sheets at Wanamaker's White Sale, they had joked about their similar tastes. One might call the other before a party to ask, "What are you wearing?" Not to be sure they'd be turned out properly—to be sure they wouldn't be identically dressed.

But they were different, too. Funny. Cassie remembered lying in the hospital room, hearing Kate order the nurses about and thinking, until she opened her eyes and saw the red hair, that Julia was there. Friends could be mirrors or windows, and the best ones could be both. Sometimes being with them was like catching a reflection in a windowpane, seeing out and in at the same time. Julia and Kate.

Cassie was startled awake by the phone. Calls before seven meant bad news. Peter pulled the pillow over his head. The phone was on his side of the bed, but he wasn't going to answer. Cassie reached across his shoulders, trying not to disturb him, and answered softly, out of consideration and fear.

"Cassie. It's me. We're back!"

Kate. The relief, like the news, felt good.

"I woke you. Sorry. I forgot to look at the clock. To me it's afternoon. I've been up for at least three hours. I'll hang up. Call me later."

"No, hold on. I'll pick up in the kitchen."

The phone hadn't wakened Sara, so Cassie could talk in peace.

"Welcome home! Tell me about the trip," she said, filling the coffeepot. She wouldn't be going back to sleep now.

"The short version—great. How about coming for lunch, and I'll tell you more. Whenever you can get here. I have to go out, but I'll be back at ten."

These days it was a feat for Cassie to get out by ten, much less back from somewhere. She tried to think what she had planned to accomplish that day. What did it matter? If the day turned out to be as hot as the one before, she wouldn't do much anyway. "I'll be there."

The coffee smelled good, really good, for the first time in weeks, no, months. Maybe she wouldn't have to keep crackers by the bed anymore. She'd forgotten to tell Kate not to make ham sandwiches— and forgotten to tell her the news. Oh well, if she could drink coffee again, maybe she'd be able to eat ham.

Peter wandered into the kitchen in his pajamas.

"Coffee. Pour me a cup?" He walked to the dining room window to see if the paper had been delivered. "Damn. He's late."

"No, you're early."

He looked at his watch. "Guess so! Did I hear the phone?"

"You tried hard not to..."

"Who in hell would call at this hour?"

"Just Kate."

"Kate. I do swear, Cass. For a polite girl you have the rudest friends."

"She apologized. She's still on European time!"

"I suppose you told her..."

"I forgot."

Peter looked skeptical.

"I'll tell her this afternoon. We're having lunch."

"Another day shot..."

"I'll let her know we're looking. She'll hear about deals in Gladwyne, I'm sure. And now she can watch Sara while I look."

"Good point. I guess I'll shower and head in early. Don't forget to pick up my shirts. I'm down to the last one."

There was no car in the drive, so Cassie parked in front, walked around to the back, and used her "convenience key" to let herself in. She made herself a glass of instant iced coffee, but there was no cream and she couldn't drink it black. She'd wait. With Sara on her hip, she wandered through the darkened front rooms.

Kate sometimes joked about her house being "very grand." It was not only bigger than Cassie's, but finished, the way houses were when people weren't worried about money anymore. Tasteful—with comfortable sofas and loveseats in traditional style, swivel armchairs, thick new carpets, mirrors with brass frames, silk flowers and clusters of candlesticks on the mantelpiece. The fruitwood tables had no marks or character, held no pictures or books or treasured objects. Kate and Ben might have ordered the showroom displays as is, complete with groupings of framed prints on the walls. The first day Cassie had visited, she wondered if the delivery trucks had just departed.

With baby furniture and snapshots of Tricia being added almost weekly, the family room was beginning to look like one. She put Sara down in Tricia's playpen and thumbed through the copy of *Elle* that was lying on the table. Her French was rusty and she read more for feel than content, assuring herself that she could survive in France, if she ever got there.

When she heard the garage door, she went out to help with the bags, relieved to see Kate looking like Kate, not like the women in *Elle*. She wore a short, striped shift, one she had bought in the spring, and sandals. She had gathered her heavy mahogany hair and fastened it loosely on top of her head in a mature style, but the tendrils that spilled out around her face called attention to her freckles—made her look too young to be so settled.

"I knew you wouldn't be back by ten!" Cassie said, taking two bags from the trunk.

"I kept running into people." Kate could never do a quick errand in town. Too many people liked her, liked to talk to her.

"That's OK. I read your magazine."

"*Your* magazine. I bought it for you yesterday at the airport." Kate put Tricia in the other corner of the playpen with Sara and they went out for another load. "Why aren't you in your suit, out by the pool?"

"I got as far as fixing iced coffee to take with me..."

"And there was no cream. It's in here somewhere. Start looking."

"So you did end up in Paris?" They laughed. The trip—a gift from Ben for bearing him a child—had been delayed a year because she wouldn't leave the baby. Kate had joked in July that Ben wanted to take her off to Paris to get her pregnant—he wanted a son. Kate was twenty-three with lots of time, but Ben, at forty-five, felt his ticking away.

"We started in London. Dinners, the theater, and lots of time in bed."

"So you were right. Then where did you go?" Cassie filled the cookie jar and took one to each of the girls while Kate divided and wrapped the week's meat for the freezer.

"Switzerland, where we spent all the time we could outdoors under that sky. Such a blue you've never seen."

"Did you take pictures?"

"Oh, sure, but there's silver in the air, that shines everything it touches, that'll never show on film...how I loved it there." Tricia, who'd whimpered about being been put in the playpen, began to cry. "Oh, baby, your mother's here. I missed her so, and I knew I was coming back. Think of her, Cassie, not knowing."

Cassie couldn't say she'd ever really considered her baby's view of the world. She just fed and dressed her, kept her warm or cool, clean and dry. She remembered holding Sara when she was tiny, thinking 'This child needs me to survive.' Remembered how she lost her breath, how her heart raced at the thought. She had overcome her fear by doing what she had to, but it never seemed as easy as for Kate.

Kate lifted Tricia over the edge of the pen and held her close.

"Poor child. I'm going to have to love you extra for a long time to make it up to you."

Now Sara was starting to fuss. Cassie tried putting herself in her daughter's place. She wouldn't want to stay in the playpen, alone. Better to take her out, respond to her need, not just let her cry until she gave up.

"Sara's ready for a swim, I think. Can't we finish the rest later, while they're napping?"

"If you don't want to save that time for sunning."

"It's too hot." Besides, it was September. Sunning was for June, when she could look forward to summer, think of herself tan and thin. There was little point now.

In the pool, they bobbed their babies between them, and Kate told her about France. About the chateaux where they stayed, the vineyards. About Paris, the *Folies*—"embarrassing"—the lingerie Ben had insisted on buying her—"I feel so foolish in it. I'm not the type for black lace"—and the food. Cassie was hungry.

After lunch, in the shade by the garden, Kate asked about the Cape.

"It must have been great seeing Julia after so long."

A momentary breeze passed, and with it a pungent scent Cassie knew and disliked. Chrysanthemums had bloomed in the sun along the fence. Summer was over.

"It should have been, but Julia was strange. When we arrived I thought it was going to be like old times—no, better than old times. But Alan's feeling down about a friend of his who's dying..."

"I thought we were talking about Julia," Kate said, passing a basket of grapes.

"We are! They have this fantastic house—old and slanty, with lots of cozy rooms...very romantic."

"It doesn't sound like the sort of place Julia would like. Is it what she wants?"

"I'm not sure she knows, so I certainly don't." And Cassie wasn't sure she wanted to. She told Kate about the strain between them.

"She's very casual with Gilly, and acts like her way is the only way."

"Not your imagination?"

"No. Then a friend of hers came by while we were having coffee. Maia. She was wild, dirty. I'll admit I wasn't as friendly as I might have been, but I was feeling sick that day, and that made it all worse. Julia got mad, then I picked at her in return, then she lectured me, made the whole thing seem like my fault." Cassie didn't tell Kate the rest. She pulled the last couple of grapes off the stem. "But late that afternoon we all had cocktails on the beach, the sunlight slanting and gold. Those times, when we're all close, are the ones I want to remember."

"We all push painful memories away. If we could we'd banish them forever." Kate shivered. "I'm moving into the sun."

Cassie guessed that some of Kate's painful memories concerned her family. She never talked about them, and there were no pictures of them around the house. What had she said that morning? That she'd have to love her child extra to make up for leaving her? Maybe Kate really knew how it felt to be left.

Julia, too, Cassie thought as they moved the chaises. Julia had been so sure she couldn't be a good mother because her own had been the worst. Maybe she needed to make others believe she was best so she could believe it herself. Maybe it was too hard for her. She'd made her point so now she didn't need more children.

"I don't either, really," Cassie said, thinking out loud.

"Did you say something?" Kate sounded sleepy.

"You're falling asleep. I'll tell you later."

"I'm awake. What?"

"Remember I said I wasn't feeling well at the Cape? I'm due in March."

Kate giggled, then laughed hard, holding her sides.

"It just strikes me so funny," she said, when she gained control. "Poor Ben. All that time and expense, fancy beds all around Europe, and you're the one who ends up conceiving, right here at home. March, you said?"

Cassie nodded.

"Well, even if Paris was worth his money, we won't be sharing a room in maternity."

"I'm not really ready, Kate."

"Oh, but you will be."

"We have to move."

"Then maybe with some Irish luck we'll find the perfect place for you, closer to here."

Good old Kate had read her mind.

Chapter 19

November 1968

DRESSING FOR HER birthday dinner, Cassie had to force the zipper of her favorite red wool skirt. With Sara she had put on maternity clothes as soon as she knew, so the world would, too. How different she felt this second time. She sucked in her stomach and turned sideways to the mirror. Not bad, but tonight would be her last chance to feel well-dressed until after the baby.

After the baby. When she had first started to mark time by that measure, March sounded very far off, but here it was November 20. After driving miles with realtors, she hadn't seen even one house she'd consider. She'd looked at old farmhouses—stucco, solid, but with molds and mice—and at several of the new "colonials" that were sprouting in meadows along the Main Line. A good storm could do as much damage to that crop as to the corn. The builders had skimped on details—plastered archways instead of hanging doors with moldings, slapped in flat picture windows instead of bays with window seats, built token fireplaces with cheap monochromatic brick and no mantelpieces. Kate had given her a subscription to *House Beautiful*, "to inspire you, keep you looking." Somewhere there had to be the right place, something between the "starters" and the "dream houses."

The properties that intrigued her were beyond the budget. But some had been on the market three months, and by the holidays the sellers might be ready to settle for less. She would look at some of those tomorrow. A birthday gift to herself.

That night, after a steak dinner at Coventry Forge, Peter pushed something towards her across the table. The box was the right size for the long strand of pearls Cassie had hinted she wanted. She gave it a gentle shake.

"C'mon now, Cass, no cheating." She usually said that to him. He'd tease her by shaking a box, staring into space trying to guess its contents, when she just wanted to see him open it, find out if he liked his present. This box was too light for pearls.

Airline tickets. To Florida. For Christmas. Peter was so excited about surprising her...she hoped he thought she cried because she was happy.

"So. What are you going to do?" Kate asked the next morning when she settled Sara with her. "You don't want to go, do you."

Cassie's throat swelled. "Peter talked about it all the way home, Kate. About taking me where it was warm. About being able to sail now that I'm not feeling sick. About his parents seeing Sara. We have to go."

"Well, there *could* be worse fates. And maybe your going will bring you blessings."

The first two houses were too far from the center of town, and the third needed renovations they wouldn't have money to make. This was it, the realtor, Mrs. Detweiler, assured her as they pulled into the driveway of the last one.

It was hard to tell. Rhododendrons and yews masked the first floor windows. But there was a portico over the front door—she liked that—and she could see that it had a slate roof. Promising...

"The gentleman who lives here lost his wife a year ago, and he's let everything go. The house doesn't show well, I must warn you, but I think I know what you're looking for, and it's here. Once it's aired and cleaned....Well, you'll see."

Walking into the kitchen, Cassie gagged. Garbage odors overpowered even those of old age and stale cigars. How could anyone live like this?

"Doesn't anyone care for this man?"

"His children live some distance away. But...the gentleman is failing. There are going to be hospital bills. Those children will want to settle. Right now all they can talk about is getting a good price..."

"How can they possibly expect it!" Cassie opened a few of the cabinets. Good storage space, and a pantry.

"Some people can't be told."

The rooms were dark and the furniture soiled and dusty, but Cassie could see that it had been nice at one time. She could almost feel the presence of the poor woman whose home it had been. If she ever saw it like this.... Both the dining room and the living room were large, with windows facing the street. Because it was a stone house, the windowsills were deep, perfect for plants. Stone houses were the only thing Cassie really loved about Pennsylvania.

Between the dining and living rooms was a spacious foyer, much like the one in her parents' home. The staircase didn't go straight up, but wound along the foyer walls—four steps and a landing, turn left, four more, another landing and left, and then the last four. She loved it. The bedrooms on the second floor were huge. All four with deep lighted closets—lots of room for shelves. There was a narrow staircase to the third floor, now just attic. It would be a study for Peter.

"This is it. The house I've been looking for. I'll have to talk to my husband, of course."

"Of course. Be sure to tell him the situation. Make your offer. It may be refused the first time, but if you're patient, you'll have the house. I'm certain of it."

Cassie was, too. She had to ride back to the office to pick up her car. Otherwise she'd have run to Kate's. She could have—it was only a couple of blocks away.

Peter saw the possibilities when they looked at it together on Sunday. During dinner that evening he told her he wouldn't offer anything until they listed their house and got some idea how much it would bring. He agreed, reluctantly, to list it with Mrs. Detweiler.

"If she's not concerned with getting *them* the best price, how do we know she'll do it for us?"

"She will," Cassie argued. "That house won't be easy to sell, and she's found a buyer. She's doing her job!"

Peter slowly carved white meat from the chicken, shaking his head.

"No, she should be telling you there's another interested party so you'll pay the asking price."

Cassie wanted to raise her voice to make her point, but needed to prove to him that she'd thought this out. He hadn't said no yet.

"She knows we can't," she said calmly. "But she knows we want it. Since we're giving her ours, she'll try to make up the lost commission by getting us our price. The cottage will show well."

"When you want something you can be real stubborn." Peter smiled at her the way an amused father would at a child. "I'm not sure I follow your logic, but O.K. I did put you in charge of getting us out of this house and into a new one. Do it."

For the next week Cassie worked on the cottage. She washed walls and woodwork and touched up nicked paint. And when she was finished cleaning, Cassie decorated for Christmas—pine candles on the mantle, a big wooden bowl of oranges, stuck with cloves, on the dining table. No tree. They were going away. She wished they weren't. She wanted to celebrate Christmas here, not in Florida.

But she packed up the gift for the Lawsons, some summer clothes and Sara's favorite toys, left the key with Mrs. Detweiler, and they flew out on the twenty-third. Strapped into her seat with nothing to do but read to Sara, she checked off in her head all she'd accomplished in a month. No wonder she was tired. Maybe this wasn't a bad idea. She reached over and rested her hand on Peter's.

"It will feel good to lie in the sun."

"Sure will." He answered without looking up from his magazine.

Cassie had never stepped from winter to summer before. The soft humid air on her face was welcome, and warm. Maybe she could get used to the idea of going south for the holidays. The Lawsons were there to meet them. They hadn't seen Sara since she learned to walk. If they even noticed, they didn't make any fuss. Their focus was Peter. They had accepted invitations to parties—every night but Christmas— to show off their handsome, successful son. Cassie did fine the first couple of nights, when she had to do little but nod and say "Pleased to meet you."

But on Christmas Eve at the neighbors', all anyone could talk about was the modern miracle of lunar orbit, and how the economy around the Cape would benefit—Canaveral. Not even Kennedy. Cassie went out to the patio and stared at the moon. It didn't look any different. She tried to imagine looking back here from there, passing behind to the other side and felt even farther from home. She was sure that someone else in her family would see the connection between themselves and so many shepherds who could talk only about a bright star in the East. Indoors, someone started to play "Jingle Bells" on the piano. Singing about snow and sleigh rides in a sundress seemed ridiculous.

Rain fell during the night, and Christmas blew in on a brisk north wind. Cassie shivered under the cotton thermal blanket, too cold to sleep and too cold to get up. She always had trouble sleeping on Christmas morning, wondering what might have appeared under the tree. Even their first married Christmas, spent at her parents' in Connecticut, "Santa" didn't deliver before midnight.

Cassie forced herself out of bed to put Sara, who had gone to bed in cotton summer pajamas, into a blanket sleeper, wishing for one herself. Once up, she peeked into the living room. Everything was just as it had been when they came home from the party. Nothing under the tree, no stockings by the fireplace. Cassie tiptoed back to bed, reminding herself that the Lawsons usually retired early. They had probably been too weary to do anything last night. They got up early, too. It was almost dawn....

When she woke around eight, the sun was shining, she smelled coffee, Peter was gone, and she was still cold. She took a hot bath and dressed in the green wool jumper she'd planned to wear only on the plane down and back. Peter and his parents were sitting around the glass dining table, finishing their breakfast. Peter got up and pulled out her chair.

"Merry Christmas, everyone," Cassie said. "Where's Sara?"

"Letty's feeding her in the kitchen..." Mrs. Lawson cut Peter off. "And when you've finished, and she's finished, Letty will bring her into the living room. It's cool enough for a fire this morning! We'll have a real Christmas."

Sara was still in her sleeper—but someone had changed her diaper—sitting in the rented highchair, being fed homemade oatmeal.

"Looks like she prefers that to Pablum, Letty. She can feed herself, though. You don't have to do it."

"Oh, I know, Miss Cassie, but it's fun. She's the best child."

Cassie kissed the top of Sara's head. "Good morning, button. Merry Christmas. To you, too, Letty. Thanks for seeing she got something warm in her tummy."

"No mind, Miss. Nice to have a baby 'round here. You want your breakfast? Miz Lawson didn't ring..."

"Just coffee. I'll have it in the living room. The others may have gone in, but I want to dress Sara first."

"Y'all take y' time. Fresh pot's just brewin'."

Cassie wanted Sara dressed for the pictures. Last Christmas might have been her first, but this was the first she could appreciate, might remember. She'd bought her so many cute little things, but Peter had insisted it was foolish to fly them down and back.

"Even her stocking?" It wouldn't have taken much room.

"Especially her stocking," he said. "She won't care if she has Christmas at New Year's."

Well, little one, at least you can wear your Christmas dress. White cotton, with an angel in a blue robe embroidered on the yoke. In her tights and little blue velvet shoes, she looked like one herself.

"Better put this on, too." Cassie slipped her arms into a light blue sweater Kate had knit. "It's cold today."

There were two packages under the tree, both for Sara. The first was a gift from Peter's father, a teddy bear the color of butterscotch, with green eyes like Peter's.

"Oh, he's wonderful. So round and soft," Cassie said, pressing him to Sara's cheek.

"Just like Sara," Grandpa Lawson said, looking pleased that she was.

"She is *so* fat, Cassie. Look at those legs in the tights." Peter's mother laughed. "I hope my present fits her."

"She's not fat, Mother Lawson, just curvy. Girls are like that!"

The gift was a sailor dress that wouldn't fit Sara for at least another year, maybe two.

"Oh, dear. I'd hoped she could wear it to the yacht club today. Oh, well. With the weather, we might not go anyway. Better to grow into it than out of it too soon, with something special like that. When the baby comes, I'll get him a matching suit, of course."

No doubt. Cassie wondered if she'd buy another dress should Sara end up with a sister.

There was an envelope for them, with a check for $1,000.

"We had no idea what you wanted, and you are flying back. You can buy yourselves something for the new house."

"Thank you! This will be a big help," Cassie said, and meant it.

With little idea themselves of what to get his parents, Peter and Cassie had decided on something personal—a picture of the three of them at the cottage, with the brilliant July garden as background. It was one of their best pictures of Sara, though she looked even cuter today. Cassie had found a silver Caldwell's frame with lilies at the corners.

"Oh, you shouldn't have," Mrs. Lawson exclaimed, as she took it out of the box.

She likes it, Cassie thought.

"You should have waited until the baby was born and had a real family portrait!"

"You can change the picture later, Mother," Peter said.

Had she meant they should have a painting done? Or did she mean they weren't a real family until they had a son?

It was hard for Cassie to enjoy their last days there. The next two were cold—too cold for sailing. She found a sheltered corner by the pool, where if she lay absolutely flat she could feel warm between gusts. She was tired of meeting new people—she got them confused with the ones they'd met already—and she'd run out of clothes. It hadn't occurred to her that she might need a wardrobe for the social season. Even if it had, she wouldn't have spent a lot of money on elegant maternity dresses that were right for Florida but wrong for everywhere else she had to go between December and March. Mrs. Lawson hinted that she'd take her shopping for "something nice" but Cassie declined on principle. She wouldn't be pregnant next summer. She was thinking like Julia—never again. Claiming to be too tired, she insisted that Peter go to the remaining parties. She'd stay home with Sara.

They were peaceful evenings. Letty served her dinner by the fire in the living room, and she read *The Salzburg Connection.* She couldn't remember the last time she'd been able to read a book, even a mystery, in two days.

The weather warmed and they went sailing, all of them the first day, just she and Peter the last. Cassie stretched out in the cockpit, her head on his lap and watched the mainsail for luffs.

"This is more like it," she said, closing her eyes against the glare. "The temperature's almost the same as the first day you took me sailing."

"Cooler than I counted on, though." Peter checked the compass and adjusted their course slightly to the east. "Sorry it wasn't warmer for your first holiday in the south. Can't say the trip has been worth the money."

"Even to see your parents?"

"Well, they like seeing me, though a week's too long now."

She agreed, but didn't want to be critical, ungrateful. She could remember when he used to say it was too short. The baby stirred and she put Peter's hand on her belly to feel it.

"I hope this one won't feel that way about visiting us!"

"Just might. Feels like the restless type." Peter pulled his hand away and trimmed the jib.

"I think we disrupt your parents' ordered life," she went on, "With Sara and all. It's a strain, I'm sure."

"They've adjusted."

"Oh, I know," Cassie said, staring up at his strong jaw. "Pretty well, considering. Have they always been so..." She didn't want to say cold. Or stuffy. "Formal?"

"I guess." Peter kept his eyes on the course ahead. Even after five years together, it was hard to get him to talk about his parents. The first time they had sailed this boat together, she had felt sorry for him, sensing that his wealthy life had been a very lonely one. She had thought then that once he felt closer to her, felt appreciated, he would be more open. Happier. But he hadn't changed much over their years together. Neither had her feelings for the Lawsons.

On New Year's Eve Peter and Cassie celebrated Christmas and being home. Sara loved opening packages—wooden puzzles, a couple of books, a blackboard, even a garage with an elevator. Which she enjoyed more—the sound of the bell when the elevator reached the top or the cars shooting out and down the ramp—Cassie couldn't tell. She liked it. That was what mattered. After a few minutes of play, Peter threatened to disconnect the bell. He liked his book, *White Sails, Black Clouds*, better than the shirt. Cassie thought he'd look wonderful in yellow, but he still preferred white.

Before midnight they went to bed and made love. Peter never approached her when they stayed with his parents, so Cassie welcomed his attention, however restrained. He wasn't any more relaxed during this pregnancy than the last. As many times as she assured him nothing would break, he still seemed afraid to touch her. The life they'd created was keeping them apart.

Julia called shortly after midnight.

"Sure sounds quiet there." Not where Julia was. Cassie could hear loud music and the soft hum of background voices.

"It is. We just got home today."

"Oh, yes. Florida this year. How'd that go?"

"I'll write you the details."

"Sure. I guess Peter's right there. Listen. I wanted to make the new year official, that's all. One of these years we should spend it together again."

"Next year! In our new house."

Maybe next year would be better.

It began with good news, 1969. Mrs. Detweiler called on the third to say she had a deposit in hand on their house, for their price. And again on the fifth to report that their offer had been accepted on the Gladwyne house. Best of all, Cassie wouldn't have to wait until the February closing to start work. The sellers had agreed to let them begin because Mrs. D., bless her, had told them renovations had to be completed before Cassie's delivery.

They couldn't, of course, with so much to do, but she and Kate walked to the house the next day and made a list and a schedule. The first weekend Cassie and Peter ripped out the "sculptured" wall-to-wall carpeting, stained with who knew what, and the next week Cassie and Kate began sanding the wide-board floors.

They painted, beginning downstairs and working around the second floor, nursery to master bedroom, until Cassie went into labor—a week early, on the morning of March third. She had steamed all the ribboned bouquets and horse-drawn carriages from the walls, but new wallpaper would have to wait. Her son would not.

After a week, Peter brought Cassie and Alexander home from the hospital to the cottage and her mother, who had flown down to stay with Sara. Things would be orderly and tranquil, and even if she had to listen to her mother's lectures, Cassie welcomed her offer to stay on as long as she could be a help. Maybe Zander had arrived early because Cassie had tried to do too much. If so, she owed it to him to rest and make plenty of milk so he could grow fast and strong.

Some mornings Kate took Sara to her house to play and stayed for lunch when she brought her back.

"I like Kate," her mother said one day as they did the lunch dishes. Her mother washed, as always, and Cassie dried. "She has a good head on her shoulders and such a nice way with the children."

"She's been a good friend to me."

"You'll be strong enough to give her a hand when her baby arrives. That's what's lovely—the way you help each other. If I'd had a friend like that, I wouldn't have had to hire that tyrant Mrs. Miller. Do you remember her?"

Cassie didn't. Her mother said Cassie had tried to sneak past the hired nurse to see her newborn brother Chris.

"Not that she thought you meant him harm, but you weren't clean. Imagine! She, after all, thought she knew best. Of course I knew that you only wanted to see him..."

Her mother tried to stop a tear with her wet wrist.

Cassie dabbed her mother's cheek with the corner of the towel and put her arm around her.

"You miss Chris."

"It seems only yesterday that I brought him home, and now..." She shook her head. "He's fine in California. But I worry..."

Vietnam. Very likely, Cassie knew.

"He might not have to go." Though maybe her mother didn't think that was good. Cassie knew her father wished he'd had the chance to fight for America, and would probably be proud if his son did.

"I'm lucky to have you," Cassie said, changing the subject. "Julia couldn't ask her mother," she said, her guard down.

"As if she'd have been much help."

Cassie heard the clock ticking in the corner of the dining room as she waited for her mother's second sentence, the shot at Julia. None came.

Cassie told her how helpful Alan had been and about Ingrid.

"And this friend is a nurse? I wouldn't expect Julia to know any nurses. Actresses, but not nurses."

"She's changed, Mom." Cassie told her mother about New York, the Cape house, Julia's painting. "We'll be going up again in July. She called me in the hospital to congratulate me and invite us."

"All of you?" Her mother moved the canisters and thoroughly wiped the counters. "That will be quite a houseful."

"We'll manage."

"You young people certainly share your lives. I don't imagine Julia will have more children..." Her face didn't harden when she said Julia's name.

"What makes you say that?"

"I don't think she's the mothering kind."

Cassie couldn't argue, didn't want to. But she was surprised at what her mother seemed to know.

"Probably not. She just wants to paint."

"She always was talented. She should make the most of that. Have you seen any of her paintings?"

"No...." What had changed? Was it that Cassie had Kate to balance Julia's bad influence? Or that she had a family and had settled into the kind of life her mother had always wanted for her? Or that she had asked her to come and help? Here they stood, drying dishes, talking to each other like friends. No lectures. Cassie hoped her mother would stay another week, but she left as soon as Cassie could drive again.

The next day, Cassie began searching for wallpaper, though she promised her mother that she wouldn't hang it until they moved in.

But they didn't move until late June, and she had only unpacked a few boxes by July.

Chapter 20

July 1969

THE AIR WAS still and the bay flat glass. Fog, thinning over the land, hung thick and grey over the water, feeding on its surface. Gilly ran down to cool her feet, and Sara let go of Cassie's hand and followed. This year she could swim and they could relax.

"It's going to be a hot one," Alan said, rocking the umbrella spike into the sand.

"More like August than July." Cassie remembered hating days like this at camp—no wind, nothing to do. But it was just the kind of day she'd longed for since March. "I hope it won't be too hot for Zander."

"Here in the shade he'll be fine," Alan said.

Peter arrived in the car with the baby, the Portacrib, lunch, snacks, juice, beach toys, and towels.

"Gone are the days when I used to grab a towel and a book and stroll down to the beach," said Cassie, embarrassed by their clutter at the side of the road. "I'd better help."

"I'll give him a hand," Alan said. "If you keep an eye on the girls."

The girls hunkered by the water's edge, their little bottoms almost touching the wet sand, watching something in the water—maybe minnows. They were getting along fine. Cassie thought of them as friends, but they were really strangers. With no memories of last summer, Gillian and Sara were getting to know each other all over again.

Julia was at Castle Hill. She didn't have class on Saturday, but she still had to work. She worked every day, she said, and never came down to the beach until late afternoon.

The men made their way down the narrow path through the beach grass, Alan leading the way. He carried the baby, cradling him close on one arm, gently cupping Zander's tiny head in his strong hand. Peter dropped the pile of towels at Cassie's feet and fussed with the Portacrib.

"The fog had better burn off and make all this worth it," he said. "There you go, Alan. Set him down."

"Back or stomach?" Alan asked.

"Stomach," Cassie answered, digging in the baby bag for Zander's favorite wooden rattle.

The men settled in beach chairs, but Cassie stretched out flat.

"Keep an eye on Sara, will you, Peter? Since you're sitting."

"Sure thing." He'd brought his usual supply of magazines, *Fortune, Time,* and *Sports Illustrated.* He'd read them in that order, probably all in one day. Alan had brought a folder and a pad, so he planned to work. For now, though, they were talking—or Peter was, about investments. Cassie closed her eyes.

Zander's squawk woke her, then she heard Sara's squeals. Alan was playing with the girls, tossing them into the air and scooping them out of the water when they landed. Sara was happy, but Zander wasn't.

Good thing he was in the shade. Lying in the sun, Cassie was covered with sweat. She got up and lifted their son out of the Portacrib.

"How can you just sit there and let him cry?"

"I was about to get him," Peter said, without looking up. Maybe when he got to the bottom of the page—or the end of the article.

"Poor baby. Are you hot? I'm taking him down to cool off." Cassie wet her own face and hair, then held her damp hand to Zander's brow. He whimpered and flailed at her.

"Mommy, Mommy," Sara called.

"The water's great!" Alan looked cool, relaxed. "Come join us!"

"In a few minutes, after I feed him."

The tide was going out. At least when it turned the breeze would come up. She moved the empty chair into the shade and took a bottle of water out of the bag. Might as well try that first. The baby took it eagerly. "Such a thirsty boy! Peter, would you pour me some juice?"

He poured a glass for her, one for himself, and settled again in his chair. "How's the water?"

"Wonderful," she said, downing her juice quickly. Zander finished the bottle and was temporarily content. "The tide's going out fast. Why don't you swim now and read later." If Peter went now, he could keep an eye on the baby while she swam.

"I'm almost finished."

It was too hot to sit and wait. She carried Zander down again and sat at the edge of the water. She dribbled some over his toes, then dipped his hand in it, the way she did at bath time. The water was almost as warm. She took off his diaper and waded in with him on her hip, talking to him softly all the way.

"Looks like you have another water baby," Alan said. "Sara sure loves it."

"You've been taking good care of her. Having fun, Sara?"

Sara came over and tugged at her arm, begging to swim with her.

"Mommy can't now, sweetheart. I have to hold Zander."

"I'll take him for you," Alan said. "Go ahead."

Cassie paddled a couple of minutes with her daughter, who liked to be spun around on the surface of the water. But when Sara saw Gillian, Alan and her baby brother leave the water, she wanted to go with them. Cassie watched until they were settled on the beach then floated on her back, alone in waist-deep water. Free.

After lunch the girls were hot, cranky and ready for naps.

"I get to sit here every day," Alan said. "I'll walk them up."

Cassie welcomed his offer. "That's so nice of you! They're so tired, why don't you take our car. Peter, the keys?"

Peter fumbled in the pockets of his shorts until he found the keys.

"Here you go," he said, tossing them to Alan.

Cassie watched him walk to the car, a little girl holding each hand.

"Julia sure has him trained!" Peter remarked as they drove off.

"Don't you think he enjoys spending his days with Gilly?"

"One of them has to. Poor guy hardly ever sees his wife."

"Neither do you, with your work."

"Well, his schedule is hardly rigorous." Peter flipped the pages of his magazine, modeling idleness.

The dig at Alan surprised Cassie.

"He's at the theater every night all summer. And he teaches all year."

"While the rest of us work."

Cassie couldn't be hearing him right.

"Teaching isn't work?"

"Not real work."

"Come on, Peter." He had to be baiting her. He couldn't believe what he'd said. The trouble was, she knew he might, but she couldn't tell. He could be smiling because he realized how ignorant he sounded, or at her, because she'd responded exactly as he'd expected her to. Baiting her was one of his favorite games, but today she didn't feel like playing. The beach was too perfect, their time there too short.

"Well, if he had a *real* job one of us would be at the house right now, and since I have to stay with Zander..." She pulled down the left side of her bathing suit and drew her son close. Peter stuffed his magazine into the beach bag.

"OK. I'll take a swim, then walk up and spell Alan."

Cassie rose to her elbows and peeked at Zander. The breeze that had wakened her, cool on her feet, lifted the straw-colored curls on the back of his head, but he slept.

"Nice nap?"

The voice at her other side was not Peter's, but Alan's. She turned over and sat up, looking around for the other children.

"Lovely. Where are the girls?"

"It took them a while to settle, but they were quiet when I left. Peter said he'll bring them down when they wake up." The yellow lined sheet in his lap was half-filled, and two more pages lay on the sand next to his chair, weighted with a stone.

"Looks like you've been here a while. What time is it?"

"Not quite three. I brought iced coffee—one of my writing crutches. Want some?" He must have read her mind.

"That would taste great." She watched him pour it, light with cream, from a large thermos.

"Sugar?"

"This is fine. I meant to tell you earlier how much we enjoyed the play last night. Maybe next year we'll see one of yours? Is that what you're working on?"

"One I started last summer. It's slow going."

"Well, this is your work time," Cassie said, picking up her book. "I'll read and let you get back to it."

"No, no. It's not a matter of how much time I spend. This one's giving me trouble." He picked up the pages from the sand and put them in a folder with the pad. "You're my excuse to take a break. Besides, Julia will be down soon. She wouldn't like to find me ignoring you. Unless *you* want to read."

"Not now." Cassie closed her book. "*Bleak House* wasn't the thing to bring along."

"It's a *great* book! I read the first page six times. That description of the fog. What a writer..."

"But Dickens is best in long sittings, and all I have these days are snatches."

"Zander's a lot of work?"

"No, he's easy enough by himself. So is Sara. Keeping *both* of them happy is what wears me out. There never seems to be time to read, to think, to do anything for myself."

"Maybe that's it." Alan doodled designs with his finger in the sand, drawing each over the one before. "Julia doesn't think she could keep two children happy."

Not and paint, too, Cassie thought. "She doesn't want another?"

Alan shook his head slowly.

"But you do."

"Yeah," he said, staring at the sand. "I really do. Holding your son today..." He looked away, out over the bay.

Cassie saw him touch the corner of his left eye. She didn't want to embarrass him, so was quiet, to let him continue or drop it.

"Damn. It catches up sometimes."

"I understand."

"Can you? With Sara, Zander..."

"I waited a long time for Sara, remember, after you and Julia had Gilly." But Cassie hadn't been forced to give up her hopes. Still, she understood. "It's hard, wanting something from someone you love, something they won't, or can't, give you."

Alan took off his sunglasses and looked into her eyes. He was silent, as if waiting for her to say more. So was she, with nothing more to say.

Zander woke up when the others arrived—Peter and the girls and Julia, with wine and cheese. Even in jeans smeared with paint and with her hair tied loosely on top of her head with twine, Julia looked elegant.

"*Hel*-lo. Stopped at the house and found Peter, of all people, in charge." She leaned down and gave Alan a kiss. "Wangled an afternoon off, eh?"

"Half. How was your day?"

"Very productive. Everything clicked. Breakthrough time." She crossed her ankles and lowered herself to the sand next to Alan's chair. "You'd think I'd be tired, but days like this give me so much energy. How'd the kids do, Cassie?"

"They've been fine. Zander likes the beach, thank God, and the girls are like old friends." Cassie rubbed cream into her lips. The sun was lower in the sky now but felt hotter. She shivered. Enough sun for one day. She put on a shirt and moved under the umbrella with Zander.

Alan poured four cups of wine and Peter passed them.

"To more days like this," Julia said, coming over to touch her cup to Cassie's.

Alan left for the theater at six, carrying a sandwich for his supper. It was eight by the time Julia and Cassie had bathed and fed the children, tucked them in, and made dinner. Peter sat in the yard, facing west, not for the sunset but the radio reception, listening to a baseball game on the portable. He didn't respond to the first or second call to table.

"I'll just take a plate out to him, Julia. He'd rather eat there, anyway, than have to talk to us when the game's on." Cassie told Peter they'd decided to let him enjoy the ballgame while they talked. "He's happy," she said, closing the screen door quietly.

Julia shook her head. "Whatever pleases Peter. Still the way it is, Cassie?"

Cassie wondered when she'd ever have ready answers for Julia's questions.

"Well of course I try to keep him happy."

"The children, too."

"Sure." Cassie watched a deliberate, silent Julia pick the walnuts out of her chicken salad and eat them one by one. "You choose things for a salad because the flavors blend. Why do you eat it that way?"

"Because I feel like it."

Julia lived by those words—leaving school, leaving New York, leaving her husband and child alone all day while she painted. It seemed like such a selfish way to live, but Alan encouraged her independence.

"Do you only do things you feel like doing?"

"Mostly."

"And you don't feel like having another baby."

"We went through this last summer, Cassie." Now Julia was spearing pieces of melon. She glared across the table. "Stay out of it."

Cassie was about to tell Julia that she could see why, that with two children there wouldn't be room in her life for painting. But maybe with Alan's help....

The floorboards squeaked under Peter's bare feet as he crossed the kitchen. The refrigerator motor clicked on when he opened the door to take out another beer.

Julia flinched as the screen door slammed shut behind him. "And if Alan involved you," she said, swigging her wine, "He shouldn't have."

"He didn't. Zander..."

"Opened the wound." Julia said quietly.

Cassie tore off another hunk of bread from the baguette.

"It must hurt him, Julia."

"And what do you suggest? That I have another child against my will, so he can have a son? And if the second is a girl, do I go on, and on? Is that why you decided to have another, Cassie? Because Peter wanted a boy?"

"Peter wasn't going to accept anything but a boy this time!" She joked, but Julia didn't laugh.

"Care for more?" Julia pushed the salad bowl toward her, but Cassie pushed it back. Julia stood up and took it to the sink. "Isn't it sad," she said, scraping the last few walnuts into the garbage, "That daughters can't be enough for their fathers."

"I don't believe that," Cassie said. Alan obviously cherished Gilly.

Peter came in again.

"Game over?" Cassie didn't want him to hear them talking about fathers.

"No," he said, slipping his plate into the soapy water. "But the bugs are fierce, and I don't want to miss dessert."

"The cake's over there." Julia nodded toward the end of the counter, "And the knives are in the far right hand drawer. Help yourself."

Cassie moved to slice him a piece, but then handed him the knife. He sat down at the table and ate his cake with one hand, holding the radio to his ear with the other, while Julia washed and Cassie dried.

In the "parlor," Julia flopped down on her *rya* rug in front of the fireplace.

"Habit," she said, lighting a cigarette. "There's usually a fire."

"I'd sure miss TV," Peter said, flicking off his radio. The signal didn't make it from Boston past the chimney.

"You would. No sports," Cassie said.

"We have one upstairs—mostly for old movies—but there's no point. If the wind changes during a commercial, we miss the ending."

"I still can't believe you live here year-round, Julia," Cassie said.

"Most days I don't either." Julia tossed her cigarette into the fireplace. "Bored, Peter? We could play cards, gin maybe." Julia knew Peter hated cards. She sounded like the perfect hostess while trying to get rid of one of her guests.

"No, I'm going to turn in early, read in bed. It's been a tiring weekend."

"Suit yourself. It's certainly more comfortable there," Julia said.

"We have a long drive tomorrow, Cass. Don't stay up too late." The empty chair rocked behind him as he patted her head and started upstairs. She heard the latch click as he closed their door at the back of the house.

"So, you can't get used to living here?" Cassie asked quietly.

"Oh, I'm used to it." She flicked her cigarette in the direction of the fireplace, not caring where the ashes fell. "I just don't like it much."

"You were so sure you would."

"Things were different back then. Alan and I were closer."

"You don't see each other much this summer."

"Even that would be OK, if I didn't feel trapped when we're together."

"Because he's trying to persuade you to have a baby?"

"No, he's given up. If he *did* pressure me I could get angry, but he's so damned nice he makes me feel like a bitch. I'm only happy when I'm painting."

Cassie slid off the deacon's bench to the rug and lay propped on one elbow.

"I never think about being happy. Between the children, the house, meals."

"Don't insinuate, Cassie. Things wouldn't be different if I cared more about all that."

"I wasn't *insinuating*."

"No, you just worry about everyone else. As always. I can't be like you."

Cassie watched Julia run her hand back and forth, making the rug look light, dark. It still looked new, as it had in the Village, in front of the professor's fireplace. In the room that had felt so warm that afternoon in December. This one seemed cold on a summer night without a fire.

"I keep telling myself if I feel good about my work, things will be better with Alan. Summer is fine here—classes, time with other painters—but winters...I honestly don't know how I'll get through another one."

Julia got up, left the room and came back with a small ochre package. She passed it to Cassie.

"Peter's gone. Have one."

Cassie sniffed the package.

"Just clove cigarettes! Trust me. Very nice."

Cassie took one from the pack, and lighted it from Julia's match. It *was* nice, but odd. Like smoking and sucking a Lifesaver at the same time.

"Did you think I'd try to slip you some pot?"

Cassie didn't know what to think.

"Does pot help?" Cassie could tell from Julia's stare that the question caught her off guard. Cassie stared back, hoping she'd answer truthfully. She didn't want to judge, only to understand.

"No. Well, sometimes. I mean, I don't use it to help. Or need it. I'm not hooked, or anything." Julia lowered her eyes. "Have you been stewing over that, too, since last summer?"

"I was worried..."

"Oh, Maia. She's too much. Sure, I smoke a little grass with her every now and then, but nothing more."

"No LSD then..."

"No, though Maia's tried to persuade me. She says it's changed her life, her work, opened her mind to the world. Frankly—I know you'll laugh—I'm afraid to."

"You?" Cassie did smile. It wasn't like Julia to admit to fears. "I'm glad to hear it."

"You didn't have to worry." Julia touched her hand. "It's good to talk to you. Maia's here, but she can't understand about Alan and Gillian. She doesn't have a family."

"But she understands your need to paint."

"And you listen."

Cassie did listen—while Julia told her about her work, about the techniques she'd mastered last summer on her own, the things she wanted to try this year in class. And as she talked about those things, she sounded passionate, happy, like the Julia she'd met nine years ago.

"This would all mean more to me, Julia, if I could see your paintings. I would really like to."

"They're down at the Center." Julia slid the matches between the cellophane and the pack, crossed her ankles and stood up in one fluid move. "But since we're being honest, even if they were here, I wouldn't let you. No one can see them yet."

"Not even Alan?"

Julia shook her head.

"Maia?"

"Sure. She's my best critic. More..."

"So Maia's *someone.* "

"Hey!" Julia said, putting her arm around Cassie's shoulder. "We never had our cake! Time for a bedtime snack," she called over her shoulder as she disappeared into the kitchen. Cassie wasn't that hungry, but Julia brought back the cake and two forks.

"Your sinful cake!" She would rather have had a plate, but they'd always eaten Julia's cake together in bites. In the past it had seemed a mark of their closeness. Tonight Julia brought it out now as a defense. Cassie ate a bit and tried again to close the distance. "So you were saying that Maia is more. More what?"

"I don't know Cassie. Don't press me." Julia scraped off a hunk of the dark chocolate icing and let it melt in her mouth, then licked her fork deliberately. "Honest, maybe?"

"Alan wouldn't be?"

"How can I be sure? He has his own script. And if my plans don't fit that..."

"Plans?"

"Yes, plans. To paint. To be discovered. To show. Who knows? Nothing specific. But not to have another baby. Maia doesn't pressure me. When I'm with her I feel optimistic, alive."

Cassie had felt diminished with Maia.

"She relates to you as another painter."

"She relates to me, period. She understands how I feel. No one else does."

"Really!" Cassie took another bite of cake. "I'm trying, Julia. I listen. You've admitted that. And you just told me Maia doesn't understand about your family."

"Mmm. But you *are* your family, Cassie. You never think about what you want, so you don't get where I am. Sorry, but it's true."

Cassie couldn't respond. And if even if she knew how, Julia had brought down the curtain. Talk about scripts. Here they were, having the best talk they'd had in years—about Julia for a change—and she had to turn it around, make it about Cassie.

"We'd better save the rest of this for Alan. He'll want some when he gets home." Julia took the cake to the kitchen. Cassie followed her with her dirty ashtray.

"No point waiting up. He's always late, and Peter says you're starting out early." She led the way to the stairs, turning out lights on the way, then turned and gave her a hug. "Anyway, thanks for listening."

PART III

Chapter 21

September 1969

summer   narrow bed under slanting eaves   wool throw soft on my bare skin   a dream   he is there   I open my eyes   he kneels there   whispers my name   Cassie   his lips brush my ear   Cassie   I want him   can't want him   I push the blanket away   pull him close   see myself in his eyes   Cassie   I let myself love him back

WITH THE SUN hot on her face, she lay still—aware of a dream, of her body, of her breathing. Shallow. Fast. Trying to hold on to what felt like joy, Cassie kept her eyes closed. When she opened them and saw Peter asleep beside her, they filled with tears. Not from the sun, from the sadness. Only a dream. Nothing had changed. Everything had.

Cassie was glad to be in the new house, nearer to Kate, who helped her paper, paint, and forget. They measured, cut, pasted, taped, rolled and talked—about children, neighbors, clothes, TV shows, recipes. A month passed and still—some days once, some days more—a memory of the dream surfaced, stirring ripples of sadness.

She flipped through *House Beautiful*—the last issue of her birthday subscription. The living room was now as striking as many in the magazine. Who would believe that only a year ago whole sections of dingy wallpaper had dangled from the walls. It had been hard work, hanging the ivory grasscloth, matching the seams. Only Cassie noticed the places where they didn't match.

Her eye followed a swath of October sun from the polished oak floor to the Oriental rug, over its ruby and sapphire flowers to the hearth, to one of the andirons. The shining brass reminded her of a July sun slipping into the bay at Truro. Maybe the dream had begun there—in Alan's eyes, or in something he said. No. If she looked for meaning in every gesture, she might find it, and she didn't want to. The dream would never be more.

Long shadows took over and the sun dropped behind a steely cloud. Cassie switched on the lamp next to her and turned to the recipe pages. She and Peter were so fortunate. They should celebrate Thanksgiving in style.

She invited Peter's parents and hers to the dinner—a feast, with soup and sorbet and two kinds of stuffing in the turkey. She replaced traditional squash with minted carrot puree, served green beans—garnished with toasted almonds—instead of turnip, added a clove of garlic and extra butter to the mashed potatoes, and tossed the baby onions in heavy cream before sprinkling them with freshly cracked black pepper. With silver serving dishes spread on the sideboard and beeswax candles glowing smokeless in the wall sconces, they toasted the holiday, good health, and grandchildren with a '66 *Nuit-Saint-Georges*.

On the fourteenth of December, Cassie splurged on a tall tree and set it in the foyer, where its fragrance filled the house. No wonder pagans had worshipped evergreens and used them to banish evil spirits in the dark months of the year. While Peter worked in his study, she spent her evenings wrapping, and soon color-coordinated packages with generous bows surrounded the tree.

December days were for baking. Mornings she let Sara help cut out the bells and sprinkle them with red and green sugar, press almonds into the Swedish dreams, or punch down the dough for the *limpa* bread. Cassie saved the difficult recipes for naptime, when she could concentrate, when the children wouldn't hear her curse as the *spritz* snaked out of the cookie press in horseshoes instead of round wreaths, when the sheet of spicy *pepparkakor* dough stuck for the third time to the rolling pin. By the twentieth of the month she had filled six canisters with cookies.

She took an assortment along to the light show to keep the children happy while they waited. The girls sat at the base of the bronze eagle, talons shiny from small hands that dared to touch. Kate and Cassie, with Zander on her hip, stood in the shadow of its wings. An expectant crowd filled Wanamaker's courtyard and lined the rails five floors up.

"High time you saw this," Kate said. "After five years in this town."

The house lights went dark and with the first trumpets of "*Adeste Fideles*," Christmas lights flashed on, changing in time with the music. Cassie hugged Zander close. He wouldn't remember the show—he was too young—but she wanted to plant joy and nurture it, so he would keep it inside, like the little tree inside her glass ball. He and Sara loved to have Cassie shake it and smiled each time the tree appeared in the settling snow. Cassie smiled, too—each time returning in memory to Rockefeller Center with Alan and Julia, listening to carols in the snow. Her New York souvenir was at home on the mantle, out of reach. She was here—indoors, warm, in Philadelphia. She bit off a point of a *pepparkakor* star. Too thick, but the flavor was fine.

Kate and Ben came Christmas Eve for *smörgåsbord*, scaled down to Cassie's time and tastes—no head cheese or fresh ham, but lots of meatballs, bread, cheese, beets, and herring. Ben circled the table, joking that she had served some of his favorite Jewish foods. Cassie smiled. Holidays should be times when barriers fall, making way for shared traditions. She didn't have any Swedish music, so instead of dancing after dinner they all sat in front of the fire eating cookies and drinking *glögg*. Ben wanted to stay until it was gone, but Kate had promised to send her babysitter home in time for midnight mass. She pulled him up from the sofa at ten.

Peter helped to clean up the kitchen—as he usually did when they entertained—then began bringing down the children's presents from the third floor.

"I don't know why you just don't put these things under the tree as you finish wrapping them," Peter remarked after his second trip.

"I've told you! Because Santa has to bring them," she whispered.

Cassie had even wrapped presents from "Santa" in different paper from the rest—paper from the North Pole, she'd pretend—part of the magic of Christmas morning.

"You're such a damn stickler, Cass."

"If I really were, we'd wait until midnight to put these out."

"*You* would." Peter yawned. "But I'm going up now."

"We haven't filled the stockings," she said, grabbing his hand.

"You can do it." He kissed the top of her head, slipped his hand from hers and started up the stairs.

Cassie watched him go. "But we should do it together," she called after him.

"Christmas is your holiday," he said, passing behind the tree and then out of sight.

"By default," she muttered. Not by choice. It should be our holiday. Cassie hoped his childhood Christmases in Virginia had been more exciting than the one she'd spent in Florida with the Lawsons. But she'd guess they hadn't. Poor Peter. Maybe he didn't help because he, too, wanted to be surprised on Christmas morning.

She sat down on the floor in front of the fire and fingered one of the small packages, remembering what was inside, missing Peter trying to guess. Missing her parents. She looked at her watch and went to the phone, wishing as she dialed that she could be in Connecticut.

Her brother answered. Cheerful. Her mother had written that he was in love, and Cassie hadn't even met the girl.

"I wanted to stay *here* this year, our first Christmas in the house," she told him. "You'll have to come down soon and see it." Cassie knew he wouldn't have more leave before spring. "Can you get Mom and Dad off the dance floor? I want to wish them a Merry Christmas."

Aunt Tina came to the phone first. She raved about the house, though she was sure the pictures she'd seen didn't do it justice. Pictures never did. She asked about the children, then to speak to "that handsome husband of yours."

"Peter's gone to bed, but he sends his best." Cassie said, as she often did for Peter, though he rarely had. "Give Uncle August a hug for me and wish him Merry Christmas." If she were with him she'd have to admit that she didn't have much time to read these days.

A perfect Christmas took a lot of time. Cassie remembered the days when all she had to do in December was read, wait, and watch. That was when she learned—to string lights on the tree, tie bows, make meatballs. She could still see her mother, hands in a big bowl, mixing the meat with bread—soaked in milk and squeezed dry—onions cooked in butter until they were golden and translucent, egg, salt and pepper. She'd dip into the mixture with two fingers, pick out a little bit, and roll it into a ball between her palm. When they were an inch across— though she never measured—she'd roll them into the frying pan so they wouldn't flatten on one side, shake the pan to get them brown all around. Two hours for that part. Maybe not—days, hours, minutes always seem longer when you're waiting. Then she'd add thirty allspice, water to cover, and leave them to simmer two hours more, sighing as she put the lid on the pan that there would be none left over.

Cassie wondered if her mother ever felt tired of doing it all. She had never said so.

"Now that you've called, Christmas Eve is perfect." Her mother sounded joyful as she did every year.

Cassie told her about their evening, how much Kate and Ben had liked the food.

"Especially the meatballs. None left, as always."

They laughed. Her mother told her about the snow there, what Aunt Tina was wearing, how lovely Chris' girl was, and her name—Stephanie. They wished each other a Merry Christmas.

"We miss you, dear," her mother said, and put down the phone. Cassie could hear "*Nu är det Jul igen*"—"now it's Christmas again"—the Christmas tree song. The spirit was supposed to last until Easter. She shouldn't have called, shouldn't have interrupted their celebration.

"No dancing. Our tree's in the foyer. I'm sitting by the fire. Peter made *glögg* though—almost as good as yours." She hoped her father hadn't heard her voice waver. She didn't want him to know that Christmas wasn't perfect here. "Start the record over and go back to your dancing. Merry Christmas, Daddy."

She hung up, and the gay sound of her family's voices disappeared. Her house was silent. She filled her cup with the last of the *glögg* and tipped the bowl to scoop out the cluster of swollen raisins and soft almonds left in the bottom.

In one of the boxes of books she'd unpacked before Thanksgiving she'd found *A Christmas Memory* and put it on the coffee table, but she hadn't found time to sit down and enjoy it again. She slipped the book out of its brick red case and read Capote's memoir of Christmas shared. Read it from beginning to end. Read through tears about "a message confirming a piece of news some secret vein had already received."

The dream was her message. The news: she wasn't happy—might never be happy—with Peter. But to have dreamed of making love to Alan...where was her loyalty? To her friend, to her own husband? What kind of person could feel joyous, even for a moment, after dreaming such a thing? At least she knew it was wrong. Peter was a good man. If she tried she could make things right. She just had to hold on.

The year's last daylight was almost gone when the Goodmans arrived to celebrate the New Year.

"Very posh." Julia tramped in, her shiny rubber boots dropping clods of snow. "Like your parents'."

Cassie wanted Julia to notice the ways her house was different, not how it was the same.

Alan walked all around the tree, admiring the ornaments. He ran his hand along a branch, and the balsam needles bowed, then sprang back. "Soft," he said, sounding surprised. "And it smells great!"

Sara was sitting in the corner of the sofa, staring at the television set. She barely looked up when Cassie handed her a gingerbread man.

"Sara loves Sesame Street. Do you, Gilly?"

Gilly nodded and climbed up next to Sara.

"She doesn't know a thing about it," Julia said laughing. "No TV. But Alan loves kids' shows. Want to join them, love?"

Alan had spotted Zander, peeking over the edge of his playpen, and didn't answer.

"Hey, look at this guy! Standing up!" Alan grinned at Cassie. "Can I take him out?"

"We're going on a tour," Julia reminded him.

"It's OK." Cassie wanted Alan to pick him up. "He's been in a shy stage lately, so he may fuss, but he can come with us. The girls are fine here."

Julia stuck her hands in her jean pockets, shrugged and sighed.

Cassie took them through the house, hardly daring to look at Alan. Her son was content, intrigued with Alan's beard. Zander was getting big, but looked small in Alan's arms. They were so different—one dark, one fair. Only curls in common.

Julia ignored them, and when the tour ended—in the kitchen— she told Alan to take Zander back to the living room. Cassie wanted him to stay.

"Can I get you anything before you go? Coffee? Beer?"

"He has his hands full. He can wait 'til Peter gets home. Scoot." Julia pushed him toward the dining room. "What time will that be?" Julia sounded curious, not eager.

"I don't know." Anxious about being alone with Alan and Julia, Cassie had asked Peter to catch an early train, and he'd promised. She was annoyed that he wasn't here and that she thought he had to be. "I'm sure that as soon as the children are fed and ready for bed, he'll arrive," she thought out loud.

"We'll help," Julia assured her. "The three of us can have them ready early."

Three of us. For the second time in a week Cassie thought of the Christmas in New York, of their picnic on the floor in front of the fire, of their gifts to each other. Now they were about to begin another year, in her new home. Some things had changed—others never could.

By six the children were scrubbed and cuddly in fresh flannel sleepers, but Peter wasn't home. Cassie brought out the walnut cheese spread and a round of drinks, and they waited. Her attempts at conversation failed. Alan was playing on the rug with Zander. Julia watched them intently, and Cassie tried not to. When she did the joy from the dream welled up, and made her throat ache. She swallowed the sadness with her Scotch and tried to pay more attention to the girls, who were happily drawing pictures. Gillian's scrawls of color filled the paper, spilled over onto the newspaper Cassie had put down to save the table. She might end up an artist like her mother. And Sara, who scribbled in small patches, careful not to go over the edge? Enough. Both she and Julia would feel better with Zander tucked away.

"Past his bedtime," she said, lifting her son from Alan's lap. "Can't wait any longer for Daddy."

When she came down, Alan was sitting on the couch, one arm around each girl, looking for Lowly in a Richard Scarry book. Cassie noticed that his glass was still half full, and her own was almost empty. She'd better find something to do in the kitchen and slow down.

Julia had begun to set the table. "Is Peter always this late?"

"Most nights," Cassie said. Julia was putting the forks in the wrong place, but it didn't seem important. It was almost seven. "He'll be here soon." Cassie knew he would be. So she half-filled her glass again, dropped in three ice cubes, and cooled her rage with a generous gulp when she heard the car pull into the garage.

"About time," Julia said, as Peter politely kissed her hello. "We've been here three hours, and the market's been closed for four! You're a model host, Peter."

He loosened his tie and lifted the lids of the pans on the stove the way he did every night, offered to fill drinks, asked Alan about the drive down, told him how far down the market had closed for the year, kissed Sara goodnight, and never said he was sorry.

At least the dinner hadn't been ruined. Perfect, Cassie thought, as he sliced the rack of lamb, pink and juicy. She took the first sip of the Pomerol. It would do. Robust, smooth. The Scotch had dulled her palate to the subtleties.

"So, Alan. How's your play coming?"

"It's not. I don't have time to write during the school year."

"You have every weekend," Julia said.

"Every weekend."

The conversation sounded to Cassie like a record playing at slow speed, like there was an echo.

"Must be satisfying, writing," Peter said. "Making people do what you want them to."

"I don't."

"What *they* want to do?" The wine made Cassie brave, and she looked into Alan's eyes. They were dark, shining, deep and warm.

"Not always." He smiled, and looked away. "I look for some tension among the characters," he said, buttering a roll. "Then build on that, sustain it until I find some resolution."

"Tension is good, then?" Peter seemed genuinely interested in the process.

"Hard for Cassandra to imagine. She hates conflict."

Julia didn't have to talk about her as if she as if she knew her better than anyone else, as if she weren't there. But she was right. Cassie had spent hours trying to dispel the tension Julia and Alan had brought with them. It had surfaced in almost everything Julia had said since they arrived.

"There has to be *some*. That's what makes it work."

Some. But for Cassie there was enough in their coming. And then Peter's being late, breaking his promise, the damn dream. No resolution in sight.

"Peter," she said, "I think you should open a second bottle of wine."

Something was tight around her waist. Pantyhose, and a slip. She'd slept on her right side. Her brain had shifted, heavy, and settled into the pillow. She rolled onto her back to let it center itself again and to think about New Year's Eve.

Some details came back. Alan talking about his play. She remembered that, but not dessert. The sound of the champagne cork was clear...and the ball turning into two as it descended on Times Square. Alan's midnight kiss.

Her dress lay crumpled beside the bed, her shoes on top of it. Peter was still asleep. Seven o'clock. She could hear small voices in Sara's room. She'd better get up. Have some juice. Make herself decent before she had to face anyone.

The kitchen smelled of stale lamb grease and fresh coffee. Julia, wearing a man's robe of burgundy silk, stood at the sink, finishing up the dishes from the night before. Better to meet her than Alan.

"You shouldn't be doing the dirty work."

"The least I can do. It was a great party."

"Was it?" Cassie eased down slowly. She might as well be straight with Julia, who poured two cups of coffee and brought them to the table.

"The dinner was gorgeous. I ate too much, and I have a hangover."

Julia didn't look it. And if she did, why was she up so early?

"This will help," Cassie said, taking a small swallow of coffee.

"Your head, maybe." Julia wrapped her robe closer. "What about the rest of it?" she asked as she retied the sash.

Cassie's head was throbbing, and Julia's probes wouldn't help.

"I don't know what you mean. Did I say something last night I should regret?"

"Was there something *to* say?" Cassie should have thought before giving Julia something to fish for. She shook her head slowly, though it hurt, trying to find a way out.

"Cassie, why don't you admit that you're miserable?"

"Because I'm not!" Tears felt good in her too-dry eyes, but the tightness in her throat made it hard to speak. Coffee didn't make it go away. "How could I be miserable. When I have so much..."

"I see. The children, the dream house..."

Cassie wished Julia hadn't said dream.

"And Peter..."

"Peter," Julia muttered his name. "Who doesn't do a goddamn thing."

"Julia, that's not fair. He works very hard, for us," Cassie said, as she had to herself so often since September. "You've just never liked him."

"I've never liked the way he treats you."

"You're spoiled..." Cassie stopped. Better to leave Alan out of this. She got up so Julia couldn't see her eyes and dropped a couple of slices of bread into the toaster.

"Alan, you mean? Believe me, I know. And sometimes I put him through hell, but I don't take him for granted."

"You think that's what I do to Peter?"

"You *are* in bad shape. He takes *you* for granted. I tried to tell you years ago, Cassie, how you were changing. Back then you wouldn't admit it. Please face it now. You're being consumed." Julia put her hand over Cassie's. "It's hard for a friend to watch."

If she said anything, Julia might guess the rest. Maybe Julia was right, but Cassie needed to think it through.

"Can't you talk to me?" Julia took a tissue out of the pocket of her robe and handed it to her.

Cassie just shook her head.

"Too bad...last summer I thought we were getting back to being honest."

"We were..."

"But?"

We might never be there again, Cassie thought. "I'm not ready," she said. "But thank you." She did feel better. Maybe because of the coffee and toast, maybe because she'd admitted there was something to talk about. Maybe just because Julia was there. Some things had changed, maybe others never would. "And for doing the dishes. I couldn't have faced them this morning."

"I knew that." She looked at the clock. "I've got to get Alan up and moving. I wish we didn't have this brunch in New York. If you and I only had more time..."

Cassie was glad they didn't. Last week she'd been annoyed that Julia had accepted another invitation that would cut short their visit. Now she was glad they had to go, so she didn't have to sit around with them all day, wondering what she might have said or done, wondering what they were thinking.

"But this summer come for longer—a whole week if you can. Even if Peter doesn't want to, *you* come. Promise."

Cassie couldn't promise anything.

Peter settled in the living room with his coffee and the newspaper. Glad the Goodmans were gone, no doubt. He liked to take it easy on his days off. Put his feet up. Enjoy being at home. Cassie glanced in between trips to the dining room cabinets to put away the china and crystal—the young lord, content in his castle, ignoring the prattle of the children at his feet. He takes them for granted, too, she thought, listening to him grunt when Sara spoke to him. She decided to take the children out for air when she'd finished her chores. Peter could come or not.

January first and the rhododendron leaves in front of the house had curled tight against the cold. But walking with the sun on her face and hollowing seats in a snow bank for the children warmed her and cleared her head. When they smiled, with cheeks as red as their rubber boots her anger began to melt, but it wouldn't be gone until Peter said he was sorry. She coaxed Zander and Sara from their "thrones" with a promise of cocoa before their naps.

Peter had stretched out on the sofa for an afternoon of bowl games.

"We have to talk," she said, turning down the sound.

"What about?" He put his hands behind his head.

"Last night." She sat down in the wing chair by the fireplace. "You promised to come home early."

"I had work to do." He looked at the television not at her.

"You could have called." Cassie got up and blocked his view. "Could have said you were sorry."

"I didn't think of it."

Matter-of-fact. Just like that. With no sense that was the worst thing he could say. She turned away so he wouldn't see her tears.

"That's the trouble," she said, picking up her Christmas tree ball, pressing the cool glass to her chin.

"I'm surprised you gave me a thought—sitting here getting quietly crocked with your friends."

"Our friends..."

"Yours—Julia and her hippie husband." He swung his feet around and sat up.

"You used to say you liked him." She turned the ball upside down. Had last night changed his mind?

"He's harmless. But you get weird when they're around, Cass. Like our good life isn't good enough."

That *was* how Julia had sometimes made her feel. Cassie flipped the ball and watched the snow fall around the tree.

"They make me uncomfortable in my own home! I can't talk to them..."

"Or to me?"

"You're my wife. Of course I can talk to you."

"But you don't. A comment here. A comment there. That's not talk. Most of the time you hide in your study."

"Goddamn, Cass, I do have to work to pay for these little galas you like to throw, so you can have the best of everything."

She put the ornament safely back on the mantle so she wouldn't throw it at him and went to the window. "So they're *my* parties, too." Her gardens, because she was the one who liked flowers? Her birdbath, because she liked to entice the birds to their yard? "And you never enjoy them."

"I do..."

"The dinner last night. Did you think that was good?"

Complimenting the cook didn't come naturally to Peter. Where he came from one expected good meals. After all, one paid for them.

"Your dinners are always good, though last night was touch and go."

She could feel her face growing red, her pulse pounding in her temples.

"How dare you! We're lucky any of it was edible by the time you got home!"

"Come on, Cass. You were several sheets to the wind. Oh, Julia tried to cover for you. Rescued your *soufflé* while you gabbed with Alan."

"And you? What did you do?"

"Followed your orders. Uncorked the champagne. You don't remember, do you?" He smirked at her. "I'm not surprised. By that time you were sounding more than a little incoherent."

She'd be damned if she'd ask him what she'd talked about.

"Listen," he said, patting the sofa, inviting her to sit next to him.

Maybe he was going to tell her. His voice had softened. Maybe he was going to apologize. She sat down, and he put his arm around her shoulder, pulling her close and shaking her gently at the same time.

"Everyone has a night like that now and then," he said. "Be glad we were entertaining friends and not my clients." He went to the TV and turned the sound back up. "No harm done."

He still hadn't said he was sorry.

Kate came the next morning to help take the tree down.

"The Swedes make this a celebration, not a chore—*Knut* they call it. But I'm always sad to see it go."

"There's more to your mood than that, isn't there? Another unsettling visit with Julia?"

"No, Julia was fine." Except for whatever was going on between her and Alan. Cassie had never even asked. "We sat right here yesterday, drinking coffee, talking. She said some things...I don't know how I can be her friend."

Kate didn't pry, just waited.

Cassie studied the patterns in Kate's green fisherman sweater, the one that matched her eyes. Twisted cables, crossed lines. Then she told her. About New Year's Eve, the fight with Peter, her feelings—the ones she could name—and finally, about the dream.

"Well, you mustn't tell Alan." Kate sounded as sure of that as Cassie was most of the time, except when she was near him. She told her that, too.

"Then perhaps you should stay away."

Kate was so damned wise.

"But Julia's already asked me to come for longer this summer."

Kate blinked an owl's slow way. "Surely you won't..."

"I don't know. Maybe if everything's right again..."

"How do you mean?"

Cassie didn't know. Was right forgetting about the dream? Or letting herself slip past its smoky surface. Was right listening to Julia echo the voice inside that told Cassie everything was wrong? Or to the voice that told her everything could be OK again, if she'd forget the dream. Back again where she'd started. Whenever she tried to take one strand and follow it, it tangled with the others, leaving her in a hard knot like the ones that dotted Kate's sweater.

"Perhaps you shouldn't try so hard to forget the dream."

A new way of looking at things. Cassie flushed at the thought of letting herself remember.

"Dreams are part of us, Cassie. You're pushing and pushing, trying to keep a door closed, but it's Cassie you're shutting out. Let her in. Listen to what she has to say."

"Maybe I've opened it by telling you."

"Leave it open, so her coming and going won't be such a struggle."

Chapter 22

January 1970

IN THE WEIGHTLESS moments before sleep, Cassie waited. She would lie still as her mind scanned memories, grey streaks passing on either side. Sometimes her dreams grew in layers, clear and sharp as crystals, on a string of trivial details from her day. Other nights, faces tumbled by, clustering like thunderheads until a storm began, noisy and flashing with people from her present and past, in unpredictable pairs—then ended with them dancing, whirling around a pale yellow room with French doors and voile curtains waving in warm spring air.

Cassie woke from her dreams refreshed, but the monotony of her existence, building like humidity dragged her down again. By noon she began to look forward to the escape of her ten o'clock bedtime. Striving for perfection was exhausting. Planning healthy, colorful meals. Shopping for food on Thursdays, cleaning the house on Fridays, keeping the children out of Peter's way on weekends, picking up the weekend clutter on Mondays, ironing on Tuesdays, washing everyday. Diapers, whites, diapers, darks, diapers delicates. Hours of folding.

Thank God for television. She watched "Today" while she drank the three cups of coffee she needed to get going and fight the damp chill in the stone house. One frigid morning in February, when she needed a fourth cup, she watched a local talk show through the nine o'clock hour. Sonya, the hostess, asked questions as if she cared about her guests as much as their answers. Cassie listened as they talked about politics, childbirth, diets—she had gained seven pounds since Christmas—open classrooms, open marriage. From that day on she let the children play in their sleepers until ten, while she spent the morning with her TV friends.

During the fall she and Kate had gone shopping or to lunch on Wednesdays but Cassie didn't want to buy any clothes until she lost weight and she wouldn't lose weight if she went to lunch, so she stopped going out. She and Kate still spent the dark hours of every afternoon on the phone, moving at the ends of long cords from refrigerator to sink to stove. They talked about everything they could squeeze into the "Sesame Street" hour while their daughters counted to ten and echoed the alphabet in the background.

Cassie didn't dream about Alan anymore. She'd found a man who reminded her of him on one of the soaps. She watched it every afternoon during the children's naps—non-fattening fantasies for lunch. But during the first week in March she dreamt two nights straight of strange houses—small dark rooms with Julia around every corner. Julia, who survived winter without television or a friend to talk to. After the coldest winter in ten years Ben had taken Kate to Guadeloupe for a two-week thaw. At the end of the first week, Cassie needed to talk.

"Hi, it's Cassie. I'm surprised to reach *you* at four in the afternoon."

"Teachers' hours," Alan said.

"Better than brokers'." Silence. His voice, soft as in the dream, made her want to say things she shouldn't, drove safe words from her mind. When he asked her how things were, she said OK and asked to speak to Julia, afraid he might charm the truth from her.

"Julia's away, visiting Maia. Gilly and I are on our own."

She could picture them at the round table in the Truro kitchen, Alan writing, Gilly drawing. A fire in the shallow fireplace, soup simmering over a blue flame on the black iron stove. Surviving the winter.

Julia's answer was New York. So like her to just go. Even if Peter could cope with the children...

"I called to talk about the summer."

"You *are* coming...with the children?"

"Well, I couldn't leave them here!"

"I wouldn't want you to."

Cassie knew from Alan's voice that he wanted her to come. She could make the drive on her own, but she hadn't even talked about it with Peter.

"Sorry. What?" Cassie had been listening to Alan's voice, not his words.

"A birthday party. For Zander. Did you have one?"

"Just a few balloons and a cake." She was surprised that he would remember. "Sara was more excited than he was. He's walking now! How's Gilly?" Cassie wondered if she missed her mother.

"Fun. It snowed last night, so we went sledding today. The hill on the way to the beach, remember? We just got home."

He'd probably made hot chocolate, not soup.

"Too bad the snow will be gone by tomorrow," he said.

"It's that warm there?"

"No, but the salt air and the wind take it away."

Back there wind was noticed and snow was welcome, not cursed for the nuisance it became here—ankle deep slush.

"Even Mother Nature can't deal with snow here on the Main Line."

"You sound sad, Cassie. Are you really OK?"

She'd said too much by saying so little, by talking about the weather to keep from talking about much more.

"Sure, but I should go. I'll talk to Peter about the summer and let you know. When is Julia getting back?"

"She hasn't said. It's open ended."

Maybe Julia wouldn't come back. But if Alan thought that, he wouldn't have suggested she come with the children.

"Ask her to call me when she does. I want to be sure that we won't upset her work plans..."

"You won't. Listen, Cassie." She waited for whatever he intended to say. "Take care," was all he said.

Cassie held the receiver until the high tone filled the dead space.

The breakfast dishes were still in the sink. Peter had complained last week about the piles of laundry in the living room and the dust in the corners of the stairs. Things had gotten away from her. She never seemed to get to everything that needed doing, never finished anything she began. She needed a week at the Cape. She'd tell Peter tonight.

But first she'd surprise him with a tidy house and the beef burgundy she'd frozen after their fall dinner party. She took the casserole out of the freezer and set it on the stove. When the dishes were washed and put away, she went into the living room to pick up before feeding Sara and Zander.

Cassie had imagined that after the move closer to town the family would eat dinners together, but they rarely did. Sunday nights, sometimes. She enjoyed quiet time with Sara and Zander at the end of their day. She'd offer new foods, but take them away if the children didn't like them. When Peter was there he insisted they eat everything they were given, even when it meant gagging and tears. If he were home every night she'd serve only what she knew they liked—to keep the peace. Sara wouldn't have discovered artichokes and shrimp. And Zander wouldn't be eating anything green. Now he ate peas, and green beans, and bits of lettuce—if she let him eat by himself. She watched him eating carrots—one tidbit at a time with his fingers. Peter said if she let it continue the boy would never learn to use a spoon. Everyone did eventually. Even Zander had, for oatmeal and yogurt, his favorite dessert.

Maybe Peter hadn't noticed. He rarely remarked about the children's accomplishments. Cassie noted each, however small, and recounted them to him at the end of the day as though they were her own. Sometimes she felt they were. She had nurtured, guided, coaxed and comforted to help them happen. She loved watching the children grow, while Peter said he would like them better grown, say after twelve. But he was serious about his responsibility to polish any rough edges and make them the shining assets Lawson children were expected to be.

Bathing them was not part of that responsibility, but Cassie's. Sometimes, if one child was sick or cranky, she cursed that he wasn't there to help. But most nights, when the children splashed in suds, surrounded by boats and floating animals, clean hair clinging to their small heads, Cassie was glad to be alone with them. They'd moved closer to the city so Peter could share the bedtime rituals—stories, tickling, tucking in—but when he did come home early, he sat downstairs with the newspaper, waiting for dinner and her attention, and she caught herself rushing through the sweet times. She preferred nights like this, when each child snuggled close, smelling of Ivory soap and baby powder, and listened to her read.

"Hey, who's coming?" Peter stood with his briefcase in the doorway of Zander's room.

"Goodnight stars, goodnight air," Cassie continued.

"Somebody must be coming. Everything's clean." Peter said.

Cassie went on, hoping to end Zander's day nicely, trying to keep the tension out of her voice, trying to relax her hand around his.

"Goodnight noises everywhere." The story was finished. "And goodnight, Zander." She lifted him into the crib and zipped him into his sleeper. Peter had gone, maybe to say goodnight to Sara. But Cassie found Sara already tucked in bed, humming to her teddy bear.

"Are you too sleepy for a story?"

"Daddy said sweet dreams."

"Zander had his story, and you were very patient. Now it's your turn."

"Pooh, Mommy."

Sara enjoyed rhyme and asked to hear the same verses night after night. This week it was "Us Two" by A. A. Milne. Cassie liked the rhythm, too, and watching Sara whisper the words along with her.

So wherever I am, there's always Pooh,
There's always Pooh and Me.
"What would I do?" I said to Pooh,
"If it wasn't for you," and Pooh said: "True,
It isn't much fun for One, but Two
Can stick together," says Pooh, says he.
"That's how it is," says Pooh.

When she'd finished tucking Sara in, Cassie peeked into their bedroom, looking for Peter. His suit coat and tie were on the bed, but he'd gone down. He'd be waiting in front of the evening news.

"Do you want a drink?" she asked on the way to the kitchen.

"I have one, thanks."

Cassie poured a glass of wine for herself and joined him.

"You tucked Sara in before her story!"

Peter peered over the top of the newspaper at the television. "I know. I didn't have the energy to listen to that stuff tonight."

"Well, she'd been waiting, so I had to read to her."

"I gathered."

Cassie sipped her wine through another news story. The house was quiet. The children had settled down quickly.

"Did you say goodnight to Zander?"

"I would have, but you didn't want me around."

"That's not fair! You interrupted his story, talking about something else entirely."

Peter stared at the screen, as if he didn't hear her.

"Why don't you go up now?"

"In a minute! At the break."

He didn't have to snap at her. If he didn't go now, Zander would be asleep by the time he did. If he'd do things on his own, she wouldn't have to nag. Sometimes Mother Lawson's voice echoed in her own—"Peter, do be on time..." Maybe she had just pushed him so hard so long that he couldn't give in anymore to what anyone else wanted.

"I suppose you want to eat in here." Cassie had set two places at the same end of the dining table, thinking they'd talk about the summer, but now she didn't want to talk.

"Wherever. The news is almost over. I don't care."

What did he care about? Whenever she asked about his work, he said he didn't like to bring it home. But he did every night. She knew he cared about being on the boat. But about the children? About her? She had to wonder if he'd even miss them when they went to the Cape. He'd be able to watch his news in peace.

She served dinner on the coffee table in the living room, and they ate in silence in front of a basketball game. Peter went up to his study when he was through, and when she finished the dishes at nine, Cassie went to bed.

Sometime after midnight, Peter pulled back the covers, letting in the cold air, and draped a cold leg and arm over her.

"Mmm, you're warm, he mumbled into the back of her neck."

"You're not." Earlier he'd wanted to be left alone. Now she did. "I was asleep. I'm very tired."

"You did a lot today. I noticed. How come?"

"A burst of energy. Promise of a break. I talked to Alan this afternoon," she said, more awake.

"Alan! Why?"

"I called—to ask Julia if she still wants us to come for a week this summer."

Peter pulled away. The room was dark, but Cassie could imagine his expression.

"I told you I want to spend more time on the boat this year, Cass. I'm not going there for a week!"

"I don't expect you to. Julia asked *me* to come—with the children."

"Sounds like one of her ideas. And leave me here?"

"Or on the boat! You're always complaining that you don't spend enough time..."

"Right, so I thought we'd cruise to Maine this summer."

"Two weeks on the boat with the children is out of the question."

"*One* is! I hoped your mother would take them, so we could go alone."

"Not for two weeks." Her mother would love to have them that long, but Cassie couldn't leave them. "Why don't I take them to the Cape, have my time with Julia, then meet you in Greenwich, and we'll sail to Maine together?"

"I can't take a third week to sail back down."

"I'll bet Daddy would love to do it for you." Everyone might get something out of this arrangement.

Peter snuggled close again.

"You do get some good ideas sitting around here all day."

Cassie felt her anger rising and rolled onto her stomach, tucking her hands under her thighs, stiffening against his advances.

"So, what did Julia say?"

Cassie was sleepy. She wished he'd be quiet.

"She wasn't there...she'll call when she's back." It was hard to think of words, to push them out. She was slipping away.

"From where?" Peter's voice sounded far away.

She didn't hear her answer.

Chapter 23

August 1970

CASSIE SHUT OFF the engine and sighed. Only a little after seven, and she'd made it safely, on her own. She was full of energy, though her voice was hoarse.

"Do you have a cold?" Julia asked right away.

"No. I sang all the way and gave myself laryngitis!"

"Good start, Cassandra," Julia said, laughing, with no hint of sarcasm. "Alan couldn't wait any longer. He's gone to the theater, so he'll see you in the morning."

"I stopped to have lunch with my mother."

"Say no more. How is she?"

"Very well! You knew Peter and I arranged with Dad to sail the boat back? She's actually going with him. A first! Getting adventurous in her old age."

"And so are you. What did she think of this arrangement, *les vacances sans Pierre*?"

Over lunch her mother had emphasized that she and Dad didn't take separate vacations and later wanted assurance that Peter wasn't angry about being "deserted." Cassie told her that he didn't want to come, didn't want to spend his vacation with Julia. She had nodded knowingly and dropped the subject.

"She understands." That part, anyway.

As they unloaded the car, Cassie tried to figure out what it was about the house that seemed different.

"The house hasn't changed," Julia said when she asked. "It's the barn! Come on. I can't wait to show you."

Walking down the gravel drive, Cassie noticed that the sliding stable doors were open—with large new screens to keep out the bugs. Orange nasturtiums spilled over the rims of new window boxes.

"You've turned it into a guest house!"

"Hardly! Wait 'til you see the inside."

Not a guest house. A studio. The whole place, even the heavy roof beams and the floor, had been whitewashed. In one corner an old easy chair and a camp bed, both draped in white cotton, flanked a square table, painted white. Julia's throw—folded in a triangle at the foot of the bed—and her paintings were the only color in the room.

"So finally I get to see your work." Cassie bounced Zander on her hip, stalling for time, trying to find the right words for her reaction.

"Yes." Julia waited.

The paintings were startling—thick swaths and narrow lines of color on large canvasses. Cassie could only stare.

"Speechless. Obviously you don't like them."

"It's not that. They're surprising."

"Well, that's *some* reaction at least. What did you expect? Landscapes?"

"When you live here..."

"I paint what's in here." Julia tapped her chest. "Not what's out there!" she said pointing toward the doors. "I don't feel like painting meadows...or seascapes."

Cassie had guessed that Julia's work might be abstract, but these paintings were jarring with clashing colors, hard lines. If she came upon them in a gallery she would never guess they'd been created by her friend. Cassie had expected the paintings to reflect Julia's sense of where she was. Maybe they did.

"They're very strong. Unsettling."

Julia nodded and Cassie was reassured that what she'd said was at least acceptable for now. Later she might think of something more to say.

"Did Alan put in the skylights?"

"No! They were always there. I climbed up on the roof and scrubbed off years of grime to let the light in." She picked up a cloth and wiped the countertop next to the old stone sink. "This was here, too, when it was a barn...so was the stove," she said, pointing to a thigh-high pot-bellied stove in the northwest corner. "Lets me work late in the fall, early in spring."

"Never in winter?"

"Not here. In New York. Maia shares her loft with me."

Cassie wondered if Julia's need to be near Maia, as much as the cold, kept her from painting here in the winter.

"Alan had no part in this," Julia said softly. "This place is mine."

Cassie woke up and looked at her watch. It must have stopped at ten o'clock the night before. She put it to her ear. Ticking. Quiet. No children's voices. She washed up and put on a bathing suit and an old shirt of Peter's.

In the deserted kitchen a place was set at the table with a note on the plate.

Julia's painting. The rest of us are at the beach. Help yourself to breakfast, then join us.

Alan's handwriting—bold and neat. She liked it—especially the Es, like *sigmas.* She wasn't hungry, so gulped a glass of juice, grabbed a towel and a book, and hurried down the hill.

With the tide out, the rusting shipwreck looked close. Only a few people were there, and Alan and the children were not among them. Cassie found his chair, empty, surrounded by beach toys, and spread her towel. Down the beach, she spotted them, getting larger, coming closer, Zander on Alan's shoulders, the girls running ahead, running back, then ahead again, splashing in the shallow water.

"Hey, you made it!" Alan called as soon as he was close enough to be heard.

She stood up, waved back, then walked out to meet them. Sara offered her handful of small scallop shells and a starfish.

"Pretty! Thank you, love." Stooping to kiss her good morning, Cassie flushed, realizing that to kiss her son, still on Alan's shoulders, she'd have to get close to Alan. "He looks happy up there. How did you ever get all of them up and dressed without waking me?"

"We were extra quiet so you could sleep."

"You and Julia?"

"No, the children and I. Julia gets up *early* early, like five."

"Every day?"

Alan nodded.

"The barn makes a perfect studio..."

"Keeps her at it."

Cassie poured juice for the children. Zander sat down next to her, but the girls took theirs, with spoons and empty yogurt cups, down to the wet sand to make cakes. Cassie watched, thinking how much she liked being here, seeing them grow together.

"Do you mind being left with Gilly most of the time?"

"Not a bit." Alan answered quickly. He took two nectarines from the cooler, and handed her one. "The way things are when Julia and I are together..."

Cassie gave a bite of fruit to Zander. She knew how things had been, at least for Julia, last summer.

"The way things *aren't*, I should say." Alan corrected himself. "We can't even talk."

Even talk. Cassie was more curious than she wanted to be. "Since when?"

Alan didn't answer. He picked up a handful of sand and poured it slowly into Gilly's sand wheel.

"Since she met Maia?"

"You guessed it. I have to ask you, Cassie. You lived with Julia for three years. You'd know, wouldn't you? If this thing with Maia is more than friendship?"

Any more than he would? Cassie wasn't sure. She had wondered herself, thought back to their days at college and asked herself questions. Julia had never been one for touching—she kept her distance. From everyone. And Cassie remembered how angry Julia used to get when people whispered about girls who were close friends. No. Julia was honest and would be about Maia. She had told Cassie she was only happy when she was painting—once she'd been happiest when she was with Alan—and that Maia was her best critic, while Alan hadn't even seen her work. Surely that would have created enough distance to disturb Alan.

"Julia *has* changed," she said, trying to sound sure. "Have you seen her paintings?"

"Yeah, now that she's moved into the studio. Something, aren't they?" He still looked troubled. "So much going on. But she doesn't want to talk about them. At least not with me." He stood up and held out his hand to pull her to her feet. "It's getting hot. Let's take a swim."

Cassie took off Zander's diaper and walked toward the water, holding him close on her hip, feeling the noon sun hot on her face.

After midnight. Cassie lay still, listening to the breeze in the pines, as she had at thirteen, at camp—with sheets rough and damp and cabin smells of mildew, skunks, wet wool and bug repellent, when the only sweetness had been the breeze on her skin and her own touch.

So good to sleep alone again. This time naked on smooth, cool cotton, her skin scented with sandalwood soap. She kissed her left palm, where she had dabbed a drop of Alan's cologne after her shower. His scent and her own caresses ended the day's aching tension. She slept in spells, broken by the wish he was there by her bed. The window was rosy the last time she woke, the crows sounding dawn. Wide awake and chilled by the morning air, she pulled up the blanket, doubled her pillow behind her and read her book until she heard Julia go down.

Cassie dressed to join her for breakfast, but found her making a sandwich for lunch.

"You're up early! I didn't wake you, I hope. I pride myself on getting out of here without waking anyone."

"No. I was reading. Since I won't see you all day, I thought I'd join you for breakfast."

"I don't have time now to chat, Cassie."

"You want to get to work."

"Yes, I hope you understand. I like to keep my head clear in the morning."

Cassie didn't feel like chatting, either. Not with Julia, anyway.

"This week is going to be good for all of us. You get a vacation and Alan gets some company—Gilly, too. So I get to work without guilt. And see *you*, of course."

Cassie the afterthought. The day before there had been moments when she wished she had listened to Kate and stayed home. She'd squirmed during natural short silences at the dinner table, fought her feelings all day.

Today would be different. There was no place she would rather be. Kate had told her to listen to herself, let herself dream.

Julia pulled the kettle off before it could whistle and poured her pot of tea.

"I'm off," she said, dropping a couple of plums into the bag with her sandwich. With the bag in one hand, the teapot in the other, she bumped the screen door open with her bottom. "See you tonight. Enjoy your day."

Cassie crossed the kitchen and caught the door before it banged.

"You, too," she whispered, her forehead against the screen, as she watched Julia walk down the hill to the barn.

Cassie poked around, looking for breakfast makings, and decided on pancakes. In the last few months she hadn't had time or energy to mix batter, much less drop it by spoonfuls, watch for bubbles, and wait to flip. But Sara and Zander liked pancakes best, and this was vacation.

She mixed up plain batter, then stirred in chopped peaches and pecans to make it special. But even set for five the table looked empty. It needed flowers.

Walking out to the roadside to pick a few daylilies, she remembered the paper whites blooming on Julia's table in the first Village apartment. Until now, Cassie realized, whenever she came to visit, Julia had fresh flowers...even in winter.

Coffee in hand, reading in the hammock outside, Cassie didn't hear the children until Alan brought them down to the kitchen around seven.

"You're supposed to be on vacation. Why'd you get up and do all this?"

"I couldn't sleep. Besides, you did *everything* yesterday, *and* got the kids up again. The least I can do is breakfast."

"Flowers, no less," he said. He balanced Sara on two books and pushed her in close to the table. "This is nice, Cassie."

Yes, Cassie thought, slipping Zander into the high chair. It is. She looked up, just for a second, to see the smile in his eyes.

She tended the first batch of pancakes, and Alan got up from eating his to flip the second. She served him a third—he liked the fruit and nuts—and watched the warm syrup as he poured, a thick ribbon folding down, losing its edge in the spreading pool.

"Cassie." Alan was staring at her. "Where were you?"

"Don't know...somewhere in my head."

"Something you want to talk about?"

Yes, Cassie thought. Now.

"Maybe...sometime," she answered. "I don't know how."

He nodded and let her be. "Let's clean these squirts up and get to the beach." He soaped a warm cloth and washed the three sticky faces and six sticky hands while she cleared the table.

On the shady side of the road, dew clung to the fringed yellow centers of the wild roses. Cassie walked on the sunny side where their scent was stronger, even braved the thorns to pick a blossom and tuck it behind her ear. Everything was still. The first patches of breeze, stipples on the bay's glassy surface, carried the sea smell up the hill. Stopping to breathe it in, Cassie took off her sandals and carried them by the thongs, feeling the road warm under her feet. She wanted to absorb each sensation before it became a sweet blur.

The sun was almost overhead when she stood up and stretched her stiff back. The sand castle was spectacular. An innocent diversion, she'd thought when Alan suggested it. Trying not to watch him oil his dark chest, she had jumped at the idea. She'd lost an hour—and several years—creating moats, building bridges, squaring off towers, making crenels and merlons with a driftwood stick.

As her kingdom spread north, Alan's expanded south—taller castles, with sharp spires. Sara and Gilly, who'd learned the art of sand dribbling, embellished his work as he went along. Zander, like Cassie's brother years before, stomped in the pools, dangerously close to her masterpiece. Wanting Alan to see it unspoiled, she scooped up her son and carried him into the water, where they did bobs to dunk off all the sand. They came out close to the others.

"Note the distinct difference in styles." Cassie mimicked the monotone commentary of her college art lectures.

"Ah, but no conflict, even over territory."

No, Cassie thought, just fun.

"But there'll be war if I don't take these kids up for lunch. Are you coming? Or staying?"

"I should come..."

"You *should* do what you want. I can handle them and bring you something later."

"After nap time?"

Alan nodded.

For months she'd wished someone would take over the children, for just a couple of hours a day. Here was Alan offering. She'd let him, though what she wanted today was to go with him.

The castles were smooth bumps and hollows under two feet of water when they all came back at three. Cassie rolled onto her back and sat up.

"The kids slept," he said. "Did you?"

"In the sun, I go to sleep as soon as I lie down."

"Glad I don't," he said, handing her a tuna sandwich. "I'd never get any work done!"

"I don't know how you do anyway, with Gilly." Cassie got up and set her chair at the best angle for the sun.

"She plays by herself. Every now and then I take a break, do something with her. She's so good."

Cassie's children were good, or so everyone said, but now that Zander was becoming a little person, she felt a growing competition for her attention—each of them wanted all of it. She tried to be fair, but if they drew her into their disputes, she almost always ended up favoring the instigator. She fought with herself to stay clear.

"It was so different with one child."

"Gilly's a loner. Like Julia. Sara's more like you."

"How?"

"Quiet, thoughtful, but connected."

Cassie wanted to hear more.

"Listen. I've been struggling for a couple of days with a scene, and during the kids' naps I finally finished it. I'd really love it if you'd read it and give me your opinion. Would you be willing?"

Willing? Oh, yes. But what if it was like Julia's paintings? What if she didn't understand what he was trying to say?

"I know nothing about writing plays."

"But you know about people. You'll know if it works. I trust your reactions."

"What's it about?"

"I'd rather have *you* tell *me* tomorrow," he said, smiling without teasing. "If you can't, I need to rewrite."

"You'd put that much stock in what I say?"

"Sure." He took a big bunch of green grapes out of the cooler, and the children clustered around his chair. He broke off a clump for each, and they scattered again.

"I always have, Cassie."

Chapter 24

THE HALLWAY FLOORBOARDS creaked as someone passed her door. Another closed and the metal latch clicked down. There were no night sounds from the master bedroom. A play for children's theater, Cassie thought, reading the description of the characters as she settled into bed with the script.

On a darkened stage, two men seem to dangle on invisible strings. One, hunching in a contemplative pose, drones battle names and body counts. The other, too, counts aloud, moving back and forth across the stage, swigging from a bottle, rubbing his belly, boasting about women he has had. Neither man acknowledges the presence of the other, but each looks up from time to time and waits for reactions from above. For the drinker comes anger, for the thinker praise.

Then the responses cease. The men fall silent and lower their eyes. After a few moments they look up, discover each other, and begin speaking again—past each other at first, until they hear each other and begin to ask questions. Each wonders how the other lives, thinks. Their speech slows, softens, as they move closer to each other, the heavy one deliberately, the thin one with a string-twisting spin on the way. When they are close enough to touch, each breaks the other's strings so they can lie down. They embrace...then sleep.

Cassie slept through the storm, dreaming it was applause and house lights were coming on after the performance. The rain had pooled on the windowsill next to her bed and was spilling over onto the floor. Damn. No beach. She had counted on that time to talk with Alan, to ask him questions about the play, to tell him what she thought. She got up, slammed the window shut, and went to the bathroom for a towel. She left it to absorb the puddle while she read the scene again, trying to remember all of her thoughts from the night before, wishing there had been a pad in the room, that she had made notes.

"Not a great morning." Alan was alone in the kitchen. "You slept through the thunder?"

"I couldn't have!" Lightning terrified Cassie. She usually woke at the first distant rumble to hide under the covers, counting seconds until the flash, measuring the distance to danger.

"The gang is in the front room. Coloring."

"I used to like days like this," Cassie said, pouring herself a cup of coffee from the blue enamel pot. "When my parents would give me a new box of Crayolas—a big one, with copper, gold, and flesh—and a couple of clean coloring books. One summer house had a sun porch with a linoleum floor. I'd lie there for hours, using shadings, and almost all the colors to turn those flat drawings into what I thought were works of art."

"Sounds like you." Alan smiled, breaking eggs into a stoneware bowl. "We'll go nuts with the three of them in the house," he said. "We should take them into town this morning and tire them out."

Cassie didn't look forward to tromping around Provincetown in the rain, but a full day of Candyland games would be worse. She split an English muffin and dropped it into the toaster.

"While they nap we can talk about your scene. I read it last night and again this morning. I have some questions..."

"Then you *really* read it. Good." Alan divided the omelet in the pan and slid half onto each plate. "Not too heavy on the politics?"

Cassie was glad he already sensed that.

"Maybe a little. *Good* omelet. And there are loud Beckett echoes..." They almost drowned out Alan's voice. "...which I gather you intend."

Alan was quiet.

"I don't mean that to sound negative." Cassie loved the way the characters' voices could only really be heard in the silence, and the metaphor of the strings that constrained them. "There are other things I want to talk about." She needed to think more before tackling them. "Later."

"Deal. Do you have foul-weather gear?"

"On my way to cruising in Maine? Sure, but not for Zander and Sara."

"We'll pick them up a couple of ponchos at Army-Navy."

"I don't have anything for their feet."

"It's a warm rain. We'll all go barefoot."

Avoiding the crowded shops of Commercial Street, they explored the quiet streets of the West End, even the one where Julia had had her studio—the one she and Julia had never reached on *their* day trip.

They'd never climbed the monument that day, either, but she and Alan did, as a last resort to wear the children out. Gilly led the way, tugging at Cassie's right hand. Sara dragged on her left, struggling with the steps, too tall for her little legs. Cassie was short of breath, the price of her long winter of sitting.

"I'll need a nap after this," she said to Alan halfway up. She climbed sideways, her back to the outside wall of the tower. The stone steps were cold and grimy under her feet, and she didn't like heights. But Zander smiled at her from Alan's shoulders and she kept quiet, not wanting to spoil the adventure.

At the top, she looked out into nothing and wished she hadn't eaten an omelet. Alan steadied her sway with an arm around her waist.

"Damn. We've been fogged," he muttered.

The girls hooked their fingertips over the sills of the lookouts, trying to climb the stone walls for a peek.

"No climbing," Alan said firmly. "I'll hold you up, but there's nothing to see. Just fog."

He handed her Zander and lifted Sara, then Gilly, then began to laugh.

"We climbed all the way up here to peer into the fog?" Cassie started to giggle. "Could you see the top when we started?"

Alan was laughing harder.

"I didn't look! I swear! It didn't occur to me to look."

"*Not* funny, Daddy." Gilly stamped her foot.

"You're right, Gilly. It's not." They stopped laughing, but looked at each other and smiled. He hears it, too, Cassie thought. Julia in the small voice.

"It's *very* disappointing," he said. "What'll we do special to make up for it?"

"*Ice* cream." Gilly began to chant it and Sara joined in. Even Zander tried to jump up and down, copying the girls.

"Afore lunch?" Sara looked at Cassie.

"Sure," Alan said, sweeping Zander back up to his shoulders. Gilly started down. Cassie took Sara's hand, but she yanked free.

"By self, Mommy."

Cassie let her go, biting her tongue to keep from saying careful.

They walked the edge of the bay back to the car, the girls running ahead, yellow ponchos bright against the grey water and sky. Cassie was glad now to be barefoot. The water was warm on her ankles, and small crabs, the color of the sand, moved sideways beneath the glassy surface. The drizzle changed to rain again, drops like handfuls of pebbles plunking down ripples. The horn sounded at the end of the jetty, close in the dense fog. She remembered when Gilly was a tiny baby, walking with Alan and talking about this kind of silence—a hush brimming with friendly sounds.

They sat down with cups of chowder once the children were quiet upstairs. Warm and dry and happy, Cassie turned the blue mug on her palm.

"Peace." Alan raised his mug toward her.

"Peace," she repeated, and smiled.

"What this is really about." Alan riffled the pages of his play with his thumb.

"Yes." The play was an antiwar statement, but for Cassie the one scene had raised personal questions, not only global ones. "How old are the men?" she asked, not ready to share that reaction. "Is one old, one young? Is it obvious?"

"They really don't have ages." Alan crumbled a cracker into his chowder. "Well, they must, of course, but it's not important to know..."

"Good. I think it's important *not* to."

Alan looked surprised.

"If one is older than the other," Cassie continued, "it will seem like a play about generational conflict. *Only* about that, and it's much more."

"It *is* about world view," Alan said.

That was obvious. Maybe too obvious. But reading it the night before, Cassie had found deeper layers of meaning. Now it was hard to find words for them.

"For me, all of the voices are ageless, equal, even though the one from above could be heard as authoritative and older. What's stronger than the voices, anyway, is the silence. When the puppeteer stops speaking, the men on stage hear their own voices for the first time." As Cassie had begun to hear hers, with another in the background.

"They *have* to listen to each other. Neither of them can exist without the other. The hawk, the dove...no one has a blueprint for the world. They don't just *choose* to come together. They have to. To survive. No, more than that—to live."

"Move beyond the politics, Alan. That seems too simple. Perhaps you need to have them talk longer before they come together. So they each come to see things as the other one does."

Alan crossed his arms on the table and leaned toward her. Cassie could feel him listening, his eyes watching her. She folded her napkin and didn't look at him.

"I felt the puppeteer was like the past—you know, like parents, society. Manipulated by him, the lives of the characters are narrow, limiting, empty." She folded the rectangle down to a small triangle. "Within each *person*, there are different characters—like your reveler and your thinker. Each of them has to be listened to, given some space, some *say*..."

With the paper triangle, Cassie tried to stop her tears. She heard Alan's chair scrape on the floor, felt his hands on her shoulders. He was standing behind her, his touch sure and settling.

"I guess you could go either way—make the larger conflicts a metaphor. For the lesser ones. Or focus on *those* as a metaphor for the global issues. I don't know, Alan. You're the writer. Anyway, the body counts made me think about the war, but your scene made some personal things very clear. That may help you or it may not." She wiped her cheek. "Enough," she said, turning to look up at him. "You only asked for an impression."

Alan pulled one of the side chairs close to hers and sat down next to her, elbows on his knees.

"No, I wanted to know how it worked. I couldn't have asked for a better response. I reached you. *Please* go on."

"Julia might come in..."

"So? Why do you care if she sees your tears? Are you so afraid to let anyone know you're unhappy?"

Not *anyone*. Kate knew. But anybody else? Especially Alan and Julia...

"Me? Cassandra Lindemann Lawson?" She touched her shoulder blades to the back of the chair, grounding herself in the facts. "She who has everything?"

"You don't believe that."

No, but that was what she told herself on the days when the sadness seemed stronger than she was.

"You're fighting your own truth, Cassie."

Kate had said almost the same thing when they talked about the dream.

"What moved you when you read this scene were your own insights. At least as much as mine. Why don't we talk about them?"

Cassie shook her head.

"In confidence?"

"I trust you, Alan. It's not that."

"Let me guess, then."

What if he did? He was talking, but with her heart pounding like an approaching train, she had to look directly at him to hear.

"Years ago—when Gilly was just a baby—we talked about you and Julia comparing your lives."

Only an hour earlier Cassie had remembered that day, the place, that talk.

"For years you two have been kind of like the guys in the play. Each of you has learned something from the other. Anyway, when Julia compared back then, your life was better. At least she thought it was, even if she wouldn't admit it. I don't think she compares now. If she does, she won't say so. I'm sure you sense that."

Cassie's eyes filled with tears again. Alan noticed and handed her a fresh napkin.

"If you were happy, you wouldn't care what Julia thought. But Cassie, everything doesn't have to be perfect. Why do you pretend, try to protect the image? We all have faults, feelings we're not proud of. You said yourself they have to be listened to."

Cassie twisted the napkin into a long cylinder, started ripping small segments from it.

"If we don't face them, how can we learn to live with them? Or find out we can't?"

She raised her shoulder to cover her left ear, but there was no lull.

"Can you look me in the eye and tell me you're happy?"

She wished she could stop crying, say something. But she knew she could not look him in the eye.

"OK." He pulled her from the chair and put his arms around her. "OK. I didn't mean to upset you. I thought from your reaction to the scene that you might be ready to talk."

She rested her cheek against his chest, felt his beard on her temple. Oh, she was ready. But was he ready to hear the words she could say so easily?

"Trust your instincts, Cassie. They're good."

She dared to look up, for just a moment.

He grabbed her hands and kissed her.

Cassie wished his arms were still around her, to ground her. Her body was gone. She felt nothing but her mouth and his. Until her pounding heart reminded her where she was. Not in her dream. In Julia's home. She pulled her hands free and forced herself to turn away.

"I thought…" She turned back and put her finger on his lips, wanting him to say more, but words might make things worse. "Forgive me."

"I do." She touched his arm to make sure he knew. Would he sense there was nothing to forgive? "You're a good friend, Alan. The best." She was able to say that much, at least.

To thank her friends, Cassie bought a seven pound lobster for dinner and a couple of bottles of white wine. They settled in for a feast after the children were in bed. Julia looked bored but listened indulgently as Alan recounted their day in Provincetown.

"Typical," she said, when he told her the part about the monument. "Nothing lost. Cassie knows you never plan ahead. Good of you, Cassie, to trek around with the small fry in the rain."

"It turned out to be fun. And I finally saw your old place. The one with the studio, in the West End."

"So *today* you weren't feeling ill."

Today she wasn't sick. Cassie hadn't done so much in the morning for months, and she wasn't the least bit tired.

"What did you think?"

`"Your barn is better."

"True, but town is more fun."

"Cassie read a scene from my play. Gave me some really helpful comments."

"I'm glad you found a critic." Julia chewed on one of the small lobster legs.

"Have you read this play, Julia?"

"I don't comment on Alan's plays—he doesn't critique my paintings. We couldn't live together otherwise."

But Cassie remembered when Julia used to paint sets for his plays. How she used to come back to the dorm and rave about his instincts, his insights, his kind criticism. Whatever had changed, Julia didn't seem to care anymore.

"You two have always been good at working things out," she heard herself say. Earlier in the week, she would have said that grudgingly, if at all. Well into the second bottle of wine, dipping a crust of French bread into melted butter, even though everything had changed, Cassie was happy with the moment.

Alan reached for the bottle to pour the last of the wine. Julia put her hand over her glass, so he divided what was left between Cassie's glass and his own.

"To happiness," Cassie toasted.

Alan nodded.

"Wherever we find it," Julia added.

Julia was waiting in the kitchen the next morning, nursing her pot of tea.

"Where are the children?" Cassie wanted to ask 'where's Alan?'

"Off getting pastries. Alan says he hopes you'll stay the morning and leave after lunch."

Cassie didn't need persuasion. She wasn't eager to leave—or to get to Connecticut.

"Are you taking the morning off? Coming to the beach with us?"

"No, but I wanted to say goodbye before I settled in for the day."

"Do you *ever* skip a day?"

"Not anymore. It's too hard to get going again. Don't worry, Cassandra. I'm happy down there in my barn. I guess you must have figured that out by now. I assume Alan's been a good host? You *have* had fun, haven't you?"

"Oh, yes. And the children..."

"And now it's off to sea."

Julia touched a nerve. Her sarcastic tone made it sound like a prison sentence, not another week's vacation. Cassie didn't want to talk about Peter. She wanted Alan to come back.

"I'm going down to work. Why don't you put your coffee in the thermos and take it to the beach. Alan will bring the food and the kids."

Julia hugged her farewell as she always had. Cassie hoped her own response felt more than just polite.

"Smooth sailing, Cassie."

Alone on the beach, Cassie tried to name her new feelings, to find their beginnings in the week's memories. One followed another, washing over her, retreating, polishing her to an agate shine, then evaporating, water into air, leaving a dry stone at the sea's edge.

Playing in the water, building castles, climbing the monument—she had felt at times as if she were Sara's age again, starting over. Even if she could, where would she start? She had made her choices. Her life wasn't Alan's play, sent back for rewrites.

But the week had been like living without strings, joyful and free. Next week she would have another kind of freedom—time away from the children, time she no longer needed or wanted.

Alan arrived carrying a box and a bag in one hand, holding her son's with the other.

"Portuguese doughnuts. Hope you like them. They're better hot, but eating them on the beach makes up for the fact that they've cooled off."

"You're right!" Cassie savored the sugary fritter and sipped her coffee, watching the girls run up and down the beach with their pinwheels. "They're going to miss each other."

"Yeah. It's been nice for Gilly to have a friend."

"It was sweet of you to buy them the pinwheels."

"I bought you something, too." He handed her the small bag. "Sorry it's not wrapped. I had to wait for the store to open, and it was getting so late."

"I'd just unwrap it, anyway." Cassie slipped a book out of the bag. The cover was dark blue, with a white gull hovering in one corner. She opened it. The pages were blank.

"For your thoughts, Cassie. As they come."

Inside the front cover, an inscription—in bold, neat letters with Es like *sigmas*

WRITE, CASSIE

Chapter 25

BOUND FOR BAR Harbor, they argued about provisions. Peter had expected her back in Connecticut by noon on Friday to prepare the list. Savoring her last moments on the beach, she had forgotten. On the way to the airport Saturday morning, she apologized again, assuring him that she practically knew the list by heart.

"I don't want the same old things." He sulked. "I thought we'd make this trip special."

They hadn't traveled alone in at least two years. Since the children were born. Cassie missed them already. They sweetened Peter's sour silence with their smiles.

"Let's make the list together," she suggested after takeoff. "That way you can add things you'd like."

"There isn't anything." He pushed his seat back and closed his eyes. End of discussion.

Working on the list, Cassie glanced out the yellowed window. After flying over water for a while there was now land below. She pressed her forehead to the plastic for a better look. The tip of the Cape.

Truro—sand and bearberry hills shining in the morning sun. The sight of Provincetown made her want to wind her watch back and live last week over. Build sand castles with the children, climb the monument and eat ice cream cones in the rain, and talk with friends. She reached into her bag and touched the cover of her new book, its pages still blank. No, with her friend. She felt so close in place and time to yesterday yet so far away. The engine slowed, "No Smoking" beeped on, and they banked left for the approach to Boston, where they'd pick up the Bar Harbor flight.

They arrived shortly after noon, checked their bags at the airport, and took a cab to town to stock up. The streets were crowded with strolling tourists. Discouraged by long lines at the restaurants, Cassie and Peter bought a couple of Bar Harbor Bars and called them lunch. The stores looked intriguing, but each time Cassie paused in front of a window to catch the drips of her melting ice cream and look at a display, Peter urged her on with a firm hand in the small of her back.

They searched the unfamiliar market for the items on the list, eliminating some, and debating each substitution. The shopping took almost as long as it would have with the children begging for things that attracted their attention. Today it would have been the back-to-school displays, lunchbox treats—peanut butter crackers and tiny boxes of raisins—colored pencils, and composition books, the old-fashioned black and white marbled kind. The shopping consumed an hour of the afternoon, and after a half-hour wait for a cab, and another hour's drive to Northeast Harbor, they were finally on board, starved and tired. It was four o'clock, but felt like six.

Peter loaded the ice and set right to checking lines and sails, while Cassie stared at the cartons of food to be stowed. At least she didn't need to clean all the cubbies and rearrange the gear. The charters had left things shipshape for once, even bought them a small brass lantern. It wasn't gimbaled, so Peter wouldn't want to use it, but here on the quiet mooring it would be safe.

Peter hung the grill over the transom, started coals for a steak, then spread out the charts, studying them as he sipped his Scotch.

"Take a look, Cass. Where to?"

"I'd be happy to stay here for a couple of days." She loved this harbor. Against its glacier grey shore—softened with soft pine green—spars, stays and halyards were bronzed and gilded by late afternoon sun. Red and white hulls, gleaming against the dark water, seemed more than real. No, less—suspended in some dimension unnumbered. "Just look at this light."

Peter raised his eyes for a second, then went back the charts. "We have to move out early tomorrow morning. You might even have to do a watch or two if we're going to make it back in a week."

Cassie shivered at the thought of a solo watch. They'd always anchored at night to sleep. She could imagine herself sleeping while Peter sailed through the night, but not the reverse. If leaving meant she might not have to do a watch, so be it.

"We'll shoot for Camden tomorrow night." Peter laid down the straightedge. "Ambitious, but possible, especially if we get a decent breeze."

It looked like a long way and meant they'd sail without stopping through Blue Hill Bay, Jericho, and Isle au Haut to Penobscot—the stretch that looked to Cassie like the most picturesque part of the cruise.

"It would be fun to explore some of the islands around here. Deer Isle, Vinalhaven..." Familiar names from school days, when classmates had talked of their summers. From photographs, paintings by Porters. From books she'd read to the children, about Bert Dow and picking blueberries.

"Well, if you'd been willing to take two weeks away..."

His tone made her feel like a child being taught a lesson, so she turned away and went below to get the steak. They'd do the trip his way. She'd be the mate. She'd had her vacation last week.

As soon as the sun went down, Peter began to yawn. Cruising gave him an excuse not to work at night as he did at home, an excuse to turn in early. They shared the bow cabin, where they always slept with their heads close together, their feet apart, Cassie to port, Peter to starboard. He would crowd into her berth for sex and fall asleep, half on top of her, until he started to snore. She'd rouse him, and he'd put his left foot down, swing his body over the aisle, and collapse on his stomach in his own bunk, all in one breath. On the good nights, Cassie could fall back to sleep before the snoring began again.

She didn't want to turn in. She wanted to stay up and write in her new book, but if she said so it could set off a mood that might last the week, from which there'd be no escape. This is what they mean when they say don't rock the boat, Cassie thought, sliding into her bunk, carefully, so she wouldn't untuck the covers. Silly, because Peter would yank them aside when he arrived, anyway. They always mussed her bunk, when she was the one who liked tight sheets and he slept like a windmill. She *could* move to his. She couldn't make herself. There was a chance he was tired enough to go there directly.

If she could do more than just remember their first day on this boat, years ago, if she could *feel* herself back there, she might be excited again by Peter's touch, by his kiss. But his lips now seemed cold and hard, like a stranger's. She couldn't make love to a stranger, yet she couldn't refuse her husband. Closing her eyes tighter, she wished the warm feelings back, but they were gone, sucked into the dark empty space between them. She hugged Peter hard to close the gap—to keep from falling further away—moving her palms over his back, his beautiful broad brown back. How she had loved watching him swim out into the bay.

"I missed you," Peter sighed into her pillow.

Cassie turned away so he wouldn't feel her wet cheek and waited for his snoring to start.

She lit the lantern and before she turned the wick down watched the tall flame lick at the chimney. She opened her book, and wrapped herself in the Hudson Bay blanket, tucking it close around her, wondering if one could say the same thing about cold feet as about cold hands. Warm heart.

> *Saturday - We come to bed with*
> *different hopes. Make love or*
> *have sex. I don't need to have*
> *sex. I want to make love. But I*
> *can't. Not without feelings stirred*
> *through the day or evening, by*
> *a glance over the dinner table, a*
> *touch between chores.*

Words flowed onto the first page. She gazed at the grey triangle between the flame's wavering gold and still blue, absorbing its calm. When she could feel a flicker inside, her pilot for the silence, she puffed out the lantern flame and touched her way through the cabin's blackness to her empty berth.

A foghorn woke her. It was dark in the cabin. Still early, she thought, turning over, hoping for another dream before she had to get up. She opened one eye. Peter was already topside. She knelt to peek out the porthole. Grey. Nothing but thick Maine fog.

She pulled on jeans, a turtleneck, a pair of wool socks, and went up to the cockpit.

"This is sudden!"

Peter glared at her as though she had rolled the fog in personally.

"Now we'll have to take the reach. Stay inside, where there's a better chance of it scaling up."

"You don't think we should wait for it to lift?"

"It has the feel of a few days."

"Mom can keep the kids. We don't *have* to be back on Saturday."

"*I* have to be back. People depend on me. But it's going to be a bitch of a trip in this stuff. Have to know where I am every stinking minute."

"I'm sorry." She was—that he wouldn't get the rest, the relaxation he needed. But he could make her feel any adversity was her fault, so she ended up apologizing for the pressure, the delay, the fog.

"How about some breakfast? What would you like?" She could sometimes soothe him with food.

"I don't care. Something hot."

The galley warmed as she fried six strips of bacon for sandwiches. As she spread it on thick slices of toast, the chunky peanut butter melted into the yeasty hollows of the five-grain bread she'd bought in Bar Harbor. She added a spoonful of instant coffee to the hot chocolate mix in their mugs and topped them with hot milk. Ashore she'd have marshmallows.

"Here." Cassie thought she might cheer him with one of his favorite combinations. "A breakfast you can eat with one hand on the wheel."

"Thanks," he said, without looking at her.

"At least we're not becalmed," she said, still trying.

"That's something. But I hate sailing in this stuff."

So did Cassie. Peter gave her the responsibility of peering into the shortened space ahead, looking for lights, listening for horns, blowing theirs. She liked tuning her senses to signs of land—the resinous scent of evergreens, sounds of water slapping the shore or of gulls. But sometimes she looked so hard she'd imagine she saw something, then have to decide whether she really did before calling out. When she made mistakes, feeling it was better to be cautious than careless, Peter was cross.

They tacked carefully down the channel to Bass Harbor, then hardened up for a quick reach across the mouth of Blue Hill Bay. The fog thinned to haze as they headed west, and once they were in the Reach behind Deer Isle, the views were clear. Cassie got out the binoculars and scanned the shore, speculating about the lives of the people who lived in the rambling mansions with deep shingled porches and in the spare clapboard houses, sharp against green grass that sloped to sea-shined rocks.

The first day she'd sailed with Peter on the Chesapeake, she'd imagined herself living in a stone colonial, tending gardens, collecting antiques. And now she did both—and had beautiful children, good health, and time to sail the Maine coast.

She spotted two women sitting in broad wooden chairs, lunching in the sun, enjoying each other's company, and further along the coast, a pair of feet resting on a porch railing—a man in a rocker, reading in the shade, enjoying his solitude. Passing images of a summer day, captured in a lens ground just so. Focused perfectly, from just the right angle. She wondered what realities lay in the shadows or beyond the range of her vision.

"I'm getting tired." Peter hunched his shoulders.

"Want me to take the helm?"

"After lunch. If you just rub my neck, I'll be fine."

Cassie shoved the binoculars back in the case and slid closer to him.

Did the residents ignore the boats that sailed past, or did they make up tales about those aboard, from appearances, names on transoms, home ports? Cassie had played that game for years, and people they met often matched her imagined profile.

LIQUIDITY. The boat was Peter's easy out, but Cassie felt locked in. Wye East. No longer home port for the boat or for them, but Peter would never change the name of the river where he'd first sailed. Handsome man at the helm, devoted wife rubbing his neck. She had always been good at reading above deck details. Her new game would be guessing what went on below.

Sunday - When you asked me to
rub your neck I did, wondering
why I should. Then as we studied
the shoreline, an old warmth
cracked the surface of my anger.
For a moment I felt a deep
tenderness toward you, and I
began to caress your temples. Did
you feel the change in my touch?
Tears come to my eyes now—for
what was good, for all that could
have been better.

After the day's long silent sail, Cassie was delighted to be hailed when they reached Camden by a couple they had met on their honeymoon years before. Would Cassie and Peter join them for a lobster dinner ashore? "No, thanks," Peter shouted, without asking Cassie if she wanted to go. She did. For companionship, conversation.

Your silence kills my love. That
bored expression when I speak. I
want to be with people, friends.
You want to be alone. Life is
vetoes, squelches.

Even after she'd scrawled the words in big letters, spilled some of her feelings in black ink, the anger still churned inside.

Thick fog again the next morning.

"We won't be able to navigate Muscle Ridge. We'll motor outside to Monhegan," Peter grumbled.

Cassie still had to watch for boats, but had no sails to trim, no views to study. At home, when Peter was in a mood, there were things to do, things that made her look and feel useful, like dusting, polishing silver. Here, where life was stripped to the bare essentials, there was nothing she had to do.

There hadn't been in Truro, either. A week ago she'd been on her way there, feeling free, singing with the radio. Today silence, like the fog, shrouded them, permeated every crevice. Hard silence that echoed against the rocky coast. Silence that made her cold.

When they reached Monhegan, they made fast to a skiffless mooring, and Peter rowed off into the fog to find the harbormaster. In her relief from the tension of being confined to such a small space with Peter, Cassie wished for a moment he'd get lost in the fog.

This place felt lonely, though she couldn't see land. The roar of surf, crashing on the rocks outside, carried in the fog, echoed her rage, threw it back. It pounded in her chest, surged in her stomach. She couldn't eat, much less cook. Peter would have to make his own dinner. She went below to the forward cabin, stripped the berths, and made them again with the pillows apart. She put an extra blanket on hers, slid under the covers, and cried herself to sleep.

She was wakened by the sound of Peter coming aboard.

"What the hell? I hailed and hailed, making my way back here through the soup, and I find you in bed."

"I don't feel well. I need to sleep."

"Sleep. Same thing as at home. Same goddamned thing," he cursed and slammed the door between the cabins.

Then she couldn't sleep for hours. Guilt kept her awake as Peter banged pans and spoons in the galley, then the light while he undressed, then the sound of his snoring, and finally, the sea. The tide swung them broadside to the swell, and LIQUIDITY rocked violently. Now Cassie understood why there were so few boats in the tiny harbor. Peter must have known it would be like this. How could he sleep?

Again the anger surfaced—at him and at herself. She'd known where she was going, too, but never anticipated rough seas. Worse, she hadn't considered other courses—just chosen a safe one, expecting calm and company. Here she lay with neither, in the rolling dark, next to her husband, where she'd wanted to be.

Sometime during the early morning hours the tide and wind changed. A fresh northwest breeze blew September into July. Cassie woke early to write.

Tuesday - Even in sunlight,
Monhegan is desolate. Around
the harbor, rimmed with dark
tide-striped rock, perched
wherever the forbidding ground
allows, buildings cling to uneven
foundations—spare and weather-
beaten, despite fresh coats of white
trim paint. Even the Island
Inn, a rambling Victorian excess
of dormers and porches with a
jaunty cupola on top, is depressing.

Living here would be a constant
struggle against the sea and wind
and sadness. There are few trees
near this shore, so there is no
escape from the light, hard with no
soft edges. From the long sloping
roof of one house, two tiny dormers
squint out toward the harbor, like
eyes narrowed against the glare.

Even in the warm morning sun Cassie needed a sweater. Watching puffy clouds pass overhead and out to sea, she felt some of the optimism she always used to have on fall days like this. At least they were leaving the island.

On the way out, they sailed past another one—small, treeless. Manana they called it, like the fruit with a "M", but the name on the chart looked like the Spanish word for tomorrow. Tomorrow, a life of tomorrows.

Today they would sail a straight line from Monhegan to Cape Elizabeth, a close reach on a northwest wind, well offshore. Exhausted from the strain of sailing in the fog, Peter entrusted her with the helm for the afternoon so he could sleep. With little to do but wave at passing skippers and keep an eye on the compass, she concentrated on sailing the boat the way she had smaller ones when she was young, keeping the sails in perfect trim, no luffs.

Through her married years she'd tried to hold a straight course with no disturbances. In puffs of bad air, she'd fall off a bit, ride it out. Peter would do the same. Good sailors, both of them. Cassie had never considered coming about, trying a more favorable tack. She'd committed to her course early.

Nearing the whistle off Cape Elizabeth, Cassie called down to Peter, who had asked to be wakened at four.

"Nice job, Cass. Such good time we can fetch Prout's Neck by sundown. No point heading up to Portland and back down around in the morning. And currents being what they are, it's better to stay well off shore."

"We might as well have sailed straight to sea from New Jersey somewhere for all of Maine we've seen," she mumbled.

"Bad break on the weather." Peter heard, and responded. "If..."

"...we had more time." Cassie finished the sentence.

Four days. We've shared a berth,
but little else. You seem to have
no sense of my sadness. A shell
is building around me—armor
which protects me, yet destroys me
because it shuts life out.

Things Peter said didn't upset her as they had, even the day before. More than the weather had changed at Monhegan, when she had actually wished he wouldn't come back.

Restless, sleepless, she thumbed through a cruising guide, reading the descriptions of all the places they'd sailed past. Prout's Neck, it said, was the site of Winslow Homer's studio, open daily from ten to four, "for one who admires his work, worth a visit." Homer's "Breezing Up" was one of the prints in her parents' study—a favorite of her father's, a gift from his son. LIQUIDITY would be underway by ten, but she could stay up, take the dinghy at sunrise, and at least walk the path where Homer painted. She'd take the camera, get some pictures of the scenery for her father, of the studio for Julia.

Wrapped in two spare blankets, Cassie stretched out in the cockpit. Scorpio was overhead when she dozed off, and lower in the western sky each time she opened her eyes during the night. When it disappeared below the starboard rail, and only one star hung in the mauve sky over the port, she climbed into the dinghy and shoved off.

From a rock seat along the Marginal Way she watched the sun inch up and spill gold over the sea. She ate a blackberry from the cupful she'd picked along the path, opened her book and read words she'd copied the night before:

> *"The life I have chosen gives me*
> *my full hours of enjoyment for the*
> *balance of my life. The sun will*
> *not rise, or set, without my notice,*
> *and thanks."*

Winslow Homer's words. She couldn't have written them, last night or this morning. But she could feel how he might have. Could almost imagine herself writing them, in time.

> *Wednesday - The air here smells*
> *of sea mixed with the sweetness of*
> *grass and pine that grow stronger*
> *in the sun. I've missed those*
> *scents...*

She circled back to the cove, where LIQUIDITY lay on her mooring, silent still. If she went aboard, she'd wake Peter. Better to wait. If he looked alarmed when he noticed she was gone, she'd call to him. For now, she'd sit here in the sun, snap seaweed bubbles, listen to the gulls, enjoy her solitude.

Peter hoisted the main as soon as he emerged from the cabin.

"Damn." He cursed and slapped the boom with his palm. He called down to the cabin. "Cass, more bad luck. We've lost the dinghy. Cass?" He looked up at the sky and shouted louder. "Cassie!"

"Peter," she called, scrambling to her feet. "Over here." She collected her things, dumped them into the dinghy, and dragged it over the rocks toward the water. Rowing out, smooth and straight, she checked his expression over her shoulder. He looked puzzled, but not angry.

"What have you been up to?"

She produced the cup of berries, now half empty.

"I needed to feel land underfoot. Look. Brought these for your breakfast."

"You shouldn't sneak off like that."

"I didn't sneak. Should I have tapped you before dawn, when I couldn't sleep, and said 'Peter, I'm going ashore'? I thought I was being considerate."

"It was dangerous..."

"I was perfectly safe."

"What if I'd sailed off, thinking you were sleeping below?"

"I'll admit *that* didn't occur to me." Things might be worse than she thought. "Am I that invisible?"

He turned his back and hoisted the jib.

"Drop it. Let's get going."

The morning was clear, the wind steady twelve knots from the southwest, and they began the day with a slow beat offshore. Rock gave way to sand, to broad beaches, already filling with families. The sun flashed off the windshields of arriving cars, and an occasional squeal floated over the water against the wind. Cassie wished she were on the beach.

"I really miss the children."

"I thought this cruise would give you a good break."

"It has...from the wash, the picking up." Last week had been a break from that, too. "But I miss their chatter, their giggles."

"I'm enjoying the peace."

Peace. Cassie hadn't felt peaceful. The turmoil that swelled in the silence had subsided some when she went ashore, put physical distance between Peter and herself. What if he *had* sailed off without her? It would have made a great tale. But like above-deck images in her guessing game, facts were only the surface of any story. She'd said she was going to look below from now on, and there were two truths in this tale: She felt better away from Peter than with him and he might not miss her, were she gone.

She opened her book and, reading what she'd written on shore, breathed deeply. Only salt air out here. Fresh and cool. What she missed was the warm sweetness of the days the land scents made her remember.

"Keeping a log?"

"Sort of," she answered easily.

"Then you'll need the time and the compass readings."

Not that kind, she thought, touched by his helpfulness, ignoring the numbers, but smiling as he read them off. Not so much a record of where they'd been as a search for where she was, where she was going.

"You know, looking at this fix, I think we have to get serious about this sailing and go through the night."

"Not put in at Marblehead?"

"No. We can be past there by dark. You can take the evening watch, and we'll motor across the bay and through the canal."

The sun pulsed red over the land.

"Red sky at night," she said.

"Good day tomorrow," Peter answered.

"We never even had a lobster in Maine." The color of the sky reminded her. She went below to refill her mug. "Do you want coffee?"

"No. I need to sleep."

Cassie needed to stay awake. Taking a watch didn't scare her anymore. Massachusetts Bay felt more friendly than open ocean. She sipped her coffee and watched the sun melt into the purple line of the land.

"I was going to call Mom from Marblehead, check on the kids."

"Why bother? You know with her they're fine."

"Just to hear their voices."

"A couple of days from now I'll remind you of that." Peter got up and patted her head. "I'm going down to sleep. Relieve you at two."

Cassie uncapped her pen.

> *Truro - the early evening hours are*
> *the best, when the crowds and the*
> *waves grow smaller as the wind*
> *and the sun drop and the only*
> *sounds are the quiet lap of the*
> *water at our feet and the voices*
> *of the children laughing. Time*
> *hangs still with the coral sun in*
> *the western sky. We sit with sea*
> *air in our faces, silent. In those*
> *moments sun, breeze, temperature,*
> *and temperaments mesh.*

It was too dark to continue. She had to concentrate on shipping traffic and steering her way down the western shore of the bay. She resisted a desire to turn hard to port and head east, across the bay to Truro. Cassie rested one hand on her book and steered south with the other, toward her next light mark, wondering why she'd ever dreaded a solo watch.

Chapter 26

CASSIE ADMIRED THE table, set with gleaming silver—not a smudge of tarnish. The family was celebrating. She and Peter had returned safely, and her parents would sail in the morning, but the main event was her brother's engagement.

He sat with his fiancée across from Cassie. Even Uncle August and Aunt Tina didn't sit together at family dinners, but when Chris and Stephanie had refused to separate, her mother had relented.

"It's nice to see a couple so much in love," she had cooed earlier as she swirled icing around the edge of her special chocolate cake. Now she kept hopping up from the table and twittering around them, filling their water glasses, passing them warm rolls. Stephanie was small but strong—boyish, with a few freckles on her nose, which was peeling like Chris'. She said she wished her parents could be there, but they were visiting her grandmother—her mother's mother—in England. Her father was with an ad agency in Manhattan and her three brothers were all at sea on Navy ships. One had known Chris at the Academy and had introduced them.

When Cassie's mother pumped her about the wedding plans, wishing, no doubt, that she could be more involved, Stephanie said she and Chris were planning everything themselves—a small ceremony at Annapolis for family and close friends. So the two of them wouldn't get lost in the hoopla, Chris said, smiling at Stephanie when he spoke. Cassie watched them murmur quiet comments as Peter recapped the cruise. They looked like a couple who could have had as good a time in the fog as in candlelight.

Maybe she and Peter had started out wrong, years ago, when they sat here, across the table from each other, talking about wedding plans. If they'd sat side by side, might things have been different? Perhaps, but the present space between them was so much greater than the distance between their chairs.

Later, on the terrace, Cassie watched her family sip coffee from gold-rimmed cups. Sitting in a circle of wicker chairs—star and cicadas as a backdrop—she felt like a stage actress who had suddenly forgotten her lines. Claiming exhaustion from two night watches, she excused herself and went to her room.

Curled up on the window seat, her book open beside her, she wished she hadn't packed her past away in boxes in the attic. She got up and went to the dresser, looking for a scrap or two that might help her salvage what she'd lost.

> *Saturday - My box of "Baby*
> *Jewelry"—a knot of gold now*
> *coated with years of coppery film.*
> *Bracelets and a loose charm from*
> *my eighteenth birthday. The only*
> *shiny thing in the box is a yellow-*
> *gold heart, a valentine from my*
> *past, delicately engraved, with no*
> *face in the locket.*

For years Cassie had moved the box around when she cleaned out her top drawer, deciding every time to keep it. The contents weren't that valuable, but they were the remains of something that couldn't be bought back. She took out the heart and left the box in the corner, under some worn handkerchiefs.

She and Peter waved her parents off the next morning and started for home.

"I liked Stephanie," Cassie said, once they were on the turnpike. "Did you?"

"She seems nice enough."

"You and Dad were talking sailing all night, so you hardly spoke to her."

"I had to be sure he was all set, Cass. There's a lot to skippering a boat. It's a big responsibility."

Cassie knew that. But listening to the drawl she used to find sexy, she found herself wishing he wouldn't lecture her.

"Stephanie's so in love with Chris, I'm sure she didn't notice. They seem like a good match."

"How could you know that after one dinner?"

"From the way they look at each other. By the way they laugh—at the same things." Cassie looked back at the children, strapped in, separated by the armrest, playing, giggling. "Mostly by the way they talk to each other."

Peter flicked on the radio and fiddled with the dial, looking for the ball game.

"We don't talk to each other," she said softly.

"We're married!"

"So?" She turned down the volume. She hated the nasal monotone of baseball commentary.

"What is there to talk about?"

"Besides who'll drive, who'll pick up the cleaning? With the drive just beginning, she tried to hold back, but couldn't. "The weather, the dinner?"

"What else do married couples talk about?"

He was asking the question honestly. He really didn't know. And if he didn't, Cassie couldn't tell him.

Once he'd heard the score, Peter turned off the radio, and they drove as they had sailed—in silence.

Back in their stuffy house, Cassie bathed and powdered the children, then put them to bed in clean pajamas on fitted cotton sheets. Too hot for tucking in tonight.

The master bedroom was, too. Cassie took a fan down from the closet shelf, set it on the dresser, plugged it in, and watched the blades turn to grey circles. She didn't feel like unpacking or doing anything, even writing in her book. She took a shower, put on one of Peter's tee shirts, flopped down on the bed, and turned on the radio. Big bands, trombones, trumpets. Clear notes in the humid air. "Stars Fell on Alabama" and she was dancing bare-shouldered on a summer night, a gardenia on her wrist...

Cassie jerked awake, opened her eyes to darkness, looked around, trying to be sure where she was. Greenwich...the boat...the Cape...home. Her left arm brushed Peter's.

"Guess I woke you when I turned off the light." He responded as if he'd been waiting for her to wake up. "You were some picture when I came in here. Stretched out, soft music..." He put an arm over her stomach and pulled her close.

Cassie squirmed away.

"Not tonight, Peter."

"Too hot?"

"Yes, and..."

He let go and turned away. Guilt made her turn back and touch his shoulder. No acknowledgment in the dark.

"Why don't you ask me sometimes," she whispered, "what I think about things?"

"What do you think about things?"

She hated him to tease when she was serious. He made significant things seem silly.

"Don't joke about this, Peter. What *is* a marriage, really? What do you think it's supposed to be?"

Cassie had been thinking about that for two weeks. For Chris and Stephanie a chance to be together all the time. For her mother and father a castle where they ruled by divine parental right, protected by their traditions from outsiders. The same for Peter's, who even maintained the decorous distance Cassie associated with arranged royal marriages. For Julia, marriage meant confinement when she wanted to be solitary, and for Alan...

"What *is* it? A contract," Peter said. "The basis for a family."

"And now that we're a family, can we still be a couple?" If they ever had been.

"You're the one who just said no. We've *been* a couple for the last week!"

"We shared a small space, but we weren't really together." As far from it as Cassie could imagine.

"Cass, where do you get these ideas? You watch too much TV. Hell, if being together was such a big deal, why'd you go off to the Cape alone?"

"Because I wanted to," she heard herself answer, sounding like Julia. For companionship, she thought, but she couldn't make herself say so.

The next morning, while the children splashed in the shallow end of the pool, Cassie and Kate cooled their feet at the deep end.

"Do you and Ben talk much? I mean about things other than money, or who's going to the store for milk?"

"Of course. We talk, I don't know...about politics, Ben's cases sometimes. Our trips, the children..." Kate smiled in their direction.

"Are things as good between you since the children?"

"Better! Ben loves those babies—and adores me for having them."

The creamy sweetness of her iced coffee reminded Cassie of the afternoon last summer when she and Alan first talked on the beach about wanting children. Kate and Ben had been lucky. Things didn't always go that way. They could go the other. Maybe you could even stop loving someone when they didn't or couldn't deliver what you expected from them, what you longed for. What you needed.

"And since the children came along Ben's playful *all* the time," Kate said with a deep quiet laugh.

Ben was mischievous, and openly lusty. Cassie had seen him tongue Kate's ear as she rinsed dinner dishes, stroke her thigh as Peter poured brandy after dinner, coaxing her gently home, where Cassie imagined they frolicked until three on their king-sized bed.

"You look forward to growing old with him."

"Ben's old already!" Kate laughed, then mirrored Cassie's scowl. "You're in no mood for jokes."

"Peter cracks jokes when I try to talk to him. So much is missing."

"It wasn't a good vacation, then. I suspected as much when you arrived with your eyes all puffy. Want to tell me?"

"You'll say 'I told you so'."

"I won't. Promise."

Cassie told her about the Cape week, from sand castles to the monument, about Alan's play and its effect on her, about their talk.

You didn't tell him about the dream..."

"No, but I had to admit I'm unhappy. He already knew it, Kate." Alan, who saw her only twice a year. From hundreds of miles away he knew how she was feeling.

And then Cassie told her about the lifeless, grey week on LIQUIDITY.

"No wonder you're confused."

"Not anymore. Remember when you told me to listen to myself? Alan gave me a book, and I've been thinking and writing my feelings down. At first when I write them they seem like someone else's, but then seeing them there on paper, reading them out loud, makes them real. Even if I close the book, they're still there. I know now, Kate. I can't grow old with Peter."

The words floated back with the sunlight from the lapping surface of the water. Through her tears Cassie watched silver reflections dance across Kate's face.

"So what do you mean to do now?" she asked, stirring her coffee in slow motion.

"Leave, I guess. I don't know when, or how. There's nowhere to go." She dried her eyes. Tears wouldn't help. "I have to plan..."

"You mustn't go anywhere. You have your children to consider. You need some time. Ask Peter to move out, if you need to."

"I can't do that! He's worked so hard."

"So have you! But if you can't, or if he won't leave, maybe you can take my sister's place. She's going to Europe in September, and I think she was looking for a sublet."

"In Center City? I can't pay that rent!"

"She doesn't care about the money so much as having it lived in. We can work it out. Have you talked to a lawyer?"

"No..." Cassie had only just realized that she couldn't stay.

"Well, you must. Ben will give you some names."

"Kate, slow down."

"For what? You said you can't grow old with Peter. Knowing that, if it's so, you have only one choice."

Kate got up and dove into the pool. Cassie watched her shoot straight down and swim along the bottom. Kate was right. How could she stay when she'd admitted she wanted to leave? Maybe somewhere, deep inside, she'd known it before today. The idea of leaving felt scary, but it didn't feel new. Kate surfaced by Cassie's feet, smoothing her hair with her hands.

"I know," Cassie answered her gaze. "Trust my instincts."

"Right." Kate climbed out and sat down. Her arm on Cassie's back felt cool, good. "It won't be easy. You've lived in your dream of what life should be for a long time."

"Was that wrong?"

Kate shrugged.

"The big dreams are hard to shake—even after we wake up."

"You're talking about yourself?"

Kate drew one foot back and forth underwater, leaving whirlpools.

"I always dreamed about a home that felt like one. A place where I'd bring my friends and my mother would give us milk and still-warm cookies. She'd ask if they'd like to stay for supper and there'd always be enough eggs. And my mother and dad would sit down and ask what the sisters taught us that day." Kate kept making whirlpools, staring at them, resisting. But the story came anyway, in a flat, faraway voice.

"That's all she wanted, too, God bless her. I'll bet she prayed for it every morning when she went to confession. 'Forgive me Father...' For having evil thoughts about her husband, the man who gave her a black eye a week? Or for what she had done to deserve it, God forbid. The latter probably...before she lit a candle for his forgiveness," Kate said through tight lips, closing her own eyes as if praying for his damnation.

Why, Cassie had wondered over the years, in all the hours, days, seasons they'd been together, had Kate never spoken about her family? But Kate had good reasons for almost everything, so Cassie had never pried. Now she understood, but wondered how Kate had kept it in. Cassie had needed so badly to share what now seemed petty.

"I had no idea..."

"Then the goodness is winning. That's all *I* pray for now. That it keeps rising like an endless layer of thick cream for the people I love. When I used to dream of a home, it was never this grand. I could never have imagined such a place!" Kate nudged her arm and laughed. "I was sprung from hell straight to heaven!"

Still shocked by Kate's tale, Cassie didn't smile.

"It's upset you, I know. That's one reason I've never told you. But can you see why I told you today, Cassie?"

"What I have is so good..."

"No! Because my mother told *her*self for years that life could be worse. 'Sure, Dad drinks a bit, and roughs me up now and then, but he's a good man at heart. He means well and we have a roof over our heads.' I've heard all the excuses, Cassie. *She* believed enough Hail Marys would make things better, but there were never enough. What do you think *you'd* have to do—be an even better wife?" Kate watched her.

Cassie's heart pounded. She thought again of the morning she'd shoved off from LIQUIDITY. Of the sun rising gold over the water, of freedom. *Choosing* a life. Kate had.

"If you won't think of yourself, think of them." Kate lifted her chin toward the children.

Cassie had. Whenever her own sadness had threatened to drown her, she clung to their happiness, their security. Zander was chuckling now as Sara dribbled water on his head. Two weeks away from routines had been good for them. Even a week with their grandparents hadn't spoiled them.

"They're happy, Kate."

"I hated him. He used to slam home at night, waking us up when we were safely asleep, refusing to eat the dinner she'd kept warm for him, pushing her away when she tried to take care of him, slapping her around if she complained." Kate covered her face with her hands as if to black out the images. "But I hated *her*, too. For pretending it would get better."

"Do you still?"

"Mum's dead. She never knew Ben, never saw all this. Sad, but best. How could she have come here and gone back to life with him? Cruel. It would have been cruel." Kate clenched her fists and shook her head. "Hate's poison."

"She could have come to live..."

"She wouldn't have." Kate cut her off. Angry. "Not with*out* him! Her *life* was his!"

Cassie wondered if he was still alive. If so, he had no place in this life.

"Sweet dreams."

Cassie kissed the children goodnight, closed their doors gently, and went down to the living room, glad Peter decided to work late, glad for more time to think. Talking with Kate helped, but all she could think about now was how Kate had suffered and how easy her own life had been. No brutality, only comforts. All the comforts of a "real home," as Kate had called it.

But Kate had been trying to help her see something she hadn't seen. Or admit something she had. Big dreams are hard to shake, she had said. Cassie knew—especially when the dream world felt better than the real one. She felt again, just for a flash, as if she were on stage right after the curtain goes up, with the audience clearing their throats and shifting in their seats, waiting for the opening lines. She still didn't know what they'd be.

Cassie put on a stack of records, took the family photo album from the bookcase, and stretched out on the sofa. The album had been a shower gift from Aunt Tina. Cassie loved the scent and feel of the dark blue leather cover, and had diligently kept it up over the years. Six years. Cassie flipped through the pages, looking at the images of her life. Domestic dreams spread on a table—china, silver, chafing dishes, the Connecticut house blooming with white flowers. Some posed smiles and candid ones after Sara was born. Pages of Sara, center of attention. Center of my life, Cassie thought, then Zander. Years marked by birthday candles, beach days, Christmas trees.

Peter had taken most of the pictures so wasn't in many. The few she'd taken on the boat, on picnics—profiles of him staring into the distance—were evidence of his place in the family.

In the family, but not if you looked closely. No pictures of him with Zander. Only a couple with Sara, when she was very small. He held her with stiff arms, away from his body, displaying her. Firstborn. Maybe she should have made him hold Sara more.

Maybe the real world was a dream, too. She closed the album gently. In the pictures everything had looked perfect, as long as she had wanted to see it that way. Looking closely she could see now that even years ago it wasn't. Not that it had to be, but it had to be better.

The slam of the garage door, just after ten, stripped her nerve. On reflex, she went to the kitchen to offer Peter a beer, make him feel better. The thud of his briefcase, when he dropped it by the stairs, brought her to. She'd tiptoed around him too long.

"Ssh. The children," she said sharply. Kate's father.

"Excuse *me.*" He went to the refrigerator and helped himself to a beer. "Want one?" He asked after he'd poured his own.

"No, thanks." She watched him scatter the pile of mail she'd stacked on the table earlier—when she'd sorted a week's worth of junk—and pull out the magazines. He tucked a couple under his arm with the newspaper and went into the living room.

Cassie followed him, waiting for the words or the right moment to say what she had to.

He balanced the beer on the arm of the chair, slipped off his loafers, put his feet up, and opened *The Bulletin*.

"Peter, we have to talk."

He squinted at her over the top of the paper, raising one corner of his mouth.

"Look, Cassie. It's been a long, tough, hot day. I just want to sit here and unwind. Do you mind?"

Maybe she should let him be, talk to him later, when he felt better.

"I *do* mind. I'm tired, too."

He laughed under his breath.

"Of sitting around the pool?"

"Tired of that look! Of you making me feel what I do is worthless, of being expected to just be here, one of the props in your life."

"Have a bad day with the kids, or what?"

"Those children, *our* children, are the best part of my life." She thought of them sleeping upstairs and lowered her rising voice. "You act like they're a noisy, messy nuisance."

As she spoke Cassie thought of Sara, of being Sara. Had she yet sensed her father's indifference? Zander. With Peter's example, what kind of man might he grow to be?

"Are you through?" Peter's voice was low, reined. "I don't know what's eating you, Cassandra, but I'd suggest you go to bed, sleep on it. We'll talk in the morning, when you're more rational." He lifted the paper so he wouldn't have to look at her.

Cassie slapped it down.

"That's another thing! When I try to talk to you, you dismiss me, dismiss my feelings as a mood. I've *never* felt as rational as I do this minute. I can't live with your superior attitude, with you undercutting everything I am."

Cassie now wished she had a beer as she watched Peter swig his.

"I don't do that."

"Maybe without knowing it, but you do. It's not good for the children. They need support..."

"Support! What in *hell* do you call staying at the office until ten o'clock at night?"

"I think you work for your own satisfaction as much as for us. You *love* work."

"Maybe you should do a little."

"See? That's exactly what I mean about undercutting me. I *do* work, Peter. The house, the children."

"OK, and you said they're the best part of your life. That makes us even. What more do you want?"

Cassie stared at the thick damp strands of hair on his forehead, the ones that were usually combed perfectly to the right. She didn't dare meet his eyes.

"I'm not sure. You *have* worked hard. You *do*, and we have so much...but it feels empty, meaningless. Don't you ever feel that?"

"No..." He was looking at her now. His bronze eyes were cold, hard.

"Well, I do." Hers filled and her voice wavered.

Peter sighed his here-come-the-tears-again sigh.

"You want me to cut back my hours?"

"It's not the time you're away, the hours you work, when I feel it, Peter. The saddest thing is..."

He was waiting. She could stop now, not say...

"I'm loneliest when you're here."

Done. Said.

Cassie tried to breathe evenly on the way to the kitchen, where she took out two beers, one for herself, another for him. His first was empty.

She handed it to him and opened the windows wider. No breeze disturbed the stillness.

"So." He stared at the blackness beyond the screens, not at her. "Are you asking me to leave?"

She stared at the profile she knew by heart. Bless him for saying it so she didn't have to.

"Yes."

"And that is the request of a rational woman?"

Cassie nodded. She couldn't think of words, hadn't considered *every* reaction.

"*That* is absurd. You're the one with the problem. *You're* miserable? *You* leave. Now I'm leaving this room before I say something I'll regret in the morning. I only wish you'd done that earlier."

Up the main stairs, to the third floor, his study. She listened to him move away.

Then she listened—through the thunderstorm—for him to come down, until around three, when she fell sleep on the couch, unable to wonder anymore what either of them would do next.

Chapter 27

"WHY ARE YOU here?"

Sara's voice. Cassie didn't know where she was. She didn't like her dream.

"Mommy?"

A touch on her hand. Cassie opened her eyes slowly, expecting the bedroom's bright sun.

"I fell asleep here," she said, the memory of the night before a stone in her chest. "I was very tired. Daddy's still asleep?"

"He went to work."

"Did he kiss you goodbye?"

"Nope."

Hugging Sara's little round body, warm in her arms, the night's sadness and fear came rushing back. For us, little one. Whatever I have to do, I'm doing it for us. For us, she repeated to herself, snapping the back of Sara's pajama top to the bottoms. She would *not* cry in front of the children.

"No? Well, let's get Zander up." She looked at her watch. "Nine o'clock! You two must be *hungry*."

Peter's clothes were still in the closet, and his suitcase was on the shelf. He wasn't going anywhere. She pulled on shorts and a shirt, trying to add up all she had to do to be out by the time he came home.

"Pancakes, Mommy?"

"Not today, sweetie. It's too hot and too late. How about French toast?"

"*That*'s hot..."

"Gurt," Zander demanded. Sara nodded.

"Yogurt it is. Vanilla." Cassie scooped some from a big tub, sliced a banana, dividing it between two bowls, and sprinkled them with granola. She'd never had to worry about having good food for the children. Peter had always provided for them. She recognized and appreciated his contributions to their well-being. She wondered if he ever would hers.

Water erupted from the spout of the kettle and sizzled on the stove. She turned off the burner, poured herself a cup of instant coffee, and dialed Kate. Cassie didn't want to detail last night's conversation with the children there, so when Kate asked how things had gone, she asked her to guess.

"He refused to leave," Kate said at once. "I had a hunch he might. I hope you don't mind, but I talked to Ben about it. He gave me the name of someone you can call and we want you to come stay. The guest room is yours and the children can double up. OK?"

It wasn't, but she was very grateful.

"Need some help packing?"

"No, we won't bring much."

"But enough for a while..."

"Yes."

PETER—

KATE HAS INVITED US TO STAY UNTIL I CAN MAKE OTHER ARRANGEMENTS. IF YOU WANT TO TALK, I'LL BE THERE.
CASSIE

She was glad he didn't call the first night. His voice, his calm drawl, might have lured her home, telling herself the last twenty-four hours had been a bad dream. She *had* told herself that, as she listened that afternoon to the lawyer with the shiny head and the Countess Mara tie and the black striped charcoal suit. As he talked about serving papers, laying out the possibilities, telling her to steel herself, file for cruel and abusive, go for her due, she had wept.

"That's not how it was! Peter's a good man. I can't do what you suggest."

"If you want to make nice, you don't belong here," he'd said.

Her feelings, precisely. She had left the legal suite with a list of unanswered questions and a sinker weight of doubt in her stomach that kept her from eating dinner and now made it impossible to find a comfortable position. So she lay there, listening to the night sounds of Kate's house. Thinking.

Ben had convinced her that she had to go back to the lawyer tomorrow, arguing that she had to know her rights so she could protect herself. From Peter. From her husband. Ridiculous. But it had seemed less so each hour that the phone didn't ring. The silence was more unsettling than any she'd suffered at home.

The next morning, Cassie looked out at William Penn, surveying his smoggy city from the top of City Hall. Peter had an obligation to support her and the children, the lawyer said. He'd have counseled her to stay in the house, had she called him first. "But why cry. Water over the dam. Just a tricky little piece to work with. Sounds like the man's going to be tough, but the law's on your side. Trust in that."

Cassie couldn't. She couldn't sit and wait for Peter and two lawyers to arrange a new life for her. She had made a promise to herself. She had to *choose* a life, shape it for herself.

She pushed 6 and got off the elevator at the new home of Wallingford Press, which had moved its offices to the same building, the newest in Center City—all marble and fountains and chrome. The company must be doing well, she thought, scanning the directory by the elevators. If she could just find a familiar name, a contact, an old face from textbooks who had moved into trade. Someone who would recognize her, have better memories of her than she had of working there.

No one. But she stopped at Personnel anyway. They told her it was hard as ever to break into trade, especially when her skills were certainly rusty. Even her experience wouldn't make her competitive with the eager crop of new grads who had spent their summers learning to type and take shorthand so that they could send rejection letters. But her record with Wallingford was good. They'd call her if anything opened up.

Doubting they would, Cassie signed on with a temporary agency. She'd worked for them before, too, and been offered permanent employment everywhere they'd sent her. In the past she'd always turned them down, knowing that she could do better than typing gas bills or sorting lading slips for a trucking company. She'd always felt sorry for young girls trapped in dead end jobs who talked of nothing but their boyfriends and dreams of getting-married. Now she'd be back with them.

Nonsense. She'd be polishing her skills on temp time—getting paid for it—so she could get something permanent. She needed some income. She couldn't earn enough, but Ben had offered to loan her money. Whatever she took from him or her parents, she wanted to be able to pay back with interest. More than that, she wanted to support herself.

I used to support us both, she thought, riding out of town on the train. And that had felt good, even when she didn't like the work. If she hadn't left Wallingford, she'd have been in trade by now. If she hadn't left Wallingford...

She hadn't wanted to stay. She'd wanted then to spend her days cooking, rocking a cradle, making a home for her family, as her mother had done. Now she tried to remember when or why that stopped being enough, but couldn't. Before last week she couldn't admit to herself that she was tired—tired of trying so hard and feeling what she did was never really appreciated, never would be. Years ago Julia had suggested as much, and Cassie had disagreed. Keeping Julia from seeing the emptiness of her life with Peter, she'd blinded herself.

At Cassie's urging, Kate and Ben went out to a movie after dinner. They didn't have to sit here and hold her hand, wait to pick up the pieces. She wasn't going to fall apart.

She settled the children before tackling the kitchen. Twice as many children, twice as many dishes, but it seemed easy. She knew Kate's kitchen as well as her own, and felt at home. But this wasn't her home, and the extra work didn't keep her from missing hers, thinking about Peter. Wondering how he was doing, if he'd eat the chicken salad before it spoiled, if he was doing dishes, too. Maybe he'd call her when he was finished. Her throat ached with sorrow. She hoped he wouldn't hear it in her voice. If he called.

The apartment was narrow and dark, but on the first floor, with a small yard out back where the children could play if she cleaned it up. She'd forgotten city dirt. Little piles of rotting paper, dropped, blown, left. Filmy windows with soot on the sills. It would be strange living here, but she'd do it—if she had to. Kate's sister was leaving right after Labor Day, and would let Cassie have the place for half the rent, plus utilities. That gave her a week to find work, make arrangements for the children.

"I'd like to talk to you," Peter said when he called that evening. His voice didn't help her know if 'like' was a request or a demand.

"Fine," Cassie said, her heart pounding. "We're in the middle of dinner here. Can you come by in an hour?"

"No. I'd rather you came here, so we can talk one to one, without your friends."

Her friends would leave them alone, but it might be better to talk there, away from the children.

"Fine. Eight thirty."

Except for the kitchen, the house was dark. Peter was sitting at the table, drinking a beer. The sound of the spring on the screen door closing behind her filled Cassie with sadness. Familiar, yet faraway, like something she'd seen in an old movie. Black and white.

Peter didn't get up. She wanted to walk over, kiss him, on the cheek, but the moment passed, and she didn't.

"Want to go into the living room, or should we talk here?" He had called and asked *her* to come, yet he just sat there as if anything to be said would be said by her. Talking would be hard enough in the kitchen. The feeling of being home was blurring her resolve. And they hadn't done so well in the living room last time.

"Here is fine." She sat down across the table from him.

"So..."

Cassie didn't speak.

"Have you thought over the other night?" Peter asked.

"Thought it over?"

"Yes. The things you said. You might have reconsidered by now."

"They weren't the sort of things that could be 'reconsidered', Peter. And if they were, so might you."

"You mean asking you to leave? No, that's how it has to be."

"Have *you* thought about what I said? About the emptiness I feel?"

"Some. But I can't see it. *This* is emptiness." He flattened the can with one hand, tossed into the trash, and took another from the refrigerator.

"Sitting in a dark house drinking beer? Yes. It must be hard for you. And I could fix everything by coming home. Quarter of nine. I'd be cleaning up after dinner, the children would be tucked in their beds, you'd be hard at work in your study, and all would be well." She longed to come home, have everything be right. "There are different kinds of emptiness, Peter." Saying it she could feel hers replacing that longing.

"If you won't come home, what will you do?"

"I've found an apartment." Not daring to look at Peter, she ran her finger along the edge of the table, feeling the dents where Zander had pounded his cup. But she had to look him in the eye, had to be clear and strong about this. "I'm looking for a job," she said, thinking he'd be pleased.

His face showed none of whatever he was feeling.

"What about the children?"

"They're fine."

"While you're working. Who'll look after them?"

"I'll make proper arrangements," she said, puzzled by his apparent concern for the children. "The other night you said a little work might be good for me." Hadn't he thought about them then?

"It would. Being out there, having to earn a living, might help you appreciate what you have." He was still lecturing her. Sitting there in his white shirt sounding superior.

I do, she wanted to shout. Do *you*?

"Fill all that time you have to feel 'empty.' If work is what you need, I'll agree to it. As long as you earn enough to pay for someone responsible to stay here with the children."

Agree to it. All that *time*. Hadn't he listened? Hadn't he heard?

"So you still don't see." She couldn't either, now. Her eyes stung with tears. She stood up.

Peter did, too, and pulled her close against his chest. "I'm trying to see, Cass. Please don't go." He held her tight. Too tight. She could feel his locked fists digging into her back. "I want you to come home."

She could put her arms around him now, tell him she would. His need and his strength were seductive. But the tighter he held her, the more she felt the steel between them, the layer each of them wore against the other.

"I can't." Cassie pulled away and left. The door closed again behind her, the metallic spring just a sound of summer nights.

When she walked in Kate's back door, the phone was ringing.

"Peter, for you," Ben said, pressing the receiver to his side. "Are you sure you want to talk to him?" he asked softly.

Cassie nodded and took the phone.

"I've been thinking since you left. You can't drag my children down to some squalid neighborhood. If you don't want to live here anymore, fulfill your responsibilities to them, fine. But they aren't going to suffer because of your whims. You bring them home where they belong, where they'll have the upbringing they deserve."

Cassie heard the words, but couldn't respond.

"Are you there? Did you hear me?"

She heard him—and the echo of the spring. Soft, flexible. Now she had to be rigid like him. Without a word, she pushed down the button, put the receiver back in place.

Ben was at her side, handing her a brandy.

"Want to tell us what he said?"

When she finished, he sat down next to her, put an arm around her shoulders.

"It's time to play offense, dear girl. Sounds like Peter may try to win custody of the kids."

"He *can't*!" Cassie hadn't believed he would try. "*I've* raised those children."

"But he's the one who supports them."

"So it all comes down to money? There's a lot more to parenting than that. Everything can't always come down to the damn money." The brandy burned with the word in her throat, but didn't melt her cold rage.

Around eleven, Cassie called the Cape.

"What's wrong?" Alan asked as soon as he answered.

Cassie told him about the cruise, about getting up the courage to talk with Peter when they got home. She told him she and the children had been staying with Kate, about Peter's ultimatum. About her fear.

"Come here if you need to, Cassie, but don't move too fast. Give yourself space. Time to think, to do what's right."

Right. Who knew what was right? Cassie got in the center lane and stayed there, ticking off the miles from Pennsylvania into New Jersey, New York. Early in the month she'd sung them away, happy to be on the road. Today, not sure of anything, not even her own feelings, she was glad to have the hypnotic white lines to follow through quiet tears, straight and dependable.

Like Peter. Most of the time. She had loved him for that, hadn't she? Thought it would be good to spend her life with someone dependable? She could depend on his paycheck, and on his distance. When she told Kate she couldn't grow old with him, Kate hadn't even asked if Cassie still loved him.

But Cassie asked herself. Over and over, in time with the lines in the road. Did she still? Had she ever? When did she stop? Had she stopped? Was hating to hurt him the same as loving? Was loving letting him hurt her? Was that what Kate's mother must have thought? Peter had never hit her, pushed her around, but just as there were different kinds of emptiness, there were different kinds of hurt.

Last night Cassie had wanted to scream 'I hate you' to his frozen face. But hate was very close to love, they said. Did hating someone really mean you loved them? Had Peter's raw tenderness toward her the night before flipped the coin from hate to love? Was that why she *had* to leave? Couldn't hug him back? Was she afraid of loving him? If she loved him, why was she leaving? If she didn't, would she ever get used to the emptiness of not loving him anymore?

In Connecticut, Cassie noticed the day. Boats heeled on the deep royal Sound, flags stood straight out from halyards. The yellow haze was gone, and the air was clear. August had turned to September without her notice.

"Almost to Gramma's, Mommy, right?" Sara always watched for familiar landmarks. "We eat lunch at Gramma's, right?"

"Not today, Sweetie. Gramma's not home. She's on the boat, remember? Kate gave us sandwiches. Do you want one now? Mommy's going to keep driving."

"All that way to Cape Cod?"

"All that way."

Chapter 28

ALAN HELD HER close. Seconds passed, maybe a minute. Standing there without speaking, in the shade of the four cedars, Cassie shivered.

"Let's go inside." Cassie freed Sara and Zander from their car seats, and they ran ahead to find Gilly. Alan lifted the wagon back and took out the suitcases. "I'll get the rest later," he said, as Cassie followed him into the kitchen.

"Julia's still working?"

Alan turned around and put down the cases he was carrying.

"She's not here! You knew that, didn't you?"

"You didn't tell me! Last night on the phone..."

"I thought you knew."

Cassie flushed. She shouldn't feel glad. Just the two of them here. How would it look, with Julia gone? "How could I have known?"

"When Julia called Tuesday night—to say she was settled—she said she'd called you. You weren't in, so she talked to Peter."

"Peter never told me." Cassie's heartbeat raced to keep up with her fears.

"Julia said he sounded snitty. Her word. Now I can understand why. You were so upset when you called, with all that was happening, that I didn't expect you to ask about things here. But honestly, Cassie, I *did* figure you knew."

Cassie began to cry. What would Peter make of her being here?

"You didn't think, Alan. I have to go back. We shouldn't have come."

Alan put an arm around her shoulder.

"But you did. You can't turn around and drive back now! You're exhausted. Want to take a nap before supper?"

Cassie shook her head. She was tired, but didn't want to sleep.

"We'll talk later, try to figure out what you can do. Let me fix you a drink."

"No, thanks." She needed to keep a clear head. "Can I help?"

"Nope."

Sounds like Sara, she thought. Maybe Sara picked it up from him.

"Just relax."

Maybe Alan was right. There was nothing she could do right now. She'd already compounded her problems by being impulsive. She needed time to think things through. Here, at least, her problems weren't around the corner.

"Julia went to New York *early* this year," she said. "She *is* in New York?"

"She is." Alan put on his red apron. "For good."

"Oh, Alan." Cassie couldn't bring other words out of the jumble of feelings. Sadness for both Alan and Julia, knowing the break must have been hard for them, too. But she wasn't really surprised. Julia had hinted of leaving.

"No warning?" Alan's sympathies might lie with Peter.

"About a year, if I'd read the signs."

"From the questions you asked me last month, I'd say you did. Maybe you just didn't want to heed them. Not like Peter, poor guy."

"Don't say 'poor guy" Cassie."

His reflex annoyance surprised her.

"Sorry," he said. "If that's how you feel, that's how you feel. But I hate to see you blaming yourself."

"I don't. But I have to take responsibility, for things I've said and done."

"Sure, but so does he." Alan stooped in front of the refrigerator and pulled out things for salad, one at a time. Lettuce, pepper, cucumber, dressing. "So how are the kids doing, through all this?"

"OK, I guess. First they spent a week here, then one with my mother, then Kate's, now here again. I think they think the moving around is just a long vacation."

"Lucky you have places to go where they have friends."

"They do, and I do. We *are* lucky. But they've only been home for two nights in all that time. I have to get them settled soon, let things catch up. And Gilly?"

"She's OK. She's used to not seeing much of Julia, you know." He polished each plate before placing it on the table. "Want to round them up and get their hands washed? We're almost ready."

"It smells delicious, but don't be offended if Zander doesn't try it. Remember, he's not very adventurous."

"In this house there's *always* peanut butter and jelly."

Cassie didn't talk or eat much during dinner. Just listened to the children's chatter about the summer, toys, foods they liked, foods they didn't. Except for the mushrooms, Zander ate what was put on his plate, even asked for more.

"Sure thing." Alan winked at Cassie. "Gilly didn't eat her mushrooms, either. Sara, maybe you want them!"

Sara nodded and speared them triumphantly from both plates.

Gillian bragged that she would be going to school. She'd have to, Cassie thought, when Alan did.

"There's a nursery school nearby?" She wouldn't have thought there'd be many young families wintering in Truro.

"A small one. Finest kind, they say around here."

When the stories were finished, one for each child, and the kitchen was tidy, Alan lit a fire in the front room. Coffee mugs in hand, they sat on the floor, close to the hearth.

"Finest kind. They really say that?"

"When something's very good," Alan said.

Cassie nodded.

"Feeling any better about being here?"

She shrugged, staring into the fire, wanting to say yes.

"Want to tell me now what's happened since you left?"

Cassie looked up at him. "Not now. This is too nice."

Alan pressed her hand to his cheek. Her arm tingled, current coursing from his wiry beard, from his fingertips where he touched her temple with his other hand. Not a dream. She could see the firelight reflected in his eyes when their lips met. He caressed her back under her shirt, and she reached under his. She was breathing his breath, he hers. He hugged her tighter than he ever had, then put his hands on her shoulders and held her away, where he could look at her.

"I want you to know, Cassie, that since you left everything has felt wrong."

"For me, too..."

He put a finger on her lips.

"Not now. I just want you to know that I love you. Have loved you for a while now. I shouldn't say more, but I want you to know."

Cassie touched his cheek. How she loved his face. She kissed him again, wishing she'd told him first, wanting not just to echo his words, wanting to tell him differently that she felt the same way.

"Does Julia know?"

Alan shook his head.

"Until tonight, when you arrived, I'd never really admitted it to myself, much less to Julia!"

"I've wanted to tell *you* so many things..."

"There'll be time. God, Cassie, I can't believe you're here, *we're* here. I meant to say earlier, you can sleep down in the studio, if you want."

"That's probably best."

"Feels wrong, but looks right. I'll take your bag down and light the stove to take the chill off."

"Can I come?"

"Don't you want to stay here where it's warm?"

"Right now I want to be with you."

The night was cool with fall, but her hand felt warm in his as they walked down the hill to the barn.

"Looks like there are more stars than ever."

"Everything is very clear." He squeezed her hand. "September. The best month here."

"So I've heard, though I've never been able to stay."

Alan slid the door open, disappeared into the dark space, and flicked on a lamp.

"It's not too cold..." He opened the door of the stove, snapped kindling into short pieces and piled it on the grate.

Cassie looked around the room. Easel, paints, canvas, stretchers...every trace of Julia was gone. The barn was an empty white space. She opened one suitcase, took her book from the side pocket, and put it on the table, then her throw. She unfolded it and smoothed it on the bed.

Alan stared at it.

"Sorry..."

"Don't be. I was just remembering the night she gave it to you."

He stood up, took her in his arms, kissed her deeply again, and led her to the narrow bed. They lay holding each other, bodies touching, head to toe, until warmth began to fill the cold spaces. They undressed, then, and covered themselves with the throw.

"Better than the dream," Cassie whispered, caressing him, feeling his touch, moving to meet it. "Hmm?"

"The dream that I loved you."

"Tell me your dream," he said later, wiping her tears with his thumb.

"I dreamt we made love."

"When?"

"Some time ago, but it doesn't matter. When I woke up, I cried because it hadn't been real, because you were gone."

"I don't want to leave now, Cassie."

"You must. The children…"

"Only for the night."

Cassie didn't answer.

"I'll still be here—well, at the house—when you wake up tomorrow. Think of what life could be like if you stayed. This could be your first September."

Cassie couldn't think about it—not now.

"OK," he said, getting up. "You need your sleep."

Cassie pulled the throw up to her chin and watched him dress.

"So you'll be warm enough," he said, tossing two more sticks into the stove. He leaned down, kissed her goodnight, and started toward the door.

"Alan," Cassie reached for her book on the table. "Take this. Some of the things I want you to know are here."

He was reading it when she walked into the kitchen the next morning. He got up and kissed her on the cheek. Cassie pulled away, looking for the children.

"They're in the front room. I'll be careful, Cassie. That was just a friendly kiss."

"They all are." Cassie smiled. "That's the best part." She took out a mug, poured herself coffee, and joined him at the table. "Just starting?"

"Oh, no. I read it all the way through last night. I'm just looking again at some of the entries. There's some nice writing here. Reading it, I wanted to come back down, hold you, love you again."

Cassie put her finger to her lips.

He lowered his voice even more. "I sensed there were things you needed to say—that's why I gave it to you. But I didn't think how it might hurt to write it all."

"The writing didn't hurt. The talk we had here during vacation was a beginning. During the cruise, that book was a way of continuing our talk, my link to you. But I'll admit that coming face to face with the feelings on the page was painful."

"So what now?"

"This minute? Today? Sunday's a day of rest. First I'd like something to eat! Then let's walk the beach. We'll talk. I'll think, then I'll call Kate. I hope Peter hasn't been harassing her trying to find out where I am."

They walked almost to Provincetown and back, talking about their childhoods, their hopes for their marriages and their children. They replayed their mutual past, comparing impressions, feelings, getting to know each other without people in between. When it began to rain, they came home and talked through her options while they chopped vegetables and meat for a stew.

"I don't know that I should say anything," Alan said.

"I value your opinion."

"Maybe your lawyer will say otherwise, but even if I didn't love you, I'd say you shouldn't go back. Not if Peter could take the children."

"But I can't run away, Alan. I have to go back, be responsible, get a job and convince him not to try to take them."

"How?"

"I don't know. But he doesn't really *want* them so much as he wants to punish me for hurting him. And I think to be sure they're raised right—with advantages, he'd say. If he and I can just talk..."

"It scares me."

"Me, too," she said, dialing Kate. "Many ways."

"Kate? It's Cassie. Any word from Peter?"

"No, but Julia called. I thought you were with her!"

"You didn't say so..."

"No, but I was confused, and I guess I sounded like I was keeping something from her. She said Peter already told her that you'd left him, so there was no need to cover for you. She wants to talk. I just said you weren't here and I'd have you call."

"Good. I will."

"She sounded so exasperated. Said she'd been trying to catch up with you for days."

"Don't tell anyone I'm here, Kate. I'll tell the lawyer."

"Then what?"'

She stared at Alan, reading at the table, his dark curls flecked with triangles of purple light from the Tiffany lamp.

"I'd like to stay here. Something to do with a dream..."

Alan looked up and smiled.

"...but I'll be back soon. If Peter calls, you can tell him that."

"Good. Keep in touch."

Cassie went over and kissed the top of Alan's head, massaged his shoulders. She couldn't stop touching him.

"Julia's looking for me."

"She didn't know you were at Kate's!"

"Peter told her. Told her I'd left him, too. I guess she's miffed I didn't tell her first. I'll have to call."

"From here? Now?"

"Tomorrow. No more calls tonight."

"I'll go check the children," Alan said, closing his book. "Then we can go down and settle you in the barn." That night, building on all they had shared during the day, they made love again.

Rain pelting on the skylights kept Cassie awake much of the night. She turned on the light a couple of times and tried to read, but couldn't concentrate, thinking about Peter's next move, hers. And her mother must be back by now. She'd have to call there, too. Tomorrow.

But Monday she couldn't reach anyone. Labor Day. It was easy to lose track of time here—there wasn't enough. It poured rain all day. She and Alan passed the hours playing with the children, but Cassie was getting restless.

"The worst thing is that I don't know him," she told Alan over tea. "I've lived with him all these years, yet he's shared so little of himself that I have no idea what he might be thinking, what he might do."

"All the more reason to stay here, away from him."

But knowing that wasn't an answer, Cassie found herself wishing away the last day of the summer.

Tuesday it rained all morning. Alan left early with Gilly. Her toys still seemed new to Sara and Zander, so they played in peace, without television. Cassie liked the quiet, the peaceful views out over the hills. The lawyer was in court when she called, so she left a message that she'd be back in town by the end of the week, then wrote a letter to him, outlining her intentions, and another to her mother. Cassie hoped she would read it, try to understand her feelings and react like her mother—not like the matriarch of a family in which there'd never been a divorce.

After lunch, she baked a spice cake, and had just turned it out on a rack to cool when she heard the car. The kitchen was filled with smells of clove and cinnamon when she ran to the door to welcome them home.

"Julia! What are you doing here?"

"*My* line, Cassandra." She dropped her open umbrella by the door. "Your friend tried to cover, but I figured it out."

"Julia…"

"When did you move in?"

"I didn't. I drove up on Saturday..."

"Saturday. Let's see, left your husband on Monday. Five footloose days...and now a cozy domestic scene…"

Cassie grabbed Julia's arm and shook it.

"Stop it. *Stop* it and listen to me, damn it," she hissed at Julia. My kids are napping upstairs, and I don't want to shout at you. Peter told you I left him?"

"Last night. When I called the first time he just said you weren't there. After a week went by and you didn't call back, I just figured he didn't give you the message. I *never* dreamed something like this might be going on."

"Not what you think." Not exactly, anyway. "I asked Peter to leave..."

Julia raised her eyebrows and sat down. "Really!"

"He refused. Said *I* had to if I was so miserable."

"You were that."

"And it took me a long time to admit it, I know. But once I did, I couldn't stay. I moved in with Kate, then found an apartment..."

"Where?"

"In Philadelphia. And I started looking for a job, but when Peter found out he threatened to take the children. My parents were away, and he'd probably think I'd go there, so I called here..."

"And dear, sweet Alan took you in."

"Julia, I *thought* you were here. You didn't tell me you had moved to New York, either, so stop acting like you were left out of the loop!"

Julia ran her fingers through her hair with a bored expression.

"Alan said I could come. It was late at night, I was upset, and I didn't ask about you. I'm sorry. I didn't know you'd left."

"But I'll bet you were happy to hear it." She re-braided her hair over her left breast.

"I was surprised, and not. You said you weren't happy here."

"Not what I meant, Cassandra," she said, flinging the heavy plait back over her shoulder.

Julia could always read her mind, anyway. No point trying to lie. She didn't have to then. Alan and Gilly stomped in from the rain.

"Julia." They exclaimed in unison, voices in harmony.

"Cheers. Nice day. Cassie's been baking, we've been having a little visit." She smiled too sweetly.

"I think we should continue it in the barn," Cassie said. "On my turf."

Not any more. "I've been sleeping down there."

"How discreet. To the barn, then."

"I went to *school*, Julia!" Gillian tugged at her mother's raincoat.

"I'll want to hear all about it later, love, after I've finished talking to Cassie."

Running in the rain down the hill, Cassie remembered the first day they'd gone to the barn together, the day Julia had shown her the studio. No sun, no flowers today.

Julia slid the door shut behind them and looked around the room.

"You really have been sleeping here!"

"Yes!" Cassie tucked dangling clothes into her suitcase and closed the lid.

"Alan's set you up with wood, and all, and you brought the throw. God, I should have brought down a bottle of whiskey."

"We don't need it, Julia."

Julia threw her raincoat on the counter and sat down in the chair.

"The bed's yours."

If she knew...

"So Peter's threatened to take Sara and Zander. You're going to fight him, of course."

"Yes."

"How?"

"My lawyer and I have to decide."

"You're very calm. What about your fabulous house? All the antiques?"

"Peter can have them."

Julia stared through her without speaking.

"Half of them anyway, I suppose. And you'll go where?"

"I told you. I found an apartment in Philadelphia." Cassie fingered the throw. "I don't know, Julia. There are so many things to work out."

"You're planning on staying here, aren't you? Aren't you? Answer me!"

Cassie didn't, but her silence seemed like an answer.

"I don't know..." Julia mocked her. "That sounds so like you, Cassandra. We'll see who Alan chooses, you or Gillian."

"Why should he have to choose?"

"He'll have to. You don't think you'll just slip in here and take my place with Gillian?"

"You left her here with Alan!"

"Thinking she'd have his undivided attention. I didn't think she'd have to battle for it with you and a couple of other children." Julia ranted to the far wall of the barn.

"Now be fair, Julia. It's not like that."

"Isn't it?" She turned and faced Cassie from as far away as she could be.

"No. Last summer it was *fine* with you that the five of us kept each other company so you could work. You moved to New York to paint. Now you'd uproot Gillian and take her with you?"

Julia put on her coat and slid the door open.

"Maybe, to quote you. Tell Alan I've gone to P'town to stay with friends."

"Julia. Julia!" She was gone. Cassie watched the taillights disappear over the hill. She hadn't even stayed long enough to ask Gillian about school.

The rain soothed her feverish face as she walked back to the house. She and Alan had another connection now, one that threatened the one to each other. They might both lose their children. No, neither of them would let it go that far.

"Where's Julia?" Gillian asked first.

"She's gone to Provincetown."

"When will she come back?"

"Maybe in a little while," she said, tousling Gilly's curls.

"Why don't you go play with Sara and Zander," Alan suggested.

"They missed you today, Gilly," Cassie called after her. "Julia told me to tell you she's staying with friends," she said softly to Alan when Gilly was gone. "We have to talk."

"Julia's going to make trouble?"

"She's threatening to take Gilly to New York."

'Ha! Bluff, Cassie. Pure bluff. An arrangement that might last a week at most. But why? Did you tell her about us?"

"I didn't have to."

Alan nodded, knowing.

"I would have liked to."

"If she's serious, Alan, if she forces you to make a choice, I won't come back."

He reached across the table and covered her hand with his, hiding her gold wedding bands.

"We have to fight. Together. For the five of us."

"We do have to fight, Alan, but alone. We can't even think about being together."

Cassie's mood matched the day—grey and somber—when Julia came back on Wednesday morning. Determined to talk Julia off her course, she believed she had an edge. Julia was fighting for herself, against herself.

"Want tea?"

"I'll get it," Julia said, resisting Cassie's presence in her kitchen.

"Fine." Cassie sat quietly. She'd let Julia begin.

"Look," she said when she sat down. "Some of the things I said yesterday...some of them were hateful."

"You were angry." Cassie shrugged. But after the way you pushed Alan and me together last summer, knowing he needed companionship, knowing what kind of relationship I had—or didn't have—with Peter, it shouldn't surprise you that we learned to lean on each other. He's been as much of a friend as you have over the years, Julia."

"I know, but yesterday I just wanted to spoil everything—for both of you."

"Why? Don't you have what you want?"

"Yes, but I guess a small part of me still wants some of what you've always had."

"Family?"

"You know how I've struggled with that over the years. I've tried, but just never learned how to be 'family'."

"And you want the same for Gilly?"

"Gillian's perfectly at home with it. Grandparents, friends. You've seen it. She's like her father."

"*And* like you. Her imagination, independence..."

"With a mother she can't depend on, like mine."

"Don't compare yourself to her, Julia. You've given Gilly four years she'll remember. Hardly your mother's selfish lack of interest. And if you talk to her often, come to see her, what you're doing now is something she may admire you for when she's older."

"You think?"

"I hope so. But not if you take her away from Alan, the person she depends on. If you take her to New York and try to paint *and* be her mother. By trying to hold on to her, you may lose her."

Cassie got up, leaving Julia to think alone for a bit. She filled her coffee cup, poured another of tea for Julia, sliced some cake, and set the plate on the table.

"Sweets with tea. Though it's early for tea. Like old times." Julia began to pick the raisins out of her cake one by one. "They were good ones."

"But you left."

"Yes. Ran away from that place…"

"Then this one."

"But this time I'm running to something—someone, I should say."

"Maia."

"Maia. Surely you'd guessed, Cassandra, clueless as you've always been."

"I guessed, because your friendship with her became such a big part of your life."

"You must know it's more than that, but you're not judging me, *are* you?"

"Would you ever let me?"

"We all have lapses. I'm glad you caught on, finally, Cassandra. About my life and your own, before Peter destroyed your spirit."

"He didn't know me, Julia. Couldn't. We value different things."

"I tried to tell you that long ago." Julia looked around her kitchen, running her finger slowly around the rim of her cup. "This place is all Alan, you know. He's the homemaker."

"It never seemed that way. When you moved to New York…"

"New York was where it started, Cassandra."

"What?"

"My relentless quest for something else."

"When you left school to go there?"

"Maybe. Though I realize now that despite the repressive atmosphere, I was actually pretty much me at school."

"Maybe because of it? Haven't you always been at your best when you're pushing the limits, Julia?"

"It may seem like that, but no. When you decided not to move to New York…" Julia got up and walked over to the window. "You have no idea how I've been struggling, trying different styles of living, coping," she said, without turning around. "It's taken a long time, but I'm back to me at last. Ironic that I figured it out here in the fog on the moors, don't you think?"

Not at all, Cassie thought. "Things seem clearer here than any other place I've been."

"So you think *you* could be happy here?" Julia asked in a tone so different from yesterday's.

"I always have been, but I'm not planning to stay, Julia. That's the truth."

"The Cape has always been your place, though—more than mine. Julia came back to the table and sat down. "Maybe that's why…" She quickly stood up again. "Never mind. It's too late. I should be going."

There was so much to say, but they'd said all they could for this one day.

"Why don't you stay a while longer. "I'll take a walk and you can tell Alan what you've decided. And Gillian really wants to tell you about school." Cassie hugged Julia, who pulled away.

"Let's just promise to keep in touch," she said, as Cassie walked to the door.

"Always."

Cassie went alone to the edge of the bay. She'd been right to come, she thought, smelling the fresh seaweed tossed up by the storm, feeling the spray lifted by the northwest wind. After three days from the northeast, today it would clear away the thick clouds that still hung overhead. The opposite shore was rimmed with silver. She could fight Peter, if she had to, and win. If she took time, life would be better. Not this September, but another.

She walked back to the house. On the dooryard grass lay a platinum web of closely woven strands. Fairies' handkerchiefs, she'd always called them, the Cape's promise of fair weather by noon.